TILL
DAWN TAMES
THE NIGHT

TILL

DAWN TAMES

THE NIGHT

TILL DAWN TAMES THE NIGHT

~~~~~~~~~~~~~~~~~~~~~~~~~~~~~~~~~~~~

Meagan
McKinney

A DELL BOOK

Published by
Dell Publishing
a division of
Bantam Doubleday Dell Publishing Group, Inc.
666 Fifth Avenue
New York, New York 10103

Printed in the United States of America

Published simultaneously in Canada

Quality Printing and Binding by:
Berryville Graphics
P.O. Box 272
Berryville, VA 22611 U.S.A.

For Tommy

January 1, 1990

O, hush thee, my babie, the time will soon come,
When thy sleep shall be broken by trumpet and drum;
Then hush thee, my darling, take rest while you may,
For strife comes with manhood, and waking with day.

—Sir Walter Scott
(1771–1832)

THE
PIRATE

He thinks too much. Such men are dangerous.
—Shakespeare: *Julius Caesar*

THE
PIRATE

Prologue

1818
LONDON DOCKS

There was no revelry at the Green Serpent Yard tonight. Though the rotting tavern was notorious for its bad gin—and even worse company —it was almost always crowded after dark. Its customers were the kind of vermin rarely seen outside of Newgate, and they cared not a whit about the quality of their spirits. But this night, oddly enough, the crowd was sparse.

Only a subdued little gathering of five men drank in the corner, and they sat hunched together, speaking in whispers. Every now and then one deep in his cups would burst out with a chuckle, but he was soon sobered by his companions' faces. It was clear by their expressions that tonight those who laughed laughed alone.

As the minutes ticked by, they nervously watched the door as if they were waiting for the Devil himself to appear. When still no one came, they seemed to lose another bit of their nerve, but as if to silence their dread, they downed their gin in huge burning gulps, then wiped their mouths on their shirtsleeves and ordered more.

Fear was everywhere in the Yard tonight. Not only was it seen in the faces of the men and heard in the chilling clink of pewter mugs, it was as overwhelming a stench as the unwashed bodies that filled the tavern or the soiled straw that covered the floor. Even the rats seemed to sense what was in the air. At regular intervals they appeared from their dingy nooks to see what the silence was about. Rising to their hind feet, they sniffed, then prudently disappeared back into their holes.

"Wha' if he don't believe us, Murdoch? Wha' if he kills us all? I know we're in this fer the gold, but they say Vashon'd just as soon kill a bloke

as ta look at him." An aged man in the group spoke up. "Though I've
lived a good long time, I just don't know if'n I'm ready ta go tonight. . . ."

"And what about that dragon?" another man whined to their leader.
"I've heard it gives him mystical powers! I've heard stories about that
pirate that'd scare the virginity out of a nun!"

"We're fools to be here! He'll not want our information! He's slit
more throats than I can count!" Made brave by gin, this man slammed
his fist on the board.

"Than ye can count? Than ye can count?" Their leader, Murdoch, a
scurrilous-looking man of fifty, finally stood up. "Ye stupid yellow dogs!
Ye canna count ta three!" In disgust he glanced over his lackeys and
angrily announced, "I need no cowards this night! Whoever canna find
the courage ta stay, then take yer leave and be gone! But dinna be
thinkin' ye're due any gold fer yer troubles!" With that he lifted the
plank table and shoved it to the floor. Glass shattered and the board
split.

After that violent outburst, the minions abruptly ceased their complaints. Outraged, the barkeep started from his corner, but when Murdoch turned his gaze to him, the man stopped dead in his tracks.

"If ye want ta see the morrow, jack, ye'd best stay out o' this."
Murdoch opened his coat and the dull glint of a pistol showed at the
waist of his breeches.

Without further prompting, the barkeep decided to retire. He skittered from the room and dashed for his quarters.

"Now," Murdoch said, turning back to his men, "who is ta stay an'
who is ta go?"

"The only way we'll be going is with Vashon's knife in our gut." One
of the men lifted his head. His pale blue eyes stared vacantly past his
leader. A mad smile curled his lips, and he began to laugh. "So I guess
we'll be staying!"

"That's right," Murdoch pronounced, easing back to the bench. He
warily eyed the crazed young man, then kicked a broken bottle of gin
out of his way. He was just about to send one of the men to get another
round when a shadow fell across him. He glanced up and met with his
nemesis.

"V-Vashon," he choked out, scrambling to his feet. Immediately his
minions did likewise, and with slackened jaws they stared at the demon
before them. He had taken them all by surprise, and if they had been
frightened waiting for him, now that he was here, they were terrified.

Cringing, they watched him step forward. Though Vashon's attire—a dark blue frock coat and pale buckskin breeches—was restrained and costly, it was clear this man was bad company. He towered over the lot of them by at least a head. Yet his great height wasn't what sent fear crawling down every spine. Nor was it his well-muscled form. It was his expression.

Vashon's face was handsome, uncommonly handsome, but it was as hard and merciless as a Spartan's. Written deep into his eyes seemed to be the knowledge that he found the world to be an ugly place. And in his world, his wretched place devoid of beauty or peace, he looked as if he'd developed a great capacity for destruction. By just one glance it was easy to believe this man would do what he needed to, no matter how wrong, no matter how brutal. He seemed to wear his past in his eyes almost as he wore the pistol in his belt. It was hard not to further the comparison by wondering if this man, like the pistol, wasn't just as quick, explosive. And deadly.

"Vashon," Murdoch quavered, "I canna thank ye enough fer comin'. I dinna know if ye would come. . . ."

"We've come. So tell me your information."

At the plural reference, Murdoch looked to the door. A burly pirate stood there. He appeared to have twice Vashon's years, but even though his hair was gray and his gut had expanded with age, he looked quite capable of using the pistol he had aimed right at Murdoch's head.

Murdoch turned his eyes back to Vashon. He gulped. "W-w-would ye be havin' a drink with us, guv'nor . . . ?"

"I want your information. Now."

With those words, all the men held their breath, save the speaker and the man behind him holding the pistol. Even the mad henchman with the pale blue eyes quit smiling. It was obvious it wouldn't do to try this Vashon's patience.

Murdoch gulped again and summoned his courage. His voice took on an imploring tone. "I hate ta inconvenience ye, Vashon, even ta be thinkin' such things, but there is the matter o' price?"

"I'll determine if what you have is worth paying for." Vashon crossed his arms and leaned against the wall. He looked down upon Murdoch and his cohorts as if they were no better than a pack of mangy curs. His stare unglued Murdoch altogether.

"I'll tell ye then," Murdoch conceded hastily. " 'Tis no problem at all. Because, ye see, guv'nor, I know ye'll pay. Ye're a man after me own heart. I admire ye. I trust ye—"

"Get on with it," Vashon demanded, obviously disgusted by Murdoch's bootlicking.

"O' course, o' course, guv'nor!" Murdoch rattled. "I canna wait ta tell ye, for what I know'll be worth more ta ye than all yer gold!"

"Your note said something about the Star of Aran. What do you know about the emerald?"

"I know where 'tis."

Vashon stiffened. His gaze burned into Murdoch. Deadly quiet, he said, "If you know where the Star is, why aren't you going after it?"

"We-e-ell, 'tis a bit more complicated than that. . . ."

Straightening, Vashon abruptly motioned to his man. "Isaac, let's quit these lying fools."

"Wait!" Murdoch cried, following him to the door. "All right! All right! I dinna know where the jewel is! But I know where the viscount is lookin', and I know how much you hate the Viscount Blackwell!"

Vashon turned and grabbed Murdoch by his jacket. This mere gesture sent two of Murdoch's frightened men scurrying for the door. With his eyes nearly bulging from their sockets, Murdoch watched a portion of his salvation run bowlegged out into the night.

"I know all about Josiah Peterborough," Vashon calmly informed him, all the while pressing him against the wall, "and I know where he is looking. But the Star's not in Ireland. So he and you are wasting time." The pirate released him. Terrified, Murdoch slid to the floor like a rag doll.

Vashon turned to go, and with him went Murdoch's hope for gold. Desperate, he scrambled to his feet and grasped the pirate's sleeve.

"But now Blackwell is searchin' elsewhere! He's searchin' for the gel an' only I know where she is!"

With that statement, Vashon paused. Coolly he turned back. "You know where she is?"

"The viscount got a clue the gel might be in London. So he's been all o'er trying ta dig her up. He's told everyone about her an' the locket she'd be wearing. Brightson here"—Murdoch nodded to one of his remaining cohorts—"he saw a gel with that same locket an' followed her home. We was going ta give Peterborough the information, 'til we decided ye hated him so much ye'd probably pay more."

Vashon's eyes narrowed. "What does the viscount plan to do with this girl once he finds her—if he finds her? As I recall, she was only four when her father died. What could she remember about the Star?"

Looking as if he'd just escaped execution, Murdoch nervously hitched up his breeches and offered, "I dinna know wha' she remembers, guv'nor, but I do know Blackwell wants her. An' when he finds her, he plans ta kidnap her. An' surely ye know he ain't much above torture ta git what he wants. Ask old Danny here. He used ta work fer him." Murdoch motioned to the man with the pale blue eyes, who sent them a mad little smile only to turn his interest to his thumb.

"He plans to kidnap her then?" Vashon mused.

"Aye, an' as I see it, once Blackwell gits his paws on her, she ain't gonna be much use ta anyone else, tha's fer sure."

"Where is this girl?"

"She's in London."

The ominous pirate thought about this for a moment. Vashon looked as if he didn't quite believe Murdoch. His expression almost sent Murdoch scrambling for the corner.

"Go on."

Relief washed over Murdoch's features. "There now! I knew when we got this information that ye'd be wantin' it! An' old Peterborough can just go ta the Devil, said I!" Anxious to please, and even more anxious to save himself from bodily harm, Murdoch wiped off a bench with his coat sleeve. He then offered the seat to Vashon. "Can I get you to rest, guv'nor? There ain't no need to—"

"I said, go on."

Murdoch blanched and looked up at the pirate's tall, unyielding figure. He couldn't get his next words out fast enough. "She's at an almshouse, right here in London—grew up there, I heard tell."

"What else."

"We-e-ell . . ." Murdoch hesitated. It was obvious that as much as he loved his life, he loved gold more. Using the last remnants of his courage, he stuttered, "I—I hate to mention this, guv'nor, but th-there is the small detail of payment. . . ."

"Continue, I said."

He eyed Vashon uneasily. "The almshouse is called The Phipps-Bluefield Home for Little Wanderers. 'Tis between the docks and Goodman's Fields in Whitechapel. She works there now, helping the other poor lads and lassies, but we've heard tell that she's lookin' fer a new position. The owner's jus' died—or somethin' of that sort."

"Do you have her name?"

Murdoch nodded.

"Then what is it? Tell me her name and I'll know you have the right girl."

Hoping to end this night still possessing his life, but perhaps a little richer, Murdoch whispered, "I canna quite recall, guv'nor, but perhaps a wee bit of gold might—"

Without warning, Vashon grabbed Murdoch's soiled collar. His cohorts gasped in horror as the pirate forcibly pulled him up to his eye level. When Murdoch squealed like a stuck pig, Vashon said, "Tell me her name, you ass, otherwise you shall sorely regret summoning me here."

"Her name's Aurora! Aurora Dayne!" Murdoch choked.

Vashon released his hold. Murdoch stumbled to the dirty floor, coughing and rubbing his neck. The pirate studied him for a moment. He reached inside his greatcoat, and Murdoch's eyes widened with terror. The men started scrambling for cover, but Vashon only produced a bag full of coins.

"Correct answer, idiot."

With a cynically handsome smile, Vashon thumped the bag down on the floor beside Murdoch. Then, to everyone's relief, he said, "Now, tell me more. . . ."

The Phipps-Bluefield Home for Little Wanderers

Aurora wiped a small patch of soot from her garret window and looked out at the London rooftops. It was time to leave, and though she had yearned for this moment for over a year, now that it was here she felt overwhelmed by it.

"I wish you weren't leaving," a girl's voice murmured behind her.

Aurora turned and gave the girl a small reassuring smile. "If I weren't going, Faith, you would not be blessed with my room."

The girl Faith looked around the tiny room. The floor, though bare, was swept and waxed; the walls were still white from their last whitewashing. The blankets were a bit worn and patched, but still the bed was freshly made and tightly tucked. Aurora could see the girl was pleased.

"Oh, I don't want you to go . . . but I *do* cherish the thought of my own room!" Faith burst out.

Aurora laughed. "I understand completely. I remember what a palace this little room was compared to sleeping downstairs with the children."

"Yet now what will your room be like?"

Faith's question caught Aurora off guard. "I—I really don't know," she managed to say. "I suppose when I get there, it will be much the same as this one."

"Except it won't be in a shabby old orphanage, will it? It'll be in a great mansion. You'll quickly forget us."

Aurora met Faith's reproachful stare. Immediately she went to her and took both her hands in her own. "I have to go, Faith. You know I must."

A tear fell down Faith's cheek. The girl wiped it away with a vengeance. "Why did Mrs. Bluefield have to die of consumption? Now John Phipps has come along and in one year ruined everything!"

Aurora's expression filled with sorrow. They hugged and Faith wept on her shoulder. When the girl's tears were spent, Aurora pulled back and said, "Now you know, Faith, John will take good care of the Home. He really is a decent man. It's just that I . . . well, I cannot seem to get along with him."

"He's a madman."

"No, no!" Aurora exclaimed.

"He is," Faith persisted, hiccoughing. "Your leaving is driving him crazy. He's been in a fit ever since you told him you wanted to go."

Aurora didn't meet her gaze. She wanted to deny Faith's words but it was difficult. From all outward appearances, John was a steady young man, righteously bent on improving the Home now that he'd inherited, but there were times . . . there were times when he seemed a bit unbalanced. And, unfortunately, she had always caught his attention more than the other girls at the Home, so she'd seen more of his erratic behavior.

She took a deep breath and finally looked at Faith. "He wouldn't hurt anyone. You know that, Faith. If I ever thought he'd do anything wrong, I would never leave. John just doesn't like to be told 'No,' but when I'm gone, he'll run the Home in a decent manner, I promise you that."

"I know. But I wish you weren't going. He frightens me."

"There's no reason to be frightened!"

"He does strange things. Especially where you're concerned!"

"What do you mean?" Aurora asked, not sure she really wanted to know.

"Just yesterday I saw him staring at the sampler you made for Mrs.

Bluefield when you were a child. And it's such a shame for it was a beautiful sampler, too, Aurora. It must have taken you months."

"What happened to it?" Aurora whispered.

"It's gone. John Phipps stood staring at it in the eating hall. Then I watched him calmly take it from its frame and put it into the hearth like it was merely kindling. Oh, Aurora, he was so cold about it!"

Aurora turned away, sickened. The sampler had taken her nearly fifteen months to complete. Even now, years later, she could remember how painstakingly she had made each little stitch. She also recalled how pleased Mrs. Bluefield had been by it. She had stitched Mrs. Bluefield's own motto at the bottom—"Toil endeth the follies of the day." Now, almost bitterly, she thought it should have read, "Folly endeth the toils of the day."

"Aurora, must you go?"

With a troubled gaze Aurora looked at Faith. "Surely you see I must? He just will not leave me alone, and I cannot marry him. I know I shall probably never have such a chance for a husband again, but it's all wrong and I'd rather die an old spinster than marry him. Do you hate me for that?"

Sadly Faith shook her head. They hugged once more. When Aurora broke free, she gathered her willow hamper, which held all her belongings, and went to the door. But before she left, she took a lone book that sat upon her dresser and pressed it into Faith's hands.

"The Perrault fairy tales?" Faith whispered, staring up at Aurora with tear-reddened eyes. "You cannot mean to leave this behind. Mrs. Bluefield gave it to you."

For the first time Aurora lost the tight control she was holding over her emotions. She could barely keep her voice from trembling. "The children so love these stories. Once a week I've been stealing downstairs to read to them in their sleeping quarters. If John found out, he'd disapprove, but the children and I have kept it from him so far. I think you can too. In the evening he's quite involved in his prayers, you know."

"I'll read to them once a week, Aurora. I shall find a way, I promise," Faith said, the tremble in her voice matching Aurora's.

"Then God bless you, Faith. And I—I hope we meet again." With that Aurora could hold back no longer. She clutched the willow basket to her bosom and fled down the garret stairs in tears.

THE HEROINE

Anyone who braves the world sooner
or later feels the consequences of it.
—Lady Elizabeth Melbourne

THE
HEROINE

Anyone who braves the world sooner
or later feels the consequences of it.

—Lady Elizabeth Melbourne

Queenhithe Dock

Her adventure had begun.

Taking a deep breath, Aurora could hardly hide her anxiety as she looked past the main deck of the *Seabravery* toward the river Thames. It was barely noon and they were still moored at Queenhithe Dock, but in a few hours they would be sailing.

As was her habit, she nervously fingered the locket at her throat. It was an odd locket, battered and chipped, yet unique. The gold had been cast in the shape of a tiny lizard and set with chips of glittering emerald. Rubies were its eyes and its underbelly, diamonds. It was hinged, but this one's hinges were hidden and it had a clasp that only she knew how to open. Most didn't even realize it was a locket, thinking instead it was just a pendant. But inside, as his only gift to his little girl, her father had etched the last verse to a favorite nursery rhyme.

Fingering the locket now, she felt another chip of emerald missing. The loss saddened her, yet she vowed not to be melancholy. When she had left Faith and the Home, she had had her cry. Now there would be no more tears. Today she had become a lady of adventure, wild and carefree. Soon she would begin her passage, and in only a matter of weeks she would be seeing exotic places: places she had known only in dreams. London would be behind her and a whole new life would begin.

With excitement coloring her cheeks, she looked out across the river. The Thames beckoned her to go forth. As if it could speak to her, the normally sluggish river, churned up by the wind, sent frolicking waves against the ship's sides with the same excited beat as her heart.

As if still unable to believe her good fortune, she abruptly dug into her brown silk reticule to find the letter. For a moment she couldn't find it and her smooth brow furrowed with worry. It all had seemed like a dream. Was she to wake up now? Was it not true after all? Her fingers found the vellum. The letter was still there. Everything was still going to happen.

Relieved, she brought it to the light and was just about to read it once more when a loud female voice interrupted her.

"Another woman! Thank heavens! I didn't know how I would endure this crossing without another female to share my sorrow!"

Aurora looked up, and her aqua eyes widened as a plump, well-attired matron came toward her on the deck. The woman wore a black satin calash bonnet and sported a black pagoda-shaped parasol. She was obviously dressed in widow's weeds, but her gown was of the highest quality. The costly black taffeta rustled as the matron came forward to greet her.

"Do let me introduce myself, my dear," the matron announced, shading her with the parasol. "I am Mrs. Stefan Lindstrom. We'll become quite chummy on the way to Bermuda. I know, because this is my sixth trip."

"Six!" Aurora answered, amazed. "I fear this is my first."

"You shall do just fine. I know all the cures for seasickness and I hear the *Seabravery* is the finest vessel sailing. In fact, the captain tells me that the owner of the ship will be sailing with us, so I expect Captain Corbeil shall take special pains to make the going smooth. What is your name, my dear?"

Mrs. Lindstrom's last question caught her off guard and it took her a moment before she could speak up. "Miss Dayne. Miss Aurora Dayne," she answered haltingly.

"Lovely, just lovely. And you are lately of . . . ?"

Aurora paused again. "Lately of The Phipps-Bluefield Home for Little Wanderers."

"Oh! An orphan! How completely romantic!" Mrs. Lindstrom clasped her hands.

Aurora gave her a puzzled look. She didn't know at all what the matron meant. Growing up an orphan had not been the least romantic. Mrs. Bluefield, saint that she was, had seen to it that she was educated and cared for. But other than that her life at the Home had been drab, as drab as the color of the Home's serviceable linen gowns. This Mrs. Lindstrom made no sense at all.

"I'm not an orphan now," Aurora explained. "I mean, I was an orphan at the Home, but since I've come of age, I've been a teacher there."

"And a good one, I'm sure."

The matron gave her a broad smile, and immediately Aurora warmed to her. Mrs. Lindstrom was a bit too inquisitive, perhaps, and certainly prone to dramatics, but Aurora liked her nonetheless. The fact that Aurora had been a poor orphan didn't seem to put Mrs. Lindstrom off in the least and that was unusual for someone of her obvious wealth.

"So what has brought you to the *Seabravery*, Miss Dayne?" the matron asked next, seeming to burst with questions. "Are you, perchance, joining a fiancé in St. George's? I can only guess, with your petite figure and that glorious color of hair, you must have some wonderful adventure before you. Oh, how I wish I were young again! The things I would do . . . !"

As Mrs. Lindstrom rattled on about her lost youth, Aurora self-consciously swept a curl from her forehead and discreetly tucked it beneath her shabby brown bonnet. She had never thought the color of her hair "glorious." Caught exactly in a middle hue, her hair had never been fiery enough for a redhead nor pale enough for a blonde. Indeed, to her, the faded red color seemed dull. Its tint seemed to mimic her life: pallid and restrained.

With a small frown, she recalled how John Phipps had once even commented her hair was "properly quiet." But he'd been all too enamored of that "properly quiet" hair, she thought darkly. That was just what she was running from. After Mrs. Bluefield had died a year ago of consumption, the gray pallor of John Phipps's influence descended upon her life like a shroud. Though she had known him ever since her first day at the Home, suddenly, with Mrs. Bluefield's passing, there was no escaping him. His attentions had become suffocating, his presence unbearable.

Guilt darkened her aqua eyes. John Phipps was not an awful man, despite what he had done to her sampler. On the contrary, with his self-righteous piety, most thought him quite a good man. A terribly good man, she thought, still remembering how she'd been called an ingrate for spurning his offer. She might actually regret declining his offer, yet still she doubted it. Though her hair color might be properly quiet, her heart was not. And she could have never given it to him.

Even now she could recall the episode that had quite clearly proved their incompatibility. Staunchly Evangelical, John Phipps had found Mrs. Bluefield's philosophy of running the Home with mere kindness insufficient. He had become convinced that Christianity would make the lower orders more content with their paltry lot. Since there was certainly no lower order to society than orphans, he'd felt compelled to begin emphasizing the messages of William Wilberforce to the little ones, and, once, when he'd been so caught up by the Evangelical cause, he caught Aurora reading *Cinderella* to the children and publicly implored her to rethink her path, calling the fairy tale "particularly exceptionable when it painted some of the worst passions that could ever enter the human heart."

Soon after that John had proposed. He had proudly offered her a "modest, quiet, passive life in faith and charity and holiness with sobriety." Then, as a wedding gift, he had presented her with Hannah More's *Coelebs in Search of a Wife*, most obviously in the hope that it would cure her of her love for the "unparalleled vice and infidelity" of literature.

It could never have worked, and now, in hindsight, Aurora could see why Mrs. Bluefield had always encouraged her to leave the Home for a position in the outside world. She had never gone because she had felt a great debt to the Home. She would have worked there her entire life if only to repay a little of Mrs. Bluefield's kindness. But her mentor was now long departed and the thought of spending the rest of her life by John Phipps's side had become untenable. But just when her search for a position had seemed fruitless, the miracle she had prayed for happened. The letter now in her reticule had arrived. It was as if the sender had known of her situation and was generously offering her escape.

"So is it St. George's you're destined for, Miss Dayne, or one of the outlying plantations?"

Startled out of her thoughts, Aurora looked at Mrs. Lindstrom.

"Oh, I know!" the matron continued. "You're going out to Clairdon to marry one of the Sinclair boys! How many sons does Lord Sinclair have now, anyway? Eight was what I heard at last count. Quite strapping lads if I do recall . . . In fact, Miss Dayne, you couldn't do any better."

Aurora artfully covered her smile with her gloved hand. Mrs. Lindstrom certainly did go on! When she lowered her hand, she said, "I'm going to have to do much better, Mrs. Lindstrom, because I'm afraid I'm not meeting a fiancé in St. George's, and most assuredly none of the Sinclair boys. In fact, I'm not going to St. George's at all. I'm going to Kingston, Jamaica."

"Kingston! Good heavens, I didn't know the ship was going on to Jamaica."

"Yes, I'm to be a companion to Lady Perkins of Roselawn Plantation. From her letter, I suspect she is rather elderly—you haven't by chance heard of Roselawn, have you?" Aurora gave the matron a hopeful look. She had always considered herself as possessing quite a bit of fortitude. But sailing away from the only home she had ever known to a tropical island and having not one point of reference was most definitely unnerving.

"St. George's is quite a distance away from Jamaica, love, but let me think. . . ." Mrs. Lindstrom shook her head. "No, I can't remember a Roselawn, and I must say I pride myself on knowing who is who—but Roselawn and Lady Perkins—no, I simply cannot recall."

"I see." Aurora tried to hide her disappointment.

"How did you hear of this position?" Mrs. Lindstrom gave her a concerned look.

"Well"—she looked out to the muddy waters of the Thames—"it's really been quite a surprise. Lady Perkins's letter came only a week ago. It instructed me that if I should like a position, to be here today, ready to sail."

"How very brave of you, my dear, to venture so far alone! But I suppose the orphanage treated you wretchedly."

"Oh, no! On the contrary!" Suddenly Aurora's eyes misted. The Phipps-Bluefield Home might have been an orphanage, but Mrs. Bluefield had made it a wonderful place. In the years she had grown up there, as far back as she could remember, the kind woman had been her mother, her friend, her teacher. And now she was severing her last and only ties to her. Despite her troubles with John Phipps, it was painful.

"There, there, my dear." Mrs. Lindstrom watched her with a troubled expression. She patted her hand and said, "They must have been good to you then, for you to miss them so."

"Yes, yes." Aurora's words spilled out before she could stop herself. For some reason she was becoming unbearably homesick.

"But now, Miss Dayne, you'll see the world—well, at least half of it!"

"Yes." She tried to smile.

"And who knows what passion and romance you may find along the way!"

Aurora blushed. That was just exactly what she craved, but now that it was before her, she wondered if she was up to the challenge. Perhaps she really was as "properly quiet" as John had said she was.

"I'm afraid to disillusion you, Mrs. Lindstrom," she said. "My life has been rather unremarkable, and I fear even a trip to Jamaica may not change that."

"When one is young and beautiful as you are, my dear, there's no telling what adventures may lie ahead."

Aurora laughed in spite of herself. "Well, we can always hope, can't we?"

"We must!" Mrs. Lindstrom laughed in return. Abruptly, the matron released the black whalebone frame of her parasol and without further ado, she said, "Come, Miss Dayne. Though Mr. Lindstrom's been dead almost ten years, I still find I mourn him, but I cannot take the sun in these weeds. So if you'd be so kind, I should like us to find respite in my cabin. I could have my maid make us some chocolate and together we can wait to weigh anchor."

"Why—why—that would be lovely," Aurora said, but Mrs. Lindstrom had already left, her pointed black parasol leading the way like the prow of a ship.

Mrs. Lindstrom's cabin between decks was quite grand. The chests of drawers were made of mahogany and there was the slightest bit of bronze-doré decorating the corners, but still the furniture was made for a ship. The nobs and handles were recessed into the wood so that should one lose one's balance during the course of the trip there would be no sharp protrusions from the bureaux. A tiny blue Axminster carpet brightened the cabin considerably and with the portholes open, a nice breeze flowed in from the Thames. Mrs. Lindstrom's maid, upon their arrival, busied herself putting refreshments on the teapoy, which was also designed for a ship, for it sported a small brass railing around its top.

"So, Miss Dayne," Mrs. Lindstrom began once their chocolate was served, "does your cabin meet your expectations?"

"Yes, yes, my cabin is lovely." Aurora didn't mention that even her small, rather plain cabin was still far larger and more elegant than her garret room back at the Home. She took a sip of her chocolate and added, "I'm sure the fare is heavenly on this grand vessel. I can hardly believe my new mistress was so generous as to book me on it."

"Yes, that's quite extraordinary, especially since the owner is traveling with us. That makes the fare double. Less room, you know, and also, they take such greater pains."

"Do you know the owner?" Aurora asked.

Mrs. Lindstrom shook her head. Her silver sausage curls peeking out from the front of her calash bobbed like springs. "No, I only know that he is supremely wealthy—the *Seabravery* is only one of fifty ships that he owns. He also has an enormous sugar plantation on some island in the Caribbean. St. Kitts, I think or perhaps Nevis."

"He seems quite mysterious," Aurora commented while fiddling with the ribbons of her bonnet. She longed to take her bonnet off, but they surely would be sailing soon and she would have to return to the deck.

"I must say he is quite mysterious, quite the romantic figure, I hear. You see, my dear," Mrs. Lindstrom leaned forward as if she were about to tell a wicked piece of gossip, "another reason passage on the *Seabravery* is so dear is because this ship has never been plundered. Not by a pirate or privateer. Apparently there's something absolutely dastardly about this owner's reputation that has kept even the worst sort of ruffian from bothering it."

"Is that so?" Aurora asked in a hushed voice.

"Quite. I heard it from my son-in-law, and he knows everything. Absolutely everything. That's why he got me on this ship. He felt it would be the safest passage."

"Are you going home, then? Have you a house in St. George's?" Aurora anxiously fingered her locket. She was glad to change the subject. This trip had always seemed a bit too wonderful to be true, and she didn't want anything to spoil that impression. For some reason, the talk about the ship's owner made her vaguely uncomfortable.

"Yes! I've been gone six months, and though I love my grandchildren considerably, I cannot wait to see my friends. We've got quite a little group of ladies in town—oh, I wish you were not going on to Jamaica! Mrs. Ransom has a young daughter just about your age . . . what are you, my dear? About nineteen?"

She hesitated. She always loathed that question. "Yes, nineteen," she said too hastily.

"That's superb. Julia Ransom is twenty now. You two would be the best of friends!"

Aurora was once more taken aback by Mrs. Lindstrom's forthrightness. The woman was quite casual in including her within her social circle. It was as if the woman forgot to whom she was speaking. Aurora had rarely had any contact with the upper classes, but every now and again a wealthy uncle or cousin would deposit his undesirable orphaned relatives at the Home. Those guardians of any consequence always made it pointedly clear that she and Mrs. Bluefield were not their equals. But not the remarkable Mrs. Lindstrom.

"More chocolate, Miss Dayne?" Mrs. Lindstrom waved her hand in the direction of the pot.

Aurora shook her head. "Please call me Aurora, won't you?" She gave the widow a quiet little smile. She felt so relieved that she'd met her. The voyage would surely not be so terrifying while Mrs. Lindstrom was aboard.

"I know we're to be great friends." The matron seemed delighted at her offer. She patted her hand. "And you must call me Flossie. That was Mr. Lindstrom's nickname for me."

"How dear you must have been to him."

The matron smiled a sad smile of remembrance, but then she promptly brightened. "Now, Aurora, surely Captain Corbeil is ready to sail, so why don't we see what's going on up top?"

Aurora nodded and clutched her gloves. "Something should be happening by now. We must be hours behind schedule."

"Shall we go up and see if this vastly mysterious owner has arrived?" Mrs. Lindstrom brazenly winked. "Oh, I do hope he dines with us and not in his cabin. How utterly dull the voyage would be then!"

The matron straightened her bonnet and gathered her pagoda-shaped parasol. As Aurora watched, she was certain she had never met anyone like Flossie Lindstrom. When the matron sailed out of her cabin, appearing like a huge black ship bearing down on the less loquacious as if they were merely flatboats, Aurora was awestruck. She simply couldn't imagine anything being dull with her around.

The sun set behind the Tower and still the *Seabravery* had yet to leave its mooring. From the quarterdeck Aurora watched the sparks of exploding firecrackers on the docks heralding Midsummer Eve. Mrs. Lindstrom had retired to her cabin long ago, and Aurora was left to pace the decks, sure that they would not leave before dawn, yet still anxiously waiting for . . . something.

As she looked out, London's sooty nighttime gloom was chased away by the many orange bonfires lit in the streets. "Huzza!" she heard men shout gleefully. Both the Archbishop of Canterbury and the Archbishop of York had tried to impress upon their flock that it was the festival of John the Baptist they were celebrating. They had instructed them that church was the place for them on this eve.

Aurora smiled. It had certainly done no good. People continued to build their fires in the streets, eager to celebrate the summer solstice. Even now she could see through the narrow cobbled streets people dancing in pagan silhouette around the brilliant fires.

Dreamily, she rested her elbows on the railing. Tonight it seemed as if civilization had never come to England. The bonfires were the Druid Baal fires of centuries ago and Midsummer rites abounded. Hempseed was being sowed in the churchyard, and unmarried girls were taking their pincushions and hanging them up for the night in their stockings in hopes that that would bring them a glimpse of their future husbands. Caught up in the excitement, Aurora blithely wondered if she had brought a pincushion on board. She laughed at herself for being so superstitious.

On the docks she heard the snapping of more firecrackers. Boys cheered and horses shied. The commotion distracted Aurora, and she didn't see the wagons pull up to the ship's gangway until they were unloading.

At first she thought the owner had finally arrived, but it seemed unlikely that his omnipotent presence would appear in a common wagon. Captain Corbeil came to the main deck and supervised. She watched as costly silk prayer rugs from Persia were heaved aboard. Mahogany tables with elaborate caryatid legs were hoisted up also. At one point four men carried aboard a black upholstered sofa sporting legs carved to look like gilded dolphins. It was clear even to Aurora that all the furnishings were the finest specimens of current taste. And it was clear that they were being brought aboard to appoint one cabin. One very large cabin. Most obviously the owner's cabin.

Aurora looked past a man bearing a bronze urn and found the captain standing idly by the railing. From below, she could hear the pounding of hammers and the murmurs of male voices as workers nailed the furniture into the cabin to make it immobile for the voyage. Added to the celebrating on the docks, the cacophony was deafening. There was certainly no retiring to her cabin in this din, so she remained in the shadows of the masts. Yet still the captain's gaze found her.

The barrel-chested, grizzled captain had been the epitome of a gentleman all through the day. He had cheerily seen to her and Mrs. Lindstrom's every comfort; he'd been quick with a kind word or a polite joke. Yet now, caught off guard by her appearance, he looked different. It was as if she troubled him somehow, as if those worries that he'd been able to hide in the activity and brightness of daytime were now not so easily disguised in the shadows of night.

As quiet as a frightened doe, she stood by while he studied her shabby pelisse. Every patch, every threadbare edge of her garment seemed to shame him and she wondered if he pitied her. Perhaps he had somehow found out she was from the Home and felt sorry for her. But instinctively she knew that wasn't the reason. His look was too involved and too dark to be that easily explained.

It may have been the explosive celebrating down on the docks, or even the harsh banging of the workmen belowdecks, but all at once her nerves were strung taut. She forced her worried stare away from the captain's troubled one and turned to the rail. She knew that whatever she imagined she saw in the captain's eyes had to be a mistake. Mrs. Lindstrom's romantic imaginings were surely rubbing off on her.

She looked out to the Thames and marveled at how her perspective had changed. In the daylight she had thought the river a sparkling gateway to adventure. Now it looked more like the river Styx winding black and fathomless into the murky fog. Feeling suddenly cold, she wrapped her pelisse around herself more tightly and bore up against the wind.

"Miss Dayne, I'm surprised to find you up at this late hour."

Quickly she spun around and found Captain Corbeil at her side. Gone was the troubled look, and in its stead his brown eyes held a cheerful twinkle.

"I-I-I was not sleepy," she stuttered like a child. Thoroughly disgusted with her lack of composure, she took a deep breath and said, "Do forgive me, Captain. I've been nervous about the voyage, and the delay has made me only more so. In fact, I believe I'm even seeing things in my distress." She wavered a smile. Already she felt foolish. The captain was no keeper of great, dark secrets. He was a paternal and chivalrous man, concerned with her welfare and comfort. She should be gladdened to be in such good hands, not suspicious.

The chuckle booming from his chest only reassured her further. He laughed and said, "I'm sure you're mistaken, Miss Dayne. What could you be seeing? Are you displeased with the ship?"

"No, no! The ship is quite wonderful." She gave him a sheepish smile. Whatever had possessed her to think anything was sinister?

"I do apologize for the delay, however. It has been regrettable, but I promise we shall leave within the hour."

"At night?" she inquired. "Isn't that most unusual?"

The captain gripped the railing. She glanced down and for the first time noticed that three of his fingers were missing. The scars on his hand were massive and she wondered how that could have escaped her. Not wanting to be caught staring, she quickly looked up, but he gave her a reassuring smile. "I know the Thames, miss. We'll be out in the Channel in no time."

"And shall we leave the owner behind after all?" she asked, trying to divert her attention from his hand. Her question seemed to startle him, even though he quickly hid his feelings behind a facade of joviality.

"Oh no. He'll be here, Miss Dayne. That I can guarantee." Abruptly he excused himself to go below and check on his men.

She was left alone for only a minute before Mrs. Lindstrom appeared. She was in a luxurious black wool pelisse that didn't quite hide the blue brocade of her dressing gown. Her bonnet was on crooked and she looked blowsy, as if she'd just been awakened from a deep sleep and hadn't had the mind to pull her appearance together.

"There you are, my dear!" The matron called to her and waved a hand through the air. "Can you believe the racket? And at midnight!"

"Yes, it's quite something," Aurora agreed and made for her side. She was just about to speak when a further commotion broke out on the docks. As if expecting it, the captain appeared from belowdecks, and strode to the gangway. Curious, Aurora and Mrs. Lindstrom went to the railing and peered down at the dock.

Aurora had never seen such dark splendor. Below was a black japanned coach pulled by eight shiny black steeds. Its presence seemed to stamp out everything else as unimportant. Even the Midsummer revelry on Queenhithe seemed to hush and the pounding cease beneath their feet. The harness fittings were gold and a thin gold edging outlined the carriage, but there were no crests on the doors to identify the rider. Ominous was the only word for the vehicle, yet even that word was weak when it came to describing the man who appeared from inside it.

"My God . . ."

The matron gasped from the delicious horror of it all. Aurora felt Mrs. Lindstrom's hand take hold of her arm and though she wanted to comfort the older woman, somehow she found she hadn't the fortitude she thought she had. When she tried to speak, her voice would not come. As if captured by the man who was making his way onto the ship, her mouth would not form words and her gaze would not leave him.

He was tall—several inches taller than the captain, who was a tall man himself—yet the hint of barely restrained violence in this man made him appear towering. He wore a fashionable black *carrick,* his coat sporting no fewer than nine capes. Beneath this Aurora could see a white batiste shirt and trousers made out of black superfine. From just his clothes, she would have guessed that the man conducted his life well within the confines dictated by society, but when she looked further, Aurora sensed there was very little that confined this man.

In truth, he flaunted fashion, and not with just the glossed-over ferociousness of his manner. He wore his hair almost down to his shoulder blades, tying the unruly black coils into a queue at his neck, a style unheard of for nearly twenty-five years. And a tiny silver hoop pierced his left earlobe, giving him an unspeakably wicked look, so that when all the parts were put together, there seemed only one way to describe him.

"He's a pirate!" Mrs. Lindstrom gasped, tightening her hold on Aurora's arm. Aurora wanted to soothe her, but there was no way to deny what she said when, in fact, she'd been thinking exactly the same thing.

From the shadows of the quarterdeck, they watched the man step onto the *Seabravery*. Captain Corbeil went to greet him, and it was clear they were well acquainted. Now it was obvious that the terrifying man was the owner for whom they had been waiting.

In one lucid moment Aurora was sure they were attributing too many sinister overtones to this man's presence. But then, as if to point her out, Captain Corbeil's gaze slid unwillingly to her figure.

And the owner's gaze followed.

Even though he was on the main deck below, the man's overpowering presence captured her. As if by spell, he forced her unwilling gaze to meet his own, and Aurora was shocked by his eyes: so startlingly beautiful, so startlingly cold. He bestowed barely a glance upon her, but in that time his gaze was so utterly thorough she felt as if even her soul were under his scrutiny. He had such a tight hold on her that even when the moment passed and he had turned back to the captain, she couldn't tear her gaze away. Nor escape from the dread that was beginning to seep into her very bones.

"Oh, what excitement! What exquisite terror!" she heard Mrs. Lindstrom whisper to her. "In all my days! Aurora! That man is a pirate! A pirate! Oh, we're certainly in for an adventure now!"

Aurora stared at her. In dismay, she found her hand clinging to Mrs. Lindstrom's arm quite as tightly as the matron's clung to her own. Looking down, she watched the owner disappear belowdecks. Rationally, she had no reason to think anything wrong, but still she couldn't shake the feeling that something was happening. And as mad as it sounded, she couldn't dispel the frightening thought that it concerned her.

In one swell of panic, she released Mrs. Lindstrom's arm. Guided by instinct alone, she walked to the gangway and had every intention of leaving the ship, even if it meant crawling back to the Home with her pride on her sleeve. But at once she heard the clicking of the capstan and the heavy fall of water rushing off the weighed anchor. To her utter dismay, the gangplank had already been lifted, and there was nothing below her but the black glittering waters of the Thames. Appalled, she turned to Mrs. Lindstrom. The widow's face mirrored her own. In desperation Aurora's eyes wildly scanned the decks for escape, but, like it or not, there was no going back now.

Her adventure had begun.

2

"We've got her."

With that statement, Vashon tossed off his *carrick* and flung it onto the dolphin-legged settee. Kicking a chair out from under a table, he turned the chair around and sat down, his hands gripping its back.

"I think she's really quite a nice little maiden, Vashon. I hope you'll handle her with care. I don't see it to our advantage to frighten her now." Isaac Corbeil took off his gold-embellished captain's cap and rubbed his balding pate.

"How am I going to frighten her?" Vashon smiled a rare and fleeting smile. His teeth gleamed a wicked white against his evening growth of beard, and for a quick, elusive moment, he looked almost happy.

The captain sighed. "Good God, but have we done some terrible deed, Vashon? I mean, this girl's not some easy-virtued wench from La Tortué that we can haul away without so much as a by-your-leave."

"Don't be absurd. This is the best thing that's ever happened to the chit." Vashon released a mirthless laugh. "She's better off with us than at that rotten almshouse, by half."

"Perhaps, but her complexion certainly lost that pretty apricot glow when she set eyes on you."

"She'll hold up." Vashon's mouth twisted sarcastically. "Too, we may be underestimating her abilities to take care of herself. After all, she took one glance at me and looked ready to jump overboard. So at least she's a woman of action."

Isaac chuckled and shook his head. "Yes, I suppose she is."

"Besides, if you're worried about me, I'll have you know I'm certainly not in the habit of taking my pleasure with stiff, proper little virgins, fresh-faced from the orphanage."

With that statement, the captain sobered. "Nonetheless, Vashon, when you look beneath this girl's timid demeanor and worn clothing, you might just find yourself caught unawares. I did. Aurora Dayne's certainly not like that horse-faced Gideon woman we took on board today."

Vashon gave him a jaded stare. "Why would I even look at that baggage? The girl's a shabby little prig. I've seen finer feathers on a sparrow."

"Yes, but it's difficult to notice her garments once she's captivated you with that face. Already she's garnered the attention of the seamen. Her bonnet blew off in the breeze this afternoon. That sorry lot was almost dumbstruck when she turned and smiled at them before righting it again."

Vashon's eyes suddenly flashed. "She's our only hope of finding the Star of Aran. So I hope you'll see to it that they won't be bothering her. Otherwise, *I'll* see to it they won't . . . permanently."

"Ah, my good man!" Isaac laughed. "That really won't be necessary! We do need *some* crew to sail the ship!"

Vashon shot him a black look. Then his humor returned. A dark smile tugged the corner of his lips. "But I'll admit one thing about the girl. I thought spinsters who ran orphanages were supposed to be warty little hags with thin lips and even thinner figures. Now why does our Miss Dayne not fit that description?"

"Perhaps for the same reason that most think pirates who've made their fortune plundering ships are scurvy, toothless villains with the skull and crossbones hoisted on their masts—not the Union Jack." Smugly Isaac crossed his arms.

Vashon finally smiled altogether. "I suppose you're referring to me?"

"Who else?"

"Well, then, let me get out my eye patch. At least that should give that old Widow Lindstrom a thrill."

"I'm afraid that old girl already half expects something like that. I think you'll have to do better."

Both men laughed.

The captain finally looked at Vashon in awe. "I admit it now, Vashon, I really didn't think this scheme of yours would work. I had no idea Miss Dayne would actually be so anxious to leave England. I truly harbored some fears we'd have to sneak into that orphanage in the middle of the night and roll her up in a carpet."

"Why do something so messy when you can have the chit walk right into your hands? Or your ship, as it were."

"Kidnapping by any other name . . ."

"Would still smell as sweet," Vashon finished. With a vengeance he added, "Besides, should we have thrown her to Blackwell?"

Isaac stared at him for a long moment. "You know, it never fails to impress me that you can refer to Peterborough by the title Blackwell. My God, man, how that name must rot in your gut."

"Not at all," Vashon answered. "He did much to get that title. Until I've the desire to take it away from him, he may have it. In truth, I might not enjoy toying with him so much, if he had nothing to lose."

"You're a bigger man than I, Vashon. Or a colder one. I'm not sure."

Vashon smiled. "Come now, Isaac, surely my magnanimous nature has impressed you. I've saved our dear Miss Dayne from a terrible fate. Her father stole that emerald from Peterborough, and knowing him as we do, I shouldn't think the viscount would be too charitable."

"No," Isaac agreed. "Old Blackwell wouldn't be. Michael Dayne certainly picked the wrong man to rob. Have they ever found out what happened to him?"

"I heard someone say once that they thought they saw him hanging from one of the viscount's oaks. But I think that poor bloke was somebody caught poaching, not Miss Dayne's father."

"Well, if Blackwell treats his poachers so harshly, perhaps Aurora Dayne can count her blessings she's on the *Seabravery* now." As if to signal his leaving, Isaac put on his captain's cap and said, "I'll inform the crew that you're pleased, Vashon, and that everything is going as planned. They're all concerned about this voyage, you know. I'm afraid a lot of men's hopes rest on Miss Dayne's shoulders."

"Yes," Vashon agreed, turning pensive. "It's hard to believe our fortunes all hinge on that shabby little churchmouse."

"You may see her as a shabby little churchmouse, but still she's a lady beneath all that raggedy brown fustian. I hope when you deal with her, you'll remember that."

Vashon gave him a cynical smile. "Let me remind you, Isaac. Our *Miss* Dayne's not exactly the cream of society. Her father was a thief by trade, her mother, God only knows what, and she grew up a pauper in an orphanage."

"Yes, yes." Isaac nodded. "But she doesn't know about her parentage and I'm sure she'd be horrified to find out."

"Well, perhaps it's time the little miss knows who she is," Vashon stated coolly.

"I suppose. But still, she strikes me as quite an innocent. And I don't think anything can change that. Not even you."

"You underestimate me then, Isaac."

"I've never underestimated you, Vashon."

Vashon met Isaac's stare. A look passed between the two men, a look fraught with the shared agonies of the past. Uncomfortable, Vashon looked away. Making light of the captain's comment, he said, "Isaac, never fear for that little brown wren. Between you and the old widow clutching at the girl's arm, I'm sure she'll be quite safe from all my treachery."

Isaac chuckled and the tension left his face. "Yes, yes, I suppose you're right. That old Mrs. Lindstrom has been hanging on to Miss Dayne like a bulldog."

Disgruntled, Vashon reached for a brandy decanter on the caryatid table.

Isaac watched him and sighed. "How I wish I could join your celebration. But the men must be casting off the hawsers by now and I have to get this ship out of the docks before they sink it."

Vashon nodded. "Go to it then. I want to unload our chattel in Bermuda as quickly as we can so that we may begin our real business." His jaw tightened with determination. He looked down and took a long sip from his glass. Darkly he uttered, "Victory is near."

Aurora opened her eyes. For a moment she wasn't sure where she was, but then she remembered and lay back beneath the eiderdown quilt.

How could she have forgotten she was on a ship? The persistent rocking alone should have reminded her. Even now she was amazed that she had remained in her bed the entire night. Fingering the turned railing that ran along the bedframe, she mused that it certainly didn't seem enough to keep her on the mattress. Yet apparently it was. She was still in her tiny bunk.

She closed her eyes. The ship's rocking wasn't the only thing that reminded her of where she was. All at once a flood of images passed through her mind. There was a shiny black coach . . . dockside revelers . . . an ornate couch with gilded dolphins as feet . . . a kindly widow in taffeta weeds. There was also a man. He stood tall and menacing in a black caped coat, his eyes as glittering as the emerald chips on her locket.

She rolled over and clutched the pillow to her. The memories of the night before—when the "pirate" owner had boarded—were still rather unnerving. Yet surely, she told herself, the dark handsome shipowner would look less menacing in the morning light. Most likely her imagination had painted him in much more threatening a manner than he actually deserved. In fact, when she saw him at breakfast she would probably be shocked at his pallid features and stumpy proportions. The man was probably about as threatening as a gnome, and when she saw him again, she would feel quite the fool.

Reassured, she opened her eyes and looked around her. No one could doubt that her employer was a generous soul. Her cabin was designed for the finest of ladies. In spite of the dear cost of space on a ship, the compartment was even larger than her bedroom at the Home. It was wainscoted in mahogany and swathed in shades of Dresden pink and black. Complete with lights and portholes and custom-fitted bureaux, the compartment was so lavishly appointed Aurora was almost embarrassed when she saw her brown woolen dress hanging tiredly next to a pitcher and bowl of silver lustreware. In comparison to her surroundings, her garments certainly looked mean and incongruous, yet Lady Perkins had deemed her deserving of them. When Aurora thought of how she could have made the long voyage across the Atlantic, she counted her blessings. She knew it was quite common for 150 passengers to bunk in one hold, and she had even heard of families too poor to afford passage anywhere else but near the rudder. They spent the entire journey across the cold Atlantic soaking wet and ultimately died of pneumonia before they reached their destination.

She was indeed fortunate, she thought, as she looked around her cozy little cabin. Things could be much worse.

With that thought spurring her on, she tossed aside the covers and went to the pitcher. In only a few minutes she was dressed and sitting on the bed combing her long hair. When the pale red mass of curls was tamed into a knot at the back of her head, she pulled on her slippers and walked to the door. She remembered quite clearly that the galley was at the end of the passage in the aft quarters of the ship. Her only hope was that Mrs. Lindstrom would be there to join her.

Pulling open her battened door, she was surprised to find the door opposite hers open. She was even more shocked to see into the huge cabin and find, against the far wall, the unusual couch that sported the gold dolphin-shaped legs. A thick Chinese carpet with a pattern of confronting green dragons covered the floor and a huge mahogany desk stood against the far corner, obviously where the owner conducted his business aboard ship.

Seeing the owner's quarters opposite hers was a bit unsettling. She wasn't exactly sure why, but her first instinct was to scurry back into her cabin and lock the door. She found the situation even more disturbing when she felt the edge of her door and realized her door had no lock. Just a simple latch that worked from the inside and out.

Timidly she closed her door, all the while keeping her sight on the room before her. It appeared that the owner was out, but she was unnerved at the thought that he might be just on the other side of that door. He might be performing his toilet and unaware that his door was open. He might be shaving, or worse, dressing.

Aurora blushed. She had never in her life seen a man dress before. John Phipps had been quite adamant that she not even see him in his shirtsleeves until after their engagement. John had told her that seeing a man not fully garbed would most definitely put her into a state. Now, thinking of that tall, handsome owner of the *Seabravery* unclothed, she was amazed that for once in his pious little life John had been right. That *would* put her into a state.

She made her way down the short passage until she found the roundhouse. Mrs. Lindstrom and the other passengers had either already eaten or were taking their breakfast in their rooms. The galley was empty save for the chef, who quickly served her a fine meal of eggs and black pudding. Earlier Mrs. Lindstrom had informed her that as the voyage continued the meals would get progressively worse, so with that in mind, she ate everything on her plate.

When she was finished, she was eager to seek company. The quietness of the cabins and the lack of passengers made her a bit tense. She knew there weren't but nine passengers on board, and she longed to see some of them. Having spent most of her life at the crowded Home, the hollow echoes of the ship as it sliced through the waters made her feel twice as alone.

She found her way beneath the porticoed entrance to the aft cabins and went out onto the main deck. There were seamen everywhere, tying the rigging, climbing the masts, running the decks, but to her disappointment, nowhere did she spy a fellow passenger. Feeling a pair of eyes staring at her, she looked up, and the boy in the crow's nest yards above her head tipped his cap. She smiled and waved, yet immediately the boy was chastised by one of the seamen in the rigging. Taken aback, she looked to the other sailors to see if they too abided by such behavior. When she did, each and every one of them violently averted his gaze. She knew it was proper to keep a distance between passenger and seaman, but this was odd behavior indeed, especially when just the night before these same sailors had tipped their caps and nodded pleas-antly to both her and Mrs. Lindstrom.

Shrugging off an ominous feeling, she went to the rail and looked out. They were well past Gravesend by now and the Channel stretched out before them like a frothy blue jewel sparkling in the morning sun. A few whitecaps were stirred up by the wind, and though the breeze blew brazenly over her bonnetless head, she was loath to return to her cabin. Instead she watched as the English coastline gave more and more of itself up to the sea. They were going along at a fantastic pace, and she found it exhilarating.

"Miss Dayne. I hope your accommodations are satisfactory."

Aurora spun around. She was sure Captain Corbeil was her solicitor, but the smile on her lips died as she faced the *Seabravery*'s terrifying owner.

He was most definitely not a gnome. If anything, in the morning light he had grown a foot from when she had last seen him. With the sunlight flickering in his eyes, she could now see they were a vivid shade of emerald green. His eyes, despite all their promise of terrible emotions, took her breath away.

Dumbstruck, she tilted her head up to look up at him; it was all she could do to utter even the most inane conversation.

"I'm—I'm afraid we haven't had an introduction, sir."

"Allow me," he said, nodding his head. "My name is Vashon. I'm the owner of this vessel." With that, he leaned back on the railing next to her. He was very close. Almost too close. With his legs slightly apart and his elbows against the rail, he seemed very much at home. Now, as last night, he most definitely looked the part of the commander of the *Seabravery*.

"And I am Miss Dayne. But, of course, you seem to know that already," she said.

He was so near she had to suppress the urge to step back out of his shadow. She really wanted to flee to her cabin, but she told herself that she was no longer the milksop maiden John Phipps had thought her. She was a lady of adventure now. It wouldn't do to run away. After all, she told herself, what harm could come to her on this ship?

She took another glance up at him and suddenly she had her doubts. This man was anything but harmless. He was clean-shaven and well-dressed in breeches, boots, and a shirt as blindingly white as the sails above them. Yet the man's appearance still unnerved her. She found the heavy coils of his long black hair, though neatly bound, threatening. He was unlike any man she had ever seen. His silver ear hoop, glinting off the sparkling water, confirmed this. He was no John Phipps, a man as easy to run from as an unweaned puppy. Somehow she felt if she ever dared run from this Vashon, he was just the kind who would go after her. And not stop until he'd got her.

"Are you enjoying your voyage, Miss Dayne?"

She tilted her head up once more to look at him. His eyes were alight with laughter. Somehow he must have known she was intimidated and obviously found it amusing. She suddenly became annoyed.

"Everything is quite satisfactory, Mr. Vashon. Unfortunately, you'll have to excuse me now—"

Tensing, she felt his gaze lower to her throat. She unwittingly looked down and saw he was staring at her locket, deep in thought.

"Your pendant is beautiful," he murmured, his eyes reflecting the light with all the subtleties of a jewel. "And how well it suits you, Miss Dayne."

"My father gave it to me," she whispered, growing flustered. She had never met a man as brash as this one. John had been loath even to look at her locket, calling it "a pagan thing." This man was not only staring at it but admiring it as well. He looked as if he ached to reach out and touch it.

He smiled and leaned further back on the railing, much to her relief. "I seem to recall one Viscountess Blackwell having a bauble just like it," he said. "But then again, that pendant was stolen, fifteen years ago at least. I can only guess where it is now."

Aurora's eyes darkened. Was this man somehow accusing her of stealing this viscountess's locket?

"I assure you, Mr. Vashon, you must be mistaken." She fought to keep her voice even. "This necklace was my father's legacy to me, and he made it clear when he left it for me that there wasn't another one similar to it in all of England. So no one could possibly have owned one like it."

"I believe you, Miss Dayne."

Taken aback by his sudden assent, she was at a loss for words. The wind picked up and loosened one of the pins from her hair. Her hand went to her head and she realized, to her chagrin, that she'd been out in public, speaking to a man, without her bonnet. Her cheeks colored as she quickly repinned the loose curl. She said, "I'm afraid you'll have to excuse me, Mr. Vashon. I fear I must retrieve my bonnet."

"By all means," he said, a strange look crossing his face. "The sun gets hot in the tropics. A fair maiden like yourself needs protection."

A strange fluttering blossomed in her belly. She looked at him and her fingers worried the locket at her throat. For some terrible reason, her bonnet didn't seem like the kind of protection of which he spoke. And it didn't seem nearly enough. Particularly if it was to protect her from him.

She left, taking only one more glance at him. Nonetheless, she was overcome with the desire to find her cabin and hide there for the rest of the journey to Jamaica.

THE
VILLAIN

. . . this declining age, when too many worthy members of the community seem to have an alacrity in sinking.

—Captain Rees Howell Gronow: *Reminiscences*

3

Lord Josiah Peterborough, seventh Viscount Blackwell, was a stunningly handsome man. Though he was well into his forties, his dark brown hair had yet to silver, and he possessed a most arresting pair of brilliant green eyes. With title and wealth, he was one of the most sought-after peers in London. That he cut a rather joyless figure was easily forgiven, attributed to the fact that he'd been tragically widowed at a tender age. If anything, his melancholy stance only endeared him further to an already adoring society. His female admirers in particular viewed him with sympathy—well-tempered, of course, with a generous dose of erotic infatuation.

His conquests were many. At Melbourne House, Lady Melbourne had quickly declared him intriguing and insisted always that he dine next to her. The patronesses of Almack's labeled the evening a success whenever the viscount chose to attend. Lord Blackwell was accepted everywhere, even at Carlton House, and the Regent had even seen to it that he was among the guests invited to a weekend or two of debauchery at the Marine Pavilion. But though the cream of the peerage had long embraced him, there were still three things about him most did not know.

The first was his shame-filled past as the poverty-bound, untitled son of a barley merchant. Because of his complete lack of funds, Lord Blackwell's future had once looked so bleak that he'd been sent off to Heidelberg at the tender age of twenty-three in the hope that he might earn a living as a physician. Though he never finished his studies, even now, decades later, Josiah Peterborough still possessed an intimate familiarity with the human body, coupled with a horrifying knowledge of surgery.

The second was simply the fact that his heiress wife had not taken that overdose of opium, lo, these many years ago, without assistance.

And lastly, no one quite knew the exact source of his wealth. It was naturally assumed that it had come from the title that had ironically landed upon him right after the death of his step-brother. His pitifully short marriage was also a point of speculation concerning his income, for his late wife had been endowed with a fortune. But alas, neither was so.

While the Blackwell estate did bring in some funds, the viscount had become greedy during his years of penury in Heidelberg. To make money, he had turned to illicit dabblings in certain "trades." These ventures had soon proved so profitable that his lust for their income only grew more fierce. Now his empire was enormous: He owned a fleet of ships, all pirated off the seas from their legal owners; he was a crafty smuggler of Cantonese goods; he sold art purloined from the broken aristocracy of Paris; and he peddled flesh, of any and all kinds, in London's wretched Spitalfields. In short, there was not a whole lot the Viscount Blackwell would not do to make a gold coin as long as it was done discreetly. And he had been doing it all rather discreetly for a number of years.

Only of late had things become more difficult. Tonight was no exception.

The viscount was just readying to leave his London town home for Drury Lane when the missive arrived in his study. The letter was from Ireland and even before he broke the seal—a wax seal consisting of two dragons regardant—his face had already taken on a harsh expression.

"Is it from him?"

Peterborough looked up and found his new business partner, a young man named Asher, standing in his study door. Asher was slim, blond, and immaculately kempt. Some would place him in the dandy set, for he sported the most fantastic carmine waistcoats on an unnaturally corseted torso, but the viscount seemed unimpressed with this *incroyable*. Asher's tendency toward the feminine quite obviously annoyed him. Even now the viscount looked as if he wanted to throttle the man.

"I thought I told you never to visit here," Peterborough snapped. "When we began our business arrangement, I made it quite clear you're to leave a message and I'll meet you."

Asher made a moue, then entered the room nonchalantly. "Yes, yes. We wouldn't want the proper folk to think you've got bad taste in friends." Without another pause, he eased himself down on a rose damask armchair and carefully crossed his legs.

"Your news had better be worth your insubordination," the viscount stated. "We've only been doing business for a few weeks, and I can make sure that that's all there is to it." Finished with the letter, he crumpled it in his hand and vehemently threw it into the burning hearth.

"I see you've heard from Vashon," Asher said as he watched the letter flame.

"Yes" was all that Peterborough offered. His green eyes hardened and his fists visibly clenched.

"I suppose he's still taunting you with that emerald?"

"He wrote to say he's still in Ireland and getting closer to the Star all the time."

"Well, he's not in Ireland."

Peterborough stiffened.

"In fact, he's been here for some time."

"Why was I not informed of this!" the viscount demanded.

"I sent messages."

"I've been busy! You should have been more explicit!"

Asher shrugged.

Peterborough lost all patience. "Damn you! Is that the news you have tonight? If it is, you can take your leave! I'll deal with Vashon tomorrow —in the meantime I've got theater tickets and—"

"I've heard of rumors around Queenhithe," Asher interposed. "Vashon has changed tack. Some say he's found a girl, a Miss Dayne, to be exact. Does that name have any special significance?"

Upon this news, the viscount's eyes nearly bulged from their sockets. "You jest . . ."

"That is the rumor." Asher studied his nails.

"Then has Michael Dayne been found too? He disappeared with her."

"No, Michael Dayne has not been found."

Numbly, Peterborough lowered himself to sit on the edge of his desk. He mumbled to himself, "Then he didn't run away with his daughter. He left her here, right under my nose. And now Vashon has her. And with her the Star and all its power."

Hearing him, Asher released a dramatic sigh. "My God, this will always seem like a fool's quest. Why don't we forget about the Star— surely we've enough to occupy us in Spitalfields. I know I can do without this blackguard Vashon whipping at our backs."

"It's not the Star's wealth I'm concerned with." Peterborough's face took on a faraway expression. "*The Chronicles of Crom Dubh* tell of its power. Whoever possesses the emerald, it is said, will see his enemies die. I've come to believe that possessing the Star is the only way to destroy Vashon."

"Whatever did you do to him, anyway? I've heard his vengeance gets worse as the years go by. And as his own wealth increases, so does his bloodlust for you."

Peterborough ran a hand through his fashionably cropped hair. Belligerently he stared into the fire.

"Well?" Asher prompted. "What did you do? Kill his mother? Rape his sister? What?"

"Vashon is my half brother."

With this news Asher looked as if he might slide to the floor. He gripped the pink brocade arms of his chair and stared dumbstruck at the viscount. "This cannot be . . . your own brother?" he finally whispered.

"Oh, it can be and it is," Peterborough confirmed. His face grew hard. "Blackwell's son is still alive."

"How—how did this come about?"

The viscount's cheeks flamed in anger. "Vashon has plagued me from his very conception! Can you imagine how I felt, left to rot in private school while my mother remarried and gave birth to a son—a child who would have wealth and title—all the things I did not!"

"Did you kill the boy's father too?"

Peterborough spat, "Of course not. I had no designs on the title then. I just couldn't bear the position imposed upon me by my birth, and when old Blackwell died of that fever I suddenly saw that the only thing standing between me and the viscounty was a thirteen-year-old boy."

"Your brother."

"My *half* brother."

"So what became of this babe?"

"I was duped. I meant for him to be killed but the task was botched."

"You thought to kill your own brother?"

"I tried to tolerate him. And until the boy was thirteen years of age I did tolerate him. But those years I'd been sent off to Germany hardened me. I couldn't endure it any longer. That some sniveling, pampered boy was taking everything that I deserved was more than I could bear. I crept back from Heidelberg and snatched the boy from his home."

"How did he escape you?"

The viscount turned grim. "I meant to kill him, but when it came to the final moment . . ."

"You could not," Asher whispered, finishing for him. There was a definite note of relief in his voice.

"No!" Peterborough abruptly denied, piercing Asher with one of his deadly stares. "I could have killed the boy! And without a day's remorse!" In frustration he slammed his hand on the mantel. "But he challenged me! That goddamned wretch challenged me to kill him so that he could come after me from beyond the grave. And do you know what? I faltered! Out of fear! I was afraid of a boy's curse!"

There was a silence as Asher took in this news. Then the viscount continued.

"He played easily upon my superstitions, so I thought to have two hirelings do the job. But Vashon was an extraordinarily handsome boy and when they realized they could get even more money selling him to a slaver in Algiers, they told me they had killed him. I only realized Vashon was alive ten years ago . . . when he showed up at my door."

Asher finally found his tongue. "He showed up—*here*?" he exclaimed in amazement.

Peterborough nodded. "He asked about our mother. When I told her she had died quickly, he seemed almost comforted."

"Did you—did you—?" Asher stuttered.

"Don't accuse me of matricide. She died in a theater fire. Don't you remember when the Alcée went up?"

Asher almost looked relieved. "So Vashon came for his title. However did you escape relinquishing it?"

"He didn't want the title. He said he'd come to tell me of his past. All that had happened to him since I had last seen him."

Asher made no comment so Peterborough continued.

"It seemed Vashon somehow survived his ordeal in Algiers. He took great pleasure in telling me of the men he had killed. Though he had still been a boy, he had killed the first man who had tried to . . . touch him." He paused. "He explained that one to me in great detail. He only did it to see the terror in my eyes."

"But how did he make such a fortune running the streets in Algiers?" Asher asked.

"He had found his way among the pirates of the Casbah. When he came to see me, even then he claimed he was quite wealthy—and he looked it."

"So Vashon cares nothing for the title. Instead he wants to ruin you, is that it?"

Peterborough nodded. "That's why we need that emerald. And God save us if it falls into his hands. My blood runs cold when I think of how he must have killed that man in that brothel. Vashon was but a boy, but even then his retribution was swift."

"For everyone but you, eh?"

Furious, Peterborough looked away. "For everyone but me," he repeated.

Asher watched him a moment, moved by the man's frustration. Hesitantly he reached out to touch him. Peterborough saw none of this. Not the soft, trembling hand, not the young man's eyes, suddenly filled with a strange kind of longing. But before the viscount turned his head again, Asher thought better of his actions. He pulled back his hand, and once more his eyes took on that indifferent gleam. "Buck up, my dear viscount. It's clear to me Vashon could have killed you at any time. So surely you've proved yourself craftier than he. You're still alive, aren't you?"

Peterborough put his head back and laughed. "But that's his torture, don't you see? He wants to drive me insane looking for that emerald. He knows about *The Chronicles of Crom Dubh*. And he's just taunting me into racing him for it. If he gets it before I do, my life will come to an end without him even raising his hand." He groaned. "Oh, that cursed stone. I wish I'd never heard of it. How I'd like to feel Michael Dayne's neck crushing within my hands! He was the beginning of my misfortune. That wretched thief told me about the Star in the first place and then lured me into hiring him to steal it from Inishmore Castle. But I had no idea he'd be tempted into keeping the thing for himself. And now because of that stupidity, I'm fighting Vashon for my very life!"

"Yet still, your venom is equal to Vashon's—or don't you remember the men of the *Leviathan*? I daresay those few who survived certainly speak your name in hushed tones."

"That Jew, Isaac Corbeil, was the owner of the *Leviathan*. Vashon didn't own that ship then, so the demise of its crew proved nothing to him. As for my venom being as strong as his, I only know one thing and I know it as certainly as I know the feel of my mistress's thighs." The viscount's voice lowered to a whisper. "If that pirate wanted me dead, I would *be* dead."

4

Aurora stared back into the fiery red eyes. The dragon mesmerized her. She had wandered to the front of the ship only to discover the ship's handsome yet fearful figurehead—a green Chinese dragon—lashed to the prow. She marveled at it for a long while, admiring its intricate details. Each green scale seemed to ripple with movement; even its painted vermilion mouth seemed to breathe fire. It stared back with a malevolent gaze, and it appeared so real that she thought if she should touch it, it would writhe beneath its lashings. The figurehead seemed to have nothing at all to do with the name *Seabravery*, but for some reason it reminded her of the ship's owner. He too was handsome yet fear-inspiring.

A week had passed and Aurora had yet to see the ship's mysterious owner again. It was quite a feat to avoid a person in the confines of the *Seabravery*, yet somehow she had managed to do it. Her trips to the decks were rare simply because the weather had turned stormy, and she found even her pelisse was hardly enough protection against the cold blasts of Atlantic winds.

So she had mostly stayed in her cabin or visited with Mrs. Lindstrom. She had eaten with the other passengers in the roundhouse while the captain and the ship's owner had been served in the owner's cabin. In many ways it had been easy to avoid the dark, dangerous-looking man across the passage from her. And avoiding him certainly seemed the safe thing to do, even if it was rather cowardly.

"Quite skillfully carved, isn't it, Miss Dayne?"

Aurora turned around and found Miss Cordelia Gideon standing next to her. Miss Gideon was the nanny of a child, Hester Rune, who had been orphaned. Hester, she had found out, was to go live with her uncle in St. George's, and Miss Gideon was taking her there. Despite the child's good prospects, Aurora had found Hester a sad little thing, much like the children who first entered the Home. Her pity only grew more with each passing day for she discovered the child's nanny was sore compensation for Hester's loss. Miss Gideon was a haughty and cool woman who ordered Hester about as if she were a half-wit. The woman seemed to possess no patience at all, and she was a poor choice for governess for a frightened young girl. Aurora's heart went out to Hester every time she saw her.

"Why, good afternoon, Miss Gideon, Hester," Aurora finally said. "I was just exploring the ship and just now discovered the dragon."

"The dragon scares Hester," Miss Gideon stated sourly. "But every day I bring the child to it so she will no longer succumb to these ridiculous fears."

Aurora burned with suppressed ire. She looked down at Hester, and the child was desperately trying not to look up at the dragon. Instead Hester's gaze was riveted to the deck, her face frozen in a terrified frown.

"The child is only five, Miss Gideon," Aurora reminded her. "Surely you don't expect her to behave as an adult? Why, even I felt a shiver or two run down my spine when I first saw the carved dragon—"

"The girl is an orphan, Miss Dayne," Miss Gideon answered brusquely. "And being such, Hester cannot afford such childish whims. She's alone in the world now. She must expect no coddling."

Aurora stared at the woman. How well she knew statements like that. A retort was just on the tip of her tongue but she bit it back. She knew firsthand what an orphan could or could not afford, and unfortunately the answer was always, not much. They were the castaways of society, these abandoned children, and in reality Hester was far more fortunate than most. Hester, at least, had an uncle she could live with, and perhaps, later in life, earn her board as a companion to his wife. Most others were tossed to the street, only to find an end not nearly as auspicious as their beginnings.

Gently Aurora bent to Hester and touched her frock. The child was dressed solemnly in lavender today, the color of half mourning, and Aurora was glad to see it. She found nothing more dreadful than seeing a little girl swathed in black.

"Aren't you pretty today, Hester," she said. "Now tell me, how do you like this big ship? Much better without the dragon, I wager."

Hester tentatively looked up but she still did not speak.

"Tell me, Hester, do you like nursery rhymes?" Aurora continued, determined to see the child smile once before the voyage was over. "I do," she added, "and I know scores of them. Would you like to hear one? My father taught me this one and it's my favorite."

Slowly Hester nodded. Her eyes grew wide and she waited in anticipation.

Aurora smiled. "Now you have to follow everything I do. Can you do that?"

Awestruck, Hester nodded again.

" 'An angel from heaven came tumbling down.' " Aurora fluttered her hands downward. When Hester hesitantly imitated her, Aurora smiled her encouragement.

" 'And asked the way to Aran.' " She pointed north. Hester followed, pointing her tiny finger in the direction of Aurora's.

" ' "I've come to find my long lost star!" ' " She put her hand to her eyes as if shielding them from the sun. Hester did likewise.

" ' "Can you help me with my errand?" ' " She put her hands together and rested her cheek on them as a cherub would. Hester followed, then began to giggle.

Aurora clapped her hands and hugged her. It was probably the first time the child had laughed since her parents had died, and the sound was delightful. "Oh, you're terribly quick, Hester! I can see you're going to be an apt pupil!"

"That's enough of this silliness, Miss Dayne," Miss Gideon remarked, rather rudely. For some reason she looked rather uncomfortable, and her gaze kept darting to a spot behind Aurora. "It will only excite the child, and then she'll be impossible to deal with. Come along, Hester, it's time for tea." With that Miss Gideon took Hester's hand and began dragging her away.

"But—but—" Aurora stammered helplessly, looking at Hester's forlorn backward glance. *There's another verse!* she wanted to say, yet it was too late. Before she could utter a sound, the sour-faced Miss Gideon and her melancholy charge were gone.

Slowly Aurora got to her feet. Irritated, she brushed the wrinkles from her pelisse. She released a huge sigh. The woman was impossible, and the worst part of it was that Hester was the one to pay for it in the long run. Feeling almost depressed, she turned back to the dragon. To her dismay, less than three feet from her the ship's owner stood by the the far rail. He was staring at her, an odd expression on his face that looked strangely like triumph.

He smiled then, and for some reason that smile made her fingers instinctively reach for the comfort of her locket, but she couldn't find it, hidden as it was under her woolen pelisse.

"Mr. Vashon," she began uneasily.

"Miss Dayne." He nodded his head, another ghost of a smile playing on his lips. "Must we be so formal?"

"Whatever do you mean?"

"Simply that I'm called Vashon. I've no other name. So it's absurd for you to pin a title upon it."

She looked at him. He had no other name. She knew perfectly well what *that* meant. Yet it was no surprise that this barely civilized man was born on the wrong side of the blanket. The only amazing thing was that being so lowborn he'd still been able to amass such a fortune. And that was easily enough explained away simply by uttering the word "pirate." Her eyes locked with his, and again the sense came over her that he cared not a whit for society and its rules. His bastardy probably concerned him less than would a hangnail. He unsettled her. She was not such a conformist that she had been ready to embrace John and all his ideologies, yet she was not such a renegade that she refused to acknowledge her own place in society as this pirate did.

"I was pleased to find you out here, Miss Dayne." He stepped toward her. "I hadn't seen you and feared that you were confined to your cabin with seasickness. Frail women on these voyages tend to get struck down like that."

"I don't consider myself frail, Mr.—" She colored from anger and embarrassment. It wasn't proper to call him "Mr." any longer. Yet calling him "Vashon" seemed completely too intimate.

So she would simply not call him anything, she thought to herself, still burning from his comment. Frail, indeed!

"Then you haven't been seasick?"

"No, not at all," she assured him. "In fact, I've been enjoying the voyage immensely."

"Good," he said, his brilliant green eyes glancing briefly over her pelisse. "You've a long sail ahead of you, and I've seen many a woman's . . . curves waste away to nothing on such trips. I should hate to see that happen to you."

She colored again. How dare he refer to her figure! "Good day to you, Mr.—" As if she were warding off a headache, her hand went to her temple. The man was impossible to deal with on a genteel level with his lack of a name and his improper comments. "Good day to you!" she finished and began to walk away, self-righteously indignant over his familiarities.

But then his familiarities only increased. She felt him take her arm in a steely grip. Wild-eyed, she looked about to see if anyone else saw him, yet the deck was devoid of everyone, even of sailors.

"You really are a sour little prig, Miss Dayne. Has anyone ever told you that?"

She stared up at him, trying with all her might to erase the shocked look on her face. He was so close she could see just how savage and handsome he was with his long jet black hair and harsh classic features. He was so close she could smell him. And his scent was akin to the sea, fresh, exhilarating, mysterious. Much too heady, like a sip of fine wine, and she wasn't at all sure if she should have more.

Yet, while his grasping her arm was bad enough, calling her a prig was beyond redemption. Miss Gideon was a prig. John was a prig. She was a lady of adventure.

But, then again, perhaps not.

She looked up at him, and when her frightened aqua eyes met his taunting green ones, she was beset by doubts. A lady of adventure would know how to put this man off. A lady of adventure would scoff at him, as she had read in countless novels. The lady would set him in his place and move on to greater challenges. She, on the other hand, seemed only to goad him on.

"Please—please, let go of my arm," she whispered, hating how small her voice sounded. "I really must go."

"Miss Dayne, is the only way I can talk to you to lock you in my cabin?"

Her eyes opened even wider.

"Well, is it?"

"No, not at all," she choked out.

"Good." Suddenly he dropped his hold. "For such a timid little wren you certainly can be trying. I suppose you weren't given that touch of red in your hair for nothing."

Self-consciously she tucked her hair further into her bonnet. She did her best to compose herself before she asked, "So what is it you wish to speak to me about, *sir*?"

He smiled at her pointed address. It was as if he could read her mind and see how he terrified her. She prickled beneath his stare. The man really was infuriating.

"Miss Dayne, Captain Corbeil and I have invited Mrs. Lindstrom to dinner tonight in my cabin and we were hoping you would join us. I can promise only the best cuisine. My chef was tutored by Carême, and he makes all his finest dishes for me."

"I'm not sure that is the proper—"

"I assure you it is quite proper," he interrupted. "Mrs. Lindstrom is certainly a sufficient chaperon for such a paragon of virtue as yourself."

His sarcasm was not lost on her, but she was determined not to let it bother her. "Yes, I suppose Mrs. Lindstrom would be fine, but—"

"But how do you know she'll be there?" He almost laughed. "Well, why don't you scurry away to her cabin and ask her? I'm sure she'll set your mind at ease. Besides, unlike you, she's rather taken with me. I think she'll persuade you to come if just to ease the boredom of this voyage . . . and assuage a little of that bald curiosity she has about me."

She couldn't help but bristle, particularly at the word "scurry." She didn't scurry. Did she?

Coolly she said, "I suppose if Mrs. Lindstrom is attending, it would be all right for me to be there. Since I do consider Captain Corbeil quite the gentleman, I'm sure the evening will be conducted with propriety." She dared a glance up at him. She'd hoped he'd understood the comment about Captain Corbeil. When he began to laugh, she was quite certain. Though instead of besting him, she herself felt bested.

"Why not come to my cabin and let me tell you a few stories about Isaac Corbeil?" He chuckled. "Perhaps I can change your mind."

"I think not. *I* am a good judge of character." She gave him a look that should have left no doubt in his mind what she had judged him to be. Again, infuriatingly, he laughed.

"You win, Miss Dayne, but you'll still come to dinner?" His mouth turned in a slight smirk.

"I shall be there."

"Seven o'clock?"

"Seven o'clock." She nodded and turned to go.

"Miss Dayne?"

She froze. She wasn't going to let him grab her again. She had never been grabbed by a man in her life and she was not about to let him make a habit of it. "Yes?" she said warily.

"I heard what you said to the child. About the Star of Aran."

She frowned. The Star of Aran? He was obviously referring to her nursery rhyme, but why he had called it that, she was not at all sure.

"That was just a rhyme my father taught me when I was a child," she said. "In fact, it's the only thing I remember about him. Why did you refer to the Star of Aran? Is there such a thing? Have you heard of it before?"

He studied her face. "It's of no account. I thought that might be the name of the rhyme."

"You have an astounding memory then, sir, to have surmised all of that after hearing the rhyme only once."

"I remember a lot of things, Miss Dayne."

There was a long silence as if they both were at a loss as to how to continue. The man was an ever increasing enigma to her, and she truly doubted she would ever understand him, most certainly not before she reached Jamaica.

She began to turn away.

"One more thing."

"Yes?" She looked up at him. For the briefest of seconds she thought he was going to touch her cheek, but if he was, he sufficiently quelled the notion.

"That child, Hester. She's a browbeaten little waif and doesn't smile often. It was kind of you to tell her that rhyme."

"It was nothing," she answered self-consciously. "I like children. I like to see them smile."

His stare grew more intense. "If that's the case, then I would think a young woman like yourself would be spending her time starting a family rather than sailing across the Atlantic with a ship full of strangers."

Startled, she met his gaze. Her desire for a family went back as far as she could remember. Even as a child, her favorite time of the year had been Christmas because that was when the orphans went caroling at the town houses in Berkeley Square. And though Aurora, the youngest back then, shivered from the cold and the snow, she had never wanted Mrs. Bluefield to return them to Whitechapel. Instead she had wanted to stay singing in front of those open doors, to remain peeking in at the cozy family life, long after the master of the household had lifted up one of his children to put a penny in the cup for the Home.

But her longing for a family was a subject she had rarely broached with anyone, let alone this very male stranger. She hadn't even told John Phipps, for she knew instinctively that her dream would have never worked with him. And when she was truthful with herself, she knew that was why she was on the *Seabravery* now. Though a part of her was certainly running away, a part of her seemed also to be running to something. Or someone. If he existed at all.

She gazed reproachfully at the ship's owner. The man was abrupt and inquisitive to the point of rudeness. The fact that she never knew what he would say next rattled her considerably. With a great deal of effort, she tried to put on an indifferent facade.

"I've always considered my young charges to be my family, sir. I've not seen the need for anything more."

"I see."

His eyes met hers. There was the trace of a smirk on his lips. It was as if he had seen right through to her vulnerability and, if it were possible, had even followed the path of her thoughts. Unwittingly she blushed.

"Until tonight then, Miss Dayne," he said, mercifully excusing her.

"Yes," she choked, appalled that on just her second meeting with this ungodly pirate, he had somehow found her Achilles heel.

5

> An angel from heaven came tumbling down
> And asked the way to Aran.
> "I've come to find my long lost Star
> Can you help me with my errand?"

Vashon studied the rhyme again and again. Painstakingly he had written it in his ship's log. His lips moved as he read it silently now for the hundredth time. A knock on the door made him close the log in frustration. With great impatient strides he crossed the cabin and flung open the door.

"You called for me?" Isaac stepped into Vashon's cabin.

"He gave her a nursery rhyme! A damned nursery rhyme, and it is so much gibberish!" Vashon handed him the log.

Isaac read the rhyme, then rubbed his chin with the remaining thumb and forefinger of his right hand. Finally he said, "Well, old Michael Dayne was no fool. He gave his daughter the clue to the Star, but just what that is . . . Do you think she knows it?"

"I sincerely doubt it. She's not much of an actress, and when I asked her about the Star, she looked absolutely stumped—as if I were speaking Greek." Vashon took the log back and shoved it into a built-in mahogany bookcase. Frustration etched the handsome planes of his face. "When I heard her recite the damned thing to that child, I thought I would almost laugh out loud with glee! I could hardly wait to get back here and decipher it. But it makes no sense! There's got to be another verse, that's all. And we'll just have to sit patiently until we can get it out of her."

Isaac chuckled, his tanned leathery face appearing almost youthful in his mirth. "Ah, and patience is your virtue, Vashon. Especially with women. Why, I'm surprised you're not beating her cabin door down demanding that she decipher it for you. I've seen mightier women than her crumple at your feet. Not that they didn't look happy about it afterward, mind you, but you do have a rather forceful way about you —why use the kid gloves now?"

Vashon scowled at him. "We've a ship full of passengers. How, pray, should I deal with them while Miss Dayne calls for help from her cabin —throw them all overboard?"

"You've done worse."

"To some, maybe, not innocent passengers." Vashon tapped his fingers on his deck. "But don't worry. I've set up dinner for tonight and besides . . ." He stopped in thought.

"Besides what?" Isaac prompted.

Vashon smiled darkly. "She'll be ours soon enough."

Aurora dug to the bottom of her willow basket and found the gown she wanted. She shook it out and ruefully examined the wrinkles.

The dress was made of a simple blue cotton, printed with tiny white dots. She herself had embroidered the tiny peach-colored rosebuds on the neckline and sleeves. It was her best gown, but she had packed it at the bottom thinking it would be a very long time before she'd find the chance to wear it. Now, looking at its crumpled state, she wished she'd packed it at the top.

Restlessly she threw it on her bedstead. She pressed the wrinkles out with her palms, then went to fetch her comb. She'd procrastinated long enough and now didn't have much time to be ready. Still, she was determined to look her best.

All afternoon she'd paced her cabin, thinking about *him*. She'd been so close to canceling the owner's offer of dinner that she had even penned a note. But then she had torn it to little bits, unwilling to be labeled a coward. He did terrify her in a strange and inexplicable way. In their few meetings the ship's owner had been able to discover things in her that she had always held close. As if he could see what she held in her deepest heart. Sometimes she had the unsettling feeling that he knew more about her than she knew herself.

Yet as much as she wanted to avoid him, she still couldn't hide the fact that he fascinated her. His hard features and his even harder stance should have put her off. Yet somehow they didn't. She felt pulled to him. As if something in her spirit yearned for his company.

In disgust, she shook her head and grabbed her little mirror. Slowly she unpinned her hair and began combing it. It wouldn't do to dwell on the mysterious Vashon. She was still chagrined over their last encounter. That, she reassured herself, was really why she was going to his little dinner. She was determined to look as cool and unperturbed as she could, so that he would see her untouched by his abrupt behavior.

A soft knock on her door snapped her out of her dreary thoughts. Quickly she plaited her hair and thrust the braid over one shoulder. She opened the door and found her young steward there.

"Good evening, Benny," she said demurely.

"Good evening, miss," the boy said, placing the copper hip bath in the corner. But take away their veneer of civility and if he

She watched as he went back and forth from the passage bringing in her water. She was already quite fond of Benny. He was a blond lad, hardly bigger than she was, but where his movements should have been quick and full of uncontained youthful energy, they were not. One of his legs was missing, and normally the boy used a crutch, but today he went about on his peg, an elaborate piece of whalebone carved with scrimshaw. Yet the most striking thing about him wasn't his sadly absent leg, nor his handsome English face, but the tiny monkey in gold-and-scarlet livery that tenaciously clung to his shoulder, no matter how rough the ride.

"And how is Koonga this evening?" she asked, holding a finger for the little creature to grab.

"She's got Cook in a fine temper," he replied. "She broke into the pantry and stole the last drop of cream just as Cook was preparing coffee for Mrs. Lindstrom."

"Oh, dear."

The monkey wrapped her prehensile tail around her wrist then started to chatter as if rapaciously defending her character.

Benny turned his head to his little passenger and scowled. "She's going to be monkey soup, if she don't watch herself."

"Oh, not that!" Aurora laughed when Koonga gave him the most astonished expression.

"Will there be anything else, miss?" he asked when her bath was ready.

"No, no, of course not. I've already inconvenienced you enough." With a nervous glance she watched him hobble to the cabin door. She was still uncomfortable being waited on, and though Benny was hardly more than sixteen, she was sure she'd never think it proper to have a male in her cabin.

"The captain says he'll knock on your door precisely at seven, miss," the boy said after he'd handed her a stack of fresh linen towels.

"Thank you so much," she said and watched him make his way down the passage. Discreetly her gaze slid again to his peg leg. She'd been rather curious as to how the boy had lost a leg. She'd certainly had the manners to refrain from asking, but she still found it odd that so many of the crew members were maimed. The captain had his fingers missing, and even the cook sported a black silk patch over his eye. She had no complaints, of course. All the crew were clean, well-dressed, and scrupulously polite. But take away their veneer of civility and it had dawned on her that they were a rather motley bunch.

When Benny was gone, she quickly bathed. She pulled on her stockings and chemise, then lifted the blue gown over her head. The gown tied beneath her breasts and sported an inner bodice of plain drab linen that was precariously low. Her modesty was kept intact by the attached apron front, which she carefully pinned over her bosom so that the embroidery pattern would meet at the shoulders. Next she pulled on her slippers, or "straights," as she knew the fashionable world called them. Since each heelless shoe was made exactly alike, she'd had to break them in herself, and it wasn't until she walked to her dresser that she realized she had them on the wrong feet.

After draping her large gray woolen shawl across her shoulders, she pinned the mass of her hair into a large bun, then brazenly loosened a few curls at her temple. She was almost going to pin them back when another knock banged at her door. Her stomach tightened and she felt her nerves jump. It was seven.

"Good evening, Captain," she said calmly when she answered the door. Captain Corbeil was looking most handsome in a dark blue coat with gold braiding that matched his cap. Unlike his sailors who wore only gun-mouthed trousers, the captain sported white breeches and boots. He held out his arm in a most chivalrous manner and she took it, glad to have something to hang on to even for the few steps to the owner's cabin.

When they made their entrance, Mrs. Lindstrom was seated majestically on the dolphin-legged couch and sipping a sherry. In the far corner of the cabin Benny was scuttling about, setting up a gateleg table for their meal. For a moment Aurora thought they were the only two in the large cabin until she glanced over her shoulder and saw Vashon at the bookcases pouring from a set of decanters.

He looked magnificent. He was as plainly dressed as any man she had ever seen—he wore only black pantaloons, a double-breasted waistcoat in bottle green merino, and a white muslin cravat—but the severity of his costume suited him as none other would. His attire only accentuated his startling handsomeness and, too, that particular facet of his character that straddled the razor's edge of civilization.

She hardly realized she was staring at him until their eyes met. Then vivid emerald clashed with soft aqua, and a strange, foreboding tingle went down her spine. She wanted to look away, but she found she couldn't. His gaze held her captive almost as well as his arms could have. And as he gazed at her, she found something in his eyes she had never seen before. A look of total, incontestable possession. He looked at her as a pirate might his captured booty . . . or, perhaps, one of his female prisoners.

"Sherry, Miss Dayne?" he asked abruptly, breaking the spell.

"I don't . . . ah . . . thank you." She had meant to say no, but Benny was already at her side with a tiny sherry glass. She graciously accepted it and took a nervous sip. The Phippses had always strictly forbidden spirits in the Home, and in her entire life she had never tasted them before. But then, she was doing a lot of things now she had never before done. Again her anxious gaze swept distrustfully over her host.

"Oh, Aurora," Mrs. Lindstrom burst out, "I am so glad you've arrived! Vashon was just telling me all sorts of hair-raising tales! Imagine! Even now a dreadful sea serpent could be swimming beneath us—ready to devour the entire ship!" Mrs. Lindstrom eagerly scooted over on the couch so that there was room for one more.

Aurora gave the widow a huge smile of relief and gladly let the captain seat her on the couch. She wondered how she would have gotten along at all on this strange voyage if it wasn't for the audacious Flossie Lindstrom.

"I can't imagine there are actually such things as sea serpents," Aurora lightly reassured her, thankful for the reprieve. "But nonetheless, surely the Royal Navy will be there to protect us should we encounter such nefarious creatures, isn't that right, Captain?"

The captain smiled and took an elbow seat next to the ladies. "Most definitely," he answered, giving Vashon a sly grin. "In fact, if you must know, the Royal Navy is quite fond of Vashon's ships. It seems wherever he goes, the Royal Navy is quick to follow—"

"Brandy?" Vashon asked, scowling.

The captain cheerfully accepted. "Why not? If we're to be attacked by sea serpents, then I should like to go happy."

Aurora smiled and took another sip of her sherry. It burned like fire down her throat. She wasn't sure she liked the stuff, but it did make her feel a bit more comfortable, which was certainly hard to do in Vashon's presence.

"Pooh!" Mrs. Lindstrom burst out. "All this talk of sea serpents! The only reason you gentlemen are not quivering in your boots is because that terrible figurehead wards off all the sea creatures!" The vivacious widow looked as if she were anxious to devour a really choice bit of gossip. "Now do tell, Vashon. Why *is* there a dragon affixed to the prow of this ship? I suspect it's for the same reason this supposed 'packet' has a gundeck right above my cabin. For shame, Vashon! Why, this is no packet at all but a readily armed warship!"

A slow smile turned up the corner of Vashon's mouth. "This is a packet, I assure you. The gundeck is rarely used—a vestige of times past. As for the dragon, every ship I own has a dragon for a figurehead, regardless of the ship's name. I'm partial to them."

Aurora watched him while he leaned casually against the bookcases. He did like dragons. There were dragons woven into the carpet beneath his booted feet. Behind him a black-lacquer coffer was painted with rampant dragons. Even as she looked down she saw a dragon etched into the crystal of her tiny sherry glass.

"And is that the only reason?" Mrs. Lindstrom prodded.

"I also find people remember them."

"And perhaps . . . stay clear of them?"

Vashon took a sip of his drink. His smile broadened. "That's one perspective, I suppose."

"Oh, this is fascinating. Just fascinating." The widow clapped her hands. "So that's why your ships have never been accosted—all the wicked ships simply sail away when they see that fearsome dragon."

Aurora looked down at her sherry glass. Fingering the lizard around her neck, she wondered if all the good ships sailed away in fear too. That thought didn't make her rest easy, especially when she knew all too well that Mrs. Lindstrom was disembarking in St. George's, not three quarters of the way to her own destination.

"Dinner is ready, sir," Benny announced.

Captain Corbeil jumped up to assist Mrs. Lindstrom. Aurora was just about to rise from the couch herself when Vashon offered his strong arm. She was reluctant to accept his help, but something inside her refused to show him how he intimidated her. Giving him a gracious smile, she lightly took his arm and though she found it shockingly hard and massive, she allowed him to lead her to the table.

When they were seated, conversation turned to such mundane topics as the dinner wine and the cook's prowess in the galley. The meal was served on elaborate Imari porcelain, and Aurora conceded the cook was nearly a genius to be able to serve seven delicious courses on shipboard provisions. The crowning glory to the meal was a pineapple that one of Vashon's ships had brought to Queenhithe the night they left. Aurora had certainly seen the costly fruit in shopkeepers' windows, but she had never imagined she'd ever taste one. As Benny cut it, the room filled with the exotic fruit's scent, and while she was overfull from dinner, she found herself eating every slice she'd been served.

When she was finally through, she placed aside her empty fruit dish and found her host's unsettling green gaze upon her. She wondered if he thought her a glutton, but something else seemed to be on his mind.

While the ladies were being served their tea, he finally said to her, "I understand you're off to Jamaica, Miss Dayne. What takes you there?"

"My new employer lives there, sir." She felt odd answering his question.

"And who is that, if I may be so presumptuous?"

"Lady Perkins of Roselawn Plantation."

"Vashon," Mrs. Lindstrom interrupted, "have you heard of Roselawn? I have not, and I do take pride in knowing *everyone*. But you are ever so much better traveled than I—can you tell us about this place where Aurora is going?"

Vashon leaned back in his chair. He gave the captain a glance. "Yes, I've heard of Roselawn. I've heard of Lady Perkins too. I believe she's rather a tyrant. In the future I believe Miss Dayne would do well to reconsider the merits of rushing off to be in the employ of one she does not know."

"Oh, but you must be mistaken!" Aurora burst out, shocked that he could be saying such a thing about her wonderful new employer. "Lady Perkins could not possibly be as you describe. Her accommodations for me on this ship are alone enough evidence of her kindness."

"How else is she to lure a nice English girl from her home? In my experience, it's better to use honey than vinegar . . . at least at first."

"Her letter to me was nothing but gracious, and the pay she has offered is beyond generous. You must be mistaken, sir. It's not Lady Perkins of Roselawn of whom you speak."

"Your loyalty to an employer you've never seen before does you credit, Miss Dayne," Vashon said, an odd expression on his face. He seemed almost pleased by her defense of her employer, yet, too, disgruntled by her sudden show of spirit. "However, in the future if you come to realize the lack of merit in being a handmaiden to abusive old women, I hope you will acknowledge to me that I was correct."

Aurora tried to still the anger she found welling up in her breast. The man's arrogance knew no bounds! "I sincerely doubt that will occur, but even if it did, *sir*, I hardly think it likely you and I will ever cross paths again after this voyage. So there will be no opportunity to acknowledge such a thing to you."

"Oh, dear, Aurora," Mrs. Lindstrom interjected, pushing aside her plate. "What if Vashon is right about Lady Perkins?"

"But he is not right," Aurora assured her, feeling rather brazen.

"Come now, Miss Dayne," Vashon said, "You're hardly old enough to speak with such authority about what goes on in the great wide world. After all, what are you, a mere girl of eighteen?"

Aurora stiffened. How she hated questions about her age! "I may only be eighteen, sir, but I speak with the authority of good sense. And with that, I cannot believe Lady Perkins to be anything but a good and just woman."

"Eighteen?" Flossie burst out, "Good heavens, Aurora, how can you now be eighteen when you told me as we left Queenhithe you were nineteen?"

Dreadful silence filled the air as Aurora felt all eyes on her. A slow, painful crimson stained her cheeks and her gaze didn't dare stray from her fruit dish, as if it offered salvation.

"I'm terribly sorry, Mrs. Lindstrom," she began, her voice lowering with shame, "but being an orphan I was not privileged to be left with the date of my birth. So . . . I . . . must guess at my age."

Flossie closed her eyes as if unspeakably ashamed of herself. Isaac simply looked away, as if the whole display made him uncomfortable. The only one who dared stare at all was Vashon. But Aurora couldn't decide whether his fascination stemmed from delight over her humiliation or from a grudging respect for the manner in which she bore it.

"How shockingly rude of me, Aurora. Do say you forgive me and I'll never ask such wretched questions again," Flossie finally prattled.

"Please, it's nothing," Aurora answered, wanting desperately for the conversation to change.

Flossie took a deep breath. "Well, do let's settle this Lady Perkins problem. The thing to do, love, is come with me to St. George's. Write this awful woman an apology and allow me to find you some suitable employment—"

Without warning Captain Corbeil started and knocked over his after-dinner Chartreuse. The yellow green liqueur sloshed off the edge of the table right onto Mrs. Lindstrom's bombazine skirts, interrupting all conversation.

"A thousand apologies! That was terribly clumsy of me!" the captain exclaimed.

"No, no, it's all right," the widow answered, dabbing her skirts with her napkin.

"You must let me pay for the gown."

"Heavens, no! My maid can take care of this in no time. You must put such thoughts out of your mind!"

"Then I shall escort you to your cabin at once so that the damage can be undone."

Without further pause, the captain held out his arm and seemed to rush the widow along. Aurora began a fleeting farewell, but in a flurry they were out the door. To her dismay, she then found she was alone at the table with *him*.

"More tea, miss?" Startled, she looked up and found Benny at her side with the silver teapot. She practically swooned with relief.

"No, thank you. I really should be off too." She gave the boy a nervous smile and stood. She then summoned her courage and faced her host. "It really has been a lovely dinner. You were quite gracious to invite me."

Vashon rose from his chair. He looked as if there were some unfinished business that had yet to be taken care of satisfactorily.

"You needn't leave, Miss Dayne," he said.

Her gaze trailed to Benny who was ready to exit the cabin door with a trayful of dirty dishes.

"No, I really must say good night. . . ." The cabin door shut behind Benny with startling silence. Feeling a bit like a trapped pigeon, she glanced nervously about for her shawl. She had had it on when she had first entered the cabin, but at some point in the evening she had lost it.

She spied the gray wool draped on the dolphin-legged couch and quickly moved to retrieve it, but before she could get there, to her dismay she found her path blocked. She looked up and saw Vashon's brilliant green eyes twinkling with sardonic amusement.

"My cabin isn't Almack's, Miss Dayne. You needn't quit my company simply because we're alone. There are no disapproving matrons here to take away your voucher."

"Really, it's been a long evening and surely you look forward to retiring. I mustn't keep you." Ignoring his sarcasm, she tried to go around but he thwarted her every movement. Finally when she could see he was not going to let her fetch her shawl, a furrow of irritation appeared on her brow. He was almost laughing at her. As always, his easy intimidation seemed to please him enormously, and that only inflamed her ire.

"May I have my shawl—or do you possess no chivalry whatsoever?" she asked sharply. She hoped that was enough of a dressing down to make him let her pass, but she was quickly disappointed to find it wasn't. While her sudden show of temper seemed to surprise him, he also appeared to find her accusation wickedly amusing.

"I have to admit that question's never been bluntly put before me." He smiled and crossed his arms over his massive chest. "But now that it has, I do fear you won't like the answer."

Her eyes widened. The man didn't even have the grace to lie.

"I see," she said icily. "If that's the case, then surely you can see it is imperative I not stay a minute longer." She gave her shawl a parting glance, then made for the cabin door. Benny could fetch it for her tomorrow. There was no point in taking any risk now in trying to retrieve it.

She had just made it to the threshold when she heard him stride up behind her. The door was open barely six inches before his hand deftly pressed it closed once more.

"I can't allow you to leave like this. I would be remiss in my duties as host if I did."

She spun around and faced him. Her cheeks flamed; her temper flared.

"You allow me to leave, sir, or the captain shall hear about this! I'll not let you keep me prisoner here a moment more!"

"Prisoner? Is that what you think you are?" He leaned against the wall. It was an unnerving move for it only brought him closer to her. Her head tipped back to look up at him and he seemed to revel in her accusatory stare. Slowly he added, "You have a lot to learn about prisoners, Aurora."

Her name on his lips shocked her. It had a gentleness to it that she hadn't expected. In the deep, rich tones of his voice, he spoke it almost like a caress. An intimate, appreciative caress. She suddenly wanted to blush to her toes.

"I certainly know enough about prisoners not to want to learn about them from you," she answered, her voice barely above a whisper.

"Perhaps after what I said about Lady Perkins you think she can teach you better."

"As I told you before, your unfounded tales of my employer cannot turn me against her."

"Even after the Widow Lindstrom's offer? Come along, Aurora, that must seem rather attractive to you now. Tell me you have no thoughts at all of leaving the ship at St. George's." His demand hung heavy in the air, carrying much more weight than she would have supposed.

She clenched her fists at her side, then met that insolent emerald gaze. "I think very highly of Lady Perkins," she informed him. "And until I reach Kingston and my new employer proves me wrong, I shall continue to think highly of her. In the meantime, your opinions of my situation concern me not a whit. In fact, my only worry is why you've taken an interest in them. Surely you've grander things to occupy your mind than my welfare?"

She certainly expected to see annoyance on his face. He had clearly wanted her to be wary of Lady Perkins, but with this news, the tension left his face. He suddenly laughed.

"Your name suits you, Aurora. You're either fiery—or gray—just like the dawn. But I think I've seen too much gray. You definitely put too much stake in which way the winds of propriety might be blowing. But I dare say it now, the winds may be shifting."

With that enigmatic statement, he straightened and sauntered to the couch. She watched him as he scooped up her shawl. To her surprise, he held it out like a gentleman, waiting for her to allow him to place it upon her shoulders. But unlike a gentleman, when she stepped into it, he took a bit too long to relinquish it. His hands, strong and unimaginably warm, wrapped her slowly in its warmth, then they ran down her shawl-clad arms only to make her shiver at his touch.

She did not recoil as she thought she might. If anything, she almost longed for the caress again. She had never felt a man's caress. John Phipps had never touched her. Perhaps if he'd been consumed by hot, selfless passion, she might never have left him, but his passion had been a cold thing, wrought of his own greed and self-righteousness, and there had been no room in it to consider her desires. To John, she had been a thing to covet, not caress.

Now as she turned her head to glance at Vashon, she couldn't help feeling mildly disappointed that he had stepped aside. As dangerous and unexplored as it was, she almost wanted to experience his touch again. But he was already at the threshold. As if nailed to the floor, she stood watching him while he opened the cabin door and held it out wide for her to exit.

"Your bedchamber awaits, my lady," he said as if to nudge her from her spot.

"Vashon, the widow's snug in her cabin, but now what in God's name are we going to do about—?" The captain suddenly appeared at the door, yet the minute he saw Aurora his words died on his lips.

Aghast at the captain's shocked expression, Aurora colored right down to the swell of her breasts. She was making a spectacle of herself. By every appearance it looked as though Vashon was trying to get her to leave him for her own bedchamber—and that she was reluctant!

Mortified at what she supposed he thought of her character, she could hardly look the captain in the eye as she swept past him. With a swift murmuring of thanks to her host, she exited and desperately sought respite in her cabin.

After she had gone, the men exchanged few words. Vashon only said, "It's taken care of."

And the captain merely answered, "Thank God. For a moment there, I thought we were going to have to kidnap this entire shipload of passengers—starting with that damnable widow!"

6

That caress bedeviled her for nights.

Even now as Aurora stood on the fo'c'sle deck warming her face in the sun, the memory of it possessed her. She had once thought if ever she would dream of a man he would be like those gallant, fair-haired princes in one of Perrault's fairy tales. But now, much to her chagrin, her dreams seemed captured by a totally different character—the shadowy, secretive, terrifying owner of the *Seabravery*.

It had only been a touch, but for some reason she couldn't put it out of her mind. When she was asleep in her little bed, over and over again she replayed the scene with Vashon as he helped her with her shawl. But in her version, he didn't step back as he had actually done. His hand didn't leave her. Instead his large iron-strong hand swept down her arm and rode at her waist until she chanced to turn her head. Then when her eyes met his, he kissed her, kissed her as deeply as her chaste little mind could imagine.

She should have been having nightmares, especially after what she believed Captain Corbeil thought of her. But when she awoke, she was much too concerned about her dreams of Vashon and what those dreams meant for her to begin worrying about the captain.

"The captain has said we may have a storm by this evening."

Frowning, Aurora suddenly snapped out of her dark musings to look at Miss Gideon, who had spoken. She, Mrs. Lindstrom, and Miss Gideon were spending the afternoon together watching Hester. Aurora realized she must have missed some of the conversation because she couldn't remember when their idle talk had turned to the weather.

"We've had terribly fine sailing. I'm not surprised our luck is about to change," Aurora commented, hiding her discomposure as she stared out at the blue horizon. They had had fine weather in the weeks they'd been at sea. The days were now even getting balmy and no longer did they need their pelisses to walk about abovedecks.

"Our luck won't change, my dears," Mrs. Lindstrom assured them. "Captain Corbeil is more than a capable seaman. He is driven to get us to St. George's."

"And how much farther have we to go?" Miss Gideon asked. "I shouldn't like to have to endure more than one storm on this voyage."

"Isaac—ah—*our captain* told me that we should be there within the week." Mrs. Lindstrom had the grace to look flustered by her mistake. To cover herself, she chatted on. "You know, I've never seen a ship make such extraordinary time. Captain Corbeil doesn't even furl a portion of the canvas at sunset—none of that lallygagging around for him! No indeed!"

Aurora couldn't help smiling at Flossie. Ever since the night the captain had spilled his Chartreuse on Flossie's skirts, the widow had been unable to speak of anything but their fine, upstanding captain. Mrs. Lindstrom had even asked her once, on the sly, if Aurora thought it too bold to invite the captain to afternoon tea in her cabin. In spite of her age, Flossie had developed a grand, schoolgirlish infatuation for the captain, and Aurora thought it charming. She was just glad the voyage wouldn't be over too soon. At least for Mrs. Lindstrom.

Not having missed a thing, Miss Gideon gave the widow a disapproving stare. "Our captain may be extraordinary but he'd have to be God to will away a storm. The best I hope for is that it doesn't keep the child awake. I don't abide indulging a child's terrors, and I must say it's quite difficult to get one's sleep when there's wailing in the cabin."

How charitable, Aurora thought bitterly as she looked at the woman. Hardly able to keep her tongue still, she instead turned her attention to Hester. The child was staring up at the crow's nest as if she had just discovered for the first time that there was a man up there, and Aurora's heart once more went out to her. She fervently hoped the storm wouldn't be too bad, for there obviously would be no comfort for the little girl if it were.

"Miss Dayne?" Miss Gideon paused as if for effect.

Aurora turned her attention back to Hester's nanny.

"I've been meaning to speak with you about something, Miss Dayne," Miss Gideon continued. "With your permission, may I broach the subject now?"

"Of course you may. What is on your mind?" Aurora answered, a bit too tersely.

"Do you realize you're the only one continuing on to Jamaica? I just spoke with the Wainwrights this morning, and I've now tallied all nine passengers."

"Surely the *Seabravery* will be taking more passengers on in St. George's. I doubt I shall be the lone passenger."

"But what if you are? Have you thought of the possibility?" Miss Gideon narrowed her eyes. "I certainly wouldn't want to be in your situation. I could not ever travel alone with such heathens." The woman's gaze slid down the companionway to the weather deck below. There Vashon stood speaking with the Moroccan sailmaker. Even from the fo'c'sle they could hear him slip easily into French as he pointed out a rip in one of the royals.

"Vashon is no heathen, Miss Gideon," Mrs. Lindstrom spoke up. "He is more accurately portrayed as an eccentric."

"Eccentric or not, I don't believe it is right that a young woman should sail across the Caribbean with him as her only company. A lady of high morals would adamantly refuse. Don't you agree, Miss Dayne?"

Irritated, Aurora chose her words carefully. She longed to put Miss Gideon in her place, but even more than that she wanted to deny the woman's accusation in the hope that by doing so it might erase that wicked dream—and her own unbidden reaction to it.

"On the contrary," Aurora began passionately, "it is the woman of high morals who need not refuse. What has she to fear? I still believe there will be other passengers brought aboard at St. George's. However, if there are not, I can assure you that my behavior always is and always has been beyond reproach. So I don't see how it would matter a whit if I were sailing with heathens or eccentrics, for I, unlike some, cannot be led astray."

"Bravo, Aurora!" Mrs. Lindstrom burst out.

"What shocking cheek!" Miss Gideon gave them both a baleful glare. She snatched up her charge and heaved herself down the companionway.

"That is an utterly disagreeable woman! To even question your respectability is beyond the pale! I only hope the poor child's uncle is not so frightful!" Mrs. Lindstrom snapped closed her parasol as if to reinforce the point.

"Yes, so do I," Aurora agreed uncomfortably, watching the woman charge past the deckhouse.

Vashon had finished his conversation and was now leaning against the weather deck's railing. She saw that he too was watching the indignant Miss Gideon's flight.

As soon as she disappeared, he looked across the ship to Aurora, and with that one penetrating emerald glance he shook Aurora's self-righteous moral indignation to its core. Aghast, she averted her eyes and refused to be further seduced, but not before she was beset with renewed doubt. Only a moment ago she'd been utterly convinced that she could withstand any sort of treachery and keep her respectability intact. But was she being a fool? After all, there were such things as dragons—even if just in the imagination. Was she really up to taking one on all by herself?

"Do you really think we won't be taking any more passengers on at St. George's?" she suddenly asked Mrs. Lindstrom, a frown furrowing her smooth brow.

"Of course not, love. Besides, you needn't worry. There's always Captain Corbeil to look out for you."

Aurora looked across the decks once more. The captain had joined Vashon at the railing. The two men were laughing and it was obvious they were sharing some kind of joke.

Suddenly, inexplicably, she wasn't reassured.

By early that evening the captain's prediction came true. Though it had yet to rain, ominous rumbling clouds appeared on the horizon and the sea had become rough, easily tossing the ship across its churning surface. By dinnertime Aurora found it difficult to make herself presentable, for every time she tried to pour some water from her ewer, the ship would lurch and she'd miss the bowl entirely. When her face was finally washed, her cabin looked as if it had experienced a minor flood.

Dinner was quiet. Most of the passengers had either requested dinner in their cabins or were too sick to eat from all the tossing about. Only Mrs. Lindstrom and the Magoun brothers were in the roundhouse when she arrived, and that company was fleeting, for though Alex and Lee Magoun obviously considered themselves, at seventeen, quite manly, even they were not able to abide their dinners amid the roiling action of the ship. Before the meal was finished, they had already made their excuses, and Mrs. Lindstrom also soon took her leave to see to her seasick maid, leaving Aurora alone to return to her cabin.

For some reason she was a little depressed about facing that empty cabin for yet another evening. After the constant companionship at the Home, Aurora found it disheartening to spend so much time alone.

Even within the confines of the ship, she felt isolated from the rest of the passengers, especially since all their cabins were below the vestigial gundeck and hers was aft, right off the weather deck.

She lingered in the galley as long as she could, but finally made her way to her cabin. Though the turbulence had yet to affect her constitution, she still found it difficult walking down the passageway to her room. She swayed from side to side, clutching the mahogany paneling whenever a roll became too fierce. She practically staggered like a drunkard the last few steps to her door, but before she could get there, a great roll knocked her sideways and propelled her against the opposite cabin's door. She would have been all right except for the fact that Vashon's door was not securely latched. It swung open with her weight and she was hurled onto the carpet right inside his quarters.

Shocked by what had happened, she quickly got to her knees and prayed that the cabin was empty. Yet as she looked up a terrifying sight met her eyes. A fiery green dragon, more ruthless and lifelike than the one on the prow, loomed above her, ready for attack. With the rocking motion of the ship, it actually seemed to move. As she knelt on the carpet transfixed, it took her a moment even to begin to comprehend that the dragon was not real, much less make the connection that it was a painting—a painting done on the flesh of a man's naked back.

Before she could even tear her eyes away, Vashon turned and suddenly the dragon was gone from her view, to be replaced by the scowling face of the cabin's occupant.

"Shouldn't you knock first, Miss Dayne?" Vashon commented before he grasped her wrists and pulled her to her feet. The vessel dipped then, and though she suspected he possessed quite enough strength to steady the both of them, he let the ship toss them against the door, which closed with a thud.

"Your—your back—" she stammered, unnerved by his closeness and by what she had seen.

"Yes, it's called a tattoo," he commented dryly.

"But how could you have painted such a thing on yourself? It's on your back," she whispered.

"I didn't paint it—a pretty Chinese maiden put it on my back. In Peking. In the Forbidden City." He looked down at her and suddenly seemed quite pleased with what he saw. A ghost of a smile played on his lips.

"In China?" she asked, looking up at him with bewildered aqua eyes. "But if you got it in China, wouldn't it have come off by now?"

"It doesn't come off." He turned slightly and presented part of the dragon to her. "Touch it and you'll see for yourself."

She had never touched a man's back, but this one demanded she do it. The dragon was so ferocious and detailed, she could hardly believe it was on his skin. Timidly she reached out her hand. Her fingertips met with the creature's scaly tail. The thing whipped down his lower back serpentine fashion, only to disappear beneath the waist of his trousers. But though the dragon seemed much too real, all she felt was warm, smoothly muscled flesh. If she'd had her eyes closed, she would never have known the dragon was there at all.

"But why doesn't it come off?" she asked in a hushed voice.

He turned back to her. The ship lurched and he held fast to the door, steadying her between his arms. "It doesn't come off because it's not on my skin, it's in my skin. It was put there with a needle and dye."

"Then it must have hurt terribly . . ."

He suddenly laughed, and she was struck by how white and even his teeth were, and how fascinatingly handsome he was when he smiled. If he wasn't so barbarously "eccentric," as Mrs. Lindstrom put it, he would surely have women swooning at his feet. As she watched him from such close proximity, she wondered if there weren't a few swooning anyway.

"It did hurt. A great deal, in fact," he said as he looked down at her. "But this little Chinese wench was skillful with the needle . . . and when she was through I recall quite clearly her unusual methods to take my mind off the pain."

Aurora stared at him. She wasn't even sure what he was implying, but somehow she knew instinctively a proper gentleman would never speak such things to her.

The ship rolled and she was thrust against his hard, naked chest. Once more his scent—so wild and mysterious—assailed her. She didn't want to touch him again, but with her back to the cabin door he was the only thing to grab. Her one hand wrapped around his steely upper arm while her other hand met with his hair-covered torso. It was a deep roll, so deep that the one dim lantern in the room was doused by its own fuel. In the darkness she held on to him. The only illumination in the cabin was from a distant flash of lightning.

"You amaze me, Aurora," he suddenly whispered down to her.

Another flash of lightning and she looked up. His expression in the darkness was almost terrifying. He looked like the quintessential predator and she, the vulnerable prey.

"You appear to be such a timid little wren," he commented, "and yet now in this storm when the other passengers are groaning in their cabins, you've proved to have as much fortitude as you claim. I must say it should carry you through the future quite well."

"You act as if you know what is in my future," she said in a hushed voice, hardly able to keep it from shaking.

Another bolt of lightning and another roll, and he moved closer. The silver ring in his ear glinted in the flash. "I can't always tell what the future holds. It still surprises me. After all, just look what we have here." He touched her cheek and whispered, "Isaac was right. Who would have ever guessed such an unadorned little London miss such as yourself could actually be so winsome?"

His head bent down and her hand curled against his chest, but whether it was a welcoming gesture or one of despair she was never to be sure. One thing she was sure of was that he was going to kiss her. Just like in her dream. And though they were certainly ill-honed, all her womanly instincts couldn't be wrong.

His head bent farther and his hand slid lower along the wall. Propriety told her she should pull away, but there was nowhere to go. Too, his lips held such a promise, she didn't want to refuse—didn't know how to refuse. This was no dream that would melt into obscurity the instant his lips touched hers. This was really happening, and she longed to discover all the nuances of feeling she'd been missing.

He was so close she could feel his breath warm and enticing on her cheek. As her fingers uncurled against his chest, she rediscovered the pleasure of caressing him. She explored his front, textured with hair and rigid with muscle, and she never imagined mere flesh could be so hard and implacable. Beneath her hand she felt his heart drumming against his ribs, and she was amazed to find it quicken as he drew her to him. Her own heart beat wildly as his arm encircled her waist. At last the moment seemed to come when they would meet, and even the ship seemed to steady for their encounter. But before it could even begin, it was over.

Vashon's head shot up and Aurora realized belatedly that someone was knocking at the cabin door. The ship lurched and his hand rested on her waist to steady her. In the dimness of the cabin, she could still make out an irritated scowl on his face as he snapped, "What is it?" to the door.

"Vashon!" Benny's voice rang out from behind the door. "The captain is having a time of it in this storm! He sent me to see if you could help!"

Reluctantly Vashon dropped his hold on her and went to a nearby chair. She could barely see the flash of white as he donned his shirt. "Tell Isaac to keep that anchor weighed and that I'll be right there," he called.

"Very good, sir!" Benny shouted before they heard the telltale scrape of his peg leg as he left the afterhouse.

In the silence that followed as Vashon pulled on his boots, Aurora didn't know whether to flee or remain rooted where she was. Her mortification at what almost happened grew by the second; the only thing that hid it was the darkness of the cabin and the impending doom of the storm. As the ship made a precarious roll, she heard him mutter a curse. Grim-featured, he reached for her and pulled her aside of the door.

"Stay here and wait for me until I get back," he ordered.

"I most certainly will not," she whispered, unable even to look at him. It galled her that he would even ask such a thing. What kind of a woman did he think she was?

He nodded and released a mirthless chuckle. "Then I suggest you get to your cabin while you still have one." With that, he slammed the door behind him, and she listened as he made his way forward until the thud of his boots gave way to the howl of the wind.

The night was spent in abject misery. The storm didn't abate until well after dawn, and though the *Seabravery* seemed to have survived with no great damage, Aurora suspected there wasn't a soul on board ship who had slept through the turbulent night.

She most certainly had not. In fact she was up and dressed by the time Vashon returned from the decks. Amid the now gentle rocking of the ship, she heard his weary footfalls as he made his way past her door. She'd almost been tempted to speak to him, to open her door and say something about their encounter the night before. But she quickly stopped herself. There were no appropriate words. After all, she admonished herself, what was there to say? Nothing had happened, really, and the worst was not what he had done at all. The worst was what she had wanted to happen. She'd spent the night wondering if deep down she hadn't truly wanted him to kiss her, wanted that exotic, dangerous man to put his lips on her own and show her just what she would have missed if she had married John. But, as she told herself now, that certainly required no comment or apology from him.

When he was secluded in his cabin, she collected herself, then ventured forth to see to Mrs. Lindstrom's welfare. The widow's maid was prostrate with seasickness when she arrived, but Aurora was happy to find Flossie up and making herself tea on the porcelain stove with no apparent ill effects herself.

They had just sat down to take some refreshment when Captain Corbeil knocked on the cabin door. He seemed pleased to see them both so well, though he did take note of the moans of Mrs. Lindstrom's maid from her tiny bed in the corner. The captain, looking spent and aged from his ordeal with the weather, didn't stay long, but before he left, he gave them some news at which Aurora didn't know whether to be happy or horrified.

It seemed that the storm had purchased them some luck and driven them farther west than they thought. They were now only two days away from St. George's.

7

Their early arrival at St. George's caused some confusion. Messengers had to be sent all through the island to notify the relatives of passengers that the *Seabravery* had docked. Though it took most of the day, Aurora watched as one by one the passengers left for their homes. The Wainwrights with their three-month-old baby were the first to depart in a curricle. The Magoun brothers, practically falling over each other, said a lingering, wistful farewell to Aurora until their phaeton arrived from their father's plantation near Hamilton.

The best farewell, however, came inadvertently from Miss Gideon. From the weather deck Aurora watched as the carriage pulled up to the dock for the governess and her charge. Aurora was loath to see little Hester go, until she saw a man spring from the carriage and eagerly assist his wife's descent. When they finally caught sight of Hester, the couple paused as if they weren't sure how to proceed, but before another moment passed, the man bent down and scooped Hester into his arms while his wife laughed and wiped the tears from her eyes. Suddenly Aurora knew Hester was going to be all right; she would indeed be one of the lucky ones. She was even more convinced of it when the carriage made ready to depart and Miss Gideon was hoisted up top to sit with the driver. After the voyage, the woman was now put back in the position of servant, and her influence on Hester's life would be lessened. And this didn't seem to suit the woman at all. She looked as disagreeable as ever when she was forced to hold on for dear life while the driver sped away to parts unknown.

With amusement dancing in her eyes, Aurora turned to see Mrs. Lindstrom standing by the companionway with her maid. The little servant still looked deathly pale from her bout with the storm, but she proudly held on to her mistress's hatbox and seemed quite happy to have begun resuming her duties.

"Oh, my dear! Can it be that we may truly never meet again?" Flossie rushed over to her and grabbed both of Aurora's hands. "How I wish you'd change your mind about this Lady Perkins and come with me instead . . . the Graftons need a governess and I know the—"

"I couldn't impose," Aurora answered, shaking her head, "and besides, I couldn't let Lady Perkins down. She expects me. Please don't worry." She squeezed the widow's hands. "I promise I'll be just fine. It would be foolish of me to put so much weight in *Mr.* Vashon's knowledge of the local nobility. I'm sure he's wrong about Lady Perkins."

Flossie studied her, then heaved a huge sigh. "I suppose you're right. Even with his riches, Vashon is an unlikely sort to hobnob with the peerage. But you will write and let me know how you fare? I'll be worried sick until I hear from you."

"I'll dash off a note the second I arrive." Aurora gave Flossie a hug, and arm in arm they walked to the gangway. The widow took only a moment to scan the empty docks before bursting out with an oath.

"That rascal Robert! He's not here yet and it's ten to one he's deep in his cups! If he hadn't been with me all these years I'd fire him and procure another driver this instant."

"Is he just coming from the town house?" Aurora asked.

"Yes. He's got to know the *Seabravery's* arrived." Flossie twirled her parasol in agitation, then summoned her maid. "Go find him, will you, Jane, and if he's too besotted, acquire me another carriage. I'll be waiting in the private room at the Somers Island Inn."

"Yes, mum." Jane curtsied and promptly descended the gangway.

"Is there anything I can do to help?" Aurora asked. "Perhaps Captain Corbeil can assist you with your baggage."

"No, no, I've already refused his escort. What an ingrate I would be to ask for it now." Flossie snapped closed her parasol and Aurora wondered if the widow wasn't going to miss the captain more than she let on.

"Does the *Seabravery* come regularly to St. George's?" Aurora couldn't help but ask.

Flossie looked away and Aurora thought she saw a hint of sadness around her eyes. "Apparently not" was all the widow said before she snapped open her parasol once more. "Listen, love, I'm sure I've a wait on my hands at the inn. Why don't you join me and we'll have a cup of tea? You need to get off this ship for a while anyway. They won't be sailing today."

"Wonderful! I should love to get off this ship for a while!" Aurora laughed. Together the women descended the gangplank, but once on the dock, Aurora paused.

"Oh, dear, I've forgotten my reticule," she said. She looked up the steep gangway, then back to Flossie's plump figure. "I can't ask you to reboard, and I can't have you waiting for me on these docks. Show me the Somers Island Inn, and I promise I shall meet you there in a minute."

"It's straight ahead, love. You see the painted sign of the ship crashing on the rocks? That's it. You cannot get lost. In the meantime, I shall secure a private room for us."

"I won't be a moment," Aurora assured her before she once more fled up the gangway.

It took her hardly any time at all to be back in her room and to secure her brown silk purse. She was just about to quit her room when out of the corner of her eye she spied a set of keys lying on her newly made bed. She recognized them instantly as Benny's. They were the keys he used to get into the storerooms to supply the passengers' cabins with fresh linens. Thinking surely he was missing them, she dropped them into her reticule and quickly went to search him out.

Most of the men slept in the fo'c'sle, except the captain and Benny. They had cabins in the deckhouse right in the middle of the ship. Aurora meant to see if Benny was about and if not, to slip the keys beneath his cabin door. But she didn't quite get that far. The captain's door was open a crack, and inside she could hear Vashon and the captain having a lively conversation. She certainly was not the type to eavesdrop, but when her name was mentioned, she couldn't help stepping nearer the door, curious about their discussion.

"There's no chance Aurora will still take the widow's offer?" she heard Vashon say.

"She hasn't requested her trunks be moved. I think we're in good stead," she heard the captain answer. "But, of course," he added wryly, "we've you to thank for that whole folly. You take such perverse pleasure in scaring the girl, Vashon, you almost scared her right out of our hands."

"Being browbeaten by a bitter old woman is no life for a girl like her. I just want her to eventually see that she's better off sailing with us—and hopefully working with us—than wandering where the path of her life was sure to lead her. If not Lady Perkins, then some other hag would have employed her. And made her miserable little life even more miserable."

"But Lady Perkins doesn't even exist, man! She's a figment of our imagination. Why torture the girl?"

Aurora's knuckles whitened as she clutched her reticule. What in God's name were they saying? That Lady Perkins didn't exist? *Her* Lady Perkins? She couldn't believe it. Horrified, she looked about to see if anyone else had heard this news. But the narrow passage was still empty. Turning back to the door, her heart thumping like tympani in her chest, she moved forward to listen.

Vashon mused, "I suppose I do enjoy tormenting her a bit—I've never encountered such a stiff vestal prig—where did they grow her? But nonetheless, when we leave tonight, that brittle facade of hers should crack like a mirror. I almost can't wait to see it . . . and find out what's behind it."

Captain Corbeil sighed. "I must tell you I dread the next few days. Aurora's a quiet little thing, all right, but something tells me she isn't going to go along without a fight."

"I'm up to the fight." She heard Vashon laugh sarcastically. "My only fear is that she'll disappoint me." He suddenly changed tack. "How are the supplies coming? I don't want to wait a second longer than necessary to get this ship out to sea again."

"The water's all we're waiting for now, and the men tell me the barrels are already on the docks. They should be loaded within the hour."

"Good. We set sail at eventide then. With our most precious passenger, Miss Dayne." Suddenly Vashon laughed again, and the sound sent a chill down Aurora's spine. She couldn't believe what he was saying, but when the captain spoke, it seemed all too true.

"Yes, finally we're to get this damnable plan under way. I must admit, it's about time."

In shock, she stood in the passage and took in the captain's words. Unable now to deny what she'd heard, she felt the horror of her situation hit her like a brick wall. It was all a trick. The voyage was a sham set up for her benefit. Lady Perkins didn't exist. She was being kidnapped. And even the captain was in on this horrible deed. Vashon, she could believe would do such a dastardly thing as kidnap her—but for what reason she still didn't know—yet the captain, the good, kindly, chivalrous Captain Corbeil? It just couldn't be. He seemed like such a fine man . . . how could he truly be a party to this?

As she tried desperately to comprehend the situation, she failed to hear the scrape of chairs against the planking. By the time she heard footsteps, she'd already lost precious moments. The captain's door flew open, and she found herself looking up into Vashon's assessing emerald gaze.

Without wasting another second, she picked up her skirts and ran. She wasn't sure what the reasons were behind this man's plan, but after hearing what she had heard, she did know one thing: They meant to kidnap her. And she was not about to let that happen. But he cornered her as easily as if she were a wounded doe. He pressed her back against Benny's door, and though she still meant to escape, for the moment she was trapped.

She looked up at him. Their gazes locked.

"What have we here?" Vashon uttered before he slowly moved toward her. He searched her frightened face and she could see he knew she'd heard everything. Pensively, he watched her, as if calculating the next move.

"What reason—?" she rasped at him, fear making her mouth go dry. "What reason could you have for doing this? I have no money. You know that. No one will pay ransom."

"We want no ransom. Just some information. In the meantime, let me take you to your cabin. After we sail, we'll talk." He spoke calmly, forcefully, as if he expected her total obedience, as if she were no more than one of the *Seabravery's* boys before the mast.

"We won't!" she suddenly cried out and snatched her arm from his outstretched hand. Behind him, she could see the captain come up, a troubled expression on his face. She wanted to plead with him to help her, but in his deep brown eyes she saw no mercy for her situation.

"Aurora, I'm sorry you had to find out this way, but there's no escaping now," Vashon said harshly, obviously trying to head off any rebellion. "We've got you. You're ours. Until we're satisfied we have the information we desire, any attempts to flee will not be tolerated."

She clutched her little silk reticule and tried to think, to grasp exactly what was happening. Lady Perkins was no elderly woman in Jamaica in need of a companion. And Lady Perkins's letter and the trip on the *Seabravery* had been a grand attempt to take her captive. Now that she had fallen into their clutches, they were planning to set sail. For Jamaica still? She doubted it. They would take her elsewhere, someplace she didn't know, where she couldn't go for help, or escape. It was all too horrible to believe, let alone fight against. And all she could think of was that somehow, some way, it was all a mistake.

"You must have the wrong girl," she said vehemently in a last attempt to reason with him. "There is nothing you can get from me that could be worth all this effort. I have no information on anything but the orphanage in which I was raised. You cannot do this. It's a terrible error. You'll surely come to regret it."

"No, we have the right girl." Unexpectedly Vashon touched the jewel-studded locket at her throat. He picked it up and held it to her gaze. "There's only one of these, Aurora. Michael Dayne, your father, gave this to you before he fled England, taking the Star of Aran with him. That's what we need to talk about—the Star. That's why we had to take you."

Her last hope that this was all a tragic mistake died with his words. She didn't know much about this Star of Aran he spoke of, but they did have the right girl. They even knew her father's name. Panicking, she licked her lips and searched the passage again for someone who might help.

"Let's go to your cabin, Aurora. If you cooperate, we'll see to it that you come out of this for the better."

She looked up when Vashon took her arm in a steely grip. He had just begun to lead her away like the prisoner she was when she dug her slippered heels into the floor boards and confessed, "But I don't remember my father. I can't help you. I won't cooperate."

"We'll see about that" was his ominous statement before he pushed her toward the companionway.

Suddenly her composure snapped. All her life she'd been reared to appreciate and emulate gentle, civilized behavior. Mrs. Bluefield had taught her well, for not only had she been educated in art and literature, but her manners had been carefully molded until they were impeccable enough for the unlikely prospect of calling upon the Regent.

Yet now she realized with brutal clarity that if she didn't fight right at this moment, if she succumbed to her instinct for equanimity, they would kidnap her and she would be in their hands until they saw fit to release her . . . or worse.

Her gaze flew up to her escort and she studied every hard line of his face. Vashon was not to be underestimated. They had labeled him an eccentric only because they were too uncomfortable to see him for what he really was—a man unbounded by society's rules—quite possibly a pirate. All too clearly she remembered the painting of the dragon on his back. They'd been fooled by his veneer of self-restraint and manners, but beneath it all lay that dragon, that symbol of power and violence. If she didn't take on that dragon now, she would have no chance when the *Seabravery* left port.

Viciously she twisted her arm and tried to release herself from his grasp. Her reticule fell to the floor and the articles within it scattered across the passage. Her bonnet slipped to her back and several curls slid from their pins. He seemed taken aback by her sudden obstinance and that gave her a moment of advantage. She wrenched her arm free and lifted her skirts. She was at the entrance to the deckhouse before he could grab her by the waist and drag her back to the companionway.

"This is futile, Aurora—can you really think to fight me?" Vashon tightened his grasp at her waist and laughed. Suddenly her fury exploded.

"What kind of man are you?" she shrieked.

All at once instinct mingled with memory, and she lashed out, trying desperately to free herself from his hold. She'd seen enough little boys fighting in the Home to easily recall how to mimic them. Her thinly slippered feet began kicking at his shins, and her arms flailed wildly against his chest. He only laughed harder at her impotent vengeance until one artless kick landed her knee right in his groin. The shock on his face almost mirrored hers when she felt him drop his hold. He bent over and his eyes took on a glazed appearance. Temporarily stunned, all he seemed capable of doing was staring viciously at her and doubling over in his pain. Though she wasn't exactly sure what she had done to him, she'd seen enough quarreling boys bent over with just such an injury to know he'd recover all too quickly. Her priority now was to flee, and she once more gathered her skirts and ran for the weather deck.

But Vashon recovered much more quickly than those little boys. He caught up with her just as the captain blocked her passage to the exit. She was sure the look of betrayal on her face was enough to give Captain Corbeil nightmares for a month, but just as she reached him, Vashon pulled her away. His hand caught the back of her dress and she resisted with such force, the rear seam ripped clear to her waist. Her drab little gown was now practically falling off her, and she had to add protecting her modesty to this battle as well as protecting her life.

"You—villain!" she cried at him and skidded out of reach. Her name-calling didn't seem to bother him a bit. He was still panting from her previous attack, and his complexion was definitely several shades paler. His humor seemed to have been quelled, but now there was a fire in his eye, as if she had forced his hand, and he was damned if he was going to lose.

"I didn't want to do this," he murmured before he stalked her. "I thought you of all women would prefer to go along in a dignified manner. But I see you're not the woman I thought you were."

"And you—!" she cried to him, "and you!"—she turned accusingly to the captain—"are not the men I thought you to be!"

Vashon backed her against the passage wall. She clutched her dress to her shoulders, but when he moved over her she was forced to drop one hand in order to fend him off. He easily took both her hands and her gown fell off her shoulder. With a moan, she looked down and saw her bosom barely covered by the thin binding of her chemise. She looked up and saw that he saw it too. The fire in his eyes only burned brighter.

"Let me go," she demanded in a quick, panting whisper.

"We will," he answered, brushing a loosened gold-red curl from her shoulder. "When we have what we want." His knuckles grazed her collarbone, and the feel of her skin seemed to please him, for he was reluctant to draw back his hand.

"Even if I had this information you wanted, I'd never give it to you now. Do you understand me? Never. Not after this treatment," she vowed, defiance coloring her eyes a vivid sea green.

"Ah, we'll see about that." He laughed darkly. "I haven't even tried to persuade you yet. Let's just get out of port, shall we? Then you can make all these vengeful promises . . . and I'll see what I can do to make you break them." His fingers slid along the hollows of her throat, and she leaned back against the wall and closed her eyes, trying desperately to shut him out.

How could she have ever dreamed about this beast? What was wrong with her that he could have made her believe even for a second that he was anything but ignoble? His finger caressed the upper swell of one breast and she violently met his gaze. But he hadn't completely fooled her. Beneath that veneer she'd seen glimpses of this man before—this *pirate*. Now he was taunting her. He wanted to see her crumple like the shrinking little maid that he thought she was. But he wasn't counting on one thing. There were no longer any rules. He'd erased them the minute she'd found out about her kidnapping. And now she was not going to play fair.

She bent her head and bit his hand as hard as she could. He jolted back and cursed heartily. Behind him she could hear the captain laugh.

"Just what you deserve, Vashon!" he called out. "I knew you'd underestimated her."

Vashon shot him a quelling look, and as he did so, she tried to slide from his grasp. With all her remaining strength she pushed him off her, but he had her in hand and slung across his broad shoulder in a matter of seconds. She struggled and kicked; all she fought was the air. Her bonnet slipped again and with it, a hail of horn hairpins hit the planks. Her tresses tumbled down his back like a rich gilt-red robe. As she watched the floor, her bonnet fell altogether, and he seemed to take great relish in crushing it beneath his booted feet.

"*Stop!*" she finally demanded, beating at his back. She pulled on great handfuls of his white linen shirt as if that would prevent him from taking her away, but it didn't. He strode to the companionway, now the complete victor, and she knew there was nothing within her power to stop him.

She hadn't counted on help, however. They were almost to the hatch when suddenly she heard a familiar voice. She lifted her head and through the tangle of her hair she saw Flossie Lindstrom rushing toward them from the weather deck, her deadly pagoda-shaped parasol aimed directly at Vashon.

"Unhand her this instant, Vashon! Whatever are you thinking of!"

Surprised, Vashon barely had enough time to see his attacker before he took a hefty jab in the ribs with the end of the parasol. He grasped Aurora only harder, and though she suddenly resumed her struggling, he gave no quarter.

"Get her!" he barked at the captain who was still standing in his cabin's threshold, his jaw slack from disbelief. Reluctantly, Captain Corbeil moved forward to try to stop the widow and received several knocks on the head for his trouble. He finally wrestled the lethal parasol out of Flossie's hand, but still the widow would not give up.

"What is the meaning of this, Isaac?" Flossie demanded, her normally pink cheeks red from anger. "What are you both up to that you would allow Aurora to be abused this way?"

"Take that hazardous busybody to my cabin," Vashon ordered ominously, his patience at an end. "And take that," he pointed to the black parasol that the captain held in his hand, "and see that it is thrown overboard." With Aurora still helplessly slung over his shoulder, his face took on a look of utter exasperation, then he disappeared down the hatch.

Dismayed, Flossie turned to the captain. She looked about to rebuke him once more, but she then saw the pistol he held so expertly in his hand. Isaac's expression was stern and troubled and completely without compromise. Grimly he motioned for her to go down the hatch. With a look of utter betrayal on her face, Flossie picked up her skirts and rebelliously comported her generous figure down the companionway.

8

"You won't get away with this, Vashon," Flossie informed him as Isaac bound her, hand and foot, to a chair. She looked almost comical, her full black-swathed figure being subjected to the puny confines of a rope. "I have people in St. George's! They'll find you!" she threatened.

Vashon stood by the door coolly watching the proceedings. Overhead they heard the footsteps as the ship was prepared for sail. Looking confident of a quick departure, Vashon gave the widow a derisive snort. "I've eluded better men than your milk-fed relations, madam."

"Aurora and I were expected at the inn. When I don't return, all of Bermuda will be out looking for you!"

"And how will they know enough to look for me? Most of the passengers on this ship saw you disembark. The only thing anyone will know for sure is that you left the inn and were never heard from again. They'll think you slipped from the docks and drowned."

"No! They know the *Seabravery* left early, and when Aurora's friends come looking for her, they'll piece everything together and know that we were kidnapped!"

Vashon began to laugh. Flossie appeared as if she would go into apoplexy at any moment.

"Is this true, little wren?" Vashon looked to Aurora.

She stood against the wall, her hands bound around the black japanned bedpost of Vashon's bed.

"Will all the fine peacocks of London come scouring the seas for you?" He lifted one black eyebrow.

As their gazes met, Aurora's expression remained cast in marble. She refused to show any fear. Yet they were truly in a desperate situation. There wasn't a soul in the world that would come looking for her. Aurora had nobody, absolutely nobody to miss her. Vashon was right, but she'd be damned if she'd confirm it.

"My fiancé will come," she informed him. "And he'll know something happened to me when I don't return his letters. He'll seek out Lady Perkins, and then he'll know whom to look for." She shot Vashon a venomous look, then turned away as if he were beneath her contempt.

Vashon's eyes narrowed. A cynical smile graced his lips. "There was no indication of a fiancé when we inquired into your situation. Who is this man? An illusion, I think. If you were engaged to be married, why were you so eager to be off to Jamaica and your new position? No, I think you're making that up, *Aurore,* and I tell you now, lying, especially from you, is not going to be looked upon kindly on this ship."

"It's the truth," she said calmly, refusing to show her fury. "John Phipps asked me to be his wife. When he inherited the Home, he had every intention of marrying me."

"Then what stopped him?"

The question hung in the air like a net ready to fall. Aurora fumbled for an answer.

"John needed to sort out some problems. After the previous owner's death, he felt the Home needed to be run differently. I left so that he could get things in order. He'll be after you as soon as—"

Her words died as Vashon walked up to her. She flinched when he caressed her cheek, now burning in outrage.

"This man let you sail clear to Jamaica so that he could more easily settle his business problems? I think not." His gaze swept her figure, then lingered where her dress fell from her shoulders and hung tantalizingly at her bosom. Unable to help herself, Aurora clutched the bedpost as if it would shield her from him.

"Aurora, let me tell you a secret," he finished. "No man is that patient . . . or that stupid."

"I'm not making this up! John Phipps will be after you, and with the Royal Navy, too!"

"So be it. But if I'd cowered every time someone threatened me with the Royal Navy, I'd never rise from my bed in the morning." He took a deep breath. "Now, ladies," he said to both of them, "Isaac and I must get this ship out of port before another catastrophe occurs. When we're out to sea, you'll be released and attended to by Benny. If all goes well and Aurora cooperates, then you'll be let go at the next port. That will be San Juan. . . .

"However, if Aurora does not cooperate"—Vashon gave her a penetrating look—"then you'll both be taken to my island, and you'll stay there until she does."

"Where is this island?" Flossie demanded.

"Le Mirage de la Mer is aptly named. It's truly the mirage of the sea, and no one has yet to map it. So my telling you where it is will do you no good."

Flossie sighed in despair, then turned her wrath upon Isaac, who was standing above her. "How could you do this to me? I thought—I thought—" she sputtered, then composed herself. "A curse on you, do you understand me? I thought you were a gentleman."

"Flossie," Isaac said, his voice full of annoyance, "when you left the ship, why did you reboard? Why didn't you just stay out of this? I told you I'd try to visit—what were you doing here? Were you looking for me?"

"Certainly not!" she spouted. "I was searching for Aurora. We were going to have refreshments at the inn, and when she didn't arrive, I worried that she might have somehow gotten lost. Never in my wildest nightmares did I suspect you were kidnapping her. Oooooh, and I trusted you! I even asked you to tea in my cabin during this voyage! Whatever was wrong with me?"

With that statement annoying him further, Isaac strode to the door. Vashon gave both women a warning stare, then he too left the cabin.

When the men were gone, Flossie immediately turned to Aurora. "Oh, love, did that—that—*villain* hurt you? I must tell you I was never so shocked in my life to see him flinging you over his shoulder. Are you sure you're all right?"

Aurora gave her a wry smile and said, "My dress and my sensibilities are damaged, but nothing more. I'm so sorry you came back. How I wish, like Captain Corbeil, you were out of this."

"What does he want? I'll admit that I've heard pirates love beautiful captives, but this seems so planned, so premeditated. And Isaac! I cannot believe he'd do something this shocking without a good reason—to just take a young beauty and—"

"Vashon doesn't want me. He wants information, information I fear I do not possess." Aurora frowned and sat on the edge of Vashon's huge bed. "But maybe a lie will appease him, and he'll release us."

"Love, if there's one thing about Vashon that's certain it's that he does not look like a man easy to placate. No, I'm not at all sure lying is the answer. When you're caught, as you surely will be, it will go hard on you."

"Then I'll find another way to free us," Aurora announced, grasping at every possibility. "Eventually we've got to pull into port. When we do, I'll escape and bring help."

"As desperate as that sounds, my dear, that may be our only chance." Flossie gave her a concerned look. "But let's just pray our next port isn't Le Mirage de la Mer. With a name like that, the place must be impossible to find, let alone escape from."

"I'm afraid it does appear that way," Aurora answered bleakly, just as the ship lurched away from the dock.

Aurora stared out the thick, leaded ports that spanned the stern of the ship. Worry darkened her eyes. Flossie had long since been freed from her chair and escorted back to her former cabin by Isaac, but Aurora remained tied to Vashon's richly draped bed, still captive within the Babylonian splendor of his cabin. Benny, with Koonga well in tow, had come and brought a pot of tea, but he'd been under orders that only Vashon could free her, so she had mutely stood by, her hands still bound to the bedpost, while he set up her refreshment on a nearby teapoy.

Now all she waited for was the pirate. He didn't disappoint her. In a matter of minutes after Benny left, she heard Vashon's commanding footsteps in the passage. The cabin door swung open and she was finally alone with her nemesis.

In silence he entered and closed the door. He gave her a penetrating glance, then calmly went to a chest and retrieved a fresh linen shirt. As she watched him change, she noted with some satisfaction the ugly rent in the garment he had on. She also saw the slight gash on his side, right where the muscle of his torso gripped his ribs. The wound still trickled a bit of blood. Flossie's parasol had certainly met its mark.

Her satisfaction was fleeting, however, especially when he turned his naked back to her and presented her with the dragon. The taut, well-defined muscles of his shoulders rippled beneath the beast as he pulled on his shirt. His long black queue partially hid the serpent's eyes, but when they did spy out at her, they filled her with a raw, overwhelming terror. This man was like no other she'd ever had to deal with. The only thing she knew for sure about him was that he was dangerous.

"If I'm to be held prisoner on this ship, I should like to return to my own cabin," she announced, desperately trying to keep her voice even.

Upon her unexpected statement, he turned and met her gaze. A smirk appeared on his fine lips. "We'll have a long talk, *Aurore,* then I'll see how to proceed."

"If it's my cooperation you seek, you'll not gain it this way." She gave a tug on her bound hands, then abruptly looked away, as if he were no longer worthy of her attention.

Her snub seemed to irritate him. He went to her and took a lock of her hair that was on the far side of her face. He got her attention back when he slowly pulled the curl across her mouth. She was forced to turn and face him, or risk a painful tug.

"Let me make things perfectly clear," he whispered down at her, his eyes brilliant with annoyance. "It's not I who has to win your cooperation; it's the reverse. If you want your hands untied, you will earn the privilege. If you desire your own cabin, you will earn that as well.

"Lastly, let me tell you this: If all goes well, I promise you every luxury on this ship will be yours for the asking. If things don't go well . . ." His insolent gaze raked once down her figure. That one gesture was more of a threat than all his words.

She fought back her rising hysteria. She was no match for this man. By the looks of him, his entire life must have been one of rape and pillage and murder. No doubt he took anything or anybody he wanted to have, then gloried in his conquests. How could she fight him? What weapon did she have to use against him? Physically, she was less than half his size; the top of her head barely skimmed his shoulder. Her strength was puny compared to his. He was obviously a man of great power, one who had fought many an ignoble battle. Beside him she was insignificant, a little brown wren fluttering against the jaws of a lion.

But one part of her was not insignificant. Her will could fight him even if her body could not. Many thought her retiring and unspirited. John certainly had. But deep down she had always believed that was not so, and that was how she'd summoned the courage to leave the Home when she had. She'd always thought that if given the chance she would have just as much spirit as the heroines in her novels John so disapproved of. It was now the time to prove it, even if just to herself.

She looked up at Vashon and saw the glint in his eyes. He was pleased to see her so terrified. If she became hysterical, he'd doubtless be overcome by wicked glee. Suddenly her anger boiled over. Right then and there, beneath this vile pirate's heavy-lidded stare, she swore to make her will the equal of his. Or die trying.

"I should like my hands untied," she commanded in her most brittle voice.

He dropped her tress and leisurely brushed the remaining red-gold strands off her moist mouth. He seemed to enjoy the task, for he took an abominable amount of time doing it. Her lips seemed to burn with his every touch.

She stared at him, her eyes snapping with anger.

Finally he taunted, "Why don't you try saying 'please'? That always puts me in an amenable mood."

She turned away. Even in her lowly station in life, she had never had to endure such humiliation. Begging this wretched villain to untie her was beyond the pale.

"You won't say it, Aurora?"

She still refused to look at him. It would choke her to have to say "please" to this barbarian.

He laughed. "All right then, stay there. I can't wait to see your face when I undress for bed. If you blush so easily when I'm without a shirt, you should have a nice fit of vapors when you see my choice of bed-clothes."

Her gaze darted to his.

"Still unsure?" His hand hedonistically rubbed the dark hairs on his chest that were exposed by his untied shirt.

"I won't be bullied. Not by you. Not by anyone."

"Well, well, we're going to fight, are we?" he observed. "Then why don't I take a little nap now and we can test those missish nerves?"

Without pause he pulled off his fresh shirt. Her eyes widened at what he seemed about to do, but still she held her ground. She calmed herself by remembering that she'd seen his bare chest before. This worked, even when he sat on a nearby chair and pulled off his boots. But when he bent to release the first button of his trousers, her panic overwhelmed her. She turned her head away. It was all she could do not to squeeze her eyes shut.

"Come now, *Aurore,* that's not much of a fight."

She heard a garment fall to the ground. With a rustle of fabric, the garment was kicked aside. Was he now naked and standing just a few feet behind her? The thought left her face as white as a sheet.

"What have you to say, *Miss Dayne*?" he taunted. "One word and you'll be untied."

She shuddered. Still she held her ground. She just wished she had the courage to look at him.

"Are we refusing to cooperate?"

She turned her head further away and twisted the bindings on her hands. What would he do to force her to comply with his wishes? She didn't know, but she was determined to stay where she was. Forever if necessary.

"All right. We can't go on like this forever . . ."

Suddenly she heard him run. His bare feet pounded on the floorboards as he took a flying leap at the bed. He landed squarely on the mattress. A scream escaped her lips. Unable to stop herself, her gaze flew to his well-muscled form. To her chagrin, she watched him toss back his head and laugh until tears welled in the corners of his eyes.

His pants were still very much on. She looked over to where he had stood and saw the waistcoat he had dropped on the floor. He had made her look a fool. At the moment she was too astonished at his trickery to even be angry.

But quickly she felt him grasp her wrists. She tried to pull away, but he had knelt at the end of the bed and was slowly pushing her hands down the bedpost. When she was forced to lower herself, he took her hair in a gentle knot and pulled her head just inches from his. With a very somber expression on his face, he warned, "You're all too easy to frighten, little wren. A twelve-year-old boy could do a good job of it." He forced her even closer. "But I'm not a twelve-year-old boy. And I know how to truly frighten little women like you. So I suggest that we drop these games and you cooperate . . . or you'll see how frightening I really am."

She tried to turn away, but his hand held her hair too tightly. She meant to hold out, but all at once a strange expression flitted across his handsome features. He suddenly looked hungry and covetous—as if she in her innocence possessed some kind of treat he'd never tasted before.

Fear as tangible as the blood in her veins pumped wildly through her body. He wanted her. As John Phipps had wanted her. But Vashon's manipulations were much more dark and sinister than John Phipps's had been, for this man could make her desire him in return, and, unwillingly, she already felt herself responding. Her belly grew taut and her nether regions melted and pulsed. He reached for her, and though they weren't even touching, his mouth seemed to pull at hers. She was all too aware of the dangers he presented. With one kiss he meant to punish her, free her, and enslave her all at the same time. His lips just opened for the kiss, and she buckled.

"*Please*," she choked out, despising him as she had never despised anyone.

His eyes flew open. One jet black eyebrow lifted derisively. He looked thoroughly displeased, as if he'd been more looking forward to her punishment than to her cooperation. " 'Please untie my hands,' " he prompted, goading her in his annoyance.

"Please—untie—my—hands—" she stiffly repeated.

It worked. Her bindings were off in seconds. Finally free, she stumbled back from him and groped for the door handle. Yet she found her hands too numb and clumsy to open it. She began to rub some life back into them, but before she could manage, he stopped her.

"It's locked," he said.

She spun and faced him. "I cannot return to my cabin?"

"Not yet. Come here and sit down." He motioned to the dolphin-legged couch.

When she didn't move, he grabbed the torn edges of the back of her dress and pulled her to the couch as if she were a kitten held by its scruff. He eased himself down next to her and raised his bare feet onto a nearby chair, then he leaned back and perused her.

"What are you looking at?" She gave him a baleful stare and indignantly pulled her disheveled gown back onto her shoulders.

"I was just thinking that we're not that far away from St. George's. And until we are, I believe it's best you stay here with me. I've no inclination to go after you, should you decide to swim back."

"I cannot swim."

"Good."

"But because I haven't that avenue of escape, that doesn't mean I'll endure these indignities forever." With a great show of self-possession, she again shoved up the shoulders of her gown. But it was no use. No matter how she pulled and adjusted and stretched the coarse linen of her dress, she still despaired at the sight of her sheer cotton chemise. Finally she was forced to use her hands. With her arms crossed over her chest like a shield, she barraged him with accusatory glances.

Her silent reprimands only seemed to irritate him. Piqued, he said, "The first thing you can dispense with, Miss Dayne, is this infernal guarding of your maidenhood. I promise you, no one on this ship is going to snatch it away."

She gave him a look of utter disbelief.

He only laughed.

"I won't have you or any other man looking at my . . . undergarments," she retorted, refusing to lower her hands.

That all-too-familiar smirk appeared on his lips. "What is it you're attempting to hide? Have you, like so many fashionable women these days, developed a penchant for bust improvers?"

She gasped. "How—how—*dare*—you even mention—such a thing—"

"Then release your hands."

"I most certainly will not!"

"I hate to crush you, my dear Miss Dayne, but I've seen a woman's chemise before, and while yours *appears* to be fetchingly well endowed, I assure you the mere sight of it doesn't inflame me beyond all control."

She shot him a shocked look, then damned the uncontrollable color that began suffusing her cheeks. She cared not a whit that he was left unmoved by her state of undress, but it was infuriating that he could turn things around and make it look as if she did. Yet despite his taunts, she was determined to retain what was left of her dignity. Her hands clutched at her dress until her knuckles were white.

When he noted her stiffening posture, his annoyance only seemed to increase. He gave a discouraging glance to the small teapot that Benny had brought in, then a grim smile twisted his mouth. "Perhaps it's some spirits we need. A little brandy should do the trick—that should loosen you up, get you talking. Perhaps even take out that infernal stick that's up your—"

"No!" she interrupted, refusing to let him finish whatever crude remark he was about to make. "I don't want any spirits. I just want to know what you're up to. In fact, I demand to settle this now so that you can turn us back to St. George's."

Ignoring her, he went to his bookcase and opened one polished mahogany door. Behind it were several decanters. He picked one that contained a brilliant amber liquid. With two cut-crystal tumblers also in hand, he walked back to the dolphin-legged couch.

"Have a drink, Miss Dayne," he ordered.

"Your wretched liquor won't affect my tongue. So I demand that you tell me your business immediately."

"Ah, that's very good." He laughed and poured a healthy two fingers into one tumbler.

"This serves no purpose. I refuse to speak a word until I understand what is going on—and until I'm treated with more deference."

"I'll treat you with deference. This was Napoleon's finest." He put the tumbler right before her. "Come along, *Aurore*, my prim little maiden. If these spirits won't affect you, then you have nothing to be afraid of. Take them."

"I don't want—" she protested, but before the words were out, he took one of her hands down from her chest and wrapped it around the tumbler. She watched while he eased himself down on the couch once more.

"What is going on aboard this ship?" she asked as soon as he was next to her. In her haste to seek some answers, she ignored the fact that her shoulder was bared when one side of her dress fell to her elbow. "Why all these plans to kidnap me when I don't know a thing about this Star of Aran?"

He crossed his arms over his massive chest and studied her as if she were some delicate, delicious prey. The creamy skin of her collarbone seemed to draw his gaze like a jackal's.

"I'll tell you everything you want to know," he said slowly. "But first let me again remind you of your need to cooperate." His gaze flicked over the tumbler in her hand. "I told you to drink that. When your glass is emptied, we'll begin."

She stared down at the tumbler in her hand. What she should do was toss its contents right in his handsome face. But an action like that would only delay their conversation further, and she wanted to know what was going on, and as quickly as she could.

With a passionate hostility for him growing in her breast, she took the brandy in one defiant gulp. The fire it ignited in her throat almost suffocated her, and she spent the next entire minute suppressing a violent cough in the most discreet, ladylike manner she could. But when she had finally collected herself, she slammed the tumbler down on the table next to her and faced him, her eyes demanding answers.

"More?" He held out the decanter, the shadow of a smile crossing his lips.

"No," she said in a hoarse whisper.

He smirked and poured himself a drink. Stretching out, his long form took up most of the couch, and she was forced back against one scroll arm. Cast in her tiny section of the couch, she was sure she had never been abused by anyone as she had been abused by him, and yet, too, no matter how she wished to deny it, she was sure no one had ever intrigued her as he did. Even now, with his one arm lolling over the back of the couch and the other resting on his torso, he had to be truly the most magnificent creature she had ever seen. His hair, long, dark, and gleaming, made her almost ache to reach out and touch it, to see if those curls could possibly be as heavy and thick as they looked. His chest, covered with a fine mist of perspiration, made her wonder if it would feel cool to the touch or, instead, warm and hairy and slick. She studied his profile next. For a baseborn criminal, he possessed a strong jaw, a classic Roman nose, and a startlingly patrician brow. If she didn't know better, she would have thought him bred to much higher concerns. Certainly, if he bowed at all to society's fashions, he could easily be mistaken for one of the gentry. Perhaps even a peer.

"Have some more," he suddenly said and leaned toward her with the decanter. She was about to refuse when his leg brushed intimately against her. Even that slight touch unnerved her. It conjured up that dream she had had of him—and all the uncontrollable feelings she'd felt while having it. Now she was this man's prisoner. And what he wanted from her, she didn't even know yet.

Numbly she looked down at the full glass being thrust into her hand. Though it had been torturous going down, the drink had made her feel braver by half. She had already lost one battle of wills to this man, but she was nowhere near to surrendering the war; she needed all the courage she could get. She took another sip and spent another moment choking discreetly into the back of her hand.

"What do you want, then?" she finally asked, ready for the answers.

"I want to know where the Star is, Miss Dayne. The Star of Aran. If you tell me that, you can go free."

"What is it?" she whispered.

"It's an emerald—as big as your fist. Your father stole it from the Viscount Blackwell—"

"My father! He did no such thing!" she gasped, shocked at his words. Her father was no thief. Though her memories of him were few, her father was a kind man, a man who had taught her nursery rhymes and given her jewelry. Such a generous, noble soul couldn't possibly be a criminal too. This pirate was grievously in error.

"You don't like that, do you, me besmirching your father's character?" He smirked. "Isaac was right again. He said you'd have a difficult time believing it."

"My father didn't do such things, I tell you. You're mistaken." She glared at him.

"But he did do it. He stole that emerald, then put you out of harm's way in that almshouse. So where did he take it, *Aurore*? Do you know?"

"The Home was not an almshouse, and my father did not steal. You're mistaken."

He suddenly grew impatient. He took her jaw and forced her to stare up at him. "We can quit this playacting of gentility, Miss Dayne. You're the product of a thief and an actress-*cum*-prostitute. The only reason

you and your father have the same last name is because he did not
object to your using it. It has nothing to do with your legitimacy."

Her face turned dead white. "What are you saying?"

"I'm saying that you, my dear *proper* Miss Dayne, are a bastard."

She tore from his hold, nearly choking on her denial. "I won't hear
such lies!"

He turned deadly serious. "They're not lies. I'm telling you the truth.
Your mother was an actress in a halfpenny theater in Bethnal Green,
and she died giving birth to you, her only child. Your father raised you
and probably even regarded you with some affection before he stole that
emerald and took off for parts unknown, leaving you at that orphanage.
What I want to know is, where did your father say he took the emerald?"

Aurora hardly heard him. She couldn't believe what he was saying.
Her entire being rebelled at it. She was not some bastard whelped in the
back of a dingy theater. She was the proud daughter of—?

The picture was blank. There were no faces of her parents for her to
remember, nothing except the vague impression of a man who could
have been anyone: rich man, poor man, beggar man, *thief.*

She closed her eyes. No, it could not be true. She remembered as a
young girl Mrs. Bluefield reciting a line of a poem to her the one and
only time she had ever summoned the courage to ask about her parents.

> Oh hush thee, my babie, thy sire was a knight,
> Thy mother a lady, both lovely and bright.

It had been the best thing to say. All her life Aurora had ached to
believe those words, and by saying them, Mrs. Bluefield had given her
the courage to believe they were true. She'd worked extra hard on her
manners, her decorum, her studies, all in the secret hope that one magical day the knight and the lady would arrive to retrieve her. And all the
lonely years she'd spent as an orphan would be proclaimed a terrible
mistake.

> . . . thy sire was a knight,
> Thy mother a lady, both lovely and bright.

Irrational tears sprang to her eyes. She quickly turned away so that
he wouldn't see them. She knew she was not the only child Mrs. Bluefield had recited the poem to. Even she herself, once a teacher, had used

the line to answer some of her children's questions about their back-
grounds. All of them had wanted to believe the rhyme. And for none of
them, not even herself, was it true.

"You're a wretch to be telling me these shameful lies," she said, her
voice shaking with emotion.

"It's time this superior facade of yours came tumbling down."

"If I'm superior, it's because I have some honor and righteousness of
spirit." She whipped around and faced him, her fury momentarily un-
leashed. "Unlike you, who couldn't look a snake in the eye!"

He paused, as if her anger surprised him, then he laughed mockingly.
"Still the rigid little ice maiden, I see. Remind me, Aurora, when we
reach the heat of the Caribbean, to chill my wine next to you."

She shot him a nasty glance.

He sobered. His face suddenly went rock hard. "Now I want to get
back to business. Where is the Star?"

"Even if this vile accusation were true about my father, I was hardly
more than a babe when I last saw him. How could I know where this
Star is?"

"He taught you that nursery rhyme. He told you where it was in
those silly lines. So where is the Star? Tell me and you'll be free."

She looked at him for a moment, pushing her hurt far down inside
her to a place no one else could see. She could feel the spirits taking
their effect, and she was glad for their release. Though her thoughts
became more muddled, the liquor helped her better disregard his threatening proximity. "My father did not steal that emerald. I'll never believe it."

"Well, you must. Michael Dayne was indeed a thief, and a good one
at that."

She grew quiet. She wished she had some proof of her father's good
character in order to show Vashon he was wrong, but she had nothing.
Only her lizard locket, which he had already tried to convince her had
belonged to someone else. "Do you really know about my father?" she
asked in a pitiful whisper, suddenly feeling a crack in the brittle shell
she kept placed around her.

"Yes." He watched her.

"Then where is he now? Is he still alive?" Her eyes glistened with
hope. She didn't want to believe Vashon knew anything about her dear
father, but after all the years of loneliness, of having no connection to
anyone on this earth, she'd certainly take a father who was a thief over
no father at all.

"It's unlikely," he answered slowly, his eyes searching her face. "He hasn't been heard of since he abandoned you at that orphanage."

Her gaze dropped to the floor. She couldn't bear for him to see her disappointment. "You know nothing about him, but you accuse him of being a thief. Where is your proof?" she demanded, trying to cover up her vulnerability. "You dishonor my father and yet you have no proof."

Without warning, his hand slid to her throat. She shivered from the warmth of his fingers tracing over her pulse. Reverently, he picked up the lizard-shaped locket that hung around her neck.

"This is how I know," he said in a hushed tone, his gaze locking on the lizard. "This pendant was made for Lady Blackwell for the day she married. It's well known that your father stole it from her husband. It identifies you as Michael Dayne's daughter more eloquently than this," he touched a lock of her hair. "Your father, I'm told, had the same color hair."

"There are others who possess this hair color," she reminded him.

"But there's only one pendant. I told you that the first time we spoke."

"So you say my father's nursery rhyme tells where this emerald is?"

"Yes. I'm sure of it. The clues are there." He let the necklace fall.

Slowly her hand crept to her throat. As was her habit she fingered the locket, but this time her reaction wasn't out of nervousness. Now it was out of protection. With a slow sureness, she began to realize that she had a tool to use against this man. She wouldn't believe the wretched thing he was saying about her parents. But above all else he seemed to want this emerald, and if by some chance it was true that the whereabouts of this jewel were hidden in the words of the nursery rhyme, then she would see to it he never deciphered it. For she and she alone knew that the rhyme had another verse. A second verse that was engraved inside her locket.

"Tell me everything you remember about your father. We can begin there," he said.

She swallowed. She had to keep the locket from him. But for now, as long as he and everyone else thought her lizard was merely a pendant, she was safe. "I'd like some more brandy," she said.

His brow lifted at this request. Silently he complied.

When her glass was filled once more, she groped for some appropriate answers. She knew she had to tell him enough to satisfy him, without telling him too much. In the meantime, it was best to keep her knowledge of the rhyme to herself. She'd save that as a bargaining chip, particularly if circumstances worsened. She took a sip of the brandy and glanced at him. She hated to even speculate how much worse things could get.

"I don't remember anything about my father," she began, unable not to add, "except, of course, he was *most* noble. But in any case, my memories of my father won't find you the emerald. It's obvious this jewel is in Ireland. By its name it belongs to the Aran Isles. Though I know not which one."

"The Star came from there, that's true. But it's not there now. I've looked. *Others have looked*," he added enigmatically.

"But if you're hoping to find the location through the rhyme, the rhyme makes no sense. How can you hope to decipher it?"

He stared at her until she felt singed by his gaze. "You're the key to that, Aurora. You're going to decipher it for me."

A tingle of fear crept down her spine. "And what if I cannot? What's to become of me then?"

He leaned closer. "We'll just have to make sure you stay useful then, won't we?"

It was all she could do not to blurt out right then that there was another verse. He frightened her. The uncertainty of the voyage frightened her. But she knew she had to remain strong. Her survival depended on it. If she handed him her trump card, then her worth to him would be speculative at best. And what did pirates do to worthless captives? Make them walk the plank? Abandon them on a sandy little cay? She took another fortifying sip of the brandy and fervently wished she'd read Defoe's *The Life and Strange Surprising Adventures of Robinson Crusoe.*

"You're going to be three sheets to the wind if you keep gulping that down."

She looked at him, only half hearing his comment. Fanning her face with her hand, she wondered how this enormous cabin could have grown so small. She was suffocating. If she didn't get some air, she thought she might retch. Rising unsteadily to her feet, she walked toward the stern and opened one of the ports. The breeze whipped at her hair and the sea spray cooled her cheeks. She placed her tumbler on the sill and looked out in the distance to where St. George's melted into the turquoise horizon. Already they were so far from the island there was no getting back. The thought panicked her all over again.

"Vashon," she finally said, "you must believe me that I don't know the whereabouts of the emerald. If I did, wouldn't I have found it myself?"

She felt him come up behind her. His hands took her upper arms in an iron caress.

"You would have, that's true," he answered, his voice a deep rumble against her back. "But I can see you've had no knowledge of the emerald's existence, so how could you look for something you didn't even know about?"

"But I know about it now, and still the rhyme makes no sense to me. I can't decipher it for you. So you must let Flossie and me go."

"I won't."

"Why?" she demanded.

"Because you're hiding something."

She whipped around and faced him. His eyes were as hard as the emerald itself. "What are you saying?" she gasped.

"I'm saying that you're keeping something from me. I can see it in your manner. You know something you're not telling me."

"And if I did know something, what would you do if I told it to you?"

"I would discover if it was true."

"And then, if it was, would you let Flossie and me go free?"

"If that's all you knew, perhaps."

She turned back to the open port. The cooling breeze was no longer working. She felt hot and her thoughts were difficult to articulate. Slowly she said, "How can I believe you after all that you've done to me today? You're not an honorable man."

He laughed darkly. "Perhaps not, but there are worse characters out there who want the Star quite as badly as I do. I can only tell you that any information is best put in my hands rather than in theirs."

"Or best left in my own."

His hands tightened on her arms. "Listen to me, Aurora, I've gone to a lot of trouble to get you. And I'll keep you until I get what I want, however long that may be. Are you willing to endure that?"

"I cannot trust you. I have no choice but to take the risk."

"You have another choice." As if she were a doll, he flung her around to look at him. "Tell me what you know and I shall be generous."

"And if I don't?" she said with a rebellious set to her chin. "What shall you do about it? Torture it out of me? Well, perhaps you misjudge me. Perhaps I've more fortitude than you think."

"And perhaps you haven't. You know, in some cultures torture is elevated to an art. It needn't even hurt, it just needs to bring a man . . . or in your case, a woman . . . to his breaking point."

"My breaking point shall be elusive indeed." She stared up at him, her eyes glittering with the sheen of defiance and intoxication.

"Your breaking point, my little maiden, is all too obvious," he answered pointedly.

Their gazes locked and they stood for a long moment in mute combat, the primeval understanding and hostility of the sexes flowing between them. Finally she declared, "That's not so," but as if mocking her statement, he merely lifted one black eyebrow, then abruptly caught her up into his arms.

She fought to be free from his hold, yet her movements were softened by the brandy, and she quickly found she was no match for him at all. His hand rode at her back while his other hand stroked the tangle of her hair. She made to cry out, but before she could, his mouth stifled her protest. His lips found hers, and once he had them he refused to relinquish her no matter how hard she pushed him away. Eventually his kiss became so deep and thorough that his tongue broke the barrier of her teeth, and he thrust himself again and again into her mouth until she moaned in despair. His hands became as brutal and unrelenting as his mouth, and beneath the linen of her gown she felt him cup her buttocks as he pressed her closer into his embrace.

But the final shock was his other hand moving up her torso. She had never ever had a man touch her breast, and when she realized that was what he was about to do, she knew she wouldn't last. Feeling as if she might faint, her vision blurring, she fell limp against his chest. She waited for his assault, but her surrender seemed to bring about a very different reaction. He stiffened. As if he felt he'd proved his point and was afraid that he might indeed break her, he tore his lips from hers and his hands fell away. Left without support, she quickly grasped the casement of the ports, all the while sobbing and panting her dissent.

It took quite a few moments for her to calm down, but finally she did. Her face was as pale as a wraith's, but this only enhanced the luminosity of her eyes and fragility of her coloring. With her hair atumble and her breath coming in short, sporadic bursts, she looked like quite the little girl lost.

But as usual she was not to be underestimated. Her hand quickly found her glass of brandy still resting on the sill, and with a passion and bravery she had never known before, she flung the contents into his hard, handsome face.

"You evil man."

As still as death, he stared at her, the brandy running down his cheeks and nose. Just by his look she was sure no one had ever done such a thing to him. She was also sure he had killed those who had done far less. In the back of her mind she wondered if he might try that with her. Though she could see the jaws of death opening, she doubted he would go that far. As he had just proved, his torture for her would be far less physically damaging, and far more unendurable.

With barely leashed fury he wiped his face with his hand. Surprising her with his swiftness, he reached out and grasped her chin so that she would look up at him. "I don't know where the Star of Aran is, but it's not in St. George's. So we have nowhere to go but to sail to Mirage. And when we get there, there'll be nothing to do but watch the tide roll in and roll out. In short, I have time, Miss Dayne, to await your information. All the time in hell. Think about it."

He twisted away his hand and walked to his wardrobe. Finding a linen towel, he dried his face and thrust his arms back into his shirt. When his boots were on, he slammed out of the cabin. Only when the door was firmly locked behind him did she sink unsteadily to her knees and gasp her relief.

9

The isle of St. George's was but a bump on the horizon when Vashon appeared on the quarterdeck. Evening had fallen and the sun had sunk low in the sky, painting the waves with a brilliant wash of golden red. A good breeze snapped in the sails above and the pale pink shell of a full moon could already be seen topping the mizzen mast. It was going to be a fine night for sailing, but Vashon either didn't care or was oblivious to this fact as he leaned stiffly against the railing. A hardness was in his eyes that even the beautiful seascape couldn't soften, and he cut a fierce figure as his long thick hair blew in the breeze and his earring gleamed red from reflecting the dying sun.

Deep in thought, he stared out to the east where a school of porpoise arched through the sea, playfully swimming alongside the ship. Yet the sleek black-and-white animals could have been the ship's trailing bilge water for all Vashon seemed to notice.

"How goes it?" Isaac asked quietly, stepping from the binnacle, where he had just logged their position.

Vashon shot him a glance, then resumed his staring in the direction of the porpoise. "It didn't go quite as I thought it would. But nothing has gone well this entire damned day."

"No, it hasn't. Flossie Lindstrom's so mad, the old girl almost swooned into a faint when I told her she couldn't see Aurora." Isaac turned his guilty gaze seaward. "I wish to God that widow had stayed off this ship."

"I expect you to keep her under control."

"She'll stay locked in her cabin. I promise you."

"Good." Vashon released a deep breath.

For the first time Isaac seemed to take note of his sour disposition. "And Aurora? Is she—?"

"She's in my cabin. Where she will stay until she cooperates."

"She could hold out a long time."

"She could."

Isaac frowned and took a moment to stare out to sea. When he seemed to have gathered the courage to speak his mind, he eyed Vashon, then commented, "I don't see how you two can compatibly share one cabin."

"And one bed?" Vashon flashed him a surly glance.

"That too," Isaac finished quietly.

Vashon riveted his gaze to the blushing horizon. "Her comfort and destiny are up to her. I've informed her as much."

"She's certainly got more backbone than we first thought. I expect she'll be quite obstinate. It'll take a great effort to win her over to our side—"

"She's fragile, naïve, and overly protected. I could break her in one night if I chose it."

Vashon's harsh words seemed to take Isaac aback. He stared at the younger man's profile as if unsure of his next move. "I've never known you to condone rape, Vashon."

Vashon only grimaced.

"God knows," Isaac continued, "where our travels have taken us we've seen enough women shattered and abused that way. But you of all people have never been one to resort to it. In fact, I remember well the night we found that beaten slave girl in Barbados. You nearly strangled the drunken sailor who had forced her down to the beach."

Vashon remained silent.

"It might kill her," Isaac stated softly.

"I know that," he snapped. He ran an agitated hand down his jaw. "This is a damned vexing situation."

"Ah, I see your dilemma. You use too much force and she'll crumble like a Roman ruin. Not enough and she'll fight you to her last breath. Yes, that is perplexing." The captain nodded. "Quite a new dilemma for you. After all, subtlety is not your forte. You usually have the touch of a machete."

"She's only a woman, Isaac. I'll have her in my palm eventually."

"But you've got to admit she's unlike other women you've known. You can't just throw her to your mattress and be assured she'll be purring in the morning. No, my sorry friend, you'll have to devise a new method for her."

Vashon's mouth took on a grim set. "I only know one thing."

"And what is that?"

"Peterborough wants that emerald. And because Peterborough wants it, I swear I'll be the one to get it first and nothing—not oceans, not continents, not even that tight-laced little chit in my cabin—is going to stand in my way." Vashon pounded his fist on the railing and left, totally ignoring the captain's worried expression.

The cabin was dark when Aurora awoke. She had no idea of the hour except that it was night. Through the open stern ports, the stars glittered across a velvet sky like a dusting of diamonds. She could hear the waves beat against the ship as the *Seabravery* cut through the water, neither the fatigue of its crew nor the dark of night keeping it from its destination. An ominous dread built in her chest as she rose to a sitting position. The counterpane fell away, and with a shaking hand she flung her hair across one bare shoulder, then looked around.

After Vashon had gone, she'd tried to come up with some kind of plan. She'd opened her locket and read the nursery rhyme over and over in the hopes that it might clue her in to the whereabouts of the Star and thus bring her her freedom. But it had been no use. The rhyme was just as silly and meaningless as it had always been, perhaps even more so now that she was trying to find some hidden intelligence in its lines.

When the rhyme offered no ostensible salvation, she'd turned her worries to Flossie. She was sure the kind widow was all right, but it was vexing being kept apart from her only ally on the ship. She prayed the captain was treating his captive better than Vashon was treating her. Every time she thought of that pirate's ruthless kiss, she trembled in anger. His threat had been all too clear. Submit or retreat, he had told her, neither of which she was ready to do.

She spent the better part of an hour trying to devise an escape. She even went so far as to search the cabin for a weapon, something she could use to force him to turn the ship around. But her search had come to naught. The bookcase held nothing of any use, and the one intriguing cabinet she found was locked. Undaunted, she kept looking, for a key, for anything, but she couldn't even find a razor tucked in the trunk where he kept his smallclothes. With defeat temporarily staring her in the face, her liquor-fogged state finally got the better of her. Too tired to pace, too sleepy to think, she'd slumped on the edge of Vashon's mattress.

Her thoughts morosely turned to what he'd said about her parents. He was wrong, she'd told herself, snuggling deep into the feather mattress of his huge japanned bed. She fell asleep to the words ". . . thy sire was a knight, thy mother a lady, both lovely and bright," but her dreams soon turned to nightmares wherein the words were proved false.

Now groggy and with her head feeling as if the slightest noise might crack it wide open, she rose to her feet. The door to the cabin opened just as she was able to clutch her gown to her chest. She turned around only to find Benny sheepishly lighting the wall lanterns near the bookcase.

"Benny!" she called out to him, her voice still thick with sleep. "What—what hour is it?"

"Four bells. Ten o'clock, miss."

She ran a shaky hand through the heavy tangle of her hair. "Do you know if I can return to my cabin?"

"Vashon told me to serve you in here, miss."

She shot the boy a reproving glance while Koonga chattered on his shoulder oblivious to her wrath. As if she'd whipped him, Benny limped to the threshold. Guiltily she looked away. "Is Vashon going to keep me captive in here forever, or do you know, perchance, if he's ever going to free me?"

"No, miss," he answered obliquely before bringing in a tray laden with food from the passage.

In a perfunctory manner, he set up her meal where the cold tea service had been, all the while trying to keep Koonga from the sugar bowl. It was then that she realized he'd been in the cabin before. While she had been asleep he had taken away the teapot. Gone, too, was Vashon's discarded torn shirt.

Warily, her gaze slid to the bed. The black satin-striped counterpane was mussed and tossed aside. When she had awakened she remembered pushing the luxurious covering off. What she couldn't recall was ever putting it over her. So who had done that? Benny? Or had the cabin been visited by another as she slept?

She closed her eyes and composed herself. She blushed every time she pictured Vashon standing over the bed as she slept. Scouring her memory to see if she could recall his returning to the cabin, she couldn't find anything. There was only a black, nightmarish void.

"Benny!" she called out hastily, halting the youth in the doorway.

"Yes, miss?"

"Benny, if I may not leave here, would you be so kind as to bring me my things from my room?"

"I'm not sure, miss . . ."

"Vashon did not disallow me my clothes, did he?" she asked incredulously.

The boy almost colored. "No, miss."

"Then would you bring me my things? I need to attend to my toilet."

Benny paused only a moment. "I'll bring you your things, miss," he said before limping to the door.

When Benny had gone, Aurora held out one last hope. There was nothing in the cabin she could use as a weapon, but perhaps among her belongings she might find something.

In less than a minute Benny returned. He put her willow basket on the bed and laid out her comb and hairpins on Vashon's massive mahogany bureau. When he had seen to all her belongings, he departed again, once more locking the door behind him.

Finally alone, Aurora rushed to her willow basket and dug through to the bottom. There was nothing there of even the slightest use except a precious pair of steel embroidery scissors Mrs. Bluefield had given her on her sixteenth birthday. She studied the small stork-shaped scissors, even testing their sharp points. But the picture of her holding Vashon hostage with a froufrou pair of embroidery scissors was just too absurd.

Defeated for the moment, she changed into one of her drab linen gowns and absentmindedly put the scissors in one of the skirt's serviceable pockets. She wasn't sure what to do now. It seemed all her options were gone.

Desperately trying to think and growing more agitated with her lack of ideas, she paced the carpet until she swore the dragons woven into it were looking threadbare. She glanced about the cabin for something to occupy her, and that was when she spied her comb and hairpins on Vashon's bureau, lying intimately next to his own comb and shaving strop. She was most certainly not going to be on this ship long enough to get used to sharing that villain's bureau! In a wave of panic she rushed up to the bureau and swept all her belongings off it. Combing out her hair, she quickly knotted it and used all her pins to pull it tightly to her nape. Then she hastily deposited her comb inside her willow basket.

More time passed, and she finally had to force herself to settle on the couch. But once there, she found herself growing sleepy again. She looked over at the dinner Benny had brought her, but she knew a full stomach would only further increase her drowsiness. Sitting on the couch, she stared at the cabin door until her eyes fairly glazed over.

At some point in the night she must have dozed. When she awoke, her head lolled against the thickly padded scroll arm of the couch, and her feet were tucked beneath her. Her eyes opened slowly, rebelliously. With a heavy-lidded gaze, she assessed her surroundings, made foreign by the distance of slumber. It wasn't until she turned her head that she saw him.

At first all she really saw were his trousers. They were black and finely cut, molding themselves perfectly to the slim hips and well-formed thighs of their wearer. He was standing so close that she had to look up even to see his torso. Finally when her head was tilted back as far as it could go, she met that ferocious green gaze and it nearly sapped her of all her strength. He really was a hard character, this pirate. She could see it in his eyes. Human frailty touched him not at all. She wondered what in this man's life could have ever turned him so completely cold and unyielding.

"Sleep well, Miss Dayne?" A shadow of a smile crossed his lips. Suddenly she knew he had been in the cabin when she'd slept before. But had he or Benny placed the counterpane over her? Benny, most likely. Somehow she just couldn't picture this fear-inspiring man performing such a tender task.

"Is it time for another interrogation?" she asked smartly, all the while trying not to squirm beneath his green stare. "If not, I insist on being allowed to remove to my own quarters."

"In good time."

He dismissed her and went to his bookcase. From the waist of his trousers he procured a key. He opened the cabinet that she had found locked and revealed a veritable arsenal. Hung on the door were six brutal machetes that each looked as if it could cut off a man's leg as easily as it could slice through cane. Three pairs of silver-handled dueling pistols were ensconced on the top shelf, and at least seven finely tempered sabers were propped on the shelf below them. There were kegs of powder and boxes of lead balls. In short, there seemed to be enough ammunition and weapons for a man to wage his own private war. Aurora was completely aghast.

Vashon pulled down a brace of pistols. He checked to see they were loaded, then tucked them in the waist of his trousers.

"Why are you arming yourself?" she asked. She couldn't help adding sarcastically, "Have your men had enough of your tyranny and decided to mutiny?"

He flashed her a wicked grin. "No, we have visitors."

Her eyes widened. "But it's night. How could you know?" At once she turned to the aft ports. Dawn was breaking and the sea and sky had melted into one dove-colored canvas. The only blight was the large silhouette of a ship bearing down on them from the east. A shiver of inexplicable fear ran down her spine. Even at that distance she could see it bore no flag.

She quickly shrugged off her trepidation. The approaching ship was the closest thing to salvation she might have. And it could hardly be worse than the one she was on. Perhaps it wasn't flying colors in order to defend itself. It was quite possible the *Seabravery* was renowned in these waters as a pirate ship. Certainly, from what she had gathered, the *Seabravery*'s owner was well known as a pirate.

She stole another glance at the ship on the horizon. There sailed a chance for freedom. If she could bolt from the cabin, perhaps she could signal it to rescue her and Flossie.

She nervously looked at Vashon. He had relocked the cabinet so there was no chance of her procuring a weapon. She would just have to be quick and catch him unawares. If she were lucky, she could be on the weather deck calling for help before he could stop her.

Her gaze riveted to his figure as he unlocked the cabin door. There would be only a second for her to slip through it, but she had to give it one desperate try. The bolt clicked open and he stepped back to pass through the door. That was her opportunity. She flew to the passage and had two steps outside the cabin before he caught her. She cried out as he pulled her by her wrist back into the cabin. She dragged on the ground, trying to free herself, but his grip on her arm was like iron. She pulled at his fingers but they stuck like glue. Finally, in a last futile attempt, she reached into her pocket and produced her scissors, digging them into his hand. He grunted and immediately let go. She scrambled once more for the open door, but he had it shut before she even reached it. He had her scissors before she could even raise her hand to use them again.

When she backed against the closed door, she noted that she had left him with a vicious scratch on the back of his hand. But his reaction to his wound was less than satisfying. Far from appearing hurt—or even irritated—he took one glance at the tiny embroidery scissors in his palm and rolled his eyes in amusement. He then went about his business as if the entire incident hadn't happened.

"I mean to escape," she called out defiantly. "As you can see I'm not unwilling to inflict injury. So why don't you let me go before I get my hands on a real weapon and truly do you harm."

He stared at her, a sarcastic smile gracing his lips. "You're right, Miss Dayne, what a fool I've been to think I could best you." Mocking her, he put one of his pistols in her hands and made a great display of showing her the trigger.

Shocked, she looked down at the pistol in her hand. Now she didn't know what to think.

"Go on, do your worst," he instructed as she, dumbstruck, held the gun to him.

"What are you trying to prove?" she asked, her voice shaking.

"Come along. If you want to be free, shoot me. Otherwise, I've got to meet the ship that's fast approaching."

"Are you out of your mind? Do you want to be killed?"

"The question is, Miss Dayne, are you a killer?" He taunted, "Come along. Shoot me."

She couldn't believe this man. He was daring her to shoot him. But could she? Could she live with herself if she actually killed him? When she didn't move, he laughed, and she almost wondered if she couldn't. She despised him as she had never despised anyone. Yet could she shoot him?

"Pull the trigger. You'll be on the deck in a second if you do."

Slowly she lowered the pistol. As much as she wanted her freedom, she couldn't have his blood on her hands. And that was just what he was counting on. He took back the pistol as if he'd never given it to her. Striding to the door, he was almost out of the cabin before she grabbed his sleeve and forced him to listen.

"You won't lock me in this cabin again! I'm determined that Flossie and I shall be on the approaching ship and away from here this very hour!" She was so furious she could hardly hold on to him. He took her every plan and rendered it impotent.

He paused and pressed her to the door. "Miss Dayne, believe me, you don't desire to be on *that* ship."

"I do! Even a lowly packet would be preferable to this floating pirates' den. Let me out of here! This instant!" she hissed, her eyes locking on his.

"You want to leave?" He pressed her closer to the door. "Fine. You shall meet the illustrious captain and crew of the *Bleeding Heart*. If it's still your desire to depart with them, then I shall not stop you."

"Do you truly mean—?"

Before she could finish, he grabbed her. He turned pensive while he looked at her bound hair. An idea suddenly occurred to him and he chuckled. Before she could stop him, he released a pin from her hair and let one long lock fall to her bosom.

"Let's give the men of the *Bleeding Heart* some booty, shall we?" His lips turned up in a cold smile, and he took her tiny scissors and snipped off the gilt-red tress. With it held fast in his palm, he then opened the cabin door and pushed her ahead of him onto the weather deck.

10

The *Bleeding Heart* grew more ominous as it approached. Backlighted by the ruby dawn, the ship appeared almost black, like a great oily raven swooping down on the noble *Seabravery*.

Aurora watched from the quarterdeck while the men of the *Seabravery* readied their ship for a confrontation. There was tension in the air as men scrambled down the ropes and up the companionways, but Aurora had the distinct feeling that her ship's able seamen had seen confrontation before. In fact, some seemed to almost relish what was to come. Such as Vashon.

She watched him on the quarterdeck. Every now and again he would shout an order, switching elegantly from French to Spanish or to whatever language the particular seaman whose attention he had could understand. But when the *Seabravery* was prepared to his satisfaction, Vashon seemed almost pleased to see the dread ship approaching. His eyes were alight with anticipation, and his step seemed quicker and full of purpose. When he caught her staring at him, he actually smiled, but it wasn't a cheerful, encouraging smile. It was a covetous, disturbing one, as if she were the Star herself, and he knew no one else could have her.

"Still hoping she'll rescue you?" Vashon walked by and shot a glance at the *Bleeding Heart*, which was now only a few hundred yards away.

Aurora surveyed the oncoming ship one more time. It actually wasn't black, but there was so much pitch slopped on its bow that the ship appeared black. When she looked further, she noted that the sails were tattered around their edges and they were a dirty shade of gray, in stark contrast to the *Seabravery*'s crisp, bleached canvas sails. But the true sign that the *Bleeding Heart* was not destined to be her salvation was the ship's flag, which its crew was just now hoisting up the mast. The flag consisted of a smiling skull, and beneath it bony hands held out a bloody heart. Shocked by the gruesome image, Aurora couldn't stop her sharp intake of breath.

"I see you're having a change of heart." A smile twisted Vashon's lips.

She suddenly longed for even the security of his wretched cabin. "I take it the approaching vessel is a pirate ship," she blurted out.

"Your powers of observation are phenomenal, Miss Dayne."

Angered by his sarcasm, she added, "And it's no wonder that ship is coming this way. You know what they say, 'Birds of a feather . . .'" Abruptly she turned away and focused on the *Bleeding Heart*. She was devastated to realize there would be no escape there, but then, suddenly, an awful thought occurred to her. She turned back to Vashon and put her hand on his steely arm. "You—you aren't perchance thinking to hand Flossie and me over to them? Perhaps to persuade them not to attack?"

He looked down at her delicate hand on his arm. He covered it with his own large one, and said, "You sound almost hopeful, *Aurore*. Should I?"

She gasped. "You cannot . . . they're pirates!"

"And what am I?"

"A pirate." Her eyes darkened and her gaze locked with his. He laughed.

The situation was hopeless. She was caught between the spider and the web. "How do you know these men?" she asked in a strained voice.

"Ah, let's just say they're old acquaintances."

She should have bitten her sarcastic tongue, yet she couldn't stop herself from saying, "What, old chums from pirate school?"

His laughter only grew louder. "Now that you know who you're up against, who do you choose to go with? Them or me?"

She looked away and reluctantly made her decision. "I suppose the *Seabravery* would be the lesser evil. At least she flies the Union Jack."

"Not always."

She abruptly looked at him, then followed his gaze toward the spanker. She blanched. In place of the flag that had previously flown there, a black banner was now unfurled, painted with the image of a dragon regardant. It was the exact dragon tattooed on Vashon's back.

She put her hand to her temple to think. Somehow she had to escape this terrible ship. But now she had to make sure she didn't land in hands worse than the ones she was already in. It was going to be a hellish task.

"What? No scathing comments?" he taunted. "No maligning of my character, no calling me traitor?"

"Why should I? You've now revealed your true colors." She tore her gaze from the spanker. "I suppose you only hide behind Britain's flag when you're running from the Royal Navy."

"Ah, there it is. So are you calling me a coward, Miss Dayne?"

She set her jaw and refused to look at him.

He only laughed. "You may not believe this, but the *Seabravery* is the best of my fleet—all of which make legitimate runs from London to New York, and all of which fly the Union Jack."

"From time to time. Only when it suits you, I presume."

"Aye. When it suits me, which is all the time."

"But not now," she said harshly.

"No, not now," he answered as he glanced at the banner, "because more run from my flag than from the Union Jack."

"The *Bleeding Heart* isn't running." She looked and saw that in a few minutes the two ships would meet.

"The *Bleeding Heart* doesn't look like much, but it matches the *Seabravery* in gun power. If she so chose, right now we could be blowing each other from the water."

"But they fear the dragon too much?"

He studied her. His gaze flickered down her petite figure, his eyes warming appreciatively where he found the drab linen running taut across her bosom. With an enigmatic expression on his face, he touched one red-gold curl that had freed itself from her hairpins and now graced her temple.

"Let's just say I've precious cargo on board," he finally said. "Cargo the *Bleeding Heart* would be loath to destroy." With that, he caged her in his arms. Standing behind her, he locked his hands on the railing on either side of her bodice, and whether she wanted to or not, together they waited for the *Bleeding Heart* to come about.

The evil-looking ship soon came alongside the *Seabravery*. The crew of each ship stood deathly quiet at the railing, facing each other like soldiers waiting for the command to attack. Aurora looked down at the weather deck. Captain Corbeil stood at the deckhouse nervously rubbing his crippled hand. Meanwhile the captain of the other ship turned his attention to Vashon.

"Vashon!" the pirate captain yelled across the water. "How good it is to see you, *mon ami!*"

Vashon grinned. Aurora could feel his heartbeat at her back. It quickened.

"Azzedine, *salaud*! What do you want? If you're looking for your keeper, I believe we left all the sharks in the reefs of Bermuda."

The captain of the *Bleeding Heart* laughed so hard he had to hold his stomach. Eventually he called out, "Vashon, I was always a man to appreciate your humor! But I think Peterborough will not be amused at your description!"

"Tell Peterborough there's no blood for him to feed upon on this ship!"

"I told him you wouldn't cooperate!" The captain laughed and shook his head. He was a short man, swarthy and unkempt. There was an exotic air about him, with his flashing black eyes and smooth, coffee-colored skin, and Aurora surmised he might be Moroccan or Algerian. He was almost handsome, but even from her distance, she could see he possessed several rotten and missing teeth.

"And who is the pretty one, Vashon?" the pirate called out. He turned his stare on Aurora, and it was so abominably crude that she found herself pressing back into Vashon's chest.

"Ah, this is my little gem, Azzedine." Vashon put his arms around her and made a great display over relishing the scent of her hair. "And you'll never guess where I found her!" he shouted. "At an almshouse in London! One must never overlook the mundane, my friend. You never know where you'll find treasure."

Aurora flinched. She desperately wanted to break free of Vashon's hold, but for the moment she was trapped. If she fought to be away from Vashon, he just might grant her desire and give her to the *Bleeding Heart*. Instinctively she knew she was better off aboard the *Seabravery*. She remained still and endured the gentle assault.

"I want you to meet Aurora, Azzedine!" Vashon continued. "This is Miss Aurora Dayne, a prized passenger of the *Seabravery*. We should not like to lose her company too soon."

"I see that," Azzedine remarked, his eyes turning serious. "And if I had such a lovely companion, I think I would be sorry to see her go! But I'm supposed to take her, Vashon. And for that I request permission to board so that I may negotiate her price."

With these words Aurora pressed even further into Vashon's chest. He was supposed to take her? Was every pirate on the high seas out to kidnap her? Unconsciously she clutched at Vashon's arms. Vashon chuckled and pulled her to him. She was so close she could feel his chest rumble when he laughed. She still despised Vashon. He seemed to enjoy her panic considerably.

"Azzedine!" he called out happily, "By all means, come aboard! Break your fast with us! But I warn you, she's not going with you! I'll see you dead, Azzedine, as sorry as that would make me!"

Azzedine chuckled again. He waved to Vashon, then the crew of the *Seabravery* made ready for him to board.

"They still talk about you in the Casbah, Vashon. The women still miss you, the men still hate you." Finished with his meal, the pirate captain Azzedine laid down his fork and rubbed his belly. He looked almost self-satisfied. If he could kidnap her and escape on the *Bleeding Heart*, Aurora was sure he'd call it a perfect day.

As if Vashon didn't want this chamber pot of a man in his personal quarters, she, Vashon, and the Algerian ate instead in the roundhouse, where the passengers out of London had taken their meals. To Aurora those carefree days seemed like weeks ago.

The chef had made a huge, elaborate meal as if the ship were hosting royalty rather than a grimy, predatory corsair. But despite the delicious fare, Aurora found she had no appetite. All through the meal she felt the Algerian's gaze crawling on her. Though it was clear Vashon held Azzedine by a tight leash, it was all too obvious that Azzedine longed to achieve his mission. But since even he seemed to know he was no match for Vashon, the captain of the *Bleeding Heart*, by the inexplicable camaraderie of outlaws, could only accept Vashon's hospitality, then take his leave.

Vashon ripped the Algerian's gaze from Aurora with a harsh stare of his own, leaned back in his chair, and smiled. "Ah, the Casbah," he commented. "I must admit I still have fond memories. Is the Rue Ben Ali still as narrow and treacherous as I remember? You could hide a thousand thieves along that street and never find even one."

"Ah, yes," Azzedine added slyly, "and I forgot to mention that the dey still hates you too—even he could not find you after you stole into the palace and into the arms of his eldest daughter."

Vashon laughed. "And is there still a bounty on my head? It's no wonder I was forced into legitimate business. The dey's scimitar is sharp, *c'est compris*?"

"The bounty still holds, Vashon, and you know I'm not above collecting it myself."

"If you could," Vashon answered easily.

"Yes, if I could." Azzedine sighed. "But since I cannot, perhaps I will bring the dey to you instead. You know he still boils with rage whenever someone even mentions the name Vashon. It was quite clever of you when he offered one hundred pieces of gold for your head to offer five hundred pieces for his."

"I'm still insulted that he didn't think me worth more." Vashon made a great display of looking wounded and suddenly both men laughed.

But not Aurora. She sat next to Vashon, pushing the fried plantain around on her plate. She found all the talk of the Casbah ironic. She had read once that Algiers was referred to as "the White City" because of the Casbah's blindingly brilliant stucco-on-brick houses that cascaded down the hillside to the city's teeming port. It had always struck her as odd that a place with a name as pure and magical as the White City was really the shelter for pirates, smugglers, spies, and other villains.

But if the Casbah was truly such a notorious place, the two men before her would certainly fit in. One pirate appeared as though he'd just as soon steal a leper's cane as shake a man's hand. But as wicked as Azzedine looked, Vashon looked more so. He gave off the aura of a man unafraid of confrontation. Long after the likes of Azzedine put their tails between their legs and fled, Vashon would keep going. Aurora suddenly realized that that was the most frightening thing about him: Vashon was not afraid to die. Men instinctively knew this and kept their distance. But what could force a man to value his bravado over his life? She came to only one answer: a man who had needed that bravado to survive.

"So, Vashon," Azzedine began, drawing all eyes to him, "what am I to tell Peterborough if I show up empty-handed?"

"You mean *when* you show up empty-handed," Vashon corrected.

Azzedine laughed. "Ah, my mistake, *mon ami.* There was never much I could get by the dragon. But what shall I tell him? Peterborough really wants the girl. I wish you would let me have her." Once more the pirate turned his glittering black stare on Aurora. She glared back at him, but still she felt like a fatted calf on market day.

"You can't take her, Azzedine, but I will offer this." Vashon nonchalantly produced the tress that he had cut from Aurora's head. He tossed it across the table. "Give this to Peterborough with my compliments. And tell him he need no longer search for the Star. It's already mine."

"I will," Azzedine agreed, "if that is the only choice you give me." His stare grew more bold, and Aurora nearly felt like retching. The

Algerian was little better than the scum she used to scrub from the
Home's only hip bath. Just the thought of his touching her was enough
to make her want to jump overboard. And clearly, he wanted to do
much more to her than merely touch her.

"Azzedine, 'thou shalt not covet thy neighbor's ass.' " Vashon once
again got the pirate's attention. Azzedine's gaze obediently flew from
Aurora to the *Seabravery*'s owner.

"That's better," Vashon commented dryly, obviously not liking the
way the pirate had been assessing what Vashon deemed to be his property.

Aurora met Vashon's eyes and her cheeks flamed with anger. She
couldn't stand another minute of this torture. She was not chattel, and
she refused to let anyone treat her as such. She was hardly thankful for
Vashon's intervention. In fact, as far as she was concerned, the one
pirate was little better than his wretched comrade.

Abruptly she stood. "I do hope you *gentlemen* will excuse me, but I
find I really must attend to my toilet." Just as she spoke, Azzedine
picked up the lock of hair from the table. He brought it to his nose to
experience its scent, and she was overcome with fury. She didn't like
having parts of her person going to some man named Peterborough. If
Vashon was not going to give her over to the *Bleeding Heart*, then she
was ready for a little rebellion.

"Aurora, where do you think you're going?" Vashon demanded in a
tone of voice she had heard all too frequently from John Phipps.

She walked to the galley door. Her eyes narrowed defiantly. "I'm
going to my cabin. And I don't need to be accompanied."

"How can you be so rude to the *Seabravery*'s only guest?" Vashon's
lips twitched in a smile. "Sit, Aurora, and finish your meal."

"I'm not hungry."

His jaw tensed. "If you continue like this, my love, there won't be
much of you with which to barter."

"What a vile tragedy then, most especially for you, sir." She shot him
a rebellious glance, then made to exit, but before she could she heard
Vashon bolt from his seat. Her arm was taken in a viselike grip, and she
was forced into the passage, away from the prying eyes of the Algerian.

"Aurora," Vashon whispered down at her, "I'll grant that you may
go this time, but I warn you, this behavior won't be tolerated in the
future. You may go to my cabin, but do not stray. The men of the
Bleeding Heart are all too anxious to claim their booty, and I don't
think you'd find their company all that . . . enjoyable."

She thrust her arm away and spat, "You needn't worry, sir. I've no desire for the company of pirates." Her flashing eyes gave little doubt that he was included in that group.

"Pirates or not, you heed my words, *Aurore*." He shook her lightly.

"I understand . . . but then again, perhaps I don't." She taunted, "Perhaps I'd be better off on the *Bleeding Heart*. Perhaps this Peterborough you speak of would at least know that one does not treat a human being like a piece of merchandise to be bought and sold to the highest bidder—"

He grabbed her up in his arms, cutting off her words. He shook her until her head seemed to spin. "You listen to me, you little baggage! You're better off on this ship than anywhere else! And if you're ever so foolish as to contemplate running to Peterborough, you think again! I've seen Peterborough burn a man to death by stuffing oakum into the poor bastard's mouth and setting it aflame. Peterborough laughed the entire time. So you praise almighty God that He put you in my hands, because you could be far, far worse off!"

"Stop . . . stop!" she demanded breathlessly, trying to wrestle from his hold. When at last she was free, she looked up and saw his face hardened with anger. A sob escaped her lips and she wondered how to answer his gruesome story. It didn't seem possible that a man as horrible as this Peterborough could exist, but every time she looked into Vashon's emerald eyes, she saw that he spoke the truth. And now, because of her father—a father she hadn't even known—she was at the center of the maelstrom in this pirate's violent world.

Shaken, she tried to think of some sort of denial. But there was none. He knew this man Peterborough, not she. If Vashon told her the man was a monster, she had no choice but to believe him and continue on this treacherous journey until escape was at hand.

"It was not my intention to frighten you, little wren." Softening at her pale features, he stepped toward her in the narrow passage, but she warded him off with an accusatory glance.

"It was your every intention to frighten me," she remarked stiffly, "and it has been from the moment I boarded this ship. You're an uncivilized, licentious criminal whose only pleasure seems to come from bullying those weaker than you—but you won't be bullying me for long."

His eyes suddenly warmed. "Ah, there's that spirit I see so little of. You know, *Aurore*, you should be glad I've kidnapped you and made you fight, otherwise you'd have withered and died at that almshouse."

"It—was—not—an—*almshouse!*" she hissed.

He burst into appreciative laughter and when she could stand it no more, she picked up her skirt and sped to the solitude of his cabin, still hearing his laughter long after she had shut the door.

11

Once in the cabin, Aurora fumed and paced the dragon-covered carpet.
What a mess she was in—did she give that plunderer her rhyme and
have faith that he would release her and Flossie unharmed? Or did she
continue to endure his lascivious behavior in the hope that she might
gain the leverage to bargain with him? She didn't know. She needed to
speak with Flossie, but he was keeping them well apart.

She bit her lower lip and thought about her limited avenues of escape,
but the noise from the ship next to them distracted her. Outside the
open ports she could hear the men of the *Bleeding Heart* carrying on
aboard their ship. She heard laughter and the strains of a fiddle being
played. Obviously the seamen were having a grand time while their
captain was being entertained aboard the *Seabravery.*

She went to close the ports, yet just as she was going to do so,
something odd caught her eye. Vashon's black satin bed-curtains, which
were usually tied well back from the bed with heavy gold-tasseled cords,
now were completely closed. It was strange, especially since the bed-
curtains were only used in a cold climate, not in the balmy summertime
Atlantic.

Frowning, she couldn't think of a reason why Benny would have
closed them. She stared at them for a moment wondering what she
should do, then timidly stepped to the black-draped bedstead. It was
probably silly of her, but she knew she wouldn't feel safe until she
discovered for herself that there was no one behind those curtains.

Her hand reached out and she grasped one edge of the heavy Chinese
satin. She meant to quickly whip it back and expose whoever might be
lurking there, but before she had the chance, a meaty arm reached out
from the black shimmering depths and pulled her off her feet.

"What 'ave we here?" a voice said before she was taken into a bone-
crushing grasp. The stench of a wet dog emanated from the man's damp

clothing. His beard held drops of sea water, but even wet, the graying, scraggly mass still looked as though it was the perfect haven for nits.

"Release me!" she screeched, trying to pull from the man's hefty arm. Her heart seemed to pound in her ears, she was so terrified.

"Ye sound another word, fair lady, and I'll slit yer throat from ear to ear."

A glittering knife appeared in the man's other hand, and he held it deftly to the pulse in her neck. She moaned and stilled her trembling hands. She was so frightened she could almost feel her blood thrum through her veins. If she dared move an inch, the blade would prove lethal.

"Tha's it, now. Speak softly," he instructed when she had ceased to move, "I've a few questions for ye."

"You're from the other ship, then?" she whispered. She hardly knew why she was asking. The men of the *Seabravery* were never so dirty and unkempt.

When the man nodded, she nearly fainted from horror. She didn't know how the ruffian was going to manage to sneak her off the *Seabravery*, but if he'd managed to steal aboard undetected, she didn't doubt he could do it. Then what would become of her? She now knew her situation would be much worse on the *Bleeding Heart*.

"Whose cabin is this?" he demanded.

"This is Vashon's cabin."

"Ah, Vashon. That bastard. Me and the men of the *Bleedin' Heart*'ve had a gutful of him."

She saw hate fill the man's watery eyes. It was clear he'd had a confrontation with Vashon before . . . and lost.

Desperate to reason with the brute, she asked, "Dare you come here and risk his fury then? You must know he won't be pleased to find me missing."

He released a phlegmy chuckle. "I dare this for a jewel as big as me nose. I aim to be a rich man afore this is over, and I hear ye're just the maid to help me." He pulled her off the bed. His rough hold had already left her bruised.

"But you must listen! I can't help you! I don't know where the Star is!" she protested, trying desperately to sound unafraid.

"Oh, ye'll help all right. Peterborough knows a thing or two about how to get a wench to talk. We'll get the Star's whereabouts out of ye— and perhaps a little something more, eh?" He laughed and squeezed her waist. When she pulled back, the tip of the knife was stuck further into the hollow of her throat. "Ye are a pretty little package . . ." he whispered, bringing her further against his chest. He licked his lips, and that frightened her more than any of his words. His gaze snaked over her figure until her skin crawled.

"Vashon will hardly let you escape," she said, trying to pull the man's eyes up to her face. "I daresay from what I've seen of him he'll know quite well how to deal with the likes of you."

"Vashon will be too dead to do much, lovey." His hand moved up her rib cage and she had to swallow her bile.

"How—how do you know that?"

"Azzedine's orders. Once Vashon's dead we'll take the ship . . . and its pretty cargo." He looked down at her meaningfully. His salty finger tried to touch her lips, but she pulled back in horror. This only angered him. "Too foin fer me, lovey?" he asked before slamming her down onto Vashon's mattress.

"No!" she cried out, but quickly the knife was pressed again to her throat. She struggled with the man as he tried to lie atop her, but even so she was no match for him. He was stocky and muscular, and when the tip of his dagger threatened to pierce her skin, she knew the battle could not be won. But still she fought him. She sobbed and kicked away his hand as he pulled at her skirt. Yet he only laughed. Her resistance seemed to arouse him further. He had hold of her pantalets before she could stop him. When she heard that garment tear, she let out a low moan. He was going to rape her; there seemed no way to stop him. But just as she felt his knife dig into her flesh, the pirate sailed off her and landed in the corner.

"Say something, Robert," Vashon said, looming over the man. "Say something to make me spare your life."

Aurora gasped and raised herself to a sitting position. The door to the cabin was wide open. Somehow Vashon must have heard her struggling and burst in. Now he towered over Robert, his face a grim, angry mask.

"So what's it to be, Robert? How will you beg me for mercy?" Vashon didn't move. She could see he was not a man to act with passion. Instead he terrified by calculation. He was doing it now. Brilliantly. Robert was as white as a sheet.

"Vashon, it was Azzedine! He's the one who had me steal aboard! It's Azzedine you should kill!" Robert whined.

"And it's Azzedine who told you you should rape my captive?"

Robert clutched the knife. With his eyes fairly popping out of their sockets from fear, he stared up at Vashon. "She's a woman, Vashon! She's fair game on these seas!"

Vashon put his booted foot on Robert's wrist. The seated man groaned and let go of the knife.

"That girl is my property," Vashon pointed out. "And you know what happens on these seas when a man tries to steal another's property?"

"Vashon! Don't kill me! Don't kill me!" Robert begged. He squirmed further into the corner, and Aurora had never seen a man so terrified. The way Vashon was behaving frightened her too. He was so calm. And so angry. Though she loathed the man cowering beneath him, she couldn't stand idly by while Robert was slain. She couldn't be responsible for another man's death.

"Vashon!" she cried out, "I'm not hurt! You cannot kill this man!"

Vashon turned. He took one glance at her molested state and she could see the fury spark anew in his eyes.

"Robert, you dog, get on your feet," he said ominously.

"No! Vashon, please . . . !"

"Vashon!" She climbed down from the bed. "I'm unharmed! This man was stopped! I agree he deserves punishment, but not death! In truth he did little more than you yourself—"

Vashon whipped around to face her, and the words died on her lips. That she had accused him of doing what the cur beneath him had done seemed beyond his ability to endure. His anger looked to ready to explode. She wasn't sure what he would do next, but just as his attention was off Robert, the other pirate suddenly pulled a pistol hidden in his wet, grimy waistcoat. Aurora gasped in horror. Yet a split second before Robert squeezed off the shot, Vashon reached for the fallen knife and ran it expertly across Robert's throat. The pirate was dead in an instant.

She had never seen so much blood. It was on the floor, on the wall, on the body. And on Vashon. Without even realizing it, she was screaming, but when Vashon reached for her, she slapped him away.

"Don't touch me," she cried, hysterical. "Don't touch me with *those hands!*"

Vashon numbly looked down at his hands. They were spattered with blood. She turned away and wondered if she was going to retch. Suddenly, uncontrollably, she began to sob, but whether it was from an attack of nerves or simply the shock of seeing a man die so violently, she didn't know.

"This man's life is hardly worth your tears," Vashon told her woodenly.

"You killed him," she sobbed.

"And he would have killed you. Eventually."

"But he did not."

"Would you have rather I waited until he did?"

She wiped the tears streaming down her cheeks with a shaky hand. "I'd have rather you left me on the docks of St. George's. I want no part of killers!"

She looked at him and had never seen him so cold. His entire face, his entire body had gone rigid. But not a word escaped his lips.

"Vashon! What's going on?" Isaac burst into the cabin and wildly looked about. He took in the dead pirate slumped in the corner and Aurora's state.

"Old Robert got aboard, then," the captain said.

Vashon only nodded. He never took his eyes off Aurora.

Isaac took another uneasy glance at the body. "Well, from the looks of him, I'd say he swam from the *Bleeding Heart*. I don't know how he did it, Vashon. We were so careful—"

"I sense a disturbance." Azzedine entered the cabin and calmly looked down at his man lying in a pool of blood. His remorse seemed as fleeting as his guilt.

"We know you sent him, Azzedine," Isaac snapped. Vashon still did not speak.

"He acted on his own." Azzedine looked once more at the body, then smiled. "But take heart, *mes amis*, at least Robert was so gracious as not to bleed on your exquisite carpet."

Aurora glanced at the corpse. She could hardly believe that only minutes before the man had lived and breathed. It was true the pirate Robert was vile, but now that he was dead, didn't he warrant more respect than merely an appreciative comment that he'd not died on the rug? Or was that how these men treated their dead, as callously as they treated the living?

Azzedine wandered closer to the body. Isaac was shaking his head and mumbling something about getting Benny to clean up the mess. Vashon was still staring at Aurora. Unobserved, Azzedine bent over his man. He picked something up from the floor and it wasn't until he had it pointed at Vashon that Aurora realized it was a gun.

"Vashon, I should very much like to kill you," Azzedine stated. He cocked the trigger and Aurora felt the blood drain from her face. She waited for Vashon to act, for surely he was going to kill this pirate too, but he didn't move. He just stared down at Azzedine while the pirate readied to murder him.

It was mesmerizing, this play being acted out before her. Never had she seen a man so utterly dispassionate about the value of his own life. She watched Vashon, and as she did so, she saw firsthand that attitude that had frightened so many men. Vashon's willingness to die was terrifying.

When Azzedine squeezed the trigger, Aurora screamed. But miraculously the gun didn't fire. The weapon made a loud thump, then Azzedine broke into laughter as if he had just played a horrendously amusing trick.

"I should very much like to kill you, Vashon," the pirate chuckled, "but alas, the powder is wet in this gun. Poor Robert! He died for no reason at all. When he threatened you with this pistol, he didn't think that the gunpowder would be rendered useless during his swim to the ship."

"Azzedine," Isaac growled, "return to your ship. And count yourself fortunate that you didn't end up like your man."

Azzedine bowed. "Till we meet again, *mes amis!*" He sauntered out of the room, snickering as if he'd told some kind of hilarious joke.

When Azzedine had gone, Isaac gave Vashon a look of disbelief. But Vashon didn't notice. He was staring at Aurora.

"You could have been killed," she said to him, her voice distraught. She'd never understand this man. At times he behaved as if a demon possessed him.

"So would you rather me be killed or be a killer?" he asked.

"Are those the only two choices? Is this life of yours so uncivilized that there is nothing in between?"

A bitter expression crossed his handsome features. "There is nothing in between, Aurora. And you remember that the next time I save your life."

"My God," she moaned, putting her head in her hands. "I didn't ask for this. I don't want to be a part of this. I beg of you, release Flossie and me at the next port!"

He walked up to her, put his hands on her arms, and shook her. When she looked up, he said, "You may not have asked for this, but you were destined to be here the day your father stole from Peterborough. So forget your prim and proper little past. It was all a lie anyway. Fate has dealt you these cards. You're in my hands now, and that's where you'll stay until I get the Star."

She let out a low sob. Almost unconsciously her gaze was drawn to his hands on her arms. The splatters of blood on his fingers had dried to a dark maroon, but some was still wet, leaving a smear on her gown. She tried to hide the revulsion that crossed her face, but he saw it. Before she could pull away from him, he nearly threw her to Isaac.

"Get her out of here!" he commanded, a slight break in his voice.

Sobbing, Aurora clutched at the captain's chest. Isaac steadied her and then gave Vashon a bewildered look. But before he could say a word, Vashon repeated his order. "Get her out of here!"

Obediently Isaac nodded and pulled her out the door.

12

"What kind of man is he?" Aurora asked, wiping away a tear that had slipped down her cheek. She looked across the railing at the brilliant blue Atlantic, marred only by the disappearing silhouette of the *Bleeding Heart*. Next to her, as if unsure of how to comfort her, Isaac drummed his two remaining fingers on the polished railing. "What kind of man is he that he could kill so swiftly, then not even move to save his own life?" She brushed away another tear.

"Vashon has always been a bit of an enigma."

"Does he not value his life? That pirate Azzedine was ready to shoot him, and Vashon didn't even blink."

"He's seen a lot in his four and thirty years, Aurora. It's made him very hard. Sometimes I think it's true that he may not value his life overly much. There seems to be something missing in him, a belief in goodness, perhaps. I'm not sure what it is, but because he doesn't have it, he seems not to care whether he lives or dies. I've seen him take extraordinary risks. But those risks have paid off."

"But you've had to fight hard too or you wouldn't be a pirate like him. You're not so hardened."

Isaac laughed sheepishly. He wiped his balding head and seemed to be groping for the right words. "I'm not a pirate, Aurora. I know you must think me one, but in truth I'm just a ship's captain. That's the life I've led for the past forty years, ever since my wife Rachel was taken from me by the pox."

"I don't understand," she said. "How could Vashon persuade a good sea captain to come with him on such an ignoble venture?"

"I've been with him for almost ten years now." He laughed. "When he tells you he's in legitimate business, you must believe him. He has almost as many ships as the British East India Company. He's a very wealthy man."

"But he was and is still a pirate." Her eyes darkened. She gave Isaac an accusatory look. "And you, who call yourself an honest man, work for him."

"Well, yes, that's true. But Vashon does not pirate any longer—except for this one instance," he added hastily. "In fact, he's most happy just walking the beaches of Mirage and looking over the accounts of his London businesses."

"Then why isn't he doing that right now and forgetting this horrid search for the emerald?"

Isaac looked out to the cloudless horizon. "He hates Peterborough. He truly hates him. Nothing will stop him from getting that jewel."

Aurora grasped at a chance for escape. "But you and the crew, Isaac, surely you see the immorality of kidnapping two women simply for revenge. Act against him, Isaac," she urged, "and let Flossie and me go free."

"The crew and I stand with Vashon," he said simply. He studied his crippled hand.

"But you call yourself a moral man! And surely you cannot speak for the crew! There must be one decent man on this ship willing to help us —and I swear I'll find him!"

"You won't find anyone on this ship willing to help you escape if it means relinquishing the quest for Peterborough. Believe me, Aurora, I speak for the crew. Some of these men have been with me for forty years."

"But not forty years on this ship. Not forty years with Vashon."

"No," he answered. "We served on another ship. She was a whaler named the *Leviathan*. And though there's barely a fifth of her crew still alive, they're all on the *Seabravery* now, and they all give their allegiance to Vashon."

"This can't be possible!" she gasped.

"It's possible," he affirmed. "Take it from an old Jew who doesn't lie."

Frustrated, Aurora once more looked out to sea. There seemed a million miles between her and freedom. The closer they got to Vashon's island, the smaller her chances were of escape. "Take me back to the cabin, Isaac," she said. "I must speak to Vashon."

Isaac nodded and presented her his arm. Trembling, she took it.

When she arrived back at the cabin, the pirate's body was gone and the blood had been thoroughly scrubbed away. Vashon was not there, but Aurora told Isaac to leave her. Vashon would return eventually, and she wanted to ready herself for the confrontation.

When the door closed behind Isaac, Aurora's face turned angry and determined. She settled in to wait, sure of the words she had to say to Vashon. No longer would she be timid and afraid in his presence. She had seen him do the worst sort of deed, and now that she knew what he was truly capable of, it somehow freed her. She was finally ready to bargain with the Devil.

Benny soon brought her a meal, and this time she ate it. She bathed and changed her dress, burying the bloodied garment at the bottom of her willow hamper. All too soon she heard Vashon's voice in the passage, snapping something in French to a passing seaman.

When he entered the cabin, he didn't speak a word. He eyed her once, then took out his logbook and wrote at the tripod table. When the silence became thunderous, she finally spoke.

"The rhyme has another verse."

He looked up from his desk. "What did you say?" he asked, a wariness suddenly in his eyes.

"I said the rhyme has another verse."

Slowly he put down his pen. "Why are you telling me this now?"

"Because I want a guarantee that Flossie shall not be hurt."

He scowled. "You may not believe this, but I have never made it a practice to rape and torture old women."

"*I'm* not an old woman."

"I see that." His gaze skimmed her figure, then rested on her face. "Tell me the verse."

She shook her head. "No, I'm not going to tell you."

"Do you tease me then? Have you a need for me to get it out of you?"

She looked at him. He was alluding to something filthy, she was sure. Ignoring the comment, she shook her head again. "No. You cannot get this out of me. I don't know where the Star is, but nonetheless, I hold the key to its acquisition. You shall have that key as soon as Flossie and I are set free."

"I shall have it now." He rose from his chair and towered over her. But this time she could not be intimidated. Her face was a mask of alabaster.

"You'll never get it from me, Vashon. Unless you release me first. And if I go to Mirage, I swear you shall never know it."

He frowned. A muscle hardened in his jaw, but then, the corner of his mouth lifted in a dark smile. "I see you've heeded my advice too well."

She looked at him. "Yes. 'Forget your prim and proper little past,' I think you told me. Well, as of now I consider it forgotten. No longer am I a schoolmistress from an orphanage. From now on I'm the woman who holds the secret to all your wretched plans. And I'm the woman you must please." Unconsciously her hand rose to the emerald locket.

"And how shall I please you?" he taunted.

"To begin with, I demand my own cabin."

"I see."

She didn't pause. "At the next island, Flossie and I are to be released and compensated for this misery."

"How so?"

"You are to give Flossie enough money for passage back to St. George's, and you are to give me enough for passage back to London."

He looked as if he might laugh. "Is that all?" he asked with mock solemnness.

"Yes, that's all. For that I shall give you the second verse, and you can go after this wicked jewel on your own."

He put his hands behind his back and studied her. "But have you no sentiment, Aurora? After all, your father wanted you to have this jewel, or why else would he teach you that nursery rhyme?"

A slight frown appeared on her face. She had enormous sentiment for her father. He was the only member of her family she had ever known and every time she thought of him, a lonely ache blossomed in her chest. She wished fervently that he'd never left her, and as a child she had even nurtured the secret hope that one day he was going to appear on the Home's doorstep looking for her. But now, after all that had transpired the past few days, she wasn't sure if the sentiment she held in her heart was actually for her father or for the man she thought he'd been. All that was left was the image of the man she wanted him to be.

"If I have any sentiment at all," she answered, "it's the wish that I could prove my father was no thief. But since I can't do that, I certainly want nothing of the goods you claim he stole. All I want is for Flossie and me to be set free."

"And if I let you and the widow go, shall you not bring charges upon me for kidnapping and piracy, and see me twisted for it?"

"If Flossie so wishes it, she may. But I would very much like to forget this shadowy adventure and return to London in peace."

"And return to your dashing fiancé, John Philips, I suppose?"

"Phipps," she corrected.

"Ah, yes, of course. *Phipps*," he said with great emphasis. "I suppose you want to become Mrs. *Phipps* just as soon as you can."

She remained silent. She wouldn't marry John. If this trip had told her anything, it made most clear the fact that she was not suited for John Phipps.

"Whatever I do," she said briskly, "it's of no concern to you. What is your concern is the second verse to my father's rhyme. And you shall get that as soon as—"

"Yes, yes," he interposed, suddenly venting his annoyance. "But what you naïvely dismiss, baggage, is the fact that I won't know if this second verse of yours is truly the one your father gave you until I find the emerald with it."

"You have my word that I shall give you the truth."

He tipped his head back and laughed. She felt as if she had just told him some kind of bawdy joke.

"Whatever is so funny?" she asked, irritated.

"Your word," he mocked. "And don't you think I know that a prisoner is not above lying to get his desired freedom?"

"But I shall give you the truth and I can prove—" She almost bit off her tongue trying to stop her words. She had almost told him about the locket. Once he knew about that, she'd have no bargaining chip at all.

Suddenly his interest was piqued. He cupped her face in his hands and studied her. "How shall you prove it?" he asked.

"When the time comes I shall be able to. Just release Flossie and me at the next port and you shall have your verse."

"Is it written down somewhere, Aurora?" His gaze slid to her willow basket at the foot of his bed. He dropped his hands and walked to it.

"It's not in there," she told him, her voice rising in panic.

"But it is written down?"

She remained mute.

Suddenly his eyes lowered to her clothes. She lifted her hand protectively to her chest.

"Where is it, *Aurore*? Written on a tiny piece of paper, then sewn into the hem of your frock?"

"Of course not," she said, worry creeping into her eyes.

"Or is it tucked into the seam of your chemise? Surely it would be safe there, wouldn't it?" He began to stalk her.

"No, it isn't." She began backing away.

"Take off your dress, Aurora."

"I shall not!"

"Take it off or I'll take it off."

She stumbled over his mahogany armchair. He caught her just as she fell. His hand wrapped around her waist and it intimately wandered over her uncorseted torso.

He smiled and commented, "Ah, how I love a woman who needn't cinch up her waist." With that he dragged her to the bedstead, blithely ignoring her kicks and demands to be set free.

"It's not there!" she cried futilely when he threw her on the bed. She squirmed beneath him, but the moment she made some headway in escaping, she heard a knife rip through her dress. He stood over her as she lay panting on the mattress and he easily tore through her hem. It was the second time that day a knife had been taken to her, but right now Robert's knife almost seemed preferable to Vashon's.

"Where is it, wench?" he snarled after he'd pulled apart her gown's hem. When all she could do was shake her head, he went for the seams.

In seconds her drab linen gown was in shreds. Ignoring her violent protests, he rifled through the torn fabric, touching her in places she never dreamed she'd be touched. His knuckles grazed her thighs, her waist, her torso before he centered his attention—and his hands—on the seams just to the sides of her bust.

Outraged that he was using his search as an excuse to fondle her, she grew even more outraged when she felt herself responding. Groaning, she looked down and saw her nipples tighten and strain against the ripped linen of her bodice. When he saw it too, she wanted to slap the expression right off his face.

"I hate you," she swore to him under her breath.

"Yes, I know . . . I see how much you hate me. . . ." He began to smile.

"You play the fool if you think I'd ever desire an ignoble wretch like you," she spat.

His green eyes glittered with mirth. "Of course. You're right. Your fiancé Phyfe is the only man you could desire. That's why you're running to the opposite ends of the earth to be away from him."

"Phipps," she hissed. "His name is Phipps."

"Thank you. *Phipps*," he answered.

"And see that you remember that name, too, for when John comes to rescue Flossie and me, no doubt he will bring the Royal Navy, and we'll all see you hang at Wapping!" It was a lie, but she hoped it struck a chord of fear in him anyway.

It didn't. He raised one infuriating black eyebrow and said, "My, my. Old Phelps can truly do all that?"

Her anger exploded. She lashed out to scratch his face, but he easily captured her. He straddled her on the bed and with arms much stronger than hers he forced her beneath him. She moaned in frustration and longed for her embroidery scissors. She surely had the bravado to use them now.

"Where is your proof, Aurora?" he said, an ultimatum.

"You won't find it in my clothes, so *release me!*" she nearly screamed.

"But I have to be sure." He looked down at her heaving chest and did a poor job of hiding his smile. "How will I know you're speaking the truth until I've searched you—*thoroughly?*"

Wriggling beneath him, she tried to make him stop, but it was no use. He pulled at her gown until her dress was reduced to mere tatters, then he thrust it to the floor and began to prey upon her again. Now clad in only her chemise and pantalets, she felt as if she might as well be naked, and she expected she soon would be when his knife tore at the delicate homemade French work of her undergarments.

But suddenly he ceased. Deep in thought, he fingered the pierced cotton at the neckline of her chemise, letting his palm fill with the swell of flesh that peeked over it. She wasn't sure what he would do next, but when he put the knife down on the mattress and in its stead produced her embroidery scissors, she moaned in despair. It was an abomination that he was trying to strip her with the blade of a knife, but she'd never be able to endure his cutting away her remaining garments, inch by painful inch. Particularly when his palm felt so warm and so oddly right on her skin.

"Don't do this," she whispered, trying to pull away his hand.

"But this garment requires a finer touch." Pensively he stroked down the valley of her bosom with the sharp point of the scissors. He was so gentle she could barely feel them as they glided along her breastbone, but the cold metal and even colder gaze of the man above her sent an uncontrollable shiver down her spine.

"Please," she said, her breath coming in short little gasps, "I haven't many clothes—"

"And the ones you do have are wretched. Paupers dress finer than you, love."

"My garments may indeed be plain, but they're all I possess—"

"They're pitiful . . . yet I daresay the finest of gowns could hardly make you more beautiful than you are now."

Her eyes met his and she was shocked by his hungry stare. He had obviously had many women. And it was certainly no great surprise that a man like him would want to spend his pent-up shipboard lust on the only young woman available. But what did surprise her was the shadow of longing deep within his emerald eyes. Somehow she didn't believe he was looking at her as just another woman who could ease his physical needs, then fade into the corners of his memory. Instead she felt, if it was possible, that she somehow intrigued him; that he viewed her as something foreign, something elusive and rare with which he had had little experience. And because he had suddenly found himself so captivated, his desire to possess her became more ravenous with every passing second.

"No," she whispered just his scissors made the first tiny cut down the middle of her chemise. Her hand grabbed his wrist, but he calmly pulled her off.

He snipped again.

"This isn't right," she pleaded. She put her hands on his chest in supplication.

He ignored her.

"I'll never tell you the second verse. Do you hear me?"

Even the threatened loss of his precious emerald seemed not enough to make him stop. He looked down at her, then deliberately ripped her chemise further with the scissors. He paused only when the entire valley between her breasts appeared beneath the tear. Then, as if she was tempting him beyond control, he lifted his hand to touch her.

"Don't," she said, desperate to stop him. Her hands clutched his in an effort to push him away, but as she well knew, her strength was negligible in comparison with his. He kept going, pausing only once to look at her face.

Her expression was an exquisite blend of fear and desire. Fear, because she had watched him kill a man that very morning, and no matter how ruthless his enemies were, he had proved himself to be equally ruthless; and desire, because as she looked up at him, at this wild, handsome pirate, she was suddenly overwhelmed with the terrible knowledge of what had been missing in her feelings for John Phipps.

"Why do you look at me in that manner?" he asked, suddenly stopping.

She quickly averted her eyes. What was wrong with her? How could she feel this way about a man who hadn't any more honor than the thieves of Field Lane? She pushed away his hand and grabbed at the edges of her chemise. She must be delirious. Or mad. She glanced at him, letting her gaze linger on his angry, handsome features. She was mad, she thought as she looked away again. That was the only explanation for it.

"Now why do you turn from me?" He grabbed her chin and forced her to look at him.

"Let me go," she said, writhing beneath him.

"Not until you tell me—"

"Let me go!" she demanded. "What must I tell you? That I dislike the hands of a killer upon me?"

His face hardened and he dropped his hold. Looking at the hand that had held her chin, he vengefully grabbed at the counterpane as if he were wiping imaginary blood from his palms. "This killer saved your life, wench," he said in a low, ominous tone. "Need I remind you of that?"

She could see he was furious. He didn't like his values being questioned. It was as if the path of his life had been a conscious decision on his part, and by questioning it she had made him wonder if he'd made the wrong choice.

"I thank you for saving me from that blackguard," she conceded, "but that hardly makes you a saint."

"Aye, I'm not a saint." His gaze raked her ruined chemise. He seemed particularly interested in the area where her nipples strained against the translucent white cotton. She put her arms over her chest to shield herself, but that only inflamed him more. Tightly he instructed her, "Take off the remainder of your clothes, Aurora. I want to see this proof you so cavalierly offered."

"It's not in my clothing, I say." Somehow she was able to wriggle from beneath him. She scooted to the headboard, all the while clutching her chemise to her.

"Enough of these games. Let me have your clothes."

"I will not."

"Then be prepared to have them ripped from your body."

He lunged for her. Terrified, she sprang off the bed, but not before he got a handful of her chemise. In one smooth motion it was torn from her back. She screamed and just as she turned around to grab the bed curtains, she couldn't keep from revealing two full breasts enticingly crowned with apricot-tinted nipples.

"You beast!" she cursed, wrapping herself in the black satin while he tore apart what was left of her chemise. Not a seam was left intact as he searched for hidden clues.

"Give me your drawers," he said, tossing her chemise aside.

"I won't." Her gaze fell onto the mattress. She saw the knife he had discarded lying not three inches from her hand. She grabbed it up just as he was moving for her.

"Stay away!" She held out the knife, letting the blade catch the light.

He laughed. "Old Robert couldn't wield that knife too well. You think you can better him?"

"I shall try! You stay away!" Her hand was trembling so she could hardly hold the knife still.

"Throw me your drawers and I shall leave you be."

She stared at him in indecision. She hated to surrender her pantalets, but if he chose to attack, even with a knife, she knew she'd lose. Despising him, she slowly untied her drawers. She threw them at him with a vengeance, all the while staying hidden behind the black satin bed curtain.

When he caught them, he almost looked disappointed she hadn't put up a fight. In a perfunctory manner, he tore them to shreds and left them in the same pile with her other ruined garments.

"Are you quite through now?" she asked bitterly. His gaze slid to her willow hamper. Before she could stop herself, she cried out, "Not that! I haven't many clothes left!" But he was deaf to her pleas.

He sauntered over to her basket and tossed its contents on the floor. Like a bear searching for honey, he clawed through her belongings, making swift work of all her undergarments. She grimaced with every tear, but when he came to her last remaining gown, the blue one with the embroidered rosebuds around the corsage, she couldn't stop herself from pleading, "Please not that one. It took me months to make that one."

With that confession, she damned herself, sure he would now take particular relish in ripping the gown to pieces. He would try to prove her insignificance by destroying the things she cherished. She was almost disappointed in finding Vashon so similar to John after all. No doubt John Phipps had taken similar pleasure in burning her sampler.

When he didn't move, she looked up and found him staring at her. They stood there for a long moment, eyes locked, and just when she was certain her dress was lost, he surprised her. He ran his hand along the gown's hemline and seams, then he tossed it to her.

Amazed she looked at the gown in her hand and watched him as he rifled through the rest of her things. She was surprised again when he gathered up her remaining belongings, including her hairpins. She assumed he was going to let her have those too, since her hair had fallen during their struggle, but she was shocked to see him open one of the huge leaded aft ports and wretchedly toss all her things into the evening sea.

"Why did you do that?" she asked, thinking he'd surely lost his mind. "My hairpins, my shoes and stockings have nothing to do with your precious Star."

"From now on you'll wear your hair down and not in that proper little spinsterish knot. And you'll go barefoot like the captive you are. You're on a pirate ship now, not taking tea in the Pump Room." He strode to her and grabbed the mass of her hair. He gently pulled the last dangling hairpins from the wavy red-gold tresses and threw those too out the port. "And from now on, *my delightful Miss Dayne*, you have one dress to wear until we get to San Juan, so I suggest you heed my temper lest I choose to make a rag out of that one too."

He gave her one final warning look and took his leave, slamming the cabin door behind him. When he was gone, she sighed with relief and clutched her last precious dress to her. But, realization dawning on her, she stared in horror at the pile of rags that used to be her clothes. Cursing him, she shouted to the closed door, "You villain! You've left me without any undergarments!"

13

Hours later Aurora was still searching for another straight pin. She had dressed herself in her blue gown, but for modesty's sake its apron front required that it be pinned to her shoulders. By now she had begun to suspect that her tiny pincushion had gone the way of her hairpins. She just hoped that a few of the straight pins had fallen from it so that she could keep up her dress.

She got down on her hands and knees and roamed the carpet, hoping to discover another pin where she had found the first one. But even barefoot she didn't feel anything but the silky nap of the carpet; there wasn't another pin to be found.

In utter disgust she sat and crossed her arms over her chest. She was a mess. Her hair hung in a knotted curtain to one side of her shoulder. Her pale blue dress looked like something from the Manchester Rag Fair. Shoeless and stockingless, she hardly looked better than one of the orphans before they arrived at the Home. Mrs. Bluefield would have been appalled. The older woman had always prided herself on the neatness of her schoolteachers. She would probably turn in her grave to see her favorite employee looking so wild.

"Ah, I see we've gotten comfortable."

Aurora looked up and gave Vashon a baleful stare. He smirked and entered the cabin. She didn't even attempt to get to her feet.

"What have you done with my straight pins?" she asked, barely hiding the fury in her voice.

"Why do you need them?" His gaze skimmed over her chest. Though she held the apron front discreetly to her, it was obvious why she needed them.

"I don't have to answer why I demand the return of my property. I just want my pincushion. If you have to swim to retrieve it, then do so." She looked at him and her aqua eyes darkened with anger. She didn't know how he'd managed it, but it seemed ever since she'd been kidnapped she could hardly keep her clothes on; her dresses were either falling down, being torn away, or snipped off; she'd now come to the end of her rope. If he didn't give her just one pitiful straight pin, she truly believed she might do him bodily harm.

"I'll make you a deal." He stood over her and crossed his arms. "I'll give you a thousand gold dressing pins if you just give me the second verse or your proof of a second verse."

She narrowed her eyes and fumed. She wasn't about to give him her locket. Not now when he'd proved himself to be such a scoundrel. Only for her freedom would she condescend to help him.

"Do you take my offer?" He added tauntingly, "Wench?"

She closed her eyes. It was all she could do not to hit him. She opened them again only to stare belligerently out the aft ports.

"Aurora." As if speaking to a child, he bent down and looked her in the eye. "Let me say this then: What if I take the one pin you do have until you give me what I want?"

Instinctively both her hands went to the shoulder with the pin. Her apron front fell to one side and revealed a tempting amount of bosom before she scrambled to her feet. He laughed and she backed away to the bookcase. Her hand met with a heavy porcelain Chinese foo lion, and she threatened to throw it at him.

"You won't take this one. I swear I shall die first," she exclaimed.

"Ah, such dramatics. The theater in the Haymarket could use such a performance."

He stepped forward and, much to their surprise, she threw the lion at him. It missed. But the resounding crash was enough noise to send nervous seamen scurrying looking for cannonfire above them on the quarterdeck.

"Shall you alarm the entire ship?" he asked when the footsteps overhead calmed.

"Don't you come near me," she whispered furiously. "I won't let you have this pin!"

He stepped forward again, and this time she threw several of his dragon-etched wine goblets. The tinkling of glass must have alerted the sailors as to what was going on in Vashon's cabin. With each successive broken goblet, the chuckles from above grew more raucous.

"Stay away, do you hear?" she warned.

"You little hellion, I won't have you—"

She threw another goblet. Then another. He artfully ducked every time one even came close to hitting him; still he encroached upon her. All too soon she ran out of articles to throw. She hurled her last wineglass, then turned to run. He caught her just as she grimaced in pain.

"What is it?" he demanded as she bit her lower lip.

"My foot," she said, wincing, her face going pale. "It . . . it hurts." Inexplicably her foot did hurt. The pain shot clear to her calf. She limped once before he took her up in his arms and carried her to the bed.

Forgetting their contentions for the moment, he shoved up her skirt. He looked at the sole of her foot and she whimpered while he pulled a small shard of glass from the pad. Blood dripped down her heel; he stopped the flow with his hand.

"This is what you get when you throw a tantrum," he chastised, dropping his hold on her foot. He went to get a handkerchief and wrapped her cut foot. With that completed, he straightened and looked at his hand. His palm was smeared with her blood.

She couldn't help staring at it too. For the second time that day he had blood on his hands. But this time, it was because of a good deed, instead of a wicked one.

"I'm sorry," she said when he finally looked at her. She didn't quite know why she had apologized, but somehow the words just slipped out.

"Do you want another straight pin, Aurora?" His expression suddenly turned hard.

She set her jaw and clutched the loose front of her gown. He had helped her, but she wasn't ready to sell the Devil her soul for one act of kindness.

"Do you want that pin?" he repeated adamantly.

"Yes," she answered.

"Then kiss my hand."

She looked at him in shock. She couldn't believe what he was asking.

"Vashon—" she began, but he quickly stopped her. He lifted his hand to her face, then turned it palm downward so that only his clean knuckles might touch her lips.

"Kiss my hand," he whispered, his voice taking on an urgency she had never heard before.

She stared at him, unsure of what to do. It was madness what he was asking, but the reasoning behind it was worse. She believed he was somehow trying to force her to approve of what he had done that morning. Her condemnation had bothered him. She could never approve of killing. Yet when she looked deep into his eyes, she wondered if he was seeking forgiveness too.

Reluctantly she decided to comply. She took his hand in her own and lifted it to her lips. His skin felt warm and rough on her mouth, and the sensation was so pleasurable she almost longed to linger over it. But quickly the kiss ended. He dropped his hand, and as if he'd been absolved, his eyes suddenly cleared of their dark expression. He went to his bureau and found another pin for her. He dropped it on the counterpane, then went to his gold-painted ewer to wash. He behaved as though the entire kiss and its reasons for happening had never occurred. Astonished, she watched him, but she didn't pause long. She grabbed up the pin, fixed her dress, and scooted from the bed.

"You might as well stay there," he said as he ripped off his shirt and threw it across the dolphin-legged sofa.

She watched him pull off his boots. Nervously she asked, "Whatever for?"

"There's broken glass all over this cabin, Miss Dayne, and I'm not going to wake Benny out of his sleep to come clean it up. He can do it tomorrow."

Her gaze darted to the ports. It was late. Sometime between her search for a pin and now, darkness had descended, and she still didn't have her own cabin.

"Vashon, I have to insist upon my own . . ." Her voice faltered. As if she weren't even there, he readied himself for bed, which for him meant immodestly stripping off every piece of clothing on him. And this time he didn't protect her delicate sensibilities by keeping on his trousers. Ignoring her, he slid the black fabric of his trousers down over his hips and past the line of dark hair that dipped below his navel. Just as he was about to reveal every last inch of the dragon on his back, she turned away. Her gaze desperately sought escape, and though it was a futile effort, she couldn't stop herself from going to the door to see if it was latched.

"Good night, Miss Dayne."

From behind her she could hear him chuckle and slide beneath the covers of his decadent bed. In one breath he blew out the candles in the bouillotte lamp and they were thrust into complete darkness.

Her entire body stiffened. She was alone in the darkness with this naked man, and the floor of his cabin was littered with glass. Terrified of cutting herself again, she wasn't even sure if she could make the necessary movements to take herself over to the mahogany chair.

Blinded, she stumbled over his boots and bumped into his writing table. She clutched one of the lion monopode legs for support, then thankfully eased herself into the chair. She didn't even want to speak for fear that her words might force him out of bed.

"Comfortable, Miss Dayne?"

Her mouth went dry. Even his voice sounded *naked.*

"I'm quite well, thank you."

"You may have your own cabin tonight if you but speak the words."

She was the closest yet to giving him a confession. But to go to her own cabin now would mean he would have to relight the bouillotte lamp, and at this moment the thought of seeing him in the altogether seemed more terrifying than just staying where she was. "I'll not give you a thing until I have my freedom," she whispered.

"I see." The slats of the bed groaned as he turned over. "I suspect that chair will get rather uncomfortable by the second or third night."

"The chair will serve."

"But not as nicely as the bed."

"The bed is . . . occupied."

"I'm more than willing to share."

She choked. "No—no, thank you!"

He laughed. "All right, then. Until the morning."

Her brows knitted with worry. She hadn't thought of that. In the brilliant light of morning he would be getting out of that bed. And if it took him only a matter of seconds to take those clothes off, God only knew how long he might take to put them back on. Groaning in defeat, she crossed her arms on the table and laid her head on it to rest for the next battle.

The instant the knock sounded on the door, Vashon awoke. Like a cat that can see in the darkness, he reached for his trousers, stood, and pulled them on without hesitation. Avoiding the glass shards glittering in the starlight from the ports, he was at the cabin door before the knock could sound again.

"What is it?" he demanded, seeing Isaac standing on the threshold with a lantern.

"A problem," Isaac replied, his face lined with sleep. "Benny has just informed me one of our water caskets has leaked. We haven't enough left to make it to San Juan."

Vashon looked vaguely annoyed. "Is that what has you up at this ungodly hour? That's no tragedy, man. We'll simply stop at the next port—"

"That's what I came to discuss. The next port is Grand Talimen Island."

Vashon paused. Realization crossed his face. "I see," he said slowly.

"Shall we stop there?"

"Have we another choice?"

It was Isaac's turn to pause. "The choice is up to you, Vashon. It's your head they want there, not mine. I'm perfectly willing to see if we can make it to St. Kitts."

Vashon shook his head. "If it were just the crew, perhaps, but we've two women on board. We can't risk their lives if we run out of water. I'll take a look at the map and see if there's another route." He turned and went to retrieve his shirt.

Left alone, Isaac seemed reluctant to turn his eyes to Vashon's bed. But when he did, he looked almost dismayed to find it empty. As if to be sure, he held up his lamp and let the light spill into the corner.

"Do you think I tossed her overboard?" Vashon gave a cursory smile when he returned to the door.

"Of course not," Isaac replied grumpily and lowered the lamp. "But where is she?"

Vashon nodded to the dark recess of his cabin where his bureau sat. Aurora was slumped over it, her red-gilt head delicately resting on her forearms.

Seeing her, Isaac almost roared with laughter. When he took in Vashon's scowl, he looked as if he might burst.

"Are you ready?" Vashon commented dryly.

"By all means." Isaac coughed, giving Aurora's sleeping figure a last glance.

"I'll join you in the fo'c'sle in a minute."

Isaac nodded with mock solemnity. He chuckled and left the cabin.

Once more in darkness, Vashon turned to Aurora. The shadowy luminescence of moonlight poured over her like fairy dust and gave her figure an ethereal quality. She breathed softly, deeply, in the pagan rhythm of sleep, and he appeared drawn to her as a child is drawn to the dark of the woods in hope of finding magic.

He walked over to the bureau and bent to her still form. Without waking her, he gently lifted her into his arms and carried her to his bed.

"This is becoming a habit, little wren," he murmured before he placed her on the mattress. In response to his voice, she restlessly rolled to her side and grasped the counterpane. He bent down and pulled a lock of her hair away from her face. Then, slowly, he kissed her lips.

The kiss was brief and chaste, but still it seemed to surprise him. He looked as if he done it much against his will, and worse, his better judgment. His face hardened and he looked pensive. Standing, he gazed down at her for a long moment, not caring that it was dark and that she was in shadows.

"What kind of woman are you, Aurora Dayne?" he whispered. Appearing as if he did not like the answer, he took a deep breath and ran his hand agitatedly over his jaw. He quit the cabin, looking almost relieved to be going.

In the darkness Aurora briefly opened her eyes and saw the shadowy retreating back. She heard the thump of the closing door and once more drifted back into slumber, her dreams calling to her like angels.

Again she dreamed of Vashon. But this time the details took her breath away. She saw long black hair barely tamed by a queue and a small silver ear hoop that gleamed wickedly in the hot Caribbean sun. She saw teeth that flashed white in a fleeting and rare smile, and a face that was as tragic as it was stunningly handsome.

She dreamed he was the dragon.

From his expression it was clear he didn't trust people; he didn't trust her. But that didn't stop her from imagining what it would be like to touch him, to smell him, to feel him beside her. In her dream she desperately sought what she knew she couldn't have in real life. She wanted his every physical detail, and what she couldn't or wouldn't allow herself to picture, she didn't miss, because as if dreams had a sixth sense, she knew without a doubt those details were there anyway and as tangible as if she held them in her hands.

She was the slayer.

It was an impossible task. The dragon held Vashon so tightly she couldn't tell him from the serpent. Her insides warred to keep her from killing, but she was compelled to save him. The beast had him by the throat, and if she didn't rid him of this raging monster, he'd be destroyed.

She took her broadsword and aimed it at the dragon's back. Yet when she thrust, the dragon disappeared.

She searched everywhere for it, but it was gone. Her dream shifted and Vashon appeared, but in terror she wasn't sure how to tell him from the dragon. Instinctively she moved back from his reach; he took her anyway. His arms came around her like hot-tempered steel, and though she pushed against them, there was no escape. She was his.

He kissed her.

As if his tongue were flames, his kiss burned clear to her toes. She fought valiantly, but already her body had begun a traitorous surrender. She longed to be set free, yet everywhere she turned, his scent, like the damp scent of the wind before a storm, beckoned her back into his embrace. His touch, his nearness, his very masculinity brought her nerves to a singing, fevered pitch. Against her will her body responded in ways she hadn't even known it could. The promise of pleasure built and built until it seemed impossible to deny. Finally when his warm, strong hand scorched her breast, she could endure it no more. She cried out his name; he melted her in one sweet breathless moan. Her release came with such exquisite force, she awoke nearly weeping.

The dragon had won.

Sobbing and panicking, Aurora sat bolt upright. In the first few seconds of wakefulness she could barely comprehend what had happened to her. Never before had she had a dream so vivid that her entire body had participated against her will. In dismay she could feel a wetness between her thighs, and when her hand moved to her forehead, it was covered with perspiration. Unnerved and disoriented, she brushed the clinging red-gold tendrils of hair out of her eyes and looked down. Her hand was twisting a sheet and Vashon's scent was everywhere. Somehow during her sleep she'd been brought to his bed. The cabin was empty now, but the pillow next to her was still warm. He hadn't been gone long.

She looked down at her dress and nervously adjusted the apron front. Her hands were shaking, so she had a difficult time repinning her pins. Had he slept next to her? Had he touched her during the night? Was that why she had had the dream?

Her face paled and she thought again about the dream. While she calmed herself she became even more appalled. What was wrong with her that just dreaming of Vashon could elicit such a strong response from her? Thinking about it again, she could already feel her cheeks grow red. She wasn't quite sure what had happened to her, but she was terribly glad she was alone.

A knock sounded on the door and she leaped from the bed. She ran her fingers through the tangles in her hair, then sheepishly said, "Come in."

Benny popped his head through the door with Koonga hanging on to him like a necklace. Aurora was amazed that she'd been so deep in her thoughts that she hadn't even heard the telltale scrape of his peg leg coming down the passage.

"I've your breakfast, miss." He watched her warily as if he'd heard her and Vashon fighting last evening. With a stab of shame she looked over to where the shattered foo lion and crystal goblets lay in the corner. He looked there too and became even more wary. Nervously he placed the heavy silver tray down on the writing desk where she had begun her sleep. Koonga, sensing her master's nervousness, sent out a shrill scream.

"Vashon says you may venture abovedecks this morning, miss. Whenever you choose to go," he said above the din.

Distracted, she only nodded.

"Is everything all right, miss?"

A look of concern came over the boy's pleasant features. Already she could feel the color rising in her cheeks. It was impossible for him to know what had happened to her in her sleep, but somehow she felt he did know. In fact, the way she felt at the moment, she was sure the entire world knew, including the villain who owned the accursed ship.

"I'm just fine, Benny. You mustn't worry about me. How is Flossie?" Anxious for him to depart, she walked him to the door.

"The widow's as angry as a hornet. But you'll see how she fares yourself, miss, if you go abovedecks today. She's already taking the air on the quarterdeck."

"That's wonderful. I'm anxious to be off then."

"When shall I bring you your bath, miss?"

"My bath?" She looked down at her hopelessly rumpled blue dress. She most definitely looked like a street urchin now. She didn't even know if a bath would do much good, but it might wash away the lingering cobwebs of her dream, and that would surely do her good. "I suppose you could bring it now, if it isn't too much trouble."

"No trouble at all, miss."

"Thank you, Benny." She suddenly smiled at him and his whole face brightened. Koonga ceased her screams, and when he shuffled to the door, Benny's step seemed much lighter.

"Aurora, my God, what has that vile man done to you! Are you all right, love? . . . Love! Where on earth are your shoes?" Flossie sailed toward Aurora, her face a mask of outrage and concern. When she reached Aurora's side, she held out her arms and gave Aurora a bone-crushing hug. "That ignoble pirate! That freebooting villain! Is he the one who's taken your shoes?"

"Yes," Aurora answered, catching her breath after she and Flossie parted. "But I'm otherwise all right. You mustn't worry about me. It's you I've been concerned about."

"Oh, my dear child! You must not give me another thought. It's as if the voyage is merely continuing. I've had every comfort. Except for the fact that I've been locked in my cabin." With that, she shot Isaac a bitter, hurtful glance. The captain didn't even look up from the binnacle.

"But you, love"—she turned back to Aurora, worry flooding her bright blue eyes—"you look a sight. I do hope that wretched Vashon hasn't behaved in . . . well . . . in an untoward fashion."

Aurora almost laughed. "Untoward" was hardly the way Vashon behaved. Especially when he was ripping the clothes off her back. Nonetheless, she reassured the widow. "Vashon and I have clashed, I'll admit. But he's done no permanent damage."

"Thank heavens. I've been worried sick. I've even had to take some of Jane's smelling salts. It's a good thing we left that vexing little maid of mine behind on St. George's. The girl is forever feeling faint and this trip would have killed her."

Aurora smiled and took the widow's hand. It was trembling, so she squeezed it. Flossie had a great deal of fortitude, but she was no young woman and the ordeal was obviously affecting her. Right then and there Aurora promised herself that she would do all within her power to return her to St. George's.

"You mustn't worry, Flossie," she said softly. "Think of this as an adventure. And in no time I just know you'll be back home telling all your wonderful friends about your stay on a pirate ship."

The widow adamantly shook her head. "This would be quite an adventure, but only if you weren't in so much trouble. After all, I'm an old woman. What could they do to me? But you, Aurora, there's a whole manner of things from which you need protection. And because I'm frantic over that, this is no adventure at all."

"No, no! I can take care of myself. I've given Vashon back what he's given me. In duplicate!" She was exaggerating. She was standing in front of the widow with no undergarments to speak of, and no shoes. But she couldn't stand to see that frightened look in Flossie's eyes. Especially when it was for herself.

Flossie suddenly gave her a secret smile. She peeked at the captain to see if he was looking, then whispered, "Oh, but you did put up a brave front when he had you tied to that bedpost! And to make up that story about your fiancé! I wanted to applaud. You were brilliant. The very picture of myself at your age, if I do say."

Aurora smiled wryly. She could have had a fiancé coming for them. Flossie couldn't know how close the story had been to the truth. But after all that had happened at the Home before she'd left, John would most certainly never follow her. He was too hurt and too angry and too selfish.

"But unfortunately it was a piece of fiction, and we must develop some kind of plan to escape." Aurora drew closer. "I've been thinking, Flossie. We've almost a week to come up with a plan, and I believe when we make port in San Juan, I should—"

A cough sounded behind them. Both women looked up to find the captain at their side, an irritated expression on his face. Aurora doubted he'd had time to hear any of their conversation, but he'd definitely heard enough to put an end to their whispers.

"It's time for the widow to return to her cabin." He put a hand on Flossie's elbow in order to escort her back.

"Captain, this isn't necessary," Aurora began. "What harm is there in our having some fresh air and conversation?"

"It's upon my orders, Aurora. I'll not have you two whispering like thieves."

Aurora jerked her head around and found Vashon standing next to her. His presence was overpowering. Now that they had reached warmer waters, he wore only his boots, a pair of light chamois breeches, and a leather buccaneer vest that crossed over his bare torso. In the bright sun his hair gleamed almost as brilliantly as his earring. His eyes glittered more green than the ocean around them.

His presence brought back her dream with stunning clarity, and before she could stop herself she felt her face growing flushed. She ripped her gaze away from him, but this only made her more angry. With an icy tone in her voice she said, "It's Miss Dayne to you, sir. And I don't believe we're the ones who should be likened to thieves."

He gave her a wry smile. He nodded to Isaac. The captain tightened his grip on Flossie's arm.

"Wait!" Aurora pleaded with the captain. "What harm is there in our visiting?"

"There's no harm at all, wren," Vashon answered. "But rule number three on this ship states that prisoners shall not whisper among themselves, and if caught doing so, they shall be separated immediately."

"What?" Aurora spun around to challenge him, but by then Flossie was already being dragged away by Isaac. As the two disappeared down the companionway, Aurora nearly cursed. "Your rules," she blurted out, "can go to the devil."

He laughed. "But they already have, Miss Dayne. Or haven't you noticed?"

She shot him a disparaging look, then walked to the railing. She had hoped he would leave her in peace but she had no such luck.

"In three days we'll make port in Grand Talimen."

He joined her at the rail. She could feel his eyes on her even though she kept her gaze steadfast on the turquoise horizon. "I thought we were to anchor in San Juan," she said.

"A change in itinerary. One of our water caskets has sprung a leak. I don't want to risk going that far."

A slight furrow appeared on her brow. "Then shall we make port later in San Juan, or shall we go directly to this Satan's paradise of yours?"

He tipped his head back and laughed. Before she could stop him, his hand, warm yet rough, fondly patted her cheek. "How astute you are."

Unnerved by his touch, she stepped away. His caress brought to the boil all the feelings in her dream, feelings she knew were best left simmering in her unconscious. Again reminded of her wanton response the night before, she felt her composure falter. But she quickly gathered herself because she had a whole new set of worries now.

When they docked at San Juan, her plan was somehow to steal off the ship and bring help to Flossie. But San Juan was days away, giving her time to think of an escape and to coordinate her plans. Now that they were to make port at Grand Talimen, only three days away, she wondered if she could do anything in that amount of time.

In frustration she tapped her fingers on the ship's rail. The expression on her face must have mirrored her thoughts because, uninvited, Vashon said, "Thinking of an escape, my love?"

Her gaze shot to his. Her blush gave her away. Angry, she snatched her hand from the rail and started to quit the deck, but before she could get to the companionway his words made her delay.

"You haven't begged my permission to leave, Miss Dayne."

Furious, her entire figure stiffened. With just one glance she defied him to stop her.

"Miss Dayne, I'll have you know that rule number two of this ship is that all prisoners shall obey me. If you leave this deck without my permission, you have my promise of punishment, and you'll not see the widow again until we get to Mirage."

This threat gave her pause. She needed Flossie's help in thinking of a way for her to escape once on Grand Talimen. She couldn't afford to isolate herself now, not with three days to port.

Setting her jaw, she walked past him to the aft section of the quarter-deck. If she couldn't leave, she most certainly could pretend he wasn't around. But with his great height and handsome face, he was a difficult man to make invisible. She did her best, however, until she felt his arm sweep around her waist.

"Aurora?" he whispered against her hair.

Her eyes darkened. "What is it, you licentious tyrant?"

Her words made him smile. "Do you want me to tell you rule number one?"

She looked up at him. She didn't really want to know his despicable rules, but since she was under his domination until they arrived in Grand Talimen, it was inevitable she would learn them. Resentfully she nodded her head.

"Rule number one," he said in a husky voice, "is all ship's spoils belong to me . . . and to me alone."

He lifted her hair and as if his lips were a brand, she felt him place one fiery kiss upon her nape. Her hair was still damp from its washing, and he seemed particularly entranced by the way the delicate curls clung to her hairline. She closed her eyes, unable to bear what he was doing. His kiss only reminded her again of that wretched dream, and she trembled just from the thought of the power he had over her.

It seemed like an eternity, but finally he dropped the shiny, springy red-gold tangle of her hair and let her move from his hold. Desperate to leave, she looked up at him with pleading aqua eyes. Reluctantly he nodded his permission and she flew down the companionway as if she had wings. Suddenly Grand Talimen wasn't coming soon enough.

14

Grand Talimen Island was a seemingly benign little cay east of the Bahamas. Gone were the rocky coasts and Bermuda cedar of St. George's; in its place were luxurious fringes of white sand beaches and mile upon mile of swaying coconut palms.

At the north end, on the island's only promontory, sat the tiny town of New Providence, harbor to numerous ships going and coming from the Mayaguana Passage. Aurora watched from the high railing as the town grew in detail. Pastel pink-and-yellow buildings simmered beneath the hot sunshine, and whitewashed stone walls ran like a maze, effectively separating the courtyards of the wealthy from the hovels of the poor. The town radiated out from a decidedly civilized English circus, which was overlooked by elegant Spanish wrought iron balustrades and bricked French arcades, all proving how many times the island had changed hands. But if there were attempts at making New Providence appear refined, it was in stark contrast to the blooming frangipani, which sent a wild pagan scent as far as the approaching *Seabravery.*

Aurora looked to the docks and saw slave women in dirty madras tignons carrying baskets of green breadfruit to market. Curious, the women paused as the ship made port, resting their heavy mangrove baskets on their hips. Shopkeepers in white coats and white aprons lounged in their doorways, viewing with interest New Providence's latest arrival. When the ship finally made harbor, the exotic atmosphere surrounded her, the smells mingling ripe and sweet like mangos rotting in the sun. Fiddling with a windblown lock of hair, Aurora could hardly hold back her excitement—or her trepidation—for at last they had reached land. At last she was going to have a chance of escape.

Nervously she glanced around for Flossie. Vashon had adamantly refused them the chance to visit, so Aurora hadn't seen the widow in the entire three days it took to reach port. She had thought of a plan, all

right, but it was vexing that she'd been unable to share it. Now she
would just have to go through with it, hoping against hope that Flossie
would see what she was doing and try to help her.

Out of the corner of her eye she saw Vashon standing on the fo'c'sle.
Their gazes met and distrust clashed with defiance. Unwilling to taunt
him further, she quickly averted her gaze, turning it instead to the
crowded docks.

She didn't want him to guess that she was plotting her escape. Yet she
ached with the need to be free of his clutches. She closed her eyes and
thought of the past three nights spent in his cabin while he casually
stripped for bed. One more night of that shocking torture and she
would go mad.

"Aurora!"

She spun around and saw Flossie rushing up to her. The captain, who
usually accompanied the widow on her sojourns abovedecks, was,
oddly, nowhere to be found. Here was her chance to tell of her plan. She
just hoped there would be enough time.

Aurora calmly joined the widow, doing her best not to look anxious
and stir the curiosity of the green-eyed man who still stared down at her
from the fo'c'sle. When she grasped the widow's hands she began speaking, disregarding for the moment her good manners.

"Flossie, I have a plan," she whispered furiously. "You must help. I
shall—" The captain suddenly appeared from the companionway.
When he saw them together, he walked up. A hopeless, frustrated dread
blossomed in her chest, and Aurora fell silent.

Flossie turned around and shot the captain a scathing look. If she'd
still had her parasol, Aurora was sure she'd have popped it open with
an angry snap. Instead, disgruntled, she could only saunter away, the
concern in her eyes the only thing to betray her.

Aurora turned back to the railing, a black depression descending. She
would have to go through with her plan and just hope Flossie figured it
out. If it worked, they would be liberated. If it didn't . . . Her worried
gaze swept the fo'c'sle and the dark thunderous man who stood there.
She took a deep breath and gathered the shreds of her courage. If it
didn't, they would just have to pay the consequences. But if she tried
nothing, they would sail to Mirage, perhaps never to be heard from
again.

The crowd on the docks thickened, and for the first time Aurora
noticed the stunned looks on the faces of the bystanders as they stared
up at the *Seabravery*. Slaves began gathering in groups, staring up at the

dragon figurehead in awe as if the ship were almost legendary. It was most perplexing, especially when a troop of mounted infantry suddenly appeared rushing to the wharf only to surround the ship's gangplank. The captain joined her at the railing to view the proceedings. He shook his head and grumbled, "We're in for it now."

"I take it the *Seabravery*'s not welcome here," she said, all the while wondering how this was going to affect her plans.

The captain uttered a black little laugh. "Not welcome! About as welcome as Napoléon at Austerlitz."

Aurora looked once more at the infantry. They were dressed in silver coats with glittering gold braid draped on their right shoulders. It wasn't Britain's uniform, and she wondered if this little island, as English as it seemed, had broken off from the Commonwealth.

"What do they want?" she asked.

"Vashon," he answered simply, watching the Captain of the Guard edge his horse forward.

Aurora looked at Isaac in surprise, but before she could say another word, a cheer broke out from the docks. Groups of slaves had raised their fists and begun chanting the name "Vashon" while their overseers scowled in the direction of the *Seabravery*. She followed the white men's hateful glares up to the fo'c'sle. There Vashon was smiling his approval, until the overseers' whips were raised and the rebellion was put to a swift and vicious end.

"What has he done to merit . . . all of this attention?" she asked, turning once more toward the horse guards. She was at once stunned and dismayed. Vashon was obviously these slaves' hero, while the mounted infantry looked ready to board the ship and hang him. She couldn't understand it.

"The governor of this island has no love for Vashon," Isaac replied. "He stole a shipload of the island's slaves that were being exported to New Orleans. The governor never got his payment; the cargo was worth over two hundred thousand pounds."

"So that's how Vashon made his fortune. Peddling the black man's flesh." Disgusted, she looked away. John Phipps certainly had his flaws, but like a good Evangelical, he'd at least been a supporter of William Wilberforce's movement to abolish slavery.

She scowled. Why would it ever occur to her to compare Vashon to John Phipps? John was a saint compared to Vashon. Yet for some inexplicable reason she was disappointed that Vashon had proven to be such a blackguard.

"Vashon is the last person who would dabble in slavery," the captain said in a quiet tone. "If you ever get to know more about him, you'll see that."

She stared at Isaac. "But what did he do with the governor's ship?"

Isaac smiled. "Well, I do admit he made a tidy profit selling the vessel. I'm not saying the man is perfect. But as for the slaves, Vashon took them to La Tortué where he let every one of them go. That's why they cheered for him on this dock today. Some of those men had children on that ship. I think it heartens them to know that their sons and daughters live in freedom in Haiti, even if they still live in bondage on Grand Talimen."

Aurora turned her gaze once again to the fo'c'sle. Vashon stood overlooking the guards, his arms folded defiantly over his chest. He'd done a noble thing in giving those slaves their freedom. But because of that some men would think him a hero, and others, a villain.

He had yet to prove which he would be to her.

"Miss. Captain." The first mate, a young Frenchman named Philippe, bowed stiffly before them. "Governor Ignatio Roberto Aquila Lopez has sent a message, Captain."

"What is it?" Isaac removed his hat and wiped the sweat from his brow.

"He informs us that Vashon will be shot on sight if he should leave the ship."

"I see. What else?"

"He says he should like to bargain for him."

Isaac chuckled. "Of course."

"He asks you to meet him at the governor's mansion tonight for dinner. He will discuss with you then any provisions the *Seabravery* might need for its passengers."

"Thank you." Isaac nodded and the young Frenchman disappeared into the deckhouse.

Aurora tried to appear undisturbed by the first mate's news, but again Vashon's violent world was inescapably overlapping her own.

"Is it true, what he said about . . . shooting Vashon?" she asked.

"They won't get him."

"But—but that governor could certainly have his guards board the ship and—"

"And start a rebellion the likes of which even Toussaint-Louverture couldn't have inflamed. No, he won't do that. The governor isn't that stupid."

Feeling ridiculously relieved, Aurora suddenly had a thought. "So really the only consequence of all this is that Vashon cannot leave the ship."

"That's right." The captain studied her for a moment, and Aurora grew nervous wondering if she'd been too blatant in her question. But then the captain looked past her to the fo'c'sle. He waved.

"Vashon!" he shouted. "I've been invited to dinner! I'll be getting a better reception than you, I daresay! And a better meal too! Yours would consist only of manchineel apples!"

Vashon smiled wryly. He called back, "I don't want you to have too good a time, Isaac. You might turn me in after all."

"We'll see about that, Vashon! I'll see what Ignatio has to offer!"

"Then perhaps I should send a watchdog along with you. Flossie!" Vashon shouted across the decks, "I want you to go to dinner with Isaac and make sure he doesn't turn me in."

Flossie stood at the far side of the railing. When she heard Vashon, she merely gave him and Isaac a scathing look, then dismissed them both with a loud "Indeed!"

Vashon laughed and called to the captain, "That settles it! She's all yours, Isaac!"

Both Flossie and Isaac opened their mouths to protest. But as if neither one of them wanted to show how much the situation bothered them, they suddenly closed them. Flossie walked away, uttering another "Indeed!"

Aurora watched the display, a reluctant amusement in her eyes. She knew how taken Flossie had been with the captain until their kidnapping. It was ironic, now, to see her loathing for the man. If they went to the governor's mansion together, the sparks would fly.

But if her plan went as she hoped, Flossie would be spending the night in New Providence a free woman, not the captive guest of Captain Corbeil.

She took a deep breath and gathered herself. If Vashon couldn't leave the ship, then everything would be simpler. When she was off the ship, she and Flossie would only have another seaman to deal with. Much easier, she decided, than dealing with Vashon's iron-fisted reign.

She stole a glance at the captain. He was busy discussing something with Philippe. She turned back and saw Flossie at the prow, longingly watching the docks. Now was the time. Everyone was here. She just had to summon the courage and go forth.

She took a step from the railing and stumbled. In a rather dramatic gesture, her hand went to her brow and she took a moment to steady herself. Out of the corner of her eye she could see the captain looking her way. Pleased, she then made a great display of pulling herself together, but before she could take another two steps, she collapsed, hitting the deck with a horrifying thud.

She had meant to fall like Madame Récamier onto her scroll-end daybed. Instead she'd tumbled as gracelessly as a mare going down in her stall. Silently groaning, she knew tomorrow she would have the bruises to show for it.

"Good gracious!" she heard Flossie exclaim. "Aurora, love! Aurora! Are you all right!"

She heard a scuffle of feet and soon felt a touch on her brow. She knew it was a man's hand for it was rough and callused, yet warm and gentle. She hoped it was the captain's, but when she peeked through her long lashes she saw Vashon staring down at her, his expression a perfect blend of suspicion and concern.

Flossie suddenly appeared at her side. "Aurora! Can you speak, dear? Are you all right? Whatever happened?"

Aurora closed her eyes and moaned. She turned on her side so that only Flossie could see her. Opening her eyes wide, she implored Flossie to go along. A look of shock crossed the widow's face, but just as quickly it was replaced with an expression of understanding.

"She needs a doctor, Captain!" Flossie straightened, and Aurora prayed her thanks. "And what do you plan to do about this? I demand an answer this very second!"

"We'll take care of her. She'll be all right." Isaac looked at Vashon.

Slowly Vashon gathered her up in his arms. He frowned and looked down at Aurora's slack, delicate features.

"She needs a doctor. She must see a physician," Flossie insisted.

"We can take care of her on the ship," Vashon stated.

"No, she must be taken care of properly. This is serious, I know it."

"How do you know it?"

Flossie paused. Even with her eyes closed, Aurora could picture her groping for an answer.

"It's—it's a female malady, sir! One I've seen before!"

Aurora almost smiled.

Vashon's arms tightened. "What kind of female malady? I've only seen women behave this way when they're with child."

A dead silence followed.

Flossie appeared as if she were being forced to confront something she dreaded. "Well, is she?" she asked quietly.

Vashon looked at the captain. Isaac's face echoed the same question. *Well, is she?*

Aurora felt Vashon's body tensing in anger.

"She isn't," he answered tightly. "And if she is, I'm certainly not the bastard's father."

Aurora could hardly keep the blush from staining her cheeks. She'd never heard such conversation before, and to pretend to be in a dead faint while being the subject of it was almost unbearable.

In a much relieved voice, Flossie began to prattle, "Nonetheless, it's all your fault, Vashon. You've served her something on this vile ship that's gone bad and now she's ill. If you hadn't kidnapped her, she'd be just fine, but now the girl might die. Aurora must see a doctor, and I shall accompany her. I'll get my reticule. We'll be off immediately."

Aurora squelched the urge to laugh. Flossie was marvelous.

"I'll take them, Vashon," the captain interjected. "I'll take them to Sovens's place."

"You can't take her. Absolutely not." Vashon shook his head. "If you don't show up at the governor's mansion, we'll have Ignatio's entire army down here by nightfall. I'll take her. Send a sailor to Neville's. Tell him we need some men to take out these guards for a while."

Aurora jerked in dismay, then tried to hide it with a moan. What was Vashon saying? He couldn't take her to a doctor. He would be risking his life, and he did that only for foolhardy causes, most certainly not for sickly women. Especially those who, she was sure, he doubted were ill anyway.

"Vashon, you can't do this." Isaac's voice was thick with worry. "It's one thing to taunt Ignatio from the safety of the ship when you have a hundred seamen and the Maritime Code to protect you. But it's another altogether on his island. You can't take an army with you."

"I'll be back before you and the widow come down from Governor's Hill." He lifted Aurora in his arms. "Now send Philippe. I'll leave at dark."

Aurora was laid upon Vashon's bed and Flossie tended her brow with a cool, damp cloth. Every now and again she would open her eyes and shoot Flossie a reassuring look, but the widow's hand still trembled whenever she held the cloth to Aurora's head.

They would be fine, Aurora told herself. She would escape Vashon once they got onto Grand Talimen, and she would bring help to Flossie at the governor's mansion. They would be free that night.

Minutes passed, long torturous minutes while Aurora feigned unconsciousness. The captain came to retrieve Flossie, and Aurora heard Flossie plead to stay by her side. But to no avail. Vashon was adamant that the widow would not go with them, so Flossie was forced to leave with Isaac for the governor's mansion.

It seemed barely a moment passed before Vashon had a pistol shoved into the back of his trousers and was scooping her into his arms. She fluttered open her eyes once they were on the wharves and saw that night was beginning to fall. Torches burned in a colonnade along the docks. The guards in their silver-and-gold livery still stood sentinel on their mounts right at the foot of the *Seabravery*'s gangway, but she had to look twice at the guards. Before, in the daylight, the men had been as white as the Irish; now as they pulled aside their restless steeds to let them pass, they were as black as polished ebony.

"Neville," Vashon greeted the new Captain of the Guard, "I'm forever indebted to you. You came quickly."

The man named Neville answered in a soft island patois. "De guvnor no friend of mine, Vashon." He smiled a toothy, beautiful smile. "But neither are de guvnor's guards. I think dey take a bump on de head too personal."

"After we're gone, drop the guise and go back to your plantations. Don't stay for our return. It's too dangerous."

"We stay if you need us."

"No." Vashon shook his head. "I insist. I'll swim back to the *Seabravery* if I must."

"But what about de pretty lady?"

Aurora quickly shut her eyes and fervently hoped the night shadows had kept them hidden.

Vashon looked down at her, his expression hardening. "If she's truly ill, we may be in port for a while. If she's not, then I think she'll be swimming to the ship whether I go along or not."

All the men laughed, but there wasn't much time for levity. A horse was brought around and Vashon mounted, keeping Aurora well within his warm grasp.

Before they could depart, Neville seemed anxious to say something. Vashon pulled the horse around and faced him.

Neville finally spoke. "You know, friend, we be heroes tomorrow. Not too many on dis island get to help you."

Vashon looked at the black man. He seemed at a loss for words. "Neville," he began, "you know there's always room for you on the *Seabravery*. For you and your men. Damnation, if my ship were big enough, I'd take every last bastard on this island to La Tortué. But this time, say you'll join us. Get aboard. Philippe knows to expect you."

"Cannot, good friend. There's work on dis island. Someday dis island gonna be free."

Vashon sighed. He looked hard at Neville and closed his arm around Aurora. Reluctantly he nodded. There was nothing more to say. He urged his mount away, galloping quickly into the night.

In a few minutes they arrived at a neat little planter's cottage. A light burned through the white louvered wall of the loggia and Vashon quickly dismounted, carrying her gently toward the house.

"Who's there?" An aged man in a nightshirt that showed his skinny legs appeared at the door. He lifted his chamber candlestick and the light poured over them.

"God in heaven! My eyes do deceive me! Is that Vashon?" the man exclaimed.

"In the flesh. Sovens, old man, how are you?" Without invitation, Vashon brought her into the house.

"I can't believe it!" The gent Sovens followed Vashon with his candlestick. He looked down at Aurora, limp in his arms, and said, "But I see I'll have to put my dismay aside for the moment. What have you brought me, son?"

"She fainted aboard ship. We docked for some water and she had a spell. She may have eaten something that soured."

Aurora was placed on a soft mattress in a room that smelled oddly of limes. She opened her eyes for a moment and saw the candlelight spill onto a lime tree through an open window.

Vashon continued speaking. "I'll be honest, Sovens, she's not too fond of my company. She may be faking this." His voice lowered. "But if she's not, she must be taken care of. I cannot afford to lose her."

Aurora thought she detected a trace of tenderness in his tone, but then she thought of her necklace and the rhyme and the wretched Star of Aran. All that was what he could not afford to lose, she reminded herself bitterly. That was all she was worth to anyone.

With a great cloak of despair descending upon her shoulders, she shut her eyes more tightly and prayed for the moment she would be left alone. She would climb out the open window and run into the cane fields, losing herself in the darkness. The island was small enough that she'd find her way back to town in no time and get word to the governor about Flossie's captivity. They would be free this evening. Flossie would be going back to St. George's and she . . . she would be going back to London.

London.

She heard water splash and then the doctor washing his hands. In the silence she thought of her future. Would John be too angry to allow her to return to the Home? Or would she need to look for a position elsewhere? Or would she not return there at all, instead going with Flossie to St. George's, where she might find a family in want of a governess?

Before she could stop her musings, they went a step further, right where she dreaded to go. She'd always hated to think it, to even put words to it, but nowhere in her future did she see a husband. She knew all the reasons: She possessed neither the dowry nor the family connections to get one, and she was not such a fiery temptress that she could expect to dazzle a man into believing those things weren't necessary. Even a common butcher boy expected his wife to bring something to their marriage, if only a pen of piglets.

Yet deep down she supposed she'd always held out the hope that someday, some way, a man would come along and want her despite her lack of possessions. She supposed that was why she'd gone on this adventure in the first place. Now here she was, out in the night with a pirate whose most lofty ambition was to escape the hangman—for just one more day. And the best she could hope for in concluding this journey was to go back to London and resume the dismal existence that she'd been so eager to escape.

With that last thought only depressing her further, she heard the physician speak.

"You know, Vashon, the obvious illness for a girl of this age is—"

"I sincerely doubt she's pregnant," Vashon answered almost derisively. "I know she's not got my babe in her and I can't see another one taking her. She's so damned stiff a chap'd find more lively company in Marylebone Cemetery."

She almost shot up and slapped him. Instead she was forced to lie there, not moving, all the while enduring the doctor's all-too-hearty laugh.

"I see." Sovens chuckled. "If she's that tight-laced, I don't envy you. I'm just glad you brought her here in a faint. Do you know what it's like telling these missies to undress so that I can examine them? It's like taking the horns off a bull, that's what. They think every man is out to ravish them. . . ."

Aurora felt the doctor take the pin from her apron front. She grew rigid just trying to think of her next move. Panic was beginning to overtake her. She'd never thought about the fact that she'd have to be examined. And with Vashon looking on as if he were some sort of privileged viewer! It was certainly ironic, especially since he'd been trying to get her clothes off ever since she'd arrived on the *Seabravery*.

"Oh, damn." Sovens cursed and sucked the finger he'd just pricked on her pin. "I've got to get another candle. Excuse me, Vashon. These old eyes aren't what they used to be."

Aurora then heard the words for which she'd been praying. "Let me come help you, Sovens." Vashon moved to the door. "Perhaps you could even spare some of that monkey piss you natives call rum down here?"

She heard the doctor laugh, then the sound of footsteps leaving the room. Her heart hammered in her chest when she opened her eyes. She looked at the door. They were gone. The room was dark, the lone candle casting long shadows. But through the door she could hear Sovens fumbling around for another candle while Vashon was probably pouring himself a drink. Now was her chance. She couldn't delay.

She rose from the bed and slipped her feet to the floor. She backed away from the door, a soft curse from Sovens in the other room making her jump. She was almost to the window before she dared turn around to flee. But when the moment came, she scrambled for the window only to be captured in an unyielding embrace.

"My, my. What a miraculous recovery." The anger in Vashon's voice froze her heart.

She gasped and struggled to see him in the darkness. She pulled away, but his arms had turned to well-tempered steel. There was no escape.

"And what have you to say for yourself, Aurora? You've made me come onto this island and risk my neck—"

"No, no! I didn't think you'd come here! Just let us go, Vashon! Just let Flossie and me go!" It was all she could do to keep her voice from quaking. He was furious. She could only imagine what her punishment would be.

The dim candlelight flickered over his face; the anger in his eyes flared like sparks of emerald. "You know," he whispered menacingly, "if I'm caught here, they'll take you to be my lover. They'll hang you with me, Aurora. Right by my side. Now wouldn't that be a fitting end for us both." He laughed bitterly and pulled her closer. She could smell lime in the hot tropical air and she could smell him, a scent deeper than the night. He was angry and he frightened her, but she forced herself to harden to it. For that was what he wanted. That was what pleased him most. To see her cowering before him like slave to master.

"So was your trickery worth it then?" he whispered hotly. "Are you willing to be executed as my lover?"

With his words, her fury peaked. She remembered his earlier comments to the doctor, and though she knew it wasn't judicious to provoke him further, she couldn't stop herself. Defiantly she met his gaze and said, "I beg your pardon, but *no one* could mistake me for your lover. If you recall, I've been proclaimed a little less stirring than the corpses in Marylebone."

Without warning, he burst out laughing. His hold slackened, but not enough to free her. She was still in his arms when the doctor arrived with his candlestick.

"Up and about already?" he asked, amazed. "Why, I've never seen anything like it. Vashon, whatever cure you're dispensing, I should very much like to have it bottled for the rest of my patients!"

Aurora tried to twist free. When she couldn't, she began to plead. "Dr. Sovens, I beg of you. Help me. I've been kidnapped. Whatever you think you know of this man Vashon, you don't know anything about him. He's a pirate. He doesn't hesitate to do the worst kind of deed—"

"Come now, miss! Surely you're exaggerating! A pirate! No, he couldn't be!" Sovens winked at her, and Aurora couldn't remember the last time she'd been so completely taken aback.

"You—you don't believe me?" she gasped.

Sovens chuckled. He looked at Vashon. "On the contrary, I believe you all too well. In fact, I used to serve on the *Seabravery*. I was ship's doctor until Vashon retired me a few years back."

"Oh, my God." Aurora slumped in Vashon's arms. Her escape seemed even more hopeless now. She didn't know how she would get away again.

"But come now, buck up, miss. Surely Vashon hasn't been treating you that badly."

She summoned all the fury in her breast and said, "He's been the most appalling beast, not even worthy of the term 'gentleman'!"

"Gracious! That bad?" Sovens looked at Vashon and almost smiled. "Well, then, I wish I could help you."

Aurora straightened. She held her arms out in supplication. "But you can! Summon help. There's another lady on the *Seabravery* and—" She stopped short. Sovens was adamantly shaking his head now.

"I'm sorry, miss. Even if I did try to summon help for you, not too many would stick out their necks on my behalf."

"But you're a physician! Surely a man of your standing could gather all kinds of support!"

"No, miss, I'm sorry. I administer to the blacks on this island, and that makes my status several notches below the barber . . . who sometimes lowers himself to treat the island's cows."

She looked at him. Again she was confronted with that terrible dichotomy. Here was a man who now spent his years caring for those whom most would deem unworthy of attention; and yet he'd sailed with Vashon, no doubt a willing participant to all of Vashon's notorious pursuits. The man was both noble and despicable. Much as she'd found Vashon to be.

"Surrender?" Vashon asked, once more gaining the upper hand.

She never realized what a wretched word that was.

"Never," she whispered before he took her by the arm and pushed her to the door.

15

The governor's gilt barouche rocked back and forth as it climbed the promontory to the top of New Providence. Below, all the lights of the city twinkled through the colonnade of palms that lined the drive to the mansion. The ride was made in absolute silence as Flossie and Isaac did their absolute best to ignore each other.

It wasn't easy. For one thing the carriage was small and neither one of them possessed the slim girth of their youth. But worse than the cramped quarters were the stares they threw at each other like darts.

Flossie would attack first, unable to keep her emotions from sparking up into her eyes and hurling themselves silently upon Isaac. She stabbed him with one of her glittering, accusatory stares until he was forced to deflect it or allow himself to be unmanned. But when it was her turn to be the recipient of a particularly vile glare, she opened her eyes wide and nearly choked on the shock of it all, as if, by his retaliation, he was now even worse than the devil she thought he was—and how *dare* he look at her that way?

"I cannot believe I almost invited you to my cabin for tea! I cannot believe it!" With that outburst, she abruptly turned away and stared past the driver toward the mansion on the hill.

"Oh, will you give that up?" Isaac retorted, annoyance heavy in his voice.

"I will not! It was the most stupid thing I've ever done in a life full of stupid things! I'll never *ever* forgive myself for it! I, Mrs. Stefan Lindstrom of St. George's and London, almost invited a *pirate* into my cabin for tea!"

"To begin with," he answered nastily, "I'm not a pirate, and I'm getting jolly tired of explaining that. While you may not believe it, I'm a sea captain, I have always been a sea captain, and I intend to stay a sea captain!" When he had calmed himself, he said, "And another thing. I have never seen a woman so lacking in sense as yourself. Why, my own Rachel was half your age when she died, and she possessed more sense. People chastise themselves for what they *have* done, or what they *should* have done. But not for what they *might have done!*" With that off his chest, he hunched down into the seat and stared at the flattened calash of the carriage until they arrived.

The governor's mansion was a huge stuccoed palace to rival Marco Polo's description of Xanadu. Chinoiserie was everywhere, from the red faux bamboo chairs to the black lacquered Weisweiler commodes. In the porte-cochère fantastic birds were painted flying across the wallpaper while such exotica as Chinese export porcelain and English pastiches were displayed on fretwork pedestals. The predominant colors were scarlet and purple; the enormous pier mirrors reflected them incessantly, and also the astonishing narcissism of their owner.

Governor Ignatio Roberto Aquila Lopez stood in the entrance to the drawing room, his hand fondling the hilt of an ancient Toledo sword. When he saw his visitors, he gave his black mustache a little swipe and nodded in greeting. A battalion of slaves in canary yellow livery soon appeared and Flossie and Isaac were shown into the drawing room. Refreshments were served while a young turbaned boy fanned them with palm leaves.

The governor was the first to speak. His blunt manner was only surpassed by his obvious insanity.

"You know, of course, Captain, that my fondest wish is to run Vashon through with my sword until he bleeds to death at my feet. Now"—the Spaniard sat down and looked as if he were just about to win at faro—"what can I do to make that possible?"

Flossie choked on her tea, obviously unaware before now of the Spaniard's mental affliction.

"Well . . ." Isaac rubbed his eyes and feigned a casual assessment. He didn't seem surprised at all by the governor's irrational words. "I'm not sure, Ignatio. Vashon owns my ship. If something were to happen to him, I wouldn't have—"

Ignatio waved his hand. "Ships—ships—I can give you ships. Is that all?"

Isaac sipped his rum and grew thoughtful. "A ship would be nice, I suppose."

"Would you like a woman? There are three here on the island I like. I'll let you have one. And they're nice big women, you understand, Captain?" The Spaniard cupped his hands in a crude gesture.

"I beg your pardon!" At once Flossie stood up. She glared at the Spaniard, then turned her furious gaze on Isaac.

"What kind of man are you to sell your friends in this manner?" she exclaimed. "I don't understand any of this. For what he's done to me, I've no great regard for Vashon, but before I'd see him run through for his crimes, I'd have him receive a trial. At the very least!"

"Who is this woman?" Ignatio stood up. "Is she your wife?"

"Good God, no!" Isaac burst out.

Angrily Flossie faced Ignatio. He was so short she could look him straight in the eye. "You are a vile little toad of a man, sir, to say the things you have in my company."

"Captain." Ignatio turned back to Isaac. "I ask you again, who is this woman? I shall have her executed for speaking to me in this manner."

Concern flashed across Isaac's face. Disbelief registered on Flossie's. Isaac stood slowly as if he weren't sure how to contain the damage. "Governor, she's not aware of what she's saying—"

"Oh, yes, indeed, I am very much aware of what I'm saying," she insisted. Continuing her harangue as if she thought she'd simply misunderstood the governor, she said, "In fact, I'm so much aware of what I'm saying that I declare you both to be a couple of curs without the good breeding to watch your tongues in my presence. I demand to be taken back to the ship. If I'm to be kidnapped and held captive, you cannot expect me to endure this wretched company, too."

"I'll have that woman's head in my hands this very evening!" Infuriated, Ignatio shook his fist at Flossie. Her jaw slackened in shock. It was suddenly clear that she'd understood the little madman all along. And now she'd only provoked him further. Her hand moved to her neck in an unconscious protective gesture.

Isaac moved between them, anxiety etched in his face. "Governor, I shall have an apology for you. If you will allow me a word with Mrs. Lindstrom, I'll show her the error of her ways."

Ignatio fumed; his little black mustache, which hid so well the syphilitic sores around his lip, twitched. He didn't appear as if he wanted to go along, but finally, he nodded his head.

Smiling at the governor, Isaac pulled Flossie aside and exploded in fierce whispers. "Do you know what you've done, woman? Do you want to die? Is that it? Have you no sense whatsoever?"

Flossie shot the governor a disbelieving look. "That vile little man is out of his mind. I demand to be taken back to the ship." She opened a glittering black fan that was secured to her wrist and furiously fanned herself.

"Of course he is! I *know* that! And he has the power to do whatever he wishes. This is his island, remember? I swear I won't rescue you from the chopping block if your mouth puts you there!"

Flossie eyed Isaac distastefully. "Are there *no* gentlemen on this island?"

"Gentlemen? Gentlemen?" Isaac whispered, his voice rising in hysteria. "How can there be gentlemen when those flapping lips of yours are a constant source of irritation? I'm telling you once, shut them, or I'll shut them for you!"

Abruptly Flossie closed the fan. She gave Isaac her most vicious stare yet. "*My husband*, the dear saint that he was, would never have spoken to me like that. You are a villain, sir, plain and simple. You bring me to this madman's lair, then you insult me with your rude talk. As for those 'flapping lips,' just let me say that they will go on 'flapping' until you set Aurora and me free."

"We'll see about that. You'll be quiet if I have to make you be quiet!"

"And how do you propose to do that? You can kidnap me, you can imprison me, you can torture me, but as Louis Seize so quickly found out, you cannot keep the people silent!"

"Oh, but I have a way to keep you silent!"

"And what way is that, sir?" she asked sarcastically, not a bit intimidated.

"The way men have been keeping women silent for centuries, that's how!"

"Well then, do it! This should be quite a lesson!"

"I'll give you a lesson, all right!" Isaac moved to Flossie. Her chin jutted out, just daring him to strike her, but instead he did something altogether different. She was so surprised she couldn't even defend herself when he took her in his arms. In confusion she stared up at him, wide-eyed, until he kissed her so soundly he nearly gave her a heart attack.

When they finally parted, Flossie stood frozen to the ground, unable to even blink. Isaac looked a bit sheepish, as if, perhaps, he thought he might have gone too far, but then he mumbled testily, "Ah, at last, blessed silence," and went to seat himself once more on the governor's red satin sofa.

The governor clapped and pounded the captain on the back as if he'd been a toreador at a victorious bullfight. Flossie just stared at Isaac as if he, too, had gone out of his mind. She didn't even flinch when one of the liveried slaves entered the room and announced dinner.

In absolute silence they arrived at a banqueting room as palatial as the one in Brighton. No cost had been spared; El Greco's ascetic *Church of San Tomé* hung on the wall while ironically the windows, the floor, the table, were draped in a gaudy cerise-colored satin. Ignatio had already been seated at the head of the twenty-five-foot table, and he gave Flossie a belligerent glare. Isaac looked ill.

"May we continue, Captain, *without interruption?*" Ignatio glanced murderously at Flossie, but she was too busy staring dumbfounded at Isaac.

"Yes, yes." Isaac hastily sat.

"I want Vashon. What is his price?"

"First we must have our water."

"You'll get your water. When can I have Vashon?"

Isaac was just about to evade him again when one of the governor's guards burst into the room. The man was sweating and he wore several lengths of lacerated rope around his wrists. Agitated, he spoke in rapid Spanish, gesturing to his head where he'd obviously been hit. Over and over again, he repeated, *"El Draque! El Draque!"*

Ignatio jumped to his feet. He exchanged words with the guard, then rushed out of the room. When he was gone, Isaac left his seat and pulled Flossie out of hers.

"Where are we going?" she cried out, trying to pull her hand from his.

"Back to the ship. Immediately!" Isaac rushed her out the door.

"But why? What has happened?"

Isaac turned grim. "Didn't you hear the man say, *'El Draque'?* That can only mean one thing. They've found Vashon!"

Aurora didn't remember the road back to New Providence as being so dark. Of course, when she'd been on the road before, she'd done her best to pretend being in a faint, but her few glances then at the scenery had left her with not nearly so ominous a feeling as the one she had now.

She studied Vashon as she rode with him on his horse. He was furious. Gone were the gentle arms that had held her. Instead his grip was like bands of leather, tightening and tightening around her, until she wondered when they would stop her breath. His chest was a slab of granite against her back and his thighs slammed ruthlessly against her derrière as they rode. She had no idea what he would do once they returned to the *Seabravery*, and she dreaded even speculating about it. He didn't say another word. He didn't have to.

Though she had sworn to fight him, she had no choice but to go back with him. He had won another battle, but she vowed the war would continue, this time in town where she swore she would find a way to escape before he could drag her up the *Seabravery*'s gangplank.

"And what little schemes are simmering in that head now?" He bent his head and nipped the fleshy lobe of her ear. It should have been a playful gesture, but in his anger, his teeth almost hurt her. Chastised, she stiffened, denying the tingle that traitorously slid down her spine.

"How do you plan to get back to the ship undetected?" Her manner and voice were as cool as she could make them. She looked ahead and in the distance saw a line of glittering red fires, burning cane. Neville and his revolutionaries had been busy that night. She recalled reading once about the slave revolts in the Caribbean. She was certain if the governor wasn't careful, Grand Talimen would have a revolt to parallel Haiti's, and he would find his head on a stake being paraded around New Providence.

All at once Vashon pulled up his horse. He sat absolutely still and looked straight ahead. Lights flickered down the road from town. Before, she'd thought nothing of them, believing them to be the candle-light from the houses, but now she could see they were moving in a long, thin stream like ants.

"What is it?" she whispered, her fear blooming like nightshade.

"Torches. It could be they're looking for the slaves who started the cane fires, but . . ." He backed the horse a few steps. "I don't want to take the chance." Abruptly he dismounted and took her from her perch on the pommel. He then slapped the horse's flanks and sent the animal, tail high, galloping down the road in the opposite direction.

"What are we going to do?" she asked, watching him as if he were out of his mind.

"Come," was all he said before he grabbed her hand and ran for the cover of the canebrake.

It seemed they ran for miles. The cane sliced at her gown and whipped at her flesh. Vashon never let up. He headed for town with the sure instinct of a bloodhound, guided only by the blue light of the moon.

When they got to the edge of town, they moved in the shadows. Every bit of ground was hard-won; there were guards everywhere, their satin livery shining in the iridescent moonlight like the sleek coats of rats. They could only be looking for Vashon. From their whispers, even the governor was out looking for him tonight.

Vashon led her through the maze of slave shacks that lined the road from town. At one point she stumbled and caught herself on a door, only to see the notice that had been nailed to it. It was old and the edges of the paper were yellow and crumbled, but she could clearly make out what was on it. It was a sketch of Vashon's face, and beneath it were the words *El Draque*. Her Spanish was poor but she could read the notice of execution should *El Draque* ever be caught on the island. A new burst of fear shot through her veins.

"The ship will surely be surrounded." Vashon pulled her against a shack as four mounted guards trotted by. His face was taut as he peered down the road. "We'll have to hide until we can reboard."

A new plan began forming in her mind. To escape, she wasn't willing to risk his execution, but she spoke before her idea had even solidified. "I could go to the ship, Vashon. I could tell the captain where to meet you on another part of the island—just tell me where."

He pulled her closer. "How noble of you. I let you out of my sight and you'll be running up that hill to Ignatio's house so quickly a hare couldn't beat you. I'll pass on your offer, love."

"No, I—" *Wouldn't hurt you*, she'd meant to say, but the words stuck in her throat. For some reason they seemed too intimate, too much of a confession. She looked at him, then quickly looked away. "Where can we hide?"

He grew serious. He stared at her for a moment, then a slow smile graced his face. "Maybe we should grant your wish after all. Ignatio's going to scour this damned island looking for me, but he won't think to look in his own house." He nodded in the direction of the hill—Governor's Hill.

"You want us to hide at the governor's mansion? That's insane!" The glint in his eyes frightened her.

"Ah, sweet madness." He laughed and took her hand. They stole through the shadows of the night.

"Yes, she faked the entire thing. I suspect she was going to try to escape once he brought her to the island. Oh, but how I wish now I'd stopped her!" Flossie dabbed a tear from the corner of her eye. She stood on the railing of the *Seabravery* with Isaac, looking out to the lights of New Providence. Somewhere out there Vashon and Aurora were fighting for their lives.

"I've sent out as many men as I have. At least we know they haven't been captured." Isaac glanced at Flossie. It was obvious her tears made him supremely uncomfortable.

"No, no. It's all my fault. I should have known it would come to this. With Vashon in so much danger, it's only logical Aurora would be dragged into his trouble. Now they'll both be . . . be . . ." She drowned in a whole new wave of weeping. Isaac looked ill.

"Flossie," he began helplessly, "Vashon's been in scrapes like this before."

"With a young lady in tow? I—sincerely—doubt—that!" She hiccoughed.

"It does make things more difficult, but he'll manage. If it were anyone else, I'd be worried too, but—"

"Pooh! You're as worried as I am!" Flossie wiped her overflowing eyes with her handkerchief. She looked up and met Isaac's grim stare. "He's like a son to you, isn't he? As notorious as he is, you don't want him to die. You love him like a son."

Isaac heaved a huge sigh. As if it were as natural to him as sailing, he pulled Flossie into his arms and let her weep on his shoulder. Under his breath, he agreed.

"A prodigal son."

16

They were in the mansion.

Aurora's heart had never pounded so hard as the moment they entered the governor's empty kitchens and made their way up into the main house. Somewhere a clock rang midnight as Vashon led her through deserted passages and dodged the occasional servant.

The interior of the mansion was like a Peking nightmare. Chinoiserie was painted on the walls, carved into the furniture, cloying in the air. Even the songbirds hung in pagoda-shaped cages. Aurora was sure a night in an opium den couldn't have produced a more bizarre landscape. But if her surroundings were strange, her circumstances were even stranger. It didn't help her sanity one bit to know any minute they could be caught and executed.

Vashon pulled her into a room just as a slave girl walked down the passage with a luster. He pressed Aurora against his chest and they waited in the dark while the girl passed, the crystals of her candle holder tinkling like bells.

Aurora trembled; Vashon's embrace grew tighter. She looked down at his hands crossed against her stomach. He was a terribly strong man. She knew that by the way he always had to temper that strength whenever he touched her. Beneath him she was as fragile as a piece of porcelain. But did that great strength matter when he took such risks and laughed while he took them? Would it save him in the end? By all accounts, he seemed invincible. Yet was he?

"Vashon, surely you see we cannot stay here?" She clutched his hands. "We'll be discovered. I should go to the ship—"

"Now why would you rescue me?" he whispered against her neck. His breath felt like a feather running down her nape.

"Because—I—" She stumbled over her words. She didn't really know how to answer him. "Because Isaac told me the story about the slaves. I know you're innocent, and I can't stand by and let this governor execute an innocent man—not even if that man is you. I have more honor than that."

"Honor." He laughed cynically. "Honor in the face of death has about as much backbone as our good King George on one of his better days—that is, when they untie the babbling idiot."

"How can you be so blasphemous?"

"How can you be so beautiful?"

She looked up at him. He smiled a slow, dark smile. His hand left her waist and moved to her chin. He tilted her head back and she swore he was going to kiss her.

"You're as mad as King George," she said, pulling away from him.

"No one's that far gone, love." He grabbed her again.

"Don't!" she whispered harshly. He ignored her. His hand swept her hair and he seemed to revel in its tangled silken length. An intent expression crossed his features.

"I think you might make a temptress yet," he whispered.

"Is that your pirate's honor then? To ruin me?" She pulled away, this time fiercely.

"If I have any honor at all." He chuckled and reached for her again but now she was forewarned. She skittered back from him and fled down a steep, winding staircase. It was dark, but even in the sparse lantern light she could see him in quick pursuit. She had just turned the corner to run down a narrow, stone-paved passage when a voice sounded ahead of her. With barely enough time to stop, she saw two liveried guards appear at the end of the passage. They halted in surprise.

"What're y' doing here, girl?" one guard called out to her, his voice thick with rum. He lifted the lantern in his hand to get a good look at her. "The gov'nor's wenching night is Tuesday. Y're here on the wrong night."

Aurora froze in her tracks. Somewhere water dripped through the paving stones and its nerve-racking sound only heightened her fear. As calmly as she could, she glanced to her side. Vashon stood in the shadowy passage that she had just fled. With pistol in hand, his face was grim; his eyes filled with rage.

"That damned wench ain't here fer the gov'nor. She's a damned thief, that's what she is!" The other besotted guard moved forward, his bayonet fixed.

"You're mistaken!" she cried, her mouth going dry from terror. "I assure you, I'm no thief."

"Then what're y' doing here?" The suspicious guard walked up to her and poked her with the bayonet, making a tiny rip in the bodice of her dress. She backed away from him so that he wouldn't see Vashon. She held her arms protectively across her chest, and the guard seemed to savor her fear. "I ne'er laid eyes on y' before, wench. What ship did y' come from?" he demanded.

"The *Sea*—" She choked. She couldn't tell them *that*. Her eyes darted behind the guard to where Vashon stood in the shadowed corner. His face could have been carved from stone it was so hard and still. He was staring at her, she knew, waiting for her to betray him; waiting as a man waits on the gallows for the hangman. Yet she wouldn't betray him. Despite what he thought, there *was* honor in the world, and she considered that she herself possessed some of it.

"The *Cecilia*," she blurted out. "I've arrived from the ship the *Cecilia*."

"I never heard o' that ship docking here. I think y're lying, girlie."

"I've just gotten myself lost." Her eyes pleaded with him. "I've mistakenly found myself here. I don't even know where I am."

The other drunk guard laughed. "You're in the right place!" He lifted the lantern and showed that the passage consisted of row upon row of rusted, barbarous arm shackles.

"Where is that?" she asked with a tremble.

"This is wha' we like to call the 'dungeon,' girlie." The guard threw back his head and laughed.

"If you allow me to leave, I promise I won't speak a word of this to anyone," she pleaded.

"Let 'er go, Mick." the other guard chimed in. He took a swig from an ornate silver hip flask. "After all, she's a pretty little wench. Perhaps if the gov'nor tires of her, she'll remember the favor on a lonely night."

"We don't even know for sure if she is one of the gov'nor's wenches." The guard Mick jabbed her again with the bayonet. From the corner of her eye she could see Vashon tense.

"I implore you," she begged, feeling the situation ready to explode, "just allow me to leave and be on your way. Surely you both have more to do this night than bother with me."

"Aye." Mick took a hefty swallow from the guard's flask. She could see him getting drunker. "We've better things to do. *El Draque* is out there tonight. Y' know who that is, wench?"

She swallowed. Her hands were shaking so badly she had to thrust them behind her. Vashon's defiance was almost palpable. She knew he expected her to reveal him and gleefully watch his execution. There was no way he could win against these men, even with the pistol in his hand. He had at best one shot and there were two guards. But as much as her mind told her that betrayal was the way to freedom, she knew she couldn't do it. Her heart said she'd be betraying an innocent man, and she wouldn't have that on her conscience, even if that man was otherwise a notorious criminal. Her silence might cost her her life, but she could see no other honorable course. She'd once told Vashon that she was not without fortitude. Ironically, tonight, to save him, she was finally going to prove it.

"I don't know *El Draque*," she whispered rebelliously. Mick grabbed her by the arm as if to pull the truth out of her. She winced at the man's roughness, but then her gaze reached behind him to Vashon.

He stood in the darkness, staring at her, his eyes full of wonder. It was clear by his expression that he couldn't fathom why she had shielded him. But she knew that was because he was a pirate, unused to such things as mercy, self-sacrifice, and noble causes. To him the world was black and white. Whether it was because of lack of upbringing, or simply lack of love, he was blind to all the shades of gray that she herself saw quite clearly.

But suddenly, as she watched him, something awakened in his eyes, something that had been sleeping for a terribly long time. It was like a tiny spark of altruism coming to life after years of believing such a thing no longer existed within him. Though he was astonished by it, she could also see he didn't like it. It made him vulnerable and she knew he was the kind of man to fight that to the death.

"Well, he's gonna die tonight. The gov'nor ain't gonna take no more from that bloke. We're to see to it."

She forced her gaze back to the guards. Carefully erasing all emotion from her face, she vowed not to look at Vashon again. His very life depended on it. "Then I shan't keep you gentlemen," she said, making one last pitch for her freedom.

"No." Mick grabbed her arm. "We're gonna keep y', love. Word's out that *El Draque* may have a wench with him tonight. We'll just take y' to the gov'nor and see if y're one o' his or not."

Aurora looked up, the fear of what was to come freezing the expression on her face. "And if the governor doesn't recognize me, then what?" she said in a low voice.

"Then, girlie, y'd better be nice to old Mick, 'cause y'll be in a whole heap of trouble." Mick licked his lips and chuckled at the terror on her face.

Aurora pulled back. She didn't want to go with them, but where was her escape? Vashon couldn't help her. It would be suicide and they both knew it. She stared up at Mick. He pulled her against him. She could smell the rum on his rancid breath.

"The gov ain't gonna recognize y', is he?" he asked.

"No," she whispered, feeling the noose tighten around her throat.

"Come along, Mick. Y're scaring the poor thing half outta her mind," the other guard said.

"We're gonna be on the grind tonight, Davey!" Mick grabbed Aurora by the waist and with one meaty arm, lifted her off the ground. She cried out and struggled, but she'd never felt so helpless. Even though Vashon looked on, he couldn't help her, and even if he could have, she doubted that spark in his eyes was enough to light a fire and save her. He surely didn't care enough about her to risk his life, not even for his valuable Star.

"Let her down or die, fool."

The words, harsh and unyielding, shocked everyone. The guards jumped, surprised that they had an onlooker to their amusements. Aurora simply gasped, disbelieving what she saw as Vashon stepped from the shadows, one lone pistol in hand.

He was mesmerizing in his intensity. His eyes flamed, his lips curled in contempt. His tall, magnificent body seemed barely able to contain the anger it held. He personified fury. Davey, the more timid guard, immediately dropped his gun in surrender.

"He's only got one shot, Davey!" Mick shouted, immediately sobering. "Pick up y'r goddamned gun!"

Davey scrambled to retrieve his weapon. Vashon looked upon him with disgust.

"You think you piteous fools can fight me?" he asked, stepping toward Aurora.

"So she is y'r wench, El Draque." Mick pulled back and held Aurora in front of him. He swayed precariously, cursing the effects of his drink.

"That's right. And I don't take it well, seeing her maltreated." Vashon stepped forward. Though he was better armed, Mick stepped back again.

"Vashon, y' ain't gonna live through this night. The gov's got every

man on this island searching fer y' and I'll be getting a fat purse fer
bringing y' in."

"But you're not going to be bringing me in."

The guard's arm went around her neck. Aurora felt it tighten, but she
could hardly think about what was happening. She was too stunned at
Vashon's mad bravery. He couldn't possibly overpower both the guards,
yet he had still come forward to help her. And was it just for the Star?
Was that the only reason he had risked his life? She didn't want to
believe it. She wanted to believe it was something more, something pure
and good that might be worth the loss of his life. But that certainly
didn't fit this dark, ferocious man. The only thing she knew for certain
was that he'd been very foolhardy in coming forward. Grand Talimen
would have a hanging at dawn.

"Davey," Mick ordered, "shoot the bastard if y' have to, but take *El
Draque* to the jail. When the gov knows we got him, he'll be wanting a
word with him before he dies."

Davey looked at his prisoner. He was obviously terrified of him and if
Davey hadn't been the one in uniform, an onlooker might have thought
Vashon the one in command. "Mick, I think you should take him. I
don't—"

"Goddamn it, don't argue!" To press his point, Mick tightened his
arm further around Aurora's delicate neck. She gasped and Vashon
stepped forward. Davey was forced to be brave.

"All right, all right!" He swayed a bit as he held his bayonet to
Vashon. "You, stay where y' are!" He hiccoughed and Vashon almost
smiled.

"Come now, gentlemen. Surely you see this won't work." Vashon
relaxed the pistol in his hand. "You're both deep into your cups. You
aren't going to take me anywhere."

"We're not, eh?" Mick nearly choked Aurora. Vashon's temper flared
and he moved to take her, but Davey's nerves suddenly got the best of
him and his gun went off.

After the shot, Aurora looked up and screamed when she saw Vashon
slide against the wall. His shoulder trickled scarlet as he slumped down
on the floor.

"No!" she cried as she pulled forward. She couldn't bear the thought
that he might be dead. She couldn't bear it that he might have died in
order to save her.

Davey looked at Vashon in amazement, almost as a hunter might
look after he'd killed a rare and dangerous beast. Mick's hold on Au-

rora slackened and she broke free only to run to Vashon's side. She fell to her knees and meant to attend to him but before she could even determine if he was still alive, Mick had her back in his hold.

"I killed him, Mick," Davey mumbled in amazement.

"The gov'll be pleased. Y' just tell him he wouldn't come without a fight."

"I killed the Dragon."

"That's right, Davey, now go get the damned pistol. Just in case the bloke ain't all dead."

Through tear-blurred eyes Aurora watched Davey walk up to Vashon's still body. Timidly he reached for the gun that was just inches from Vashon's lax hand. Davey looked as if he didn't even breathe while he slowly slid the weapon out of Vashon's reach. Only when he had it in his hand did he let out a sigh of relief.

"Look, Mick, it's made of gold," Davey said just before a hand went around his neck. He screamed and another hand grabbed the wrist that held the gun. Vashon's eyes snapped open, and before Davey could even fight back, Vashon knocked him off his feet and dealt him a blow to his head that immediately left him unconscious.

"Let her go." Vashon rose to his feet, pistol back in his hand. His shoulder still bled, but he moved as if it hardly bothered him. Aurora looked closely and saw that the wound had barely grazed his flesh. It was little more than the damage Flossie had inflicted on him with her parasol.

The guard released her and scrambled to cock his gun. He was just about to shoot when Vashon knocked it away. Terrified, Mick went to grab Aurora again, to use her as a shield, but she, too, was thrust out of his path. He was left defenseless. Against the Dragon.

"Vashon! Let's bargain!" Mick backed from him, terrified. He stumbled once, the rum still taking effect. "I won't tell the gov'nor y' were ever here. Just leave me be and I won't tell the gov nothing!"

"You'll be squawking like a hen as soon as I'm out of sight," Vashon said, picking up the abandoned gun. He touched the point of the bayonet. Pleased by its sharpness, he slipped it off the muzzle.

"Vashon!" Mick pleaded, his terror sobering him, "This ain't necessary!"

Vashon only smiled. Aurora watched, unwilling to see another bloodletting, yet unable to look away.

"Spare me, Vashon! Spare me!" Mick backed against the wall. When Vashon confronted him, Aurora could no longer see everything that was happening. Her heart stopped in her chest as Mick wailed. Vashon clamped him into the arm shackles, and they rattled as Mick fought valiantly to save his life. But then Vashon thrust in the bayonet and there was silence.

He stepped away and Aurora finally had a full view of his victim. She thought to see a dead man. Instead she saw no blood, heard no agonizing cries of pain. She looked at Mick; his mouth was open in shock. He was very much alive, not hurt at all, but he didn't dare move. She almost laughed when she saw the reason for this. Mick was pinned to the wall by the bayonet impaling the fabric of his trousers. The knife, stuck perilously close to his manhood, was solidly imbedded between the paving stones into the crumbling humid mortar. With his arms in shackles, he looked like a butterfly under glass. Every time he even breathed wrong, he risked substantial damage.

"If you like your voice as you've got it now, I wouldn't move." Vashon's mouth turned up in amusement. Mick just looked at him, his face frozen with astonishment.

"Vashon. You bastard," the guard said as quietly as he could. The slightest show of anger cost him. Even Aurora could see that if he really lashed out, he'd lose the family jewels altogether.

Vashon smiled and stepped over Davey's unconscious form to get to Aurora. He took her hand and pulled her with him. "Have a good rest," he said before Mick's soft curses followed them down the passage.

"We've got to find a way out of here," Aurora said as she tended to Vashon's shoulder. The dragon on his back looked all too ominous with a smear of blood across its scales. She dabbed at the dragon and perused her handiwork. He was hardly bleeding at all anymore. The damage was light, barely a nick. All he needed was a bandage.

She lifted her eyes and stared out into the darkness. They were on a balcony overlooking the governor's lush courtyard. The palms shook in the gentle breeze, creating soft music, while lights danced across the island that spread out below them—the torches of the guards as they searched for their prey.

"We've time." Vashon put his arm around her waist. He pulled her down onto his lap and ignored her feeble protests. When she quieted, he asked, "I want to know something before we leave. We won't go until you answer me."

"Your wound is bleeding again. I've got to get some bandages." She tried to struggle out of his lap. He held firm.

"Why didn't you betray me to those guards?"

She didn't move.

"Aurora, I want to know."

Their gazes locked.

"I was in far less danger than you would have been," she said simply.

"Not so." Slowly he added, "Most likely they would have jumped you in exchange for not bringing you to the governor."

"I wasn't afraid—"

"When they'd had their fill, they would have brought you to him anyway. You would have been hung as a thief. Did you know that?"

His hand came up and roughly lingered on her cheek, but the caress was more than she could bear. She looked out over the balcony to the jagged silhouettes of the coconut palms.

"I don't understand. Why did you do it, Aurora? You could have died. For me." His words were deep and quiet.

"No, not for you," she denied, still refusing to look at him. What he wanted she wasn't going to give. She didn't know why she had felt this need to save him. He'd been innocent, she was sure of that, but it was more than just innocence or guilt. It was for the same reason she couldn't utter the words, "I'd never hurt you." They were too bare. They spoke too eloquently of what she was beginning to feel for this terrible man.

"You were protecting me, weren't you?"

"I've got to get some bandages."

"Answer me." He held her down once more.

"Vashon, don't . . ." Her voice suddenly cracked.

"Don't what, *Aurore*? Don't wonder why you saved my life tonight? Don't think about the reason for it?"

"The reason for it?" she repeated, his questions making her irrationally angry. "I'll tell you. It was for the same reason you stepped out from that doorway and saved me from those men. It was the right thing to do. It was the only thing to do. That's all it was, Vashon, a virtuous deed. And I know how you loathe that." She laughed bitterly. "Virtue. It sounds like an oath in the same breath with your name."

He took her face in both his hands and forced her to look at him. When their gazes clashed, he said cruelly, "You sound disappointed in my character, Aurora. Almost like a spurned lover."

"You are the one spurned, Vashon. I spurn you and I always will." She struggled to be free of his hold on her face.

"But you can't spurn me till I've made an offer. So allow me." He pulled her roughly to him, letting her slide between the clamp of his thighs. "Do you want to do a little strumming, love?"

She froze. His crudeness knew no bounds. She knew quite well what strumming meant; she had heard it from several of the older boys they'd taken into the Home. Though she might not be clear on all the details, she had a pretty good idea of the grand picture. It was a soiled one indeed.

"Let—me—go—" she demanded, looking at him contemptuously.

"Come along, Aurora," he baited, "a little in-and-out'd do you a world of good. Perhaps we might even loosen that stick enough to let you—"

"You vile man! You wretch! You disgusting, blackhearted villain!" She cursed and tugged on his thighs.

He wasn't about to let her go.

"Does this mean you spurn me?" he asked mockingly.

She squealed with fury. He only laughed. She raised her hand to slap him, but he caught it in midair. He forced it to her side, then thrust her against his chest. Suddenly he turned deadly serious. There was no more play in him at all.

"Don't make me into a noble man, little wren. Don't even think it."

"But why? Why can't you be other than what you are?" Her eyes suddenly filled with tears. She didn't know why he was affecting her this way. She certainly had other things to worry about now. All of hell's wrath seemed to be breaking loose around them: Cutthroat guards were scouring the island, Vashon had flagrantly decided to hide in the governor's own bedchamber, and there seemed little or no chance of their ever getting back to the docks undiscovered. Yet now, as mad as it was, the most important thing in the world seemed to be having him admit to that spark she'd seen in his eyes when she'd told those guards she knew nothing about *El Draque*.

Oh, but she'd forgotten how cold those green eyes could be.

She stared at him. He leaned closer.

"Heed my words well, Aurora. The day I turn into a noble man is the day I will surely die."

"No," she said, her voice barely above a whisper.

"If I grow soft, if you make me grow soft, my enemies will have at me right there." He thumped his finger into her back.

A shiver of dread ran through her. "This Peterborough, he's not God, Vashon."

"He doesn't have to be. A cruel man is never without friends. It's a noble man who dies alone with his convictions."

"It's not true," she whispered. "If you were to become a good man, Vashon, I swear to you, you would not die alone."

"I'm not a good man, Aurora."

"I saw it in you. It was that goodness that saved me tonight. That and only that. You thought nothing of the Star when you stepped from the shadows. Don't deny it, Vashon! You came out to save me and only to save me!"

"God damn you!" His arm tightened brutally around her waist.

"Admit it, Vashon! Admit that you can be a noble man. Change your path!" she sobbed.

His fury was so great he almost roared. "I am what you see, Aurora! And I shall prove to you once and for all, I shall never be a good man!" He took her head in an iron-fisted grip and jammed her mouth against his. She sobbed against his lips, but even that protest was silenced when he forcefully thrust his tongue past her teeth.

His kiss was at once fiery and bitterly impersonal. It was calculated for response and degradation; she felt both with searing sharpness. Tears of rage and frustration sprang in her eyes while desire stole into her body like a thief. She hated him now, more than she'd ever hated anyone. But worse, she knew she'd also never feel so strongly about any other man again.

When he broke away, his smile was humorless as she struck out at him.

"Still think so highly of me, my dear?" he whispered, catching both her forearms in one iron grip.

"Don't do this, Vashon. Don't wrong me this way. I saved your life!"

"Keep your mouth closed unless I'm kissing you," he answered callously.

"Don't!" she cried out as he dragged her into the governor's exotic bedroom, her pleas only serving to heighten his resolve.

He pulled her roughly down on the bed with him; his tall body covered her completely. His hand slipped down her chest, removing the pins of her gown one by one as he found them. She shuddered when the apron front fell away, leaving only a thin bodice of laced linen between her and his lust.

"Think me a saint now?" He looked down at her face for a long moment, seeming to enjoy her beauty and defiance. Then his mouth lowered to the lush swell of her bosom that spilled over her low linen underbodice.

She threw her head back and moaned from her inability to stop him. He kissed her flesh, leaving a hot, wet trail down her skin until her clothing forced him to stop. His fingers caught in the lacings down her front and carefully, painfully, he unlaced them. She pulled on his forearm, but nothing, not God nor man, could have stopped him now. He jerked away her bodice and reveled in her generous apricot-tipped breasts while she stared at him, her eyes filled with hurt and betrayal.

"There is a noble man in you, Vashon," she said with a sob, "but you've buried him so deep he may never be seen again."

"You should never have seen him at all" was all he said before his lips covered one nipple. She clutched him and her response melted into another sob. Her hands wove into his wild long hair and she tried to pull him away, but the pain seemed to mean nothing to him. He ignored it and continued his onslaught upon her other breast until she lost her control and shuddered beneath him.

"Ah, I see you're a woman after all," he said huskily, taking power in her reaction. She jerked away, vowing to remain cold and stiff, but he only smiled and let his hard handsome mouth slide between her breasts.

Trembling, she was unsure of how much more she could take. She desperately wanted to call for help, but that was impossible. To hide from the governor's men, she'd willingly locked herself in this ornate bedchamber with this pirate. Summoning the household servants would only get them both executed. She was trapped, and looking at Vashon's terrible, impassioned face, she knew he was only too well aware of it.

He rose above her and pulled her dress from her shoulders. She moaned when she watched it slide tantalizingly to her hips. She beat him when he kissed her, but her fists could have been beating a brick wall. He didn't surrender an inch.

"Who'd have ever thought I'd have you?" he whispered against her hair, his hand filling with her breast. She pushed against him, but her palms met the worn leather of his buccaneer vest, smooth and warm, like an erotic extension of his own skin. She quickly pulled away.

"You don't like to touch me, do you, Aurora?" His hand captured the one she'd pulled back. He taunted, "Why is that, little girl? Did no one ever hug you at that Home? Did our illustrious paragon of noble intentions, Mr. Phipps, never put his arms around you and keep you warm? What a cold little place you grew up in." He took her hand and slid it up beneath his vest. His chest was as solid as a piece of steel, his muscles as warm and rippling as a Caribbean tide.

"I—I was well regarded at that Home, Vashon," she threw back at him, tears streaking down her face. "No one would have ever mistreated me like this."

The tension in his face returned. "Ah, yes. Regard. But was it love? I was loved once . . . until those who loved me were ripped from my very soul."

"Vashon!" she cried out as he left the bed. She scrambled to cover her nakedness with the scarlet satin counterpane, then, with a slow-seeping dread in her heart, she watched him undress.

She didn't look away. There was no need. All pretenses were crumbling around them; her innocence, she realized, long since sentenced to an inevitable death. Mutely she saw the worn umber-colored vest tossed to the carpet, then his boots, then his trousers. Her gaze lifted and she stared at him, frightened yet exhiliarated by the beast before her.

He seemed born out of the glittering shadows of her dreams. He towered above her, his long dark hair falling down his back, his eyes gleaming as hard and brilliant as emeralds. He breathed heavily, his chest moving in a powerful rhythm. He reached for her. She scrambled back against the headboard. They paused and assessed each other, hunter to prey.

He stood, still as death, his hand gripping the governor's gilt bedpost. Her gaze fell lower this time and her fear exploded when she saw his manhood still swaying from his previous movement. But what terrified her even more was the dragon. Though she couldn't see the tattoo on his back, she finally saw the tail. It swept across his hip and wrapped twice around his iron-hard thigh before its spade tip disappeared in his groin. It hugged him, it possessed him completely, and it was now going to take her too.

She leaped off the bed and made a wild run for the door, her hands over her bare chest, the skirt of her gown trailing behind her, still clinging seductively to her hips. She thought he might try to grab her, but he didn't even need to expel that much effort. His foot stomped her trailing skirt, and she was thrust backward into his arms. He growled out a laugh and pulled her out of her gown. She cried and scratched and clawed, to no avail; he threw her down on the bed and subdued her like a shrewish wife.

"Vashon, I beg of you!" she panted before he eased himself on top of her.

"No more talk," he said, his hand making a studied slide down her breast.

"My God, I beg you! I'm a virgin!" she sobbed.

"Then like a festering wound, best to rip the bandages off quick."

"No!" she cried.

"Yes," he whispered.

She beat him but her efforts were futile. For as much as she flailed, as much as she twisted, there was no way to keep him from doing his worst. He pinned her down and his hand parted her thighs, caressing the creamy skin between them, his thumb brushing against the soft brown hair of her sex.

The shock of his touch nearly killed her, but it also summoned what little fight she had left. She'd meant to slap him, but in the flickering candlelight of the bedchamber, her gaze caught the glint of his earring. Her finger looped through it almost before the idea occurred to her. Immediately he stopped, suspended above her on corded arms.

"You stop this madness! This evil!" she panted.

"Go ahead. Rip it out, Aurora. It's happened before."

She looked up at him, her aqua eyes filled with fury and hesitation. He was being a monster. She couldn't let him continue. But could she hurt him like that? Rip the earring right through his ear? She looked at him, her full, pliant chest pressing against the granite of his as she caught her breath.

When her gaze moved to his ear, she saw a thick scar marred his earlobe. He'd lost that earring before. New tears pooled in her eyes. She could only think of one instance where another could get this close to Vashon to do such a deed.

"Was it another woman then?" she blurted out. "Did you get her this angry?" Her voice quavered. "Did she go as unwillingly as I?"

His eyes almost dared her to pull it. " 'Twas a beggar in the Casbah. I was only fifteen. He wanted the silver and came upon me in the darkness."

A long moment passed while she stared at her finger looped through his earring. "What did you do to him?"

"Let's just say he found he didn't need the silver after all."

She met his gaze. She didn't want to know any more.

"Go on, pull it so we may continue."

His harsh words frightened her more than anything had before it. She stilled her trembling hand, then gave a slight tug, not enough to inflict any damage. Her gaze caught his and she saw the planes of his face harden as he readied himself for the pain. Physical pain was just another facet of his black-and-white world. He'd take his pain to get his pleasure. It was as simple as that. But as she looked deep into his green eyes, she saw just a glimpse of how pain had shaped him. He'd been just fifteen and the world around him had been willing to see him bleed for a tiny bit of silver. She began to realize just how hard he'd had to fight to survive and how masterfully his cruel world had taught him.

Now it was her turn to teach him.

To hurt him was her only chance for escape. But with soul-crushing defeat, she knew she wouldn't, and the reason for it was more painful than what she'd been about to do.

With a heart-wrenching sob, she released her finger. He was obviously surprised by her surrender. He grabbed her but she wouldn't look at him. She turned away, her tears streaming down her cheeks like rivers. Softly, bitterly, she cried into the counterpane.

"Aurora—!"

"I can't hurt you!" she confessed, sobbing against his hand. "I can't hurt you," she cried like a curse over and over again.

"Aurora! Look at me!" he commanded, his every muscle growing taut from anger. But she refused, her tears still flowing, her chest heaving with her wretched newfound emotion.

"Aurora!" There was fury in his voice, yet something else, something almost like panic. "You listen to me. I won't feel for you, you tight-laced bitch! Do you hear me? I won't feel for you!" He brutally shook her, but she would not cease her crying. She held the counterpane with her hands and waited for his sexual onslaught. She almost didn't care. Her entire world had been shaken tonight. Even being kidnapped couldn't compare with this awful feeling, a feeling she knew she would rather die than admit.

"Aurora," he whispered, breathing nearly as hard as she.

She tossed her head back and forth, unwilling to meet his eyes, afraid of what her own might reveal. But finally he clamped her head between his flat palms and she was forced to look up at him. When she did, it seemed the entire island stilled.

He stared at her as if it were for the first time, as if they had no past at all. She couldn't look away, for though his hold was gentle, his eyes, his very being, had her completely captured. Her lips trembled; she was unsure of what was to come next. Slowly, hesitantly, his hand reached out and he touched her face.

"Vashon, don't . . ." she whispered as his finger traced her lips, bruised from his kisses. His thumb crossed her brow while her eyes chastised him through thick sienna lashes now spiked with moisture. He seemed almost to be trying to confirm that she was real as his fingers slid over her cheeks, tracing the path of her tears. Finally he believed it. He pulled back and stared at the tears glistening on his fingertips, and that was when she saw him—the man she so desperately sought. She found him in the slightest glimmer of remorse in Vashon's eyes.

"He's there," she said in an aching, quiet voice.

Angered, he pulled her further beneath him. She tried to caress his cheek but he pinned down her hands so that she couldn't touch him.

"Deny it. Yet he exists," she stated softly, her eyes brilliant from emotion.

"No," he rasped and grabbed her to him for a brutal kiss.

When she saw the magnitude of his rage, she thought he might hurt her after all, yet when the moment of his kiss arrived, his head lowered, not to her lips, but to her shoulder and he lay there, completely still, as if forcing himself to reconsider his course of action.

She ached to touch him, but he still had her hands pinned to the counterpane. She wriggled beneath him, and he finally lifted his head and looked down at her. Though they were still naked, lying chest against chest, heartbeat to heartbeat, she could sense him pulling away. She now knew he couldn't hurt her, and that made the thought of his leaving that much more unbearable. They had come too far.

He moved to leave the bed, but before he went, he woodenly placed a kiss upon her tear-stained cheek. Desperate to make him stay, she summoned a womanly guile she never knew she possessed. She waited for his lips to leave her cheek and just when they did, she turned her head and her lips met with his.

Their kiss was sublime. Never in her most wishful dreams did she believe a kiss could be like this: a man's heart and soul distilled into one soft motion of his lips. He made her want him with a desire that surpassed the physical, that grew and grew until she was almost made wild by it. Losing her self-consciousness, she slid her hand between them and let her palm mold to the grid of warm muscle over his torso. Her other hand reached up and caressed his beard-roughened cheek. Their kiss deepened.

Her lips instinctively parted for him. He tasted her, pushed himself into her, all the while persuading her to taste him. She was a slow pupil, but finally she succumbed and slipped her tongue out to meet his.

Her pleasure was intense and immediate, but it increased tenfold

when she realized that she had moved him also. She could hardly believe the power she suddenly possessed. He groaned against her, cup-
ping her breast as if he held the wealth of the world in his hand. She
shivered deliciously; her nipple hardened beneath his palm.

In the most fleeting of thoughts, she marveled at him, wondering
when he had changed. When had his touch grown gentle, his caress
tender? His kiss aching and sweet? She wasn't able to think so coher-
ently for long. His mouth broke from hers and dragged along her
throat. He moved lower and the velvet of his tongue traced one tight
apricot bud, the black coils of his hair falling across her chest in stark
contrast to the smooth ivory flesh beneath him. When he pulled himself
up once more, the scent of his skin filled her, again bringing to mind the
sea: salty, pungent, elemental. He looked down at her, his breath coming swift and insistent. She could feel him against her bare thighs, and
her senses, filled to the point of intoxication, barely registered what
happened next.

"Aurora," he groaned, "I think old Phipps just may be the one to kill
me. . . ."

Everything moved quickly then. His arm reached beneath her hips;
he arched her against him, awakening instincts in her she'd never
known she had. When she helplessly moaned, it seemed he could take it
no more. His knee forced apart her alabaster thighs and he slid between
them, taking her sweetness in one searing motion.

The shock far outweighed the pain. She gasped and looked up, her
eyes wide with disbelief. He stared back, implacable and devouring.
Turning her head away, she felt panic overwhelm her. He began moving
and her hysteria increased. Writhing beneath him, she did her best to
pull back, but with him upon her it was utterly impossible. She was
trapped like a wild bird suddenly caged.

"Stop, stop," she gasped, her eyes darkening with fear.

He never even broke rhythm. Instead he kissed her, his lips clinging,
persuading, seducing, with all the dark fury in his soul. She sank back
into helpless surrender, her body lifting to his as if it ached for him. She
wrapped his violent motion in the gentle embrace of her femininity, and
against her will her loins melted, tingling with the sensations of her
dream. Her hands clutched at him, trying to hang on, but the turbulent
ride became too much. Unbidden came the picture of the dragon on his
back rippling with his every thrust, and she began to fall, everything
around her sinking quietly into a deep, sweet oblivion.

Her last foothold on solid ground was her glance at him. He never blinked. His stare burned with sparks of lust, yet there was another desire there too. One that burned even brighter. It was a need of the spirit, and she wondered how he would ever satisfy that need when the dragon could not be slain. She understood that now. The dragon possessed him and always would. Her only hope was that it could be tamed. For the dark side of him would never completely go away.

She surrendered, and another truth came to her, a truth as shattering as the first, as naked as the picture of her fingers clawing down his back, clawing down that dragon in blind, wild ecstasy. She panted and cried and shook her head, but there was no denying it any longer. Vashon had confirmed it in a language more eloquent than words.

She had a dark side too.

17

A shaft of brilliant sunlight spilled across the two sleeping figures. When Peterborough entered the bedroom and threw back the heavy bed-curtains, one body stirred, the sheets twisting with his lazy movement. The young man's eyes slowly opened and he squinted in the blinding morning light.

"Viscount," he said, his voice thick with sleep.

"My good Lord Worthington," Peterborough greeted sweetly. "Does your illustrious father, the duke, know where you are?"

"No—no, my lord."

"Then imagine his disappointment when he discovers your little pleasures are hardly going to produce the family heir." With that dry comment, Peterborough whipped back the brocaded counterpane and grabbed the slender young man by the hair. He jolted him out of the bed and while the nude fellow scrambled to get to his feet, Peterborough tossed him off into the corner.

"What is the meaning of—!" Asher sat up in the bed, his words cut short when he saw Peterborough.

"Get up. We're going to Mirage."

Asher glanced at his paramour. The young man had grabbed the damask window curtains and was shamefacedly holding them to his loins. "I don't understand," he said. "I spoke to Azzedine myself. He was supposed to take care of Vashon."

Peterborough's face hardened and he eyed the young man in the corner. "I'm hardly going to explain all this with your lover staring at us from the drapery."

Asher ran an agitated hand over his jaw.

"Will you excuse us, Worthington?" Peterborough inquired politely, turning to the young earl.

Lord Worthington looked at Asher. Asher gave him a slight nod and the young man acquiesced. "Where can I find a dressing gown?" he asked.

"No time for that," Peterborough answered.

The young man was about to give the viscount a rather snubbing retort when his eyes opened wide in horror. Peterborough had a pistol aimed directly at his forehead. Before Asher could even gasp, Peterborough shot the young earl dead and drolly watched as his body slumped beneath the window, the lad's face a frozen, blood-flecked mask of horror.

"Why did you do that!" Asher cried, rushing to the young man.

Peterborough stopped him. "I want to talk to you. We have business."

"He would have left us alone!" Asher exclaimed, anguished by the sight of the dead young man.

"There wasn't time."

"Are you out of your mind? I'll be hanged for this! How shall I explain to the duke?"

"You won't need to. We're leaving. Our ship is already at the docks." Peterborough looked scornfully at Asher's nudity. The blond man's thin lily-white body looked as though it might perish in the sunshine. "Get dressed," he said.

Asher stared at him with loathing—and something else, something strangely like misplaced desire, on his face. "I wish you hadn't killed him," he said. "He was a good lad, despite his . . . waywardness."

"Don't mourn him. He wasn't your type. You're a kneeler, Asher. In more ways than one." Peterborough uttered a scathing laugh.

Asher's expression soured.

"Get dressed. I'm not going to say it again."

Asher slowly stepped over the dead earl and went to his wardrobe.

Showing a vast amount of callousness, the viscount sat in an armchair right next to the young man's bloodied corpse. He resumed conversation as if there had never been a killing. Testily, he said, "I just received word this morning that the *Bleeding Heart* has sailed to Johanna for an extended raid. Azzedine failed like the miserable bastard he is."

Asher peeked from behind the wardrobe door. "Why can't we send another—?"

"Shut up, you fool. Say good-bye to your buggering little earl here and get ready for a voyage." Peterborough shot him a look that promised all the fires of hell if he didn't comply. The viscount's green eyes sparkled with fury, and to emphasize his point, he pounded his fist on the windowsill, unconcerned with the dead young man near his feet. "I'm going to get him this time, Asher. Mark my words, I no longer care that Vashon's my brother. I'll see him dead and that emerald mine. And I'm going to do it in such a way that I'm going to make those men wish they were back on the *Leviathan*!"

"One day you'll go too far," Asher said in an ominous voice.

Peterborough laughed handsomely and kicked the corpse. The young earl's bloodied hand fell forward in a mock entreaty.

"But I haven't yet," the viscount said sarcastically, "have I?"

Turning back to the wardrobe, Asher closed his eyes. He appeared as if he wanted to fight back, at least with words. But he didn't. Something weak and terrible in him always bowed to those more forceful. And ever since he'd met this handsome, monstrous viscount, he knew he would never win.

Reluctantly he buttoned his shirt.

Vashon held her to him for probably an hour. He was quiet, almost peaceful, but his arms gripped her as if she were a present too soon to be taken away.

Aurora watched him, her gaze hungering for every detail. The tension was gone from his normally hard mouth. His eyes were sleepy and half-lidded, their emotion now cloaked only by shadow. Somewhere she heard a clock ring four times and she wanted to scream to make it stop. She wanted to run through the mansion and destroy all the clocks. Time must stop; she never wanted to leave his arms.

But time evaporated like desert rain. When Vashon finally left the bed, Aurora knew she had never seen a man so cold. The night air was hot, and perspiration slicked back the tendrils of her hair, covering her body in a fine glistening sheen, but still she shivered watching Vashon's frozen silhouette. He stood at the doors to the balcony, his arms crossed tightly across his chest. The dragon didn't move. She pulled the scarlet counterpane to her, suddenly chilled, suddenly self-conscious about her nudity.

"Vashon?" she whispered.

He allowed his head to fall back, as if he'd already begun to regret what he must say.

"Vashon," she said again, barely able to keep the quaver from her voice.

"Get dressed. We've stayed here already too long. Ignatio may give up his search for me and return."

"But we must talk—"

"Get dressed."

His tone sent one huge tear cascading down her cheek. She should have broken all the clocks after all. She knew the moment he left he would be lost to her. He was now pushing her away, and after what she'd just surrendered to him, she'd have welcomed a knife with more pleasure.

He faced her and she quickly wiped her tear away, but not before he saw it.

"This should have never happened," he said.

"But it—has—happened," she answered, her voice cracking.

"Never again. Never again."

Another tear fell. She reached for her gown with shaking hands. It didn't seem possible that only minutes before he had held her, caressed her, loved her. That tender man seemed from a dream now, a dream impossibly out of reach.

"Aurora."

She looked up. He towered over her, his naked body ominous and beautiful.

"Aurora," he began, "this . . ." His gaze guiltily roved over the governor's rumpled bed; the sight of her virgin's blood on the sheets seemed to stab him in the gut. "This was beyond my control. I never really intended . . ." Their eyes met. Too quickly he looked away.

"You never really intended what?" she whispered.

His expression turned wooden. He didn't answer. He didn't have to.

She closed her eyes. Everything was going numb—her body, her mind, her spirit. Wiping her eyes with the back of her hand, she gathered herself and pulled her wrinkled blue gown over her head. She tied the laces at her breasts and again made a search for the pins.

"Here."

She looked at him. He picked both pins out of the counterpane and held them out to her. But she didn't take them. Instead, she opened her palm and forced him to give them up. Her insides felt as if they were slowly freezing beneath his dispassionate facade, and in their place was left only a cold, empty anger. What he had done to her was unforgivable. She couldn't feel worse than she did at this very moment. There was no torture cruel enough, no pain deep enough.

With trembling hands she fastened her apron front, noting with bitter amusement how tattered and worn her pretty blue gown looked. As tattered and worn as her emotions.

"Isaac will wait for us at Dieppe Bay if he doesn't see us at the docks. If we stay in the cane, we should be there in an hour." He was restrained and instructional. Nothing more. She glanced at him and noticed he had dressed. He stared down at her bare feet, then his gaze wandered the room as if searching for something. He disappeared into an anteroom and in a moment, he came back with a pair of the governor's silk slippers. They almost fit. The governor, she discovered, was a very tiny man.

"Of course, you know he'll discover we were here," she said, her voice tight and frigid.

"Who?"

"The governor."

He paused, a wry smile twisting his lips. In silence, he walked to a pair of red-and-gold fretwork pedestals where matching Chinese vases flanked the door. He picked up one vase and walked to the bed. He tossed it upon the bed, the huge green dragon painted across it releasing its fiery stare to the scarlet upholstered ceiling of the bedstead.

"Now he'll know we were here," he said.

She looked at him, despairing for his very soul. He took her cold hand, and together they stole out of the mansion.

Dieppe Bay was a shallow inlet surrounded by coral reefs. When they arrived, Aurora could see the lights of the *Seabravery* anchored far beyond the reefs. The ship looked so unreachable, she didn't know how she would summon the energy to continue. She was exhausted. The sand in her slippers cut into the soles of her feet; her arms were slashed by cane. If she stumbled over one more coconut, she was sure she would fall to her knees and never get to her feet again.

Ahead Vashon stood in the surf, looking across the moonlit bay, searching for something she couldn't see. She fell back against the trunk of a palm, drained. She still couldn't make herself accept what had happened back at the governor's mansion. If she'd fought him harder, would that have changed the course of the night? Depression sank into her like water into sand. She closed her eyes, wanting never to think of this night again. No, fighting him wouldn't have worked. His seduction was too brilliant. When force hadn't produced the desired result, he'd simply used more subtle means. He'd convinced her that his gentleness and caring were real. But now, seeing his taut, rigid back, she knew it must have been a sham. Though something in her heart cried out that this was not so, she refused to listen to it. Instead she focused on Vashon's cold figure, and all her fears were reinforced.

Nothing would have stopped this night. She'd had that dream, that wretched, soul-consuming dream, and she'd never been able to forget it. Now she'd learned her lesson and it had been a hard one. "Soiled doves," Mrs. Bluefield had once called women like her. With a sharp pain Aurora also remembered how those same women left their bastards at the Home by the dozens.

She watched Vashon slowly wander back to where she stood. His face was in shadow when he spoke.

"The dinghy's been launched. The *Seabravery* will sail as soon as we reboard."

She didn't comment. She merely stood against the tree and gazed out at the ocean rolling in like a black cloud. She felt about as warm and alive as a marble statue.

"Aurora?" He reached out to touch her. She quickly pulled back.

"Look at me," he told her, but she refused, keeping her eyes instead on the ocean and the liquid reflection of moonlight upon it.

"You disappoint me, love." Annoyance was heavy in his voice. "I'd hoped that rigid little schoolmistress would stay away awhile longer."

His harsh words sent an unexpected wave of pain through her. She turned away. Her tears froze in her eyes. "I assure you she is back. And she will never leave again," she answered coldly.

"No wonder old Phipps let you go."

She gasped and sought his face in the darkness. His smirk was unmistakable. "What do you know of John Phipps?" she burst out, wild irrational fury burgeoning in her breast. "Nothing!" she spat. "You haven't the nobility or grace to even follow in his footsteps!"

"And was he so perfect then?"

"Yes! Yes! Utterly perfect!" she hissed, hating him more than ever at that moment. Anyone could see John was the better man. So how could Vashon possess this maddening ability to make her want him, and only him?

"So perfect that you fled without a clue to where you were going? Or to *whom* you were going?" he said meaningfully.

"If I'd known this night was to happen, I never would have left!"

He grabbed her arms. "But maybe that's the reason you did leave. Maybe you wanted this night every bit as much as I did. Maybe old Phipps wasn't the man you claim him to be—"

She snatched her arm back, then cracked her hand hard across his handsome cheek. He was closer to the truth than he would ever know, but she'd carry it to her grave before she'd ever admit it. "He was a gentleman," she lashed out, "not a *rapist*."

He grabbed back her arm, this time brutally. "And were these rapist's hands that had you moaning beneath me tonight? And are these scratches on my back from a woman desperate to run from me . . . or to me?"

A muffled sob escaped her; she refused to look at him. All her vows of no more tears crumbled in front of her.

He let go of her arm, for the moment willing to allow her some peace. He stepped back, but then commented, "Of course, this miserable adventure could have been avoided entirely if you hadn't feigned that stupid illness."

"Or if you hadn't kidnapped me—or if your head weren't wanted everywhere from here to Kingdom Come!" she cried.

"You crossed me, love. You lied and endangered both our lives. You could not expect to come out unscathed."

"This was not my fault," she whispered, cursing her voice that was supposed to stay cool and detached, cursing her face that was supposed to look so dispassionate. She looked away but not before her eyes revealed her hurt.

Gently he said, "No, it wasn't your fault. I take the blame for what happened at the governor's mansion. But all I want is that emerald. You help me find it and we'll forget this night. Forget that it ever happened."

"How?" she asked, almost hysterical. "I'll never forget it as easily as you. It was my blood we left on those sheets, not yours." As if it would purge her, she suddenly lashed out at him. She beat on his shoulders until she felt something warm and sticky on her fists. Horrified, she realized she'd made his wound bleed anew.

"Go ahead, take out your anger," he said tightly. "Then forget about it. For I swear to you, this night was a mistake. It will never *ever* happen again."

She began to cry in earnest, but whether it was because she had hurt him or because his vow cut her like a knife, she didn't know.

When the dinghy pulled up on the beach, Isaac jumped out, hardly able to contain his relief that they were both all right. He first went to Vashon, but when his gaze fell on Aurora's quiet, tattered figure, he immediately seemed to sense something was terribly wrong. His exuberance at seeing them died. With nary a greeting, they climbed into the dinghy and set out for the *Seabravery* in utter silence.

"Aurora! Love! I've been beside myself with worry! Thank God you're—" Flossie stopped dead in her tracks when the party reboarded the ship. She took one look at Aurora's face in the flickering ship's light, noting her knotted hair, her glistening sorrowful eyes, and it seemed in that instant Flossie knew everything. The stare she gave Vashon should have killed him on the spot.

Vashon ignored the widow's lethal scrutiny and nodded to Benny, who waited by the afterhouse. "Miss Dayne requires her own cabin," he said tightly. "See to it that she has her old one back."

"Aye, sir."

"Isaac." He turned to the captain. "Did Neville and his men manage to refill our water caskets?"

"Yes."

"Without incident?"

"They were back at their estates before midnight."

"Then we sail immediately for Mirage."

"Very good," Isaac answered.

Vashon then turned to Aurora. He looked as if the last thing on earth he wanted to do was to meet her hurt-filled gaze in the clear lantern light of the ship. "Miss Dayne," he said with studied control, "I suggest you retire to your cabin. You'll need your rest. When we arrive at Mirage, my pursuit of that emerald will be relentless."

"Very good," she answered acidly, mimicking Isaac.

He ignored her. "Benny will escort you."

"He will not," Flossie interjected. "I shall escort Aurora to her cabin. And this time no one shall keep me from her."

"As you wish," he conceded, his voice as cold as snow.

Aurora looked at him; their gazes clashed like fire and ice. When she finally felt Flossie take her arm and lead her away, she swore she saw something like regret in his eyes. But before that emotion could fully take hold, the dragon appeared and burned it all away.

18

When Flossie and Aurora were alone in her old cabin, Aurora sank down on her bunk and silently stared at the rafters. There seemed nothing to say. Words would never sort out the emotions that now boiled within her. Flossie seemed to sense this. She simply held her until Benny brought her things from Vashon's cabin.

When Benny left, Flossie lifted Aurora's chin and looked with concern at her tear-ravaged face. Aurora's aqua eyes seemed impossibly big for her pale, delicate features. Her mouth was drawn into a tight pain-filled crescent. Flossie looked close to bursting into tears herself.

"Aurora," she said in her practical fashion, "we must give in and find this stupid emerald Isaac told me about. Let Vashon have it. That's the only way. And when we do, you shall come live with me on St. George's and we shall forget this horrible voyage and—"

"No!" Aurora stood up and began to pace the cabin floor. Her hand went to the lizard locket and she fingered it as if it were a talisman. "I'll never give in to him. Not now."

"Listen to me, love." Flossie held out her arms. "They aren't going to kill us, we both realize that. And in light of this evening's . . . incidents, I think the best solution is to capitulate. Tell Vashon what you know and let him have what he wants. Then we can be sure no more . . . incidents will occur."

"Absolutely not. I will not help that—that—*pirate* find his plunder! Not even if my life was truly in danger!"

"But there's still a danger if this voyage continues. Have you given thought to it?"

"What danger?" she scoffed, glancing at Flossie. "Of course I worry about you, but Vashon wouldn't harm you, it's obvious he thinks too highly of you. And I dare say Isaac wouldn't do anything. In fact, I won't be surprised to find him growing fond of you."

"But what about a babe, have you thought of that? Vashon's baby?"
Aurora's face slowly showed her horror. Flossie had finally given
words to the unspeakable.

Seeing her fear, the widow sprang to her feet and took her hand.
"Never fear, my dear. It's unlikely that tonight . . . well, let's just
count our blessings that there probably won't be one. But if this voyage
continues—"

"If not tonight, then there won't be one," Aurora answered adamantly.

"But how do you know? I can see how Vashon's intrigued by you. It's
hard to keep a man like that at bay once he's already . . ." Flossie
blushed. Her eyes apologized for the indelicate nature of their discussion.

"Never again," Aurora vowed, shaking her head. And it was true.
She had let him inside, allowed him to see feelings she should have
never shown. Right now he was probably remembering their liaison and
laughing about it, laughing at her awkwardness and innocence and na-
ïveté.

But no more. If she lived to be a hundred, no man would ever see
those feelings again. If she were fortunate enough not to have to pay for
her night with him with a child, then she would forget she had ever lain
with him, forget she ever knew what it felt like to have his hands on her,
or his arms around her, or hear his heart beat against her palm.

"It will never happen again," she repeated softly.

"My little lambs didn't all survive, but Mr. Lindstrom and I had
fourteen children saying that."

Aurora put a shaking hand to her temple. Yesterday all she had
wanted to do was to try and escape. Now because of that everything
was spinning out of control.

"Oh, I shan't go on." Flossie squeezed her hand and gave her a
reassuring little smile. "I can see you're exhausted. Sleep, my darling.
We'll decide what to do when you've rested."

"I won't give in, Flossie. Not now."

Flossie turned and studied her. Not finding evidence of what she
sought, she asked gently, "Did he force you then, Aurora? Is that it?
Was he so cruel that you're willing to fight to the end to keep him from
getting what he wants?"

Aurora looked away, her guilt-ridden eyes telling Flossie more than
she wanted her to know. Vashon hadn't forced her; he'd been far too

skillful for that. She almost broke down when she thought how willingly she'd surrendered.

Rebellious tears slipped down her cheek. She would never give in to him again. Her heart was at stake now. And for that she *would* fight him to the end.

In the days that followed, like a daughter of Neptune she wandered the prow, a wild, furious sea spirit seeking revenge. The wind molded her thin blue gown to her lithe figure, outlining every curve, every sweet attraction. But her eyes, furious and now all too knowing, easily kept all at bay. While the sun emboldened the watercolor tint of her hair, sweeping it back from her face in a wild banner, and while her beautiful blue-green eyes searched the horizon, their expression as mercurial and dangerous as the ocean beneath a storm, she stood alone, unforgiving and unapproachable.

From the decks and the rigging, the men of the *Seabravery* couldn't stop staring, their gazes held in a trance while Aurora leaned back from the prow. She was like a changeling in their midst, evolving from a timid brown wren to a furious wind-borne gull. But though they were compelled to look, none dared speak to her on the chance that they, too, might find the wrath of those lovely aqua eyes upon them like the man who stood on the quarterdeck, his own green gaze punishing and devouring her with the same glance.

"She's not the girl who first boarded this ship, is she?"

Immediately Vashon's gaze tore away from Aurora. He found Isaac by the companionway, the captain's gaze also captured by the picture she made at the prow.

"And she'll be another girl yet, when we arrive at Mirage. I'll see to that personally." Angered, Vashon rang for Benny. When the boy arrived, he snapped, "Escort Miss Dayne to her cabin. This crew needs to get their minds and all other parts of their bodies back on the sailing of this ship."

"Aye, sir!" Benny moved as fast as he could to the fo'c'sle. Vashon watched as he approached, the boy's gait becoming more tentative with every step. Finally Benny paused several steps away as if unsure about his welcome. But when Aurora turned and saw him, her entire face lit up in a warm smile and Vashon's face hardened even more, as if he begrudged Benny his welcome.

Encouraged, Benny spoke. It was obvious his words angered her, but she didn't misdirect her fury at him. Instead she looked straight at its source, the man who stood on the quarterdeck, answering her every furious glare with one of his own.

"Tell Vashon that I'll not be cooped up in my cabin all day," Aurora said to Benny. "That should stir him sufficiently." She ended this statement with a goading glance at Vashon. She smiled when his annoyance showed on his handsome face.

"I'm not sure you should do that, miss," Benny warned. "He's in a foul mood. We're two days from Mirage and he's anxious to be home."

"What will he do, Benny? Keelhaul me?" She lifted her brow.

"I don't want to speculate on what he might do, miss."

She was just about to give him an answer when she suddenly noticed something was missing. "Why, Benny," she exclaimed, "wherever is Koonga?"

Benny let out a shaky sigh. "She's done taken ill, miss. I had to leave her in my cabin today."

"Goodness, what's wrong?"

"Don't know, miss." Benny's face suddenly revealed his worry. "She wouldn't eat nothing yesterday, and this morning she was curled up in a little ball. Not moving." The boy's voice broke.

"Oh, Benny." On impulse Aurora threw her arms around him and hugged him. Benny looked rather shocked, but his need for comfort seemed to outweigh his self-consciousness.

"Will you take me to her?" Aurora asked when they parted. "Perhaps I can see what's wrong."

"But, miss, Vashon said you were to—"

"A curse on Vashon!" she said vehemently. "First and foremost, we must see if we can help your little friend."

"No, miss. Vashon won't like it."

"I shall not go to my cabin willingly, Benny. Are you prepared to drag me there?"

"No, miss." Benny sent a wary glance in the direction of the quarterdeck.

"Take me to your cabin, then. We'll see to Koonga, and if Vashon doesn't like it, then I shall be most happy to butt horns with him."

"All right, miss." He relented. "I'd be obliged if you could care for Koonga. I'm right worried about her." His voice quavered.

"I'll do everything I can." Aurora took his arm. He helped her descend the companionway and they disappeared inside the deckhouse, not once paying attention to the wrathful green glare of the man on the quarterdeck.

"Where are they going?" Vashon snapped to Isaac, his gaze riveted to the deckhouse.

"Perhaps she wanted to take tea with Flossie."

"Did you see her hug him? What's going on between those two . . . ?"

Isaac chuckled and finished charting their course. "Is that jealousy I hear in your voice, Vashon, or am I going deaf now?"

"Don't be absurd. Benny's a lad, hardly seventeen."

Isaac looked as if he couldn't help himself. A mischievous glint appeared in his eyes and he added, "Of course. Little Aurora's only about nineteen. Much too old for him. Oh, but they're probably just friendly-like. You know—"

Vashon slammed his hand on the railing. "She blatantly disobeyed me by going to Flossie's cabin."

"Well, then, perhaps she's not with Flossie."

Vashon whipped around. "What do you mean?"

"Nothing, nothing, Vashon." Isaac looked about ready to burst. "Perhaps Benny and she are taking a stroll on the gundeck. She does like the boy, you know. It wouldn't be impossible that she just wanted to spend a moment with him."

"I'll tell her whose company to like!"

"You can't beat her into liking you, Vashon."

Vashon stiffened. His voice turned cold. "I don't care who she likes, or hates, for that matter. I just want her submission."

"Well, it seems clear to me you aren't getting it this way. You two get along as well as thunder and lightning."

"Then she'd better expect a little rain today." Vashon swung down the companionway and strode toward the deckhouse.

"Oh, the poor little darling," Aurora cooed softly as she looked down at Koonga shivering upon a paltry bundle of soiled rags. The little monkey stared up at her with such soulful eyes, Aurora was beside herself. She felt as if she were back at the Home, tending to a sick babe.

"Get me some weak tea, Benny," she directed. "And a little bit of hardtack. We'll see if we can't get something into this tiny wretched creature."

Benny nodded and Aurora picked up Koonga, letting the rags fall away.

"Do you need anything else, miss?" he asked.

Aurora cradled Koonga to her bosom. The little monkey trembled like a Quaker.

"All we need now is a blanket," she said, cooing softly to her charge.

Outside, Vashon was just passing by Benny's closed cabin door. He stopped dead when he heard Aurora's strange request for a blanket.

"Will this one do?"

Vashon looked at Benny's door. Again he heard Aurora's voice.

"Yes, that one's perfect. Isn't it, my darling? My dear little sweetheart?"

"Don't we need something more?" he heard Benny ask. "I've heard sometimes that bleeding—"

"Oh, no, don't even think about that now. Let's take our time with this. This should get much further along before we need to consider that happening." Her voice softened. "This is really very simple, Benny. You needn't be afraid. Something like this can occur anytime. It's beyond your control. Just be gentle with your hands and soft with your voice and I know you'll be well rewarded for it."

Vashon's eyes opened wide. He looked as if he'd just been punched. "Don't be afraid now," he heard Aurora coo. "I've been taught well. You can trust me. There, that's it. Yes, yes, that's it—"

Vashon burst into the cabin like a madman. Aurora and Benny looked up. Benny was holding Koonga wrapped in a blanket like a proud father showing off his newborn.

"Do you always make such a spectacle of yourself, Vashon?" Aurora asked coolly.

"What's going on in here? I heard—" Vashon stopped himself short as if he suddenly realized how ridiculous his thoughts were.

"Koonga is ill, sir," Benny said. "The miss here said she could tend to her. I'm sorry I disobeyed. Sir," he added helplessly.

Vashon looked down at the monkey shivering in Benny's arms. He closed his eyes, and it was clear he thought himself all kinds of a fool. "Take Miss Dayne to her own cabin and let her care for the monkey there. It's not . . . quite the thing for her to be in your cabin, Benny."

"Oh, what shocking hypocrisy," Aurora began, feeling as if she could have slapped him right in front of Benny. She looked Vashon straight in the eye, and a lesser man would have fled from the cabin with his tail between his legs.

"Take her to her quarters, Benny," Vashon ordered impatiently.

"Aye, sir. Right away, sir." Benny handed Koonga to Aurora and led her out the hatch. All the while she stared daggers at Vashon.

Benny deposited Aurora and Koonga in her cabin and promptly went to get the tea and hardtack. When he returned, Aurora coaxed Koonga to take a spoonful of the tea. She hardly noticed in the warm Caribbean heat that Benny had rolled up his sleeves, until she looked up and saw his knobby elbows pop out while he broke the hardtack.

She was, of course, taken aback by the black-stained skin at his joint. Not that she'd never seen that before; on the contrary, at the Home more boys than not had soot irreversibly ground into their knees and elbows and feet. The Home had always taken in more than its share of abused chimney sweeps' apprentices. She was just surprised to find one on the *Seabravery.*

"You were a climbing boy, weren't you, Benny?" she asked softly.

Benny looked down at his elbows and hastily rolled down his sleeves. He blushed and Aurora was suddenly struck by what a handsome fellow he was.

"You worked in Spitalfields?" she asked gently.

"No, miss. Bristol. That's where Vashon picked me up."

"How old were you?"

"Ten, miss. My mum died when I was three. That's when I began climbing."

"I see." She quickly averted her gaze, not wanting Benny to see the pity in her eyes.

Of all the cruel businesses, being a sweep's apprentice was the most abhorrent. A boy was forced to climb those narrow chimneys—naked, of course, so that he would not catch his clothes on fire from all the burning soot clogging the airflow—only to find himself trapped in a black, choking labyrinth of tunnels. If he did as he was told, he nearly suffocated from the lack of air; if he should by chance want to retreat, his master urged him higher by the pins stuck into the soles of his feet. Adding to this that the average age of a climbing boy was under six— the smaller the better, "Small boys for small flues" being a common sweeps' advertisement—she could think of no more deplorable institution. It broke her heart that dear Benny had ever been subjected to it.

"It weren't so bad, miss," Benny said. "Vashon put me out to sea. I've been on this ship nigh six years now."

She didn't want to feel admiration for Vashon, but in spite of herself she found it admirable that he'd helped Benny. Not wanting to belabor the thought, however, she quickly said, "It's only right that someone saved you, Benny. You're such a hard worker, Vashon couldn't ask for more."

Benny blushed again. She was completely charmed.

"I hope Vashon ain't too mad at me because of Koonga," he finally said.

"No, no! I shall speak to him on your behalf if you like."

"Thank you, miss." Suddenly shy, he hobbled to the door.

But before he left, Aurora couldn't squelch her curiosity any longer. Chastising herself for being so shockingly forward, she asked, "Did you lose your leg when you were a sweep then, Benny?"

"No, miss," he answered, appearing not at all bothered by her question. "I was twelve when my leg came off."

"I see," she said, unwilling to probe further.

"Vashon had it done."

She gasped. That was not the answer she had expected. "Why—why would he . . . ? I can't imagine . . ." she stuttered, tripping over her words. Her horror only increased when she saw how uncomfortable she was making Benny. She stumbled all over herself, trying to smooth things over. "But, of course, this is none of my business. I should never have asked, Benny, I'm sorry. I only meant to—"

Suddenly a terrible thought occurred to her. It was so terrible she couldn't even think it, but it persisted until it rose like an ugly specter, unable to be vanquished until she spoke the horrible words.

"He didn't do it as some sort of punishment, did he, Benny?" she asked, terrified. "I mean, I cannot believe Vashon would do such a thing, especially to an innocent child, but since we all know he's a pirate and pirates do such terrble deeds—"

"Oh, no, miss. My leg was full of sooty warts."

She looked at him. Her expression turned from pain to disbelief. She'd never heard of any child surviving that evil. Sooty warts were a common sweep's malady, and once the growths started on a boy, she'd never heard of a way to cure him.

"What a miracle you survived," she whispered.

"Yes, miss. That's what Doc Sovens said. He didn't want to cut off my leg. He'd taken me for crowbait already, but Vashon made him do it."

"You must have been terrified. Only twelve, were you? Such a brave little man to believe in Vashon so much." Tears sprang to her eyes.

"Yes, miss," he said quietly. "It's easy to believe in Vashon."

"Is it?" She hid the bitterness in her eyes.

"Aye, miss. When he visited me the morning my leg was to come off, he pulled up to my bedside with a bottle of rum. He poured me a glass, treating me just like I was a fellow man. We drank that whole bottle and I don't remember nothing. Doc Sovens even said Vashon had to hold me down on that table. But I don't remember. Too much rum. And you know, miss, I think he planned it that way. He got me stinking drunk so's I wouldn't remember a thing."

"He was right to do it," she said, her voice trembling with emotion for the boy.

"That's why it's easy to believe in Vashon. He always does the right thing."

Not always! she wanted to shout, pointing to her kidnapping and her seduction. But when she looked into Benny's expressive blue eyes, she knew she couldn't malign Vashon. If nothing else had been made clear by this entire conversation, it was that Benny's faith was absolute. He wouldn't believe her.

"Thank you for being so candid, Benny," she said, "It was cheeky of me to pry like that. I hope you'll forgive me."

He blushed again, then nodded. "If you'll just take care of Koonga, I'd be most obliged, miss."

She looked down at Koonga. The monkey's chills had ceased, and it was now fast asleep in her arms like a babe at its mother's breast.

A smile touched her lips. A terribly homely babe, she couldn't help thinking. "She'll be all right," she assured him. "She just needs a little care."

"Thank you, miss." Benny gave her a shy smile, then nodded his head.

She watched him go, her mind still on the picture of him and Vashon guzzling down a bottle of rum, doing it just so poor Benny, then only twelve, wouldn't remember the rest of that terrible day. It was a very different picture of Vashon. She'd seen Vashon fight and kill and . . . unbidden the memory of the night at the governor's mansion came back to her with heart-stopping clarity . . . yes, she'd even seen him make love. But experiencing those facets of his character had only made her want to fight him harder. She wanted her relationship with him to be about as pleasant as a fist slamming into a brick wall. She hated him.

Yet the picture of Vashon making Benny drink himself to oblivion touched her where she didn't want to be touched. She despised the feeling more than she despised him. Yet as much as she hated this man who fought and killed and seduced, she couldn't reconcile it with the picture of the man with Benny.

Because that was a man she could love.

MIRAGE

> . . . a spot inexpressively beautiful.
> —Bryan Edwards:
> *The History of*
> *the British Colonies*
> *in the West Indies (1793)*

19

"We're two weeks from Bermuda." Asher's words were nervous yet anticipatory.

Peterborough looked behind him and found Asher standing on the deck of the *Merry Magdalene*. Dismissing him, he turned back to stare at the endless sea. "We should be there by now," he snarled.

"Are you unhappy with our choice of ship? I thought you liked her." Asher walked around to stand next to him along the rail. "After all," he said, rubbing his hand along the polished teak, "the *Magdalene*'s swift and expertly handled. Better still, her crew's as ruthless as a vulture after carrion."

"That stupid captain is positive he can find Mirage." Peterborough scowled. His brilliant green eyes searched the horizon as if Mirage would just appear if he looked hard enough.

"He'll find it. We've oiled him with enough gold—he doesn't dare fail."

Peterborough hardly seemed to listen. He just looked out to the horizon like a man obsessed. "He's out there," he said almost to himself. "I can just feel him closing in on the Star. I can feel this noose tightening around my neck."

"*The Chronicles* could be wrong, you know. Even if Vashon does get it, the curse, if you will, may just not work. It doesn't pay to be superstitious."

"What do you know, fool?" Peterborough snapped.

Asher pursed his lips, obviously annoyed. "Not much, I'm afraid. Look at me, I'm on a damned pirate ship in the middle of the Atlantic and I haven't eaten anything better than lard and hardtack for days!"

"You've dined well on another course, if the noises from your cabin last night are any indication." Peterborough narrowed his eyes.

"Perhaps, but fool that I am, I still entertain thoughts of another meal altogether."

The viscount looked down at the soft male hand on his shoulder. A jaded smile curved his lips. "Your infatuations are beginning to interfere with our chase, Asher. You know, Worthington's demise can be duplicated in a much more creative manner. A night spent with me and I guarantee you'll be glad I shot you." He gave Asher a promising look. Asher blanched and removed his hand. He quit the deck before Peterborough could make another comment.

Alone, Aurora looked across the prow to the crystal blue sea below. The mountainous islands of St. Kitts and Nevis were straight ahead, and though it appeared that there were only two distinct islands, she'd learned that there were really three. What looked like another misted emerald peak on St. Kitts was actually the notorious isle of Mirage.

She'd run out of time. When they arrived at Mirage, Vashon was going to be merciless. He would get her rhyme eventually, just as he'd gotten her. He would win simply because he was the more driven.

Now it was time for her to act. To make sure he did not win. She'd lain awake all night thinking about her plan and the sacrifice she would have to make. But she could see no other way. She had to safeguard her position.

Placing her fingers at her throat, she touched the lizard locket. As long as she had it, there was the strongest of possibilities that it would find its way into Vashon's hands. He already suspected she had the rhyme somewhere. It was only a matter of time before he realized the pendant she wore was in fact a locket with the second verse engraved within it. When he had her locket, he would have taken everything from her; her body, her honor, and her past.

She slipped the necklace over her head and pulled where it caught in a tangle of her hair. Holding it tight, she closed her eyes and thought how bitterly she would miss it. It was the last thread that held her to her father. As a child, it was the only thing truly hers, not given to her by the charity of others. Now it would be lost, gone forever in a graveyard of brilliant blue. But she had to do it. If she had any self-respect left at all, she must.

She held the locket out over the railing. The sun glinted off the emeralds onto the sea below. She closed her eyes. She couldn't look. It broke her heart that she had to do it, but there was no other choice. She'd rather lose it to the sea than lose it to Vashon.

She let go. That very second her wrist was taken in a clamp and an iron-hard body moved next to her, leaning over the rail. Her eyes flew open and she heard the delicate tinkle of her gold chain as Vashon lunged to catch it. She leaned over the rail, praying that he hadn't retrieved it, but then he straightened, and in his hand, dangling precariously from its gold rope, was her locket.

He stared at her, his gaze punishing and angry. They did not exchange words. He moved his focus to her locket and studied it for a long moment, as if not sure why it was of such value. But soon his thumb found the catch and it sprang open, the second verse there for all to see.

"I hate you," she whispered when he took her arm.

"Obviously," he answered, leading her back to her cabin.

Aurora would always remember the colors of Mirage. They were simple colors—green, blue, yellow, and black—but on Mirage they left her breathless.

The green was the palms that spiked over the island's mountain until they disappeared in a sultry mist of clouds. The blue was the Caribbean that surrounded the island in as many clear tints as there were angels in heaven. The yellow was the sun that bathed everything in a translucent wash of light. And lastly there was black, the glittering jewels of volcanic sand that made up the beaches of this paradise.

Vashon fit in well. Mirage seemed to loosen him, to take the edge off his hard, dark character. When he was on his island, he seemed more savage yet more relaxed. He'd shed his meager attempt at looking civilized and wore only a pair of loose white trousers, not bothering to hide the dragon at all. His servants dressed better. But as his body grew more tan beneath Mirage's sun, he seemed more apt to smile and his laughter was heard more often.

She didn't see him often. After the *Seabravery* made port, she was taken to his house, Dragonard, and kept locked in an apartment, well away from Flossie and even from Benny. A series of anonymous servants waited on her, and her only friend in the world was Koonga, who was allowed to stay with her while the little monkey recuperated from her strange malady.

Dragonard was huge, perched on a hill overlooking a glorious, glittering black sand beach. It was shaped in a cross with large hexagonal rooms at the four ends. Her apartment contained one of the hexagonal bedrooms, and one night, across the green velvet lawn, she saw that Vashon possessed the next one over.

Her apartment, like the house, was beautiful. The furniture, from the high melon-shaped headboard of her four-poster bed to the stylish réca-mier near the window, was hewn from dark Santo Domingan mahog-any. The upholstery was sun-bleached linen, the bed-curtains a pristine undyed muslin. The only color was from the five windows that reached from the floor to the high ceiling, and though the louvers were always kept locked, she could see flame-colored hibiscus blooming just beyond the house, lush green banana trees swaying in the relentless breeze, and always the sea that colored everything turquoise, even distant Nevis.

But no prison, no matter how exquisite, is loved by its prisoner, and Aurora often paced the bricked floor, as impatient as Koonga with her captivity. This morning was like the others. Another breathtaking day outside and no way to escape and see it. Ever since Vashon took posses-sion of her locket, he had placed her under tight restraint. She had ranted and raved to be set free, but he turned a deaf ear to her. Now that she'd lost, she couldn't understand why he wouldn't let her and Flossie go, but she suspected he was having difficulty deciphering the rhyme. She knew it by heart, but still it made no sense to her. Seeping into her more and more each day was the horrible dread that he was not going to set them free until the Star of Aran was right in his palm.

Still not resigned to her fate, she tried desperately to think of an escape. But Mirage was little better than the *Seabravery*. St. Kitts and Nevis were not far off, but it would take a ship to get her there. Mean-while Mirage was Vashon's kingdom. There were no houses on the island except his and those of his servants. There was no town, no one to appeal to for help. Just as on the *Seabravery*, all she could do, day after day, was wait.

Koonga, now almost completely recovered, was getting into one bit of mischief after another in the apartment, and though Aurora felt obliged to contain her, she was grateful for at least that bit of entertain-ment. Presently the little monkey was atop her bed, fascinated by the spring of the linen canopy. Aurora was just pinning the frayed edges of her apron-front when a knock came at the door. She expected it to be her breakfast, but when servant after servant entered, their arms full of gowns, she gasped. Even Koonga stopped bouncing.

"What is this, Tsing?" she asked the elderly Chinese who ran Vashon's household. Tsingtsin bowed and explained.

"Missa, dless fo ru."

"For me?" she exclaimed. "How is this possible?"

"Vashon take flom ship. Wrong ago."

"So he stole these dresses?"

Tsingtsin bowed. "Yes, missa."

"Then I don't want them!"

"Missa! Missa!" Tsingtsin went after her as she stomped to the window. "Ru need gown, missa!"

"Tell him I don't want them!" she fumed. Koonga, sensing her mistress's sudden change in mood, began screaming and jumped on the canopy.

"Missa—" Tsingtsin began, but she interrupted him.

"I don't want his plunder. Take it back," she demanded.

"*Prunda . . .*" Tsingtsin repeated as if it were a new word to him.

"Yes, plunder," she said. "And I want no part of it." She walked to another window, Tsingtsin still following.

"But missa, Vashon not want ru go naked!"

"I promise you, he does!"

She shot him a scathing glance. Tsingtsin's eyes widened, suddenly getting her meaning.

"Is diremma!" he exclaimed.

"Yes, that's right. Is big dilemma!" she repeated, staring off at Nevis, the horizon crisp in the morning air.

"I talk to Vashon. He tell me what to do with gown."

Aurora spun around. "Yes, but you tell him that *I* told him what he can do with his dresses!"

"I tehr him ru tehr him . . . ?" Tsingtsin shook his head. "Yes, missa. I tehr him." He bowed, taking his army of servants with him and leaving the gowns.

She didn't want to look at the gowns. For about an hour she was able to occupy herself with plaiting her hair. But when her toilet was completed and Koonga was fed the last banana in the fruit bowl, the day stretched before her like a great yawning void. In her mind the pile of dresses seemed to grow and grow until there was no avoiding them.

Disgusted, she picked one up. Of course, it was exquisite. Pirates didn't steal shiploads of drab linen gowns like the ones she wore at the Home. The gown was made of aqua silk brocaded with gold threads around the hemline and sleeves. It looked like some sort of court gown, for it was faultlessly constructed with a small train and two gold tassels hanging at the short puffed sleeves.

She walked to the cheval mirror—the one topped with the gold laurel wreath surrounding the distinct *N*, the one she strongly suspected had once belonged to the Empress Josephine—and put the gown to her shoulders.

If the mirror didn't lie, the gown would look wonderful on her. The gold threads highlighted the apricot tint of her skin, and the aqua exactly matched her eyes.

She held out the gown and looked at it longingly. She couldn't wear it. That was completely against everything she believed was right. But still she couldn't help running her hand over the luxurious fabric. She was wearing the nicest gown she had ever owned and it looked like a pauper's rags compared to the beauty in her hands.

But if she had nothing else, she had her principles. So she laid the gown on her bed and waited for Tsingtsin to come and take it away.

"Vashon! Vashon!" From the kitchen buildings Tsingtsin shouted to Vashon as he cantered into the stable yard and dismounted. The bay stallion he rode was shiny, not from sweat but from seawater, as Vashon always took his morning ride along the beaches.

"Vashon!" Tsingtsin cried out again, this time running to the stables, his long graying braid streaming behind him. "Missa no rike gown! Missa no rike gown! Big diremma!"

"She doesn't, does she?" he commented, handing the reins to a black stableboy.

"She say me take back gown!"

Vashon almost smiled.

"Is big diremma! Me no take back gown without ru say so!"

"I'll take care of this matter." Vashon took the linen towel handed to him by another servant. He wiped the sea spray from his face and chest.

"Ru talk to missa?" Tsingtsin asked.

"I'll talk to her," he answered.

"She say one thing."

"What is that?"

Tsingtsin paused as if the message was complicated and he needed great care to get it right. "She say me say she say where ru can put gown." He smiled and bowed, pleased that he'd gotten it right.

Vashon burst out laughing. He gazed at the end of the house where Aurora's apartments were. Through the slats he could see the silhouette of a girl in blue standing at the window, looking at him.

"Ru want me take back gown now?"

Vashon chuckled. "Thank you, Tsing, but I think I'll let her deliver her next message personally." He tossed the towel back to the servant and strode into the house.

Aurora nearly jumped out of her skin when the door to her chamber burst open. Vashon stood on the threshold, half naked, his white trousers streaked with sand, his chest startlingly bronzed in contrast. Though she'd seen him through her windows carrying on his daily life, she'd not yet spoken to him since arriving at his house. The smile on his face nearly frightened her to death.

"What do you want?" she said bravely.

"Just a quick visit," he answered, his voice mocking. "Tsing tells me you don't like your dresses."

"Who did you kill to get them, I wonder?" she said, knowing full well she was provoking him.

"Nothing like that." He smiled a cheerless smile. "The ship was sailing from Italy. I took possession of those dresses on the direct orders of the Regent."

"You did no such thing."

He lifted one jet eyebrow. "Ah, but I did. The Regent thought Princess Caroline was on that ship and secretly ordered her sunk. I, of course, knew Caroline was still at the Villa d'Este. But being the man I am, I did as the Regent paid me to do. However, I did allow the crew to jump overboard, and you'll be pleased to know nary a drop of blood was shed."

"I don't believe you for a minute." She laughed. "Your stories contradict each other. Does the Regent want you hanged or knighted? It sounds as if the prince slaps you with one hand and pays you with another. And who in the world would believe the Regent trying to kill the Princess of Wales!"

He paused, putting a hand to his chest as if astonished that she questioned him. "Why, the Regent would, I gather. The next time I'm at Nero's Hotel playing a little faro or *jeu d'enfer*, I'll have him write me a note. I'm sure he'll do it if I tell him it's for *you*."

"How lovely," she commented sarcastically. "And I suppose next you're going to tell me these are the princess's gowns?"

"Well, not quite. Apparently, after our dear Caroline's debauched appearance in Genoa, the prince ordered the gowns for her and had them sent to Lake Como. But the princess refused them. I'm sure you can see why."

"No, I'm sorry. I cannot," she said, growing annoyed at his ridiculous story.

"They're a little tasteful for her, don't you think? And, I might add, a shade too small."

She stared at him. She'd heard that the princess was . . . stout. And that her taste inclined more to that of a circus performer than of a future queen. But his story was ridiculous! Impossible! He was leading her on, and when she fell for it, he'd make her a laughingstock.

"I will never believe you. I'm sorry." Nervously she watched him walk toward her.

"What you're saying is that you'd rather believe I took those gowns from a burning ship." He sauntered right up to her. She backed away.

"Took them off a ship I had plundered, after ravishing the fine lady who owned them and taking her as my captive." He followed her, movement for movement. She went toward the escritoire; he went toward the escritoire. She backed to the bed; he pushed forward. She scrambled for the door. He caught her.

He laughed. "You have it on your mind that I've stolen and killed to get everything I own." He dragged her to the bed. She fought him like a cat. "You think that's what I am, don't you?" He lifted her by the waist so she could look him dead in the eye. "You think I'm some kind of monster. A murdering, ravishing, thieving pirate, gorged with plunder and wading in blood."

Still panting from her struggles, she met his eye. Despite how she had promised to block it out of her mind, the memory of the night on Grand Talimen came back to her with painful clarity. Being so near to him, she remembered again how she had held him, close, desperately close. And she remembered his touch, rough yet responsive to her every desire. When she recalled how badly she had wanted him, her anger exploded.

"That's exactly what you are!" she cried.

He abruptly threw her onto the pile of dresses on her bed. Drowning in the silks and satins, she soon surfaced, only to find his hands on her, holding her down again. Her gaze clashed with his, and a dark smile played on his lips.

"Then let's play pirate, shall we?" he whispered.

Her struggles began in earnest then, but his mouth suddenly lowered and he tried to kiss her.

"You vowed never to touch me again," she said, her eyes glittering with anger.

"But, love, let's learn our lessons, shall we? Pirates lie."
She gasped. "You're just doing this to intimidate me!"

"And it's working." He smiled and his onslaught began anew. Her head turned from side to side to avoid his lips, and all the while he laughed like a madman above her. Furious, she lurched to one side and grabbed his wrist with her teeth.

He snatched his hand back in pain and she found the opening she'd hoped for. She sat up and pushed him away, angered that he'd caused her to behave like such a savage.

"You deserved that," she snapped.

"Perhaps." He stood and reached out a hand to help her off the bed. She stared at it, unsure of whether to trust him. But the look in his eye assured her that he would play the gentleman.

Taking it, she clambered down from the feather mattress. She stood and smoothed her rumpled skirt, making a nervous display of checking that her straight pins were still modestly intact. When she looked up, she was relieved to see him just watching her, his face serious and sober. It was clear he meant to keep his promise of leaving her alone and she was glad. She certainly didn't want any more tussles with him, she told herself. Yet she was surprised by the strange hollowness that filled her when she went to walk away from him.

"Wait." He took her arm.

She turned.

"Your hair . . . it's . . . mussed." He reached out his hand and smoothed her tumbled hair off her face. His fingers lingered on a stray curl, and before she could stop herself, her hand went up and touched his.

They stared at each other for a wretched amount of time, and she was held captive by the reluctance and yearning warring in his eyes. She knew he wanted to kiss her, and she knew he was fighting it as much as she was. She opened her mouth to speak, but before the words were out, his lips met with hers in a sultry, hot kiss.

She wanted to pull back. The only hold he had on her was with his lips, but suddenly, with just that simple touch, he possessed the power to drain the strength from her limbs and the will from her soul. Her heart pounded in her chest as he slowly lowered her back onto the bed. She moaned, hating him and wanting him in the same breath; he only deepened the kiss, announcing his triumph over her and his defeat over himself.

She didn't know how to fight him. The fire in his kiss only made her succumb. Despising herself, she let her lips part and he gladly entered. His tongue rode like velvet against her teeth, and she tasted the salt on his lips from his morning swim. He groaned and she felt his hand ride up her torso, hungering for the weight of her breast. A voice inside her told her to escape and deny all that she was feeling, but another voice, a voice shockingly more forward, said something else altogether. With a slight sob, she waited for his touch, needing it yet fearing it, for it held a mighty power to hurt her. She stiffened with the battle being fought within her, and somehow this seemed to affect him. His head snapped up and he looked down at her as she lay in the swirling mountain of dresses. He closed his eyes for a moment as if he couldn't believe where he was, then abruptly got off her.

She scrambled to a sitting position and watched as he took a moment to adjust the crotch of his trousers. When she realized why he needed to do this, she quickly looked away and felt the warmth of a blush stain her cheeks.

"Don't ever do that again," she choked out, not daring to remove her gaze from the thick spiral post of the bed. "Not ever again, do you hear me?"

He stiffly eased himself down on the récamier and let his legs splay out in front of him. "Don't flatter yourself."

"I don't flatter myself!" She tore her gaze back to him, then glared when she saw his smile. "What do you want?" she snapped. "Why have you come here today? Not because of the dresses, I wager."

He didn't answer.

A smug expression appeared on her face. "You can't figure out the rhyme, can you?"

"No."

She took some satisfaction in his honesty. "And you want my help with it, don't you? You think I might be able to help you decipher it?"

He refused to answer.

She was delighted. "I want you to know that I vow to keep any and all information regarding the Star to myself. However, if it makes you feel better, Vashon, I haven't figured out the rhyme yet either." She smirked. "But if I do, let me assure you, *you* will be the last to know."

He smiled wryly. "Touché."

Koonga suddenly popped her head over the canopy. Aurora looked up, and the little monkey jumped into her arms.

"She's better, I see," he commented.

"Yes. She just needed a little mothering."

"Well, perhaps you'd better tell me more about this foul rhyme or I'll keep you here so long that monkey'll be all you ever mother."

She riveted her gaze to him. "That long?" She lifted one brow tauntingly.

"A hundred years at least," he answered.

"And what about Flossie?"

"Flossie will be going home the end of this week. I've another ship at the docks here, the *Resolute*. She'll be sailing for St. George's as soon as she is fit."

Aurora caught her lower lips with her teeth. Already her mind was whirling trying to devise a plan to board the *Resolute* as a stowaway. She had to escape or risk growing as mad as he was.

"Thinking of going along, are we?" He eyed her lazily. "Well, to be sure, little wren, you will not be going. I still need you to tell me how to find the Star."

"You should let me leave on the *Resolute*, Vashon. I'll never tell you anything now. And you've no way to force me. You've already done . . . your worst."

He smiled. "There are other ways of doing that, some not nearly so gentle. Shall we test their effect on you?"

She quickly looked away. His crudeness never failed to shock her.

He exhaled a long, impatient sigh. "I can see you still plan on fighting me, and I'll give you this, *Aurore*, you fight well. But," he said emphatically, "I *will* not let you win. I *will* find this Star. And you *will* help me. So why not tell me as much as you know? If you do, I'll see you cozy in St. George's by wintertime."

"I don't aid common, plundering pirates." She still didn't look at him.

"Fine." He rose and walked to the door. Then, as if he'd forgotten something, he paused. "Just to warn you, I've decided to let you out for dinner this evening. I haven't decided on which method to use to get you talking, so in the interim, we will dine and you will ease my ennui, so to speak. Wear . . ." He looked at the mound of dresses on her bed. "Wear that one," he said, pointing to the aqua-and-gold gown on top.

"I won't," she snapped back, bristling at his tone. "All those gowns are cut indecently low. I won't wear them."

His gaze slid to her bosom, then rose to her face. "Well, since you've more than proven to me that you've no need for bust improvers, I suppose it's time to prove it to the world. Be ready at eight. If you're not dressed by the time I come for you, not only will I not consider your departure on the *Resolute*, but I'll dress you myself with my own two hands. An endeavor, I assure you, I look forward to with the utmost relish."

He smirked and glanced once more at her heaving bosom. After he left, she picked up the closest thing next to her bed, a costly French opaline table bell, and threw it at the closed door.

20

The good people of Hamilton stared in trepidation at the ship the *Merry Magdalene* when it docked in the Bermudas. The pirate Fontien was well known to the traders, for many of them had lost precious cargo when he "detained" their vessels in the middle of the Atlantic. Standing on the ship's prow, Peterborough was pleased by the nervous expressions of the stevedores as they covertly watched the ship at the dockhouse. He wanted people afraid. That had always been the best way to conduct business.

"How do you like these Bermudas?" Asher asked, joining him at the prow. "Personally, I like them," he added conversationally. "I think I'd like to find a nice beach somewhere and lie there so long my bones turn to dust. Some place quiet, mind you. Some place that doesn't rock one way just when you're about to move the other."

Peterborough wearily closed his eyes. "If we get the Star, you can settle here. How long before Mirage?"

"The captain says another few weeks. What, are we already growing tired of this madcap chase?"

"When we encounter Vashon, I hope you're still able to produce that biting wit."

Asher turned away, perturbed but growing used to the viscount's verbal jabs. He stared at the busy docks, but the viscount seemed to hold an unresistable attraction, and his gaze soon turned back to Peterborough.

Peterborough looked tired. His eyes weren't as brilliant, and there was a day's growth of beard on his jaw as if he'd been too preoccupied to shave. But there was still that edge of obsession that permeated his character and made him so frightening. Looking at him now, with his hair blowing wildly and his face tense with anger, Asher wondered if he'd ever seen it so strong.

The viscount turned his head and caught him staring. Asher quickly averted his eyes.

"I'd ask what you want, Asher, but it's all too clearly written on your face."

Asher grew flustered. "I came to tell you that Azzedine sent this along before we sailed. I forgot to give it to you." He nervously pulled out his purse and reached deep inside. He took out a locket of dark red-gilt hair. "Do you think it's hers?" he asked as he handed it to Peterborough.

The viscount touched it as if it were spun gold. "Michael Dayne had this unusual shade of hair," he whispered. "By God, Vashon does have her. I swear if we make it to Mirage, he'll not see her again."

Asher stared at him. Then shrugged as if humoring a madman.

At five minutes before eight o'clock a knock sounded at the door. Aurora opened it expecting it to be Vashon, but Tsingtsin stood there, a series of leather boxes in his hand.

"Missa, Vashon say give ru this." He handed her the boxes. With a polite bow, he left, but not before locking the doors securely behind him.

Resigned that there was to be no end to the irritations this evening, she tumbled the boxes onto her bed and made the final adjustments to her attire.

She wore the aqua-and-gold gown. Not that she hadn't thought long and hard about not wearing it. On the contrary, she'd spent all afternoon pacing the cool bricked floor of her apartment considering that very thing. But in the end, she decided not to test him tonight. There was always the slim chance he might let her leave with Flossie on the *Resolute*, and, too, she believed him all too well when he said he'd come dress her personally. She was not about to give him the pleasure.

She looked into the cheval mirror and tried again to pull up the low square neckline. Never in her life had she thought to go out in public dressed as she was now. The gown was perfect in length, but most definitely—and, she suspected, intentionally—lacking material in the corsage. She nearly spilled out the front.

Biting her lower lip, she studied her reflection. The aqua gown was a masterpiece. From the gold brocaded acanthus leaves on the hemline to the coral-colored satin lining of the train, she had never seen a gown as magnificent as this one. Vashon's ridiculous story that it had been made for the Princess of Wales was absurd, and yet the gown was truly worthy of royalty.

She went to the récamier and slipped on a pair of white satin straights. Finishing the attire with petal-soft kid gloves that reached to her elbows, she almost forgot about the black leather boxes until she spied them lying on the bed like ink spots on the muslin coverlet.

She walked to her bed and opened them. They held a treasure chest of jewels. In box after box were gold diadems, ruby tiaras, and long *sautoir* chains that held tiny gold perfume flasks. In dismay, she opened custom-made cases of jewels made *en suite*, some in diamonds, some in emeralds, some in pearls. There were elaborate parures in the Grecian taste, the Egyptian taste and the Etruscan taste, and even a *ferronière*, a large pearl pendant meant to be suspended over the forehead from gold chains that encircled the top of the head.

If she could escape Mirage with one tenth of the jewels on her coverlet, she'd be rich beyond her wildest dreams.

Her musings abruptly ceased with the commanding knock on her door. She heard the key in the lock, and then Vashon stood in her doorway. There was no other way to describe him but stunningly handsome. As always, his dress was restrained. He wore black pantaloons, immaculately polished Hessian boots, a white marcella waistcoat, and a neckcloth, fashionably high, tied in an austere India knot. With his black hair tamed in a queue, she would never have guessed him to be a pirate, except for the telltale silver hoop in his left ear.

It was obvious he was pleased to see her in the aqua gown. But she'd expected him to look rather smug and triumphant, as if he'd won another battle, so she was not prepared to see the utterly dazzled glint in his eye as he stared at her. His gaze couldn't seem to follow her closely enough as she walked toward him, away from the jewel-laden bed.

"You certainly do the gown justice, love," he said in a low voice.

It was the first time she blushed without his having insulted her. His casual endearment was hard for her to accept too. The word "love" sounded so seductive when it came from his lips. It left her with a feeling that was strange—and not entirely unpleasant.

"Shall we go? I'd hoped after dinner you might allow me a visit with Flossie," she said.

"Already anxious to be gone from my company?"

She answered him with one rapier-sharp glance. He burst out laughing.

"All right, I'll take you to Flossie. *After* dinner. But where are your jewels, princess? Didn't you like any that I sent you?"

He led her by the hand to the bed. Perusing the booty, he picked up several heavy pieces and thrust them into her hands.

"No, really, Vashon, I can't wear these . . ." she began helplessly. He dressed her with a gold arm cuff inlaid with shell pink cameos.

"How about these?" He held up two diamond ear pendants of prodigious length.

"No, no. I can't wear those."

He looked down at her virgin ear lobes and tossed the earrings to the bed.

"Vashon, really, I don't want to wear these jewels."

"I didn't murder anyone for them, if that's what's on your mind," he said rather defensively.

"I'll believe that you didn't," she answered. "Nonetheless, these things aren't for me. I'll wear my father's locket, but I'd appear foolish wearing these jewels. Even more foolish than I appear in this dress." She was embarrassed having to look at him after that pitiful confession, but it was true. She was no Princess of Wales, she was a girl who had grown up a pauper in an orphanage, and she was uncomfortable thinking of herself adorned with heavy, priceless jewels.

He studied her with that piercing emerald gaze. Then his eyes turned to the bed. He dropped the handful of jewels. "These trinkets must seem very vulgar to you."

He didn't let her answer. She thought he was angry, but then he did the strangest thing. He caressed her cheek and slowly released the pins from her hair. She was too shocked to even attempt to stop him and soon her tresses cascaded down her back like a shiny gold-red waterfall.

"They suddenly seem very vulgar to me," he whispered before laying a soft kiss upon her lips. His expression changed. His gaze dipped to her gown and he smiled a slow, wry grin. "But say you'll wear the gowns, Aurora. Ah, but you do look fetching. . . ."

She thought he might kiss her again, but he surprised her once more. He abruptly stepped aside and allowed her to pass. In amazement she turned to stare at him, but he only bowed, motioning her to exit her luxurious jail.

They dined on the marble terrace overlooking Dragonard's glorious black beach. The sun sank slowly behind the mists of Mount Soufrière, gilding Nevis in the foreground. Encircling them were two magnificent flamboyant trees, their scarlet blossoms as vivid as a flame. As they ate, the Caribbean sank into a deep turquoise twilight while a sensuous, caressing wind hinted of the scent of oranges. The breeze touched Aurora's hair and swept it enticingly off her brow. She watched Vashon from across the table. The meal, of course, was extraordinary: salads made with breadfruit and papaw, guinea fowl from the market in Basseterre, and lastly another carved pineapple, a delicacy of which Aurora could never get enough.

Vashon speared a piece with his fork. Perversely, she watched as he brought it to his mouth, then ripped it cleanly away with his teeth. For some reason, she found the whole display oddly titillating, and she watched him again, this time closely—noting how his strong jaw moved as he chewed, studying the way his lips clamped the fork, thinking about the taste of the pineapple as it squirted into his mouth.

"Enjoying yourself?"

Her gaze shot to the rest of his face. He was smiling as if he had been reading her mind.

Disturbed, she jerked her attention back to her meal, but her thoughts weren't easily diverted. Unbidden, the picture of him eating that piece of pineapple came back to her again with acute detail. She closed her eyes as if that would erase the image, but still she could see him, his tongue meeting it, his teeth crushing it.

She mentally shook herself. What kind of depravity possessed her? What was wrong with her that she couldn't rid herself of this strange fascination? Anxiously she took a bite of her own pineapple. She chewed it absently until she chanced to look at him and found that he had stopped eating, and was now staring at her with equal intensity.

She swallowed and nearly choked. Her stomach felt as though it had dropped two feet.

"What on earth are you looking at?" she gasped.

He put his elbows on the table and rested his chin on his fist. He wasn't smiling, but from the glitter of his eyes, he should have been. "I was looking at the same thing you were."

"I was not looking at you in that manner!" She tried to dismiss him, but nonetheless the glint in his eye was making her supremely uncomfortable.

"No, I assure you, you were staring at me just this way."

"I—I really don't know what you're talking about," she said, growing flustered.

"Ah, I see. Well, let me make myself plain." He lifted his fork to her, a chunk of dripping pineapple on its tip. In a rather obscene manner, he pulled it off with his tongue and sucked it into his mouth. "Is that what you were watching with such rapture?"

Even though she was blushing, she did her best to look indignant. "Ridiculous! Where is the rapture in watching another person eat fruit?"

He smiled. And what a wicked smile it was. "Believe me, I could find all kinds of rapture." He removed a piece of fruit from the fruit bowl and laid it before her like a dueling pistol. "Why don't we start with you eating this banana?"

"I haven't the vaguest idea what you're talking about."

"All the more delightful."

She gave him several distrustful glances, as if he'd suddenly gone out of his mind. She didn't understand what he was implying and it bothered her.

He smiled and took another piece of pineapple into his mouth. When he caught her eyeing him, he wiggled his tongue at her.

Disgusted with his prurient behavior, she steeled herself and went back to her dinner. He wasn't making any sense, and she wasn't going to stoop to try and understand him. The best thing she could do was to ignore him.

But that wasn't easy. Especially when his eyes seemed to linger on her every motion, from raising the fork to her mouth to her very last swallow. This went on for hours, it seemed, until she couldn't take it anymore. Abruptly she dropped her fork on her plate and stood.

"Flossie must be wondering where I am by now. I must go," she announced.

"Flossie doesn't know you're coming. Sit down." His gaze commanded her back to her chair. Slowly she complied.

"You haven't finished." He looked at her half-filled plate.

She pushed it away. "I most certainly have."

"All right. Sit there and watch, then." He continued eating, all the while appearing as if he was immensely enjoying himself, quite at her expense.

She refused to give him any further satisfaction. Ignoring him, she turned her attention to the sea that now encircled them like a dark blue band.

When he finished, Tsing delivered him a brandy and her a cup of tea. She wondered when this interminable dinner was going to end, but just as she did so, he brought something out of the pocket of his waistcoat and tossed it to her.

She looked down. Her locket glittered against the pristine white of the table linen. Slowly she picked it up.

"Are you giving this back?" she asked.

"I shouldn't. After all, it's rightfully mine."

"Is that how you rationalize everything you steal?"

He smiled and sipped his brandy. "You know, Aurora, I'd have never believed you could be so obstinate."

"It's been all my pleasure, believe me."

"But now I'm in a quandary. I need you to help me decipher this rhyme. So do I coax you with honey, or"—he studied the amber liquid in his tumbler—"do I crush you like a blossom beneath my boot?"

She stared at him, her eyes darkening with worry.

"Is big dilemma," he whispered to her, quoting Tsingtsin.

She tore her gaze away. Though the night was warm and she was in an abominably ornate gown for the climate, she suddenly felt a chill. How could she be so comfortable in this man's presence when he was such a blackguard? It would never cease to amaze her. Sometimes she almost forgot who he was and what he stood for. Then he would do something or say something that would remind her all too clearly of the terrible power within his grasp.

"How do you think to crush me?" she asked.

"I won't enjoy it," he stated and for once she believed him. But because he wouldn't enjoy it didn't mean he wouldn't do it.

"If you think to repeat more nights like the one we had in Grand Talimen, then you're sadly mistaken," she whispered defiantly.

He met her gaze. "If that night upset you, I could make it look like a stroll through Kensington Gardens."

She utterly believed him. "You're threatening me with rape?"

"I don't want to threaten you at all. I just want that emerald and the means to it. Unfortunately, you are the means."

She was silent.

He leaned back in his chair and crossed his arms across his broad chest. "What are you thinking of, Aurora? Are you thinking of an agreement? Are you bargaining with me in that head of yours?"

She shot him an angry glance. "Certainly not," she assured him haughtily. "Even a simpleton knows enough not to bargain with Old Nick."

Her superior air made him laugh. "Yes, I can see you, our tight-laced Miss Dayne, making a pact with Satan." He took another sip of brandy and chuckled. His mood seemed to improve. "You know, I've never told you this, Aurora, but you remind me of someone. Someone I once held in very high regard."

"And who was that?" she asked smartly. He couldn't be comparing her to Blackbeard and that was the only person she could think of whom he would hold in high regard.

"Her name was Miss Prendergast. Old Prinny, we called her. She was my governess—a staunch disciplinarian for whom I caused much grief." He smiled with the remembrance. "But despite all the toads beneath her coverlet and all the spiders in her desk, she persisted to the very end trying to reform me. In truth, we were quite famous friends. I think she must have secretly craved the wildness in me, and, I suppose I craved her tolerance of me—for which she seemed to have an endless supply." A moment passed and his thoughts seemed very far away, as if he were recalling it all with vivid detail. But then his eyes came back to her and he said, "Yes, you definitely remind me of her, Aurora. She was quite the little tight-laced spinster too. Even my mother thought so. I can remember her once telling our cook that it would probably take another Resurrection to get that sour look off Miss Prinny's face." He laughed.

Aurora, on the other hand, was speechless. Of all the shocking things he had ever said to her, this was by far the most shocking. She was so completely taken aback, she didn't even think that he had just compared her to an elderly sour-faced spinster.

A governess? This black-haired wild savage sitting before her had once had a governess? She could hardly fathom it. "I really don't understand . . . how could you . . . possibly have had . . . ?"

"Have had a life other than the one I lead now?" he finished for her. She nodded.

His jaw hardened; his eyes turned cold. "Well, I did. I had a very civilized life once. Until I turned thirteen."

"What happened then?" she whispered.

A grim smile touched his lips. "Have you ever heard of the term 'white slavery'?"

She was hardly able to utter the next logical question. "What does that have to do with you?"

He pinned her with his gaze and looked reluctant to speak, as if what he had to say was too ugly to even put into words. "I, my love, was a highly sought-after commodity."

Sickened, she lowered her gaze. She felt worse than when she'd heard his story about the man who'd attacked him in the Casbah. In spite of the genteel atmosphere Mrs. Bluefield had tried to create in the Home, the social ills of the times intruded. By running an orphanage, they were helplessly familiar with the many ways the world abused its children. She knew just what Vashon was describing.

Against her will, her eyes filled with tears. Was this quest for the Star revenge for what had happened to him as a child? Had Peterborough been the one responsible?

All the questions weren't answered, yet she finally believed she understood one facet of him now. That pampered boy of thirteen he'd spoken of, the one who'd had a governess, a mother, and even a cook, had suddenly been thrust into Algiers not only to fight for his very life over a tuppence worth of silver, but to fight for the most basic dignity as well. She could see how that would harden that boy toward cruelty. And how that could create the man who was sitting across from her now.

She looked up and their eyes met. Though all her good sense said to stay uninvolved, she couldn't hide the ache she felt for him. When he saw her face, his expression grew colder and her ache only grew more deep.

"My story moves you, doesn't it?" he asked, seeming to take a dispassionate interest in her tears.

"I would be less of a person if it didn't," she answered.

His stare became more intense. "You've a rare and gentle spirit, Aurora. It frightens me how vulnerable that makes you."

"Vulnerable?"

He glanced away. Slowly he said, "I want that emerald. I—" He paused. "I really think I might do anything to get it. I implore you. Cooperate. Tell me whatever might help. Assist me. Don't . . . test me."

Again that chill ran down her spine. No matter how her heart bled for that thirteen-year-old boy, she had to remember he was gone now and the dragon was there in his stead.

She wiped away her tears with her napkin. "You do a disservice to yourself, threatening me this way."

"I don't want to threaten you. I just want that emerald."

"For revenge on this man Peterborough? Did he send you to the Casbah?"

He didn't answer.

She took a deep breath. "Contrary to what they say, Vashon, revenge reaps little satisfaction."

He should have lashed out at her, but he hid his fury with admirable grace. He simply sat there and stared at his brandy. "All right, Aurora. I've noted your position." He met her gaze; his voice turned deadly. "But revenge reaps great satisfaction when that's all you have. And I *will* have revenge on Peterborough."

"Then I pity you, sir."

Their eyes held for one long moment. Silently Vashon stood. He helped her to her feet, and they left for Flossie's rooms.

Aurora's reunion with Flossie was heartening. If anything, the widow looked even better than the last time Aurora had seen her. There was a brilliant color to Flossie's cheeks, and for the first time the widow had donned a white jaconet collar to break the black of her weeds. In truth, Aurora thought Flossie looked wonderful, and for some reason she had the strange suspicion that the widow's good spirits could be directly linked to Isaac.

Their visit was brief. Aurora was uncomfortable talking to Flossie while Vashon was around, and she guessed Flossie felt the same from all the hesitating looks the widow gave Vashon while he sat mutely in a nearby chair. When they'd said all they could say in their present company, Flossie hugged her and whispered in her ear that she would never leave Mirage without her. Aurora only nodded helplessly, all the while thinking that Flossie would probably have no choice.

When they left and were walking through Dragonard's breezy passages, Aurora couldn't stop herself from thinking about the *Resolute*. The ship was way off Mirage, but she just couldn't devise a plan to get herself on it when it sailed. She was so caught up in her thoughts that she didn't hear Vashon until he grabbed her hand and pulled her to his chest.

"What has you so preoccupied you cannot even look at me when I speak?" he teased. He lifted a tress of her hair and began rubbing it in his hand.

"When you send Flossie back to St. George's, you realize she'll go straight to the authorities about you," she informed him.

He gave the curl a playful tug. "Yes, I suspect she'll do just that."

"Then you're not afraid?"

"Do you think they'll believe her?"

She paused. "She's well respected there. Why wouldn't they believe her?"

He smiled. "It's a rather fantastic story, don't you think? A woman of her age mistakenly kidnapped to an island that on most maps doesn't even exist. Even if they wanted to believe her, why should they go to the trouble of sailing hundreds of miles across the Atlantic just to confront a man who had the courtesy, when he saw he'd made an error, to deposit her safely back home?"

"She'll tell them about me. They'll go to the trouble to try and rescue me."

"Will they?" He raised one maddening eyebrow.

"Why shouldn't they? I'm an innocent victim."

"Not so innocent anymore."

Her gaze riveted to his for one sizzling second, then she looked away, unwilling to give him the satisfaction of an answer.

His hand continued caressing her curl. "Let me tell you what will happen. Flossie will inform the St. George's authorities that you were kidnapped. The first thing they'll do before they even think of sailing to Mirage will be to contact the London authorities to see if anyone has reported a young girl named Aurora Dayne missing. And what will they find? Does John Phipps miss you yet, little wren?"

Her expression turned worried. Absentmindedly she took the curl away from him. No, no one was looking for her. That had been the brilliance of his plan all along.

"Shall I show you Mirage tomorrow?" he asked softly.

"If you show me your island, might I not escape then?"

"Ah, but I love the thrill of the chase."

He tried to take her curl again. Piqued, she stepped from his arms. She realized they were right by her doors.

"I want you to breakfast with me. I'll send Tsing to fetch you," he said.

"I shall have my breakfast in my prison, thank you." She opened the double doors. Immediately Koonga ran to the threshold and leaped into her arms.

"Aurora."

She turned to look at him.

"You shall have breakfast with your jailer. Be ready when Tsing comes." To her surprise, he flipped her the key to her door. The heavy brass felt delicious in her palm. She looked up at him, her eyes questioning. He gave her a sardonic smile. "Go anywhere you like. Every road leads back to here. Besides, I'd like to see you after a night spent in the mangroves. We have creatures here in paradise even Old Nick might not have thought of."

"We'll see about that," she answered tartly, already feeling powerful now that she possessed the key to her room. She wasn't going to let him scare her. Her head was suddenly buzzing with plans. She could go to the docks and stow away. Or she could implore a servant to help her. With this key there were so many possibilities.

"Sleep well then, my love." He smirked, then watched her retire to her room.

When the doors were closed, she sank back against the door panels. Koonga chattered away, as if she'd missed her, but Aurora didn't pay much attention. She had too much to think about. Tumbling the monkey onto her bedstead, she sat down on the edge of the mattress. Koonga began to scream, so Aurora went to take her back in her arms. That was when she saw it: a brilliant red creature over a foot in length barreling toward her from the bedpillows.

She let out a bloodcurdling scream and grabbed Koonga. She had run to the corner when Vashon burst into her room, a murderous expression frozen on his face.

"Over there!" she sobbed, pointing to her now empty bed.

He looked around. It was obvious whatever she was pointing at he couldn't find.

"My God, do something! It was horrible!"

"*It?*" he asked, suddenly calm.

"It was the most wicked—looking—thing." She hiccoughed and hugged Koonga to her breast.

"Well, what did it look like?" he asked.

"It was a huge red snake! With legs!"

He suddenly laughed.

"Whatever is so funny?" she demanded. "It almost killed me!"

"Well, if it's any consolation, it didn't. Are you stung?"

She shook her head.

"The monkey?" He nodded to Koonga.

"I—I don't think so," she stuttered. "Good God, what was that thing?"

"A centipede. Quite poisonous. One sting won't kill you. However, if you get into a nest of them—"

"A nest! You mean I have a nest of those creatures in my room?"

"Probably not. They come from outside. Did I remember to give you the key to your room? I don't want to keep you in your room if you feel like wandering."

She looked at him and promptly burst into tears. Her behavior was unforgivably foolish, but that horrifying centipede had made her hysterical. She was still shaking from the whole ordeal.

"Come now," he soothed, going to her. "It's not that bad. I'm sure if you decide to roam the island tonight, you'll only find a few centipedes. Just stay away from the cane."

"You wretch! You probably put that thing in my bed! That's why you gave me the key!"

He laughed. "I didn't put it there. You were bound to see one eventually, but I must say, its appearance was certainly fortuitous." He took Koonga from her arms and put her on a nearby table. Then he gathered Aurora into his embrace. "If you're so terrified to sleep here tonight, you can come with me." He placed a heated kiss on her neck.

She broke free and cursed him. "Only you would take advantage of a situation like this! You have absolutely no character! Seducing me when I've just been through the most—" She choked. The centipede suddenly dashed from underneath the bed and once again raced in her direction. She screamed and ran back to Vashon, all but climbing onto his chest. He chuckled and lifted her up by the waist. The centipede sped to the window and in a flash disappeared through the open louvers.

She buried her head against his shoulder and quaked. She felt as if she'd just seen a glimpse of Hades. If she never again saw another one of those creatures, it would be too soon.

Lifting her legs, he carried her to the récamier. He placed her gently against the scroll end and brushed the hair out of her eyes. "Don't be frightened," he whispered, gazing at her pale features.

"I don't want to stay here, Vashon. Take me someplace where they don't have those things," she begged.

He looked as if he were contemplating taking her away all right, but when her imploring, fearful gaze locked with his, he seemed to change his mind. "I'd have to take you off the island for that, love."

"Then take me," she begged.

He ran his knuckles along the cream of her cheek, not answering.

"Take me away," she whispered.

"To my room then?"

"Do you get those creatures in your room?"

The corner of his lips lifted in a wry smile. "I'd be lying if I said nay."

She stared at him, unable to stop the emotion from roiling within her. She babbled, "Thank you for coming to rescue me. I was so frightened."

"Come along, you've been through worse. Old Robert surely frightened you." He laughed. "But maybe he didn't frighten you as much as all this."

"I'd never seen a creature like that before," she gasped.

"You'll probably not see another anytime soon."

She shivered despite the balmy evening.

Hesitating, he pressed her head against his chest and held her. Just being in his embrace made her feel less frightened. She stayed there for a long time, her hand clutching his shirt, her face buried in his muscular shoulder, and she probably could have left much sooner, but his arms felt so strong around her, his cheek so right against her hair that she couldn't pull away.

When she'd been in his arms too long, she reluctantly pulled back and glanced at him. Their eyes met and a look passed between them, a dark, agonizing look, as if they had both discovered something that neither one of them wanted to accept.

"Shall you come to my chambers after all?" he whispered, his face taut with unexpressed emotion.

She closed her eyes, shocked by the wild desire that was suddenly coursing through her veins. "And if I do?" she answered pitifully, her voice full of remorse, "Will anything good come of it?"

He stared at her, unable to answer. There was no good answer and they both knew it.

He extricated her from his arms and stiffly rose from the récamier. It was insanity, but she wanted to pull him back and beg him to stay. She curled her fingers into her palms to keep her from clutching at him.

"Tsing will fetch you in the morning. Will you be all right until then?" he asked coolly.

She nodded, her heart twisting in her chest.

"If you're frightened, my rooms are down the passage."

She nodded again, but truly, how she was feeling now, she was more frightened to run to his room in the middle of the night than she was of the centipedes.

"I'll see you at eight."

He left, and Aurora wondered how the world could turn so mad as to make her fall in love with a pirate.

21

When Aurora arrived on the terrace for breakfast, she brought Koonga with her. The monkey was certainly no complement to Aurora's new day dress, a fine sprigged muslin, but Aurora, worried about leaving her in the room after last night's scare, decided to take her with her.

Vashon did not seem pleased. He was in his usual heathen attire, bare-chested with only the thin white baggy trousers keeping his modesty, yet today he wore his hair untied and it blew back freely in the wind, making him appear even more savage than usual. As she took her seat at the pristinely laid table, his stare was as heavy as a manacle, but she ignored it, settling Koonga on the iron seat next to her.

"That creature's certainly well enough to go back to its keeper," he commented coolly.

"Yes, but I haven't seen Benny." She tucked a napkin into the collar of Koonga's livery to keep it clean, then handed her a silver bowl of bright yellow-orange mango slices.

"The way you mother her, I wonder if you want to give her back."

She overlooked his brittle tone. "Koonga's been good company for me. I think it's only natural that I should grow attached to her."

"She's a pitiful substitute for a child, is what she is. I've never seen a woman so anxious for a babe as you."

Her temper suddenly flared. She glanced at him. "The way you snipe, sir, I wonder if you're not jealous."

"Good God, you must be joking," he snorted.

She took a deep breath and refused to let him anger her. He seemed to want to bicker. She'd rarely seen him in such a mood. She wondered if it had anything to do with that awkward moment before they parted last night.

Deciding that the best way to deal with his poor disposition was to ignore it, she went to take her napkin, but stopped. Sitting on top of it was an unpeeled banana. Suddenly she felt her cheeks grow red.

"Hungry?" he asked, the corner of his mouth lifted in a too-innocent smile.

She placed the banana aside and started on her sliced mango as if the banana didn't exist. Of course, he was quite unchivalrous to torment her about her staring last evening, but then, she didn't expect him to behave any better. The worst thing about the banana, though, was that she couldn't understand what he was teasing her about, and she had the horrid suspicion that when she did, she was going to be even more embarrassed than she was right now.

Koonga, soon bored with her mango, began chattering and climbing the iron chair. Aurora tried to get her to sit still, but it was impossible. The napkin around the monkey's neck was quickly studied, tasted, and just as quickly thrown away. With no other diversion, Koonga climbed the table, and before Aurora could stop her, she set herself atop Vashon's shoulder and began picking through the thick locks of his hair.

The expression on Vashon's face was priceless. Aurora couldn't help herself, and she broke into peals of laughter.

"What on earth is she looking for?" he snapped, all the while keeping his eye on the monkey.

"I suspect she's looking for nits."

"Nits!" Vashon stood and Koonga tumbled off, catching herself on the back of his chair. "If I have any nits, that damned creature just gave them to me!"

Aurora laughed again and refrained from assuring him that Koonga didn't have lice. She took another bit of mango, suddenly feeling avenged for the banana.

When things had settled down again and Koonga was picking the scarlet blossoms off the flamboyant tree, Vashon said dryly, "If we're through with the amusements, I thought I'd show you the *soufrière* today. We've a nice little path to the top." His eyes lifted to the mist-covered emerald mountain above them.

"I'd rather you show me around the harbor," she countered, her voice bitingly sweet.

"Perhaps give you a tour of the *Resolute*?" He lifted one black eyebrow.

"That would be fascinating."

"Showing you my ships, love, won't get one out of the harbor with you aboard."

"One never knows." She sipped her tea.

"Tomorrow we might go down to the beach below Dragonard," he continued. "If you're brave enough, I might even coax you out into the bay to see the fish. They're every bit as beautiful as Mirage's flowers."

"I told you I don't know how to swim."

"Well, I invite you to cling to me if you find yourself drowning."

She looked up at him, a censorious expression on her face. He smiled and began his breakfast again. She could see it was going to be a long day.

"If you're a worthy man at all, Isaac Corbeil, you will find a way to allow Aurora on the *Resolute* when she sails." After Flossie announced this, she paced the jute carpet and glared at Isaac.

"I shall not betray Vashon, not even for a woman." Isaac glared back, looking quite uncomfortable as he perched on a delicately proportioned settee in Flossie's apartments.

"I don't understand this blind loyalty to Vashon—why, you were ready to trade his life quite readily in Grand Talimen."

"You know that was just a sham for Ignatio. I've explained that a million times." He shifted his weight. "Listen, why don't you just sit here next to me. Perhaps a buss or two on the cheek will calm you down."

Flossie froze. She clutched her chest in a rather melodramatic gesture. "And that's another thing! No more kisses! I asked you here to discuss Aurora, not to be kissed. You've already done that five times since our dinner at the governor's, and I will no longer permit it to continue."

"I rather thought you liked it—"

"Good heavens, certainly not!" she gasped. "It's the most improper, shocking display—"

"C'mon Flossie, I thought you rather liked me chasing you around the table the other day." Isaac grinned wolfishly.

"I did not!" If she'd had her black parasol, she would have bopped him on the head. "No lady of quality would have enjoyed that."

"Well, perhaps no lady of quality would. But you did. I heard you giggling the entire way around."

"Whatever are you implying? That I'm not a lady?" Her voice rose several notes.

"You look like a lady to me, Flossie, but what do I know? I haven't met too many ladies in my lifetime." He shrugged.

"Well, I am one, I assure you of that! And I do not enjoy this vulgar pursuit of yours!" She began pacing again. "So with that out of our way, I implore you to reconsider helping poor Aurora. That man will eat her alive! You can see that! I shudder to think what might happen to the child if left too long in Vashon's clutches."

"It seems to me she's holding up pretty well against him. If anything, he's the one who's falling. I wouldn't have ever thought Vashon could fall in love, and if you'd told me a year ago he'd succumb to some spinsterish little schoolteacher, I'd've thought you were plumb out of your mind. But now, the way he talks about her, I can see she's under his skin, all right."

"However does he talk about her?" Flossie asked incredulously.

"With the most passionate contempt I've ever heard him utter."

Flossie looked confused.

Isaac shook his head. "Believe me, Flo, I've never seen anything like it. Vashon has had his share of women, and there was one in Paris one summer—you know, one of the fallen nobility, a pretty thing with blond curls and an angelic expression—that I really thought he was growing attached to. But nothing came of it. He tired of her soon enough, and moved on. His relationships invariably begin with lust and end with boredom. But somehow Aurora hasn't produced that reaction. I have to admit I thought he'd change after he jumped her in Grand Talimen, but now he's almost frothing at the mouth with contempt for her."

"We will not speak of *that*," she admonished, her plump cheeks turning a pretty pink.

He looked at her, pacing back and forth in front of him. Suddenly he flung his arms around her and pulled her onto the settee. "Grand idea, Flo, let's quit talking."

"Unhand me, sir!" She wriggled on top of him; the settee groaned with their generous weight.

"C'mon, just a bit of sugar." He tried to kiss her; she tried to slap him. "That's right," he said playfully, fending off her blows. "I like my lassies with a little fire."

"This must stop, Captain!" she gasped after he found her lips for one short kiss. "We're not a couple of lovesick children! Recover your dignity at once!"

"Flo, listen here, now. No one'll be the wiser," he said when she finally beat him back.

"I'll be the wiser," she said, heaving herself to her feet without assistance. "And I'm a widow, if you'd take your hands off me long enough to see the color of my garb."

"Your man Lindstrom's been gone for years and years, Flossie. Don't you ever get lonely?"

She patted her face with a handkerchief embroidered in black. "Of course I get lonely. But I remind you I'm not a young girl. I'm not some trollop ready to go rolling in the hay."

"I know that, Flo. But . . . well . . . truth to tell, I'm nigh on to three score years, and I'd feel damn foolish rolling with either a trollop or a young girl."

"Oh, good heavens, such language!" She fanned herself with her handkerchief.

"C'mon. Old Lindstrom'd understand."

"I won't even consider such a thing with a man who is not my husband."

"Well, I'm ship's captain, and as far as the law's concerned, I've just pronounced us married." He stood.

Flossie backed against the large drum table centered in the room and fanned herself furiously with the limp linen square. "You have lost your mind, Isaac. What are you thinking of?"

Isaac's gaze wandered to the adjoining room where Flossie's bedstead stood draped in bleached muslin. "Well, I have to say I'm thinking the worst," he admitted.

"Oh, my heavens . . . I can't believe you even mean this."

He walked toward her and slowly untied his shirt, revealing a bear-like covering of gray hair on his chest. "Flossie, now, come along. You know it's been a long time for both of us. How many children did you say you had? Thirteen? Fourteen? Enough to know you damn well liked it."

"Oh, dear Lord!" Flossie swooned, placing the back of her hand on her brow and staggering backward.

Isaac caught her wide waist in the crook of his arm. His hand rose to her delicate white lace collar. "You know I've been meaning to tell you, you look quite fetching in this. It's a damned improvement to these weeds." His eyes moved lower. "And how do these weeds come off? Are there laces here, or—"

"No, no, no!" She pulled away, blushing.

"You don't expect not to take your clothes off, do you?"

Flossie just stood there, wide-eyed and flame-red.

"Well, I'll take mine off first, then when you see I'm not ashamed, we'll coax you out of yours."

"You are an unforgivably bold man, Isaac Corbeil. Your kisses were wicked enough, but this, *this!*" she said in a strangled voice.

"I'm sorry. I just don't know how to do it any other way."

"I couldn't possibly!"

"Oh, you can. Here, how about a buss to loosen you up?" He grabbed for her, but she trotted away.

"Isaac, enough of this insanity. We're too old for this!"

"Well, I know I'm not too old, and if you'd just let me have, pardon me, my way with you, you may see you're not too old either."

Flossie gasped. "Such talk! Such wickedness! Where are those smelling salts?"

"You don't need those smelling salts, and you aren't going to faint, either." He grabbed her and this time held fast. He gave her a long, passionate kiss, and when they parted Flossie looked as if she'd been drugged.

"Are you ready?" he whispered.

She sounded a weak protest. He took her hand and beckoned her into the bedroom.

The doors were closed behind them. It was quiet for a moment, then Flossie exclaimed, "No, no, Isaac! You can't corner me into doing this! And put your shirt back on!"

Two heavy thuds sounded and Flossie burst out, "Why are you taking off your boots?"

Isaac could be heard chuckling, then Flossie cried out, "Not the belt!"

The large pewter buckle hit the floorboards with a clunk.

There were more feverish denials and shocked exclamations emanating from the bedroom—until Isaac's last garment slid to the floor. Upon that, Flossie gasped, "Good heavens, Isaac. You're a Jew!"

Then silence reigned.

For at least an hour.

22

Aurora lay in her bed that night unable to sleep, her thoughts filled with images of Mirage. The day had been surprisingly wonderful. Vashon had taken her all around the island in the kittereen, introducing her to some of the island's workers: tall, muscular divers who offered armfuls of conch and spiny lobster, old men on donkeys who wove baskets from the mangrove, and pretty dark girls adorned with scarlet-and-black jumbie beads, whom Aurora was envious to see going back and forth from the kitchens *en chemise.*

Afterward Vashon showed her Monkey Hill, where Benny had found Koonga. The animals had been brought to St. Kitts a century earlier to be the pets of a wealthy planter. He told her the story of how the monkeys were occasionally hunted on St. Kitts. When too many of the creatures had become harassed by the hunters, they would then suddenly appear on Mirage, firing the speculation that there was an underground passage running between the two islands.

Next he took her to the *soufrière* atop the mountain, the boiling sulphurous pit that had once erupted to create the black beaches. They wandered through the misted jungle at the top, and she knew if she remembered nothing of Mirage in years to come, she'd remember the orchids growing on the manchineel trees, with petals in all the pale hues of yellow, pink, and lavender.

Last, as they headed back to Dragonard, Vashon stopped by a small tree and picked what looked to be, but were not, a handful of small limes. He sat with her on the sand beneath the tree and showed her how to eat them. Popping one genip out of its peel, he put it in her mouth as if it were candy. It was unimaginably delicious and as they sat eating handfuls of them, she had watched him and thought how much he loved Mirage, Mirage that was as wild and awe-inspiring as he was.

But now, as she restlessly tossed in her bed, her thoughts moved to something else, something that had nothing to do with Mirage, or genips, or *soufrières*. Something that nagged at her like an itch that was just beyond her reach. She was thinking about bananas.

Disgusted, she threw back the covers and rose from her bed, hoping to release her pent-up frustration by pacing the floor. But it didn't work. She knew she had to figure out Vashon's little joke or she would never sleep.

That evening they dined on the marble terrace again and when she arrived, just as at breakfast, there was a banana placed atop her napkin. She tried to ignore it, but this only seemed to amuse Vashon further. The entire episode vexed her, and until she knew what he was hinting at, she vowed never to go back to that terrace again.

She went back to her bed and whipped off the covers, making sure there were no centipedes beneath the pillows, then crawled into bed and stared at the blank canopy and thought about bananas.

She remembered the first banana she'd ever seen. They had taken on an entire branch of them in St. George's, and at first she'd thought they were a rather perplexing fruit. She'd tried to eat one with a fork but had found the skin too tough to cut. With a sharp fruit knife, she had finally cut the thing into slices and scooped out the flesh with a spoon. But she vowed never to eat one again, for no matter how much she liked the taste, it was an awful bother to eat.

But one day when Benny was in the galley preparing a passenger's tea, she'd watched Koonga take a banana from the stalk. The way the monkey ate it, the peeling came off as easily as butter sliding off a knife. It was astoundingly simple, and ever since then she'd had no problem with them. Until Vashon's little amusement was born.

She rolled onto her stomach, pulling her long, thick braid out from beneath her. In the striated moonlight from the louvers she spied a silver bowl on the night table brimming with polished fruit, several of them bananas. Irritated, she sat up and examined one.

The banana was really a ridiculously awkward fruit. It lacked the symmetry of an orange or the plumpness of a pear. She peeled back half its skin and almost blushed at how peculiar it looked. In fact, it embarrassed her to no end to even think about the fact that it looked like . . .

She choked.

No, it wasn't possible. Vashon couldn't have been using it as some sort of a metaphor for . . . ? Her cheeks flamed. Good God, what was he thinking of asking her to . . . ? Not in her wildest dreams did she ever imagine a woman might . . .

She choked again.

That had to be why he wanted to watch her.

Was that strangulating sound coming from her?

She looked at the banana and suddenly she was furious. Of all the vile, lascivious, lewd pranks! Her cheeks turned a brighter red, but whether it was from fury, humiliation, mortification, or all three, she wasn't sure. One thing she was sure of: tomorrow, he would pay. She'd reveal him for the licentious beast that he was and show him exactly what she thought of his little joke. With that in mind, she took a vicious bite off the tip of the banana and enjoyed it immensely.

To breakfast the next morning Aurora wore a gown of ivory gauze so sheer, if not for the blush-colored silk chemise beneath it, one might mistakenly believe its undertone to be skin. The corsage was fashionably —even daringly—low, and it clung in seductive splendor to her every curve. Perhaps at any other time she might not have had the courage to wear such a brazen gown.

But not this particular morning.

She walked confidently along the marble tiles to where Vashon sat admiring the view. He was no longer staring at the Caribbean. To her deep satisfaction, his gaze fairly locked on to her thinly draped figure, and he watched her approach with stunned approval.

If she'd really been brave, she thought derisively, she would have bent over him and with one finger, closed his gaping jaw. But this morning he would be getting more of a show than he deserved, so she merely took her seat and blessed him with a most comely smile.

"It's another beautiful day, isn't it? How lucky you are to have Mirage." She leaned her bodice against the table. His wretched emerald gaze went just where she thought it would. It was all she could do not to wrap her arms over her chest and run to her room, but she was too angry to back down now.

She lowered her eyes, and pretended to notice the banana for the first time. She watched him as she ran her finger slowly down the fruit.

His jaw dropped further. If she'd kissed the thing right then and there, he'd have probably died of shock.

She could have stuffed it right up his nose.

He closed his mouth. His eyes lifted. A vague distrust crossed his features. "You're in an oddly cheerful mood."

"And why shouldn't I be?" she asked, making a great display of placing her napkin on her lap.

"No reason," he answered hesitantly.

"I'm famished." Again, this time with excruciating exactness, she ran her finger down the banana. His gaze helplessly followed. "Are you?"

"Am I what?" he asked, his thoughts obviously elsewhere, obviously right where she thought he kept them.

"Famished."

He looked at her, challenging her. He nodded.

She picked up the banana. Slowly, as if she hadn't eaten in days, she peeled back the skin, savoring every rip. Her eyes darted to him and she was pleased by his obvious anticipation. He couldn't know that hers surpassed it. She nervously licked her lips, unaware of how this made her appear. When she looked at him again, he was entranced.

A soft, beckoning smile curved her lips, and her hand reached down to a satin ribbon tied to her dress. She grasped her stork scissors, which were tied to the end of it, and with her gaze never losing hold of his, she opened the tiny embroidery scissors and cut the banana in two.

He nearly jumped out of his seat. Though she couldn't see beneath the table, she had no doubt he'd instinctively clamped his thighs together in terror. Satisfied, she dropped the mutilated banana and stood.

"You wretch," she said, her fury overflowing. She gave him her most vile look, then prepared to stomp off, but instead of the anger she'd expected, he suddenly burst out laughing so hard he nearly fell from his chair. She turned and glared at him, unable to leave while he was so amused.

"How dare you laugh!" she scolded, her hands on her hips. "You should be skulking from my presence like the cur you are!"

"How did you get those scissors back?" he gasped between fits of laughter.

"They're mine. I took them from your desk one day while you were on the quarterdeck with Isaac."

"Well, give them back." Before she knew it, he reached for her. He chuckled and his arm went around her narrow waist, pulling her down on his lap.

"Let me go this instant!" she said, clawing his bare chest.

"So you figured it out. I'm amazed you did it so quickly. I've corrupted you, Aurora."

She colored and stabbed him with an angry gaze. "We will never discuss *that* again."

"Yes, why discuss it when we can do it. . . ."

She groaned and he laughed.

"You really are a swine, aren't you?" she said.

"That was ungentlemanly of me, but then I don't profess to be a gentleman." He smiled. "I admit, I truly didn't think you'd ever figure it out."

"Well, I have, so let me go. I want to have my breakfast." She squirmed; he held tight.

"Here?" His green gaze beckoned.

"Not with you, ever again!" She pulled back, but he kept her where she was. Her hands pressed against his bare chest, and as much as she hated to admit it, the feel of him was hard and fine.

"Are you reconsidering?" he asked, obviously noting her pause.

She glared at him. "Certainly not."

"Can't we call a truce?" His eyes turned to the damaged banana at her place. "After all, you've had your vengeance."

She looked over at the snipped banana. She'd definitely evened the score. When she thought about his expression after she produced those scissors, she almost smiled.

"Come along, have breakfast with me," he said.

"I suppose I might stay . . . if you let me go," she bargained.

He dropped his hold. She climbed off his lap.

"Where are you off to?" he snapped when she began walking away.

"I'm going to change this ridiculous dress."

"No, you're not." He stood and took her by the arm. "I like that gown. In fact, I want to see more of it."

"How odd. I'd have thought you'd want to see less of it." She looked down at the low neckline and added bitingly, "As if that were possible."

He laughed again. "You really are in fine form this morning, love. When did you acquire that scathing tongue?"

"A long time ago. When I was kidnapped by a pirate."

"How terrible . . ." Catching her by surprise, he reached over and grabbed the ribbon on her dress that held her stork scissors. With one sure rip, he took it from her, scissors and all.

"What are you doing?" she exclaimed as he walked to the edge of the terrace.

He flung the scissors far over the edge. "You don't think after the work you made of that banana I'd let you keep them to try them on me, do you?"

"But now I have nothing left," she gasped.

"You've got one thing." He tweaked her locket as he passed to return to his seat. "Ironic as that is, since the locket rightfully belongs to the Viscount Blackwell."

"Peterborough?"

He smiled, not answering.

She stared at him, curiosity getting the better of her. She wanted to ask him about the viscount, but it was clear from his expression that now was not the time. As if to change the course of her thoughts, he motioned for her to take her seat. She looked down and again became self-conscious of her dress. She needed to squelch the urge to tug up her corsage.

"I must change my gown," she insisted.

His gaze flickered over her attire, pausing slightly where the sheath was tied beneath her breasts. "No, leave it on."

She was just about to protest when he admitted, "You don't know how beautiful you look in it, Aurora. Truly beautiful. So I—ask you to leave it on."

His tone surprised her. It was almost respectful.

"Please sit and have breakfast with me." He rose and held out her chair. She was so taken aback by his manners that she found herself complying before she could stop herself.

After Tsingtsin had served, Vashon said, "I have a surprise for you today, little wren."

She glanced at him, still distrustful. "And what would that be this time? An abduction by Charon? A grand tour of Hades? To be honest, Vashon, I don't think I could endure another surprise from you."

He laughed. "Yes, I suppose I have given you a few too many. But this one, I think you'll like." He pushed a small inlaid zebrawood box across the table to her. It was such an elaborate little coffer that she was amazed she hadn't noticed it before.

"This looks too small to be filled with centipedes . . . or do they come in sizes I don't know about?" She raised one eyebrow, taunting him.

"I assure you there are no centipedes in there." He smiled. "Open it."

"Knowing you, I don't dare."

He chuckled. "Open it. It's a present for you."

"But why would you give me a present?"

"Because it's your birthday."

She stared at him, an embarrassed flush staining her cheeks. "It couldn't possibly be my birthday. You know I haven't got a birthday."

"You do now. I declare today your birthday. So open my gift."

She glanced at the box, but she just couldn't bring herself to open it. Looking up, she said, "If it was as simple as all that, I would have given myself a birthday long ago."

"But you can't give yourself one. Someone else must give it to you. And it begins with a gift." He pushed the box closer to her until it was nearly in her lap.

She didn't know what to say. Was he playing some kind of cruel joke on her, callously teasing her about her inauspicious beginnings? Or was he truly being so thoughtful as to give her a birthday because he knew she didn't have one? She bit her lip, looking deep into his eyes for any signs that he was making fun of her. When all she could see was his amusement over her perplexity, she decided to summon her courage and open the box.

With great trepidation she lifted the lid. Expecting all sorts of monsters to come crawling out of it, she was quite surprised to see instead a heavy gold-and-ruby chain nestled in a bed of scarlet satin. When she picked up the chain, she found an ornate brass key dangling on it.

"Pardon its simplicity, *Aurore*," Vashon whispered, "but what does one give a woman too beautiful for jewels?"

She looked up at him, the chain falling over her trembling fingers. In her entire life she couldn't ever recall anyone doing such a thing for her. The chain was certainly lovely, but presenting it to her as a birthday gift was probably the greatest thing she'd ever received. And coming from Vashon—Vashon who had kidnapped her and killed for her, fought with her and made love to her—she could hardly bear the emotion that was suddenly blossoming within her. Again she was reminded of that man who had helped Benny through his trials, that man whom she thought she could love. Now, as she stared across the table at Vashon, she suddenly accepted that he was the man she did love.

Tears helplessly welled in her eyes, and because she didn't want him to see them, she rose to her feet and dashed toward the house. She got halfway across the terrace before he caught up with her.

"What is it?" he asked, grabbing her into his arms. "Have I offended you so much that you must run away? Are you disappointed? Do you think the necklace paltry?"

"No, no, the necklace is too beautiful!" she cried.

"Then what is it that has you in tears?"

She glanced at him and hoped he couldn't see the desperation on her face. He'd done the most despicable things to her, seduced her, abducted her, humiliated her. But prompted by this one gesture, she knew that suddenly and irretrievably, she had fallen in love with him. And she knew, too, that with that came vulnerability, even terror.

"Vashon, why did you do this for me?" she gasped.

"I wouldn't have if I'd thought this would happen." He smiled wryly and touched a tear clinging to her lashes. "It's too easy to move you, love. You're like a child sometimes."

"Well then, I must be your perfect complement, because it's impossible to move you," she said bitterly. She looked at him and knew he wouldn't find favor with her next words. "But yet, I recall you were moved once."

Just as she expected his voice turned rigid and cold. "What happened on Grand Talimen has nothing to do with this. That night, by both our accounts, should never have happened."

She fingered the necklace, hopelessness eating away at her heart. With a sob she said, "As cursed as it is, it hasn't been that easy to forget, and I dare you to say that it has."

"It has," he said tersely.

She looked at him, but he wouldn't meet her gaze. As if trying to change the mood, he took the necklace from her numb hands and fastened it behind her neck.

"I think we should walk on the beach this morning. Are we done with breakfast?"

His fingers were rough against her skin, but still she ached for them. What had she ever done in her pitiful life to deserve this wretched, unwanted desire? Had it been running from John Phipps? Was God punishing her for turning down John's righteous offer by throwing her into Vashon's cold embrace? She looked down at the brass key dangling heavily between her breasts. She was curious about it, but she hadn't the heart to ask him about it now.

"Shall I show you Dragonard's beach?" he said softly.

"Not today," she answered, suddenly feeling ill.

He pulled her into his arms. "Let's forget this, and go down to the beach. I've something to show you."

"I really—"

"Please."

Their gazes met. She moaned and closed her eyes. How perfectly he fit the role of a rogue; though she knew better than to go with him, he dazzled her into compliance.

"All right," she said, knowing herself to be every kind of fool.

The corner of his mouth lifted in a smile. "Good." He escorted her back to the table.

23

Was there really a place as beautiful as Mirage? Or was it all something
she had dreamed, an island she'd created out of longing and imagination? Aurora began to understand more and more why Vashon loved it
so. Mirage's beauty grew every time she explored it. And at times such
as now, as she sat watching Vashon walk on Dragonard's black beach,
she wondered if the island was truly an illusion. If she embraced it too
closely, would she only hold fistfuls of sand?

Vashon left the gentle surf and returned to where she sat by the sea
grape. He walked toward her, glistening with seawater, his black locks
an exotic contrast to his broad sun-bronzed shoulders. Wet, his white
trousers were almost transparent, and as he came nearer she could see
every dark hair on his thighs, and even more, if she'd not had the
discretion to look away. There was one thing about Vashon she knew
only too intimately. No one could ever dispute his manly endowments.

"Come into the water with me," he said, holding out his hand.

She shook her head. "I can't."

"Why not? Are you concerned about your dress?"

"Partly." She tried to remain cool.

"Bother the gown. If you're really that concerned, take it off."

She gasped and looked at him. He never failed to get her attention. "I
certainly will not!"

"Shall I rip it off you? The dress is exquisite but—"

She crossed her arms protectively over her bosom and dared him to
try.

He only laughed.

"Come into the water with me, *Aurore*."

"You know I don't swim. Is this why you asked me here? To drown
me?" She raised one eyebrow.

"Don't think I haven't been tempted." His lips twisted in a wry smile. "But not today. Come along, there's a whole world for you to see out there. Let me show it to you." He pulled her to her feet.

"Vashon," she protested, "it's hardly proper for a lady to bathe in public—"

"Ah, yes, another slap in the face of propriety." He pulled her across the black sand. "You'd best be careful, they may yet show you the door the next time you patronize Almack's."

She laughed, unable to help herself. "Somehow I don't think that difficulty will present itself."

He dragged her to the edge of the surf, but she refused to ruin the costly gown. Finally in frustration he picked her up and carried her into the surf, keeping her skirts clear of the water.

"This is insane!" she said, clinging to his strong, corded neck.

"Look down, do you see them?" he whispered. She tipped her head and peered through the waist-high crystal-clear water. Several large fish, the color of rainbows, slipped through Vashon's legs. She'd never seen anything like them.

"Why, they're lovely. They look just like angels," she whispered in awe.

"Yes, angels."

She put her hand in the water. Another fish, a brilliant cobalt-colored one, flitted up and bumped her palm. Frightened, she snatched it back, then giggled at her folly. She turned to Vashon, but she wasn't prepared for the expression on his face. He was staring at her so intensely, he fairly took her breath away.

"Vashon—" she began, but he didn't let her finish. He lowered her legs until her feet touched the sandy bottom and her dress clung wetly to her hips. Then he pulled her to him and kissed her like a sinner seeking salvation, the doomed begging for redemption. In her mind she thought about fighting, but it would be useless. The way he so violently held her to him, he'd refuse to let her go.

But if she didn't pull away, she didn't succumb either. She was too afraid of him, afraid for the same reasons she was afraid of Mirage. Her entire life she'd feared being left with nothing. Her father had given her fistfuls of nothing when he abandoned her at the Home. And for all John had offered, she knew in time he'd take away the few things she did have: her poems, her Perrault, her locket; he'd immure her in her imagined virtue, and then she'd find herself more alone than she'd ever been, adrift in a desert filled with loneliness in place of sand.

Yet now there was Vashon. And as his lips demanded more and more of her own, she wondered if she took him to her, would he be the one to save her from all the loneliness? It was wrong, she knew that. He offered no family, no neat little cottage, no marriage vows, not even love. Yet what did she really know of any of those things, least of all love? The most she ever knew about love came from Mrs. Bluefield, and as wonderful as her mentor had been, Mrs. Bluefield had always been more generous with guidance and instruction than with affection. In truth, she wanted something she knew nothing about. So why did she want it at all, let alone so desperately?

When they parted, she clung to his embrace, terrified all over again, terrified of losing him, and worse, of never having him. He seemed to indulge her, for he held her and let the water lap against them, and let the exquisite Caribbean seascape melt to oblivion until she felt there was nothing but him. The moment went on for an eternity, yet too, it seemed only a second. To preserve the spell, she slid her arms around his neck and savagely held him to her, her cheek against the pounding of his heart. But she should have known it would be all too fleeting.

"Little wren, what is this?" he said, obviously surprised by her passion.

"Hold me, Vashon," she whispered against his warm, solid chest.

"Since when are you so anxious to have me hold you?" He playfully tugged on her locket.

"You were right, no one ever held me at the Home."

The confession was out before she could stop it and after it was made, she didn't dare look up and watch his reaction. She knew better than to ask things of him, because she couldn't bear to ask them only to see the frost in his eyes, only to feel him pull away. Yet she thought she might snap if he left her now, so she decided upon a rash course of action, unleashing a passion she'd never thought was in her. Her lips turned hungrily to his while her hands clutched him, clinging to his shoulders as if she were drowning.

Brutally he ended the kiss, pulling away as if he'd found himself embroiled in something he hadn't meant to be a part of.

Crumpling, Aurora looked away, out to the cool blue of the Caribbean as if it offered a balm that could soothe her.

"What is it about you?" he whispered harshly. "I feel like I'm mad when I'm around you."

"Is that what this is? Madness?" Tears burned again in her eyes. She was hurt so deeply she was surprised she could even feel hurt anymore. Of course, he was to blame. It hadn't been right for him to kiss her.

And now he hadn't even left her with the grace to feel seduced, especially when she had just so eloquently proved how much she'd wanted
him to hold her and kiss her.

"Yes, this must be madness," he whispered. "You have the uncanny
ability to make me want to kiss you even though I promised myself to
leave you alone."

"So you may break this promise and kiss me, but I may never kiss
you back?" Quietly she wiped a tear from her cheek.

"I want you to kiss me back, but I don't want to see that look on your
face."

"And what is that look?" she asked, crying once more.

"That look that demands to be loved." Angrily he turned and
slammed his hand across the water, making a long splash. "Understand
this, I can never love you, Aurora. There is no place in my life for love."

"Then your life is unworthy of living," she whispered. "But, of
course, by your every action and word you've demonstrated that you
already know that." She began to move away, but he grabbed her arms.

He held her in front of him and said, "Look, it's obvious you don't
know what to make of me, and I certainly don't know what to make of
you. So let's quit this. Good God, I don't even know why I want you.
You're beautiful, I'll admit, but I've had my share of beautiful women
and they've never had me this crazy."

Her face was taut with unexpressed emotion. "It's perfectly clear why
you want me, Vashon. I'm a challenge. A thing to be conquered. You've
never had someone like me before, and when I'm no longer a challenge—"

"But you're not a challenge." His eyes forced her to recall that painful night in Grand Talimen. "I have had you, and though the experience should have cured me, it's only made me want you more."

"Could you love me?"

He stared at her as if she had just uttered a forbidden curse.

Her voice wavered. "The question is not do you love me, nor is it will
you love me. You've made that clear enough." She looked at him and
the tears in her eyes began to fall again. "But could you—?" Her voice
broke with a sob. Bitterly, as if she herself recognized the folly of her
words, she lashed out. "But why am I asking this at all? You've more
than proved you've not the ability to love anyone."

"I'm not the man for you." He shook her. "I can't be. Don't you
understand that?"

"I've no illusions about your character."

"This is out of hand." He tipped her chin up and wiped a tear with his thumb. "The only thing to do is end this right here and now. Tell me"—he forced her gaze to lock with his—"have you any more information about the Star? If you say you don't, Aurora, I'll take you at your word, and you can sail away on the *Resolute* with Flossie."

She looked at him, her heart breaking in two. If she helped him, she would never see him again; if she didn't, this torture would continue until she was completely destroyed. Suddenly she felt as if she were faced with the decision of a quick death or a slow one.

She averted her eyes, too hurt even to answer him.

"Tell me, Aurora. Tell me what you know and you'll be going to St. George's this week."

"I—I'm not sure—" she said, her voice catching.

"What do you mean, you're not sure?"

She shook her head. "I don't know what you want. I don't know what I know."

"Then we'll go back to the house and talk. If you're honest with me, I'll know it. I'll take the information you can give and send you back with Flossie." He took her hand, his face as grave as she had ever seen it.

Woodenly she followed him out of the glittering turquoise surf, and in her grief, she forgot once more to ask him about the key.

24

> An angel from heaven came tumbling down
> And asked the way to Aran
> "I've come to find my long lost Star
> Can you help me with my errand?"
>
> Lizzy Lizard sat and smiled
> And stared across the sea
> "I know the way
> But cannot tell
> So silly, silly me!"

She was finally in the dragon's lair.

Vashon's apartments were done in malachite, black, and gold, and were executed with a richness in which even the Regent would have found himself at home. The antechamber possessed the only fireplace in the entire household, and because it was hardly ever used, it was covered with an enormous Thomas Hope fire screen of swags, rams' heads, and arrows.

Vashon motioned her to a wicked-looking chair with chimera arm supports, and unmindful of her wet skirts, she sat on the chair's costly black silk squab cushion. She watched him as he went to a gilt-and-ebony desk and rolled out a detailed map of the world. It was obvious he planned for her to show him where the emerald was, as if she could just rise and point to the spot. She suddenly knew even if she could do that, she wasn't sure she wanted to.

"Here are the two verses." He handed her a book covered in salmon-and-gold Venetian paper. She looked down and read in his handwriting the verses of the rhyme she knew so well.

"Tell me what you know," he prompted.

She closed the book. "Really, I know so little."

"You know your father's name was Michael Dayne. How do you know that?"

"I remember some things."

"What things?" He forced her gaze to meet his. She quickly looked away.

"Stupid things. All irrelevant. I remember my father taking me once to a ball at Carlton House." She shook her head. "I don't mean we went to the actual ball, of course, but I remember him taking me there when the guests were arriving. We stood in the street and watched as carriage after carriage arrived. The ladies were so beautiful all in their satins, and I remember my father was quite enthralled with the display of jewels." Her voice lowered in shame. "That was when he first taught me the rhyme."

She stood and nervously began pacing. "What might I remember, Vashon? I was too young. These things have no significance."

"Perhaps if we talk enough, there'll be one thing that has significance. Come look at the map." He took her hand and guided her to the table.

She glanced at it, then turned away. "I can't see anything. The rhyme is nonsensical. Nothing signifies."

"Look." He forced her back.

She glanced again, then sighed in despair.

He turned her head. His eyes glittered like the emerald he sought. "For some reason, I seem to feel your heart isn't in this, Aurora. Don't you want to leave on the *Resolute*?"

"Yes, yes, of course I want to leave," she admitted too hastily. Turning back to the map, she made an effort to scan it again, but her gaze wandered.

"Look at the map, Aurora."

"I can't find it, I tell you!" she suddenly burst out. She walked from the table and looked out the louvers to Mount Soufrière. For the first time since she'd been on the island, the peak had lost its luxurious curtain of mist, and without it its jagged summit looked almost skeletal.

"I thought we'd agreed this was the best course. You would tell me all you knew, and I would accept it and find the Star without you." He walked up and stood behind her. "Why am I suddenly finding your cooperation gone?"

She closed her eyes. Why wasn't she cooperating? The *Resolute* was her last grasp at sanity. If she knew what was good for her, she should be doing everything she could to appease this man and be on the ship when it sailed. After all, why was helping Vashon still against her morals? She'd done worse things. That night on Grand Talimen had proved she was as subject to straying as John believed her to be. But now, because of that night, her desire for retaliation had turned as weak as her desire for Vashon had grown strong.

She took a deep breath and faced him. "It's futile, Vashon. I can't help you. I remember too little to help. You've held me all this time for nothing."

"I think not." His eyes narrowed. "In fact, I think you know a great deal more, but for some reason, you've decided not to tell me."

"Why would I do that?" She made an attempt to laugh, but it sounded false even to her.

"I don't know why, especially when you know I'm not a man who likes to play games." He grabbed her arm. In his anger he almost hurt her. "What is it, Aurora? Why are you suddenly silent?"

"I'm not!" She tried to pull away but couldn't.

"Then tell me about your past. Tell me everything."

"There's nothing to tell!"

He grabbed her to him. "Look at me," he demanded, forcing her to stare up at him. When their gazes clashed, he said, "Tell me you're speaking the truth. By all that you hold dear, tell me that you know nothing more."

"I—I—" She looked at him, then looked away, unable to answer.

Upon her refusal she expected a great burst of fury, but as usual Vashon was most dangerous when he was calm.

He dropped his hands. His arms crossed over his chest and he studied her. She didn't even need to see him to know how cold and hard his eyes were.

"Are we through?" she whispered, desperate to retire to her room and sort out all her terrible new feelings. She should have known Vashon wouldn't let her.

"You aren't leaving here until I know where Michael Dayne took the Star of Aran," he stated slowly.

He went to the massive mahogany doors of his apartments, and she flinched when she heard the click of the lock. He turned, his back to the door. She watched him, suddenly knowing what it felt like to be dragon's prey.

"What if there are no answers, Vashon?" she nearly begged.

"Have I ever told you the story of the *Leviathan*?" he said.

She shook her head. They faced each other across the room, but in his violent mood she felt as if he were right on top of her.

"The *Leviathan* was Isaac's ship." He stepped closer. "It was a beautiful ship, running the route from Southampton to Algiers. Isaac was one of the best captains I ever saw. He took care of that ship like it was his wife."

"What does the *Leviathan* have to do with now?"

He didn't let her continue.

"One day, she was broadsided by a ship that flew the Union Jack. Isaac couldn't believe it. Even pirates had the honor to display their true standard when they fired."

"The ship was Peterborough's?"

He smiled. "Ah, I forget how astute you are. Yes, of course the ship was Peterborough's."

"And he pirated it and Isaac has never forgiven him."

"Yes."

"So on your 'travels' you and Isaac never took a ship?" she asked sarcastically. "I think you're not the man to cast the first stone."

"There's more."

He took another step forward. "As a youth Peterborough studied surgery in Germany. When the crew of the *Leviathan* wouldn't surrender, he took Isaac and removed his fingers one by one until he folded. Some would say Isaac was not a brave man to give up his ship, but he endured having three fingers chopped off. Think of it, Aurora. Each knuckle, each bone, cut away . . ."

She closed her eyes, shuddering. She couldn't believe poor Isaac had had to endure such torture. It was truly horrifying.

He seemed pleased by her reaction. "Shall I have the men come in and tell you their individual stories? Cook, for instance. Shall I have him explain to you the manner in which he lost his eye?"

"No," she gasped.

"Ah, I see this sickens you."

"It would sicken any decent citizen."

"Then certainly you see their need to avenge themselves on Peterborough."

Hating herself, she remained silent.

"Two hundred men were on the *Leviathan*, Aurora. Only twenty-six survived."

She choked back a sob.

He looked at her, triumph in his eyes. "There you are, you can't ignore those souls, can you? Those hundred men who scream from the grave for vengeance."

Shaking, she sat back down on the chimera armchair. There was no way she could hold back anything now. Not even if all her happiness depended on it.

When a moment passed and she had gathered herself, she asked, "What did Peterborough do to you, Vashon? You weren't on the *Leviathan*. I want to know what he did to *you*."

He lifted her chin. "If I tell you what he did to me, will that spur you to action? I think not. You like to help innocents, Aurora. And you know better than anyone that my innocence has long since departed."

"Tell me what he did . . ."

"Help those wretched men who went down with their ship! They need you!"

She stared at him, in awe of his manipulations. He suspected there might be a chance her feelings for him would cloud her desire to avenge Peterborough. So he directed her empathy toward the victims of the *Leviathan*. And it was working brilliantly. She couldn't get the picture of those suffering, drowning men out of her mind.

"Help them, Aurora. Only you can make sure they didn't die in vain."

She took a deep, shuddering breath and began to speak, her words uttered in a hopeless monotone.

"My father's name was Michael. He was from just outside of Hugh Town on St. Mary's, but I grew up in London. I remember a flat where we lived. West End, I think it was. The Horse Guards passed every day, afraid of more corn riots."

"Can you remember anything else about your father?"

"My father—is difficult to recall. I just remember I lived there."

"Go on."

A part of her began dying while she spoke, for with every word, her hold on him was unraveling like a thread. "There's truly so little. I recall only fragments—the sunshine spilling onto my chipped little eggcup in the morning . . . being afraid of the darkness beneath my bed . . ." Her voice dropped to a whisper. "My father reciting a nursery rhyme."

"Yes, let's discuss the rhyme." He pulled up the matching chimera chair. "Tell me everything about the rhyme."

"We rehearsed it every night, like prayers before bedtime. He made sure I'd never forget it."

"He wanted you to have the emerald."

"I suppose," she said bleakly.

Mistaking her mood, he pulled her hands into his and said, "I'm not going to cheat you out of your due, Aurora. I want you to know that. As far as I'm concerned, once I've got the emerald into my possession, it's yours. You may have it."

She laughed so bitterly, she nearly choked. "Ah, just what I've always dreamed of, an emerald as large as my fist. How warm that will keep me on those chill London nights."

He paused and looked at her. Slowly he withdrew his hands. "What are you saying?"

"I'm saying I don't care about that cursed Star of Aran. When I return to London, I shall go back to the Home and pray I get my position back. I have no need for your ill-gotten riches."

"You'll need money to take care of yourself. You can't go back to the Home."

"Oh, can't I?"

"No, you cannot. Peterborough knows about the Home, so it's far too dangerous."

"There's no other place for me to go."

He took her ruby necklace and, balling it into his fist, he pulled her forward. "Listen to me, my beautiful girl, you are no match for Peterborough. He knows your father stole the Star from him and even if he gets his hands back on it again, he'll take great pleasure in finding you and making you pay for your father's crime, *comprends-tu*? You're not going back to that Home. Flossie will take you to St. George's, and there you'll stay until I say otherwise."

"When you have your bloody emerald, you will have no more hold on me. I shall do as I please." She took his hand away, stood, and walked to the window. The magnificence of Mirage beckoned her, but somehow its luster was gone.

He rubbed his jaw and looked at her. "That orphanage hadn't much to recommend it." He hesitated. "Are you still mourning your dear Phipps?"

She refused to answer.

"Aurora." He stood. "Get it out of your head about returning to London now. If you want Phipps, you may write him and ask him to join you. But you cannot put yourself in such danger as to return to the Home."

"This is your battle, Vashon, not mine. I've made my peace with my father. I've forgiven him for his failures. What happens now concerns you, not me."

"I won't let you do this."

"And why not?" Her voice caught. Furious, she turned back to the scenery outside the louvers. She shouldn't have even asked that question. For what kind of answer did she expect? Vashon was the last man she could see making declarations of love to keep her by his side. So why was there this emptiness inside her yearning for just such a thing?

"Peterborough'll hurt you if he finds you, don't you understand that?"

She scowled. "How do you know so much about Peterborough? I demand to know your connection that's given you such a vengeance for him."

"He's my brother."

She whipped around and faced him. This fight couldn't be so terrible that it had pit brother against brother? But just by Vashon's expression, he confirmed it. His face was as implacable as it always was, but his eyes held rare emotion. She saw rage and betrayal; worse, she saw hurt that ran like a silent scar so deep and wide one had to pull back to see it in its entirety.

"What did he do to you?" she gasped, her very soul aching for him.

"We had the same mother. But *my* father was the Viscount Blackwell."

She closed her eyes, sickened all over again. Everything made sense now. Why Vashon had been so pampered as a child. And so terribly hardened as a youth. His own brother had been the reason why he'd been sent to Algiers and sold for his very flesh.

"Why did he do it, Vashon? Did he do it to get the title?" She could hardly utter the questions.

He didn't answer. She looked at him but his expression had closed. It was obvious she wasn't going to get anything more from him now.

She picked up the key dangling between her breasts, finally seeing the Blackwell crest stamped into its handle. The pieces of the puzzle came together as she saw the two rampant dragons flanking the Blackwell shield. They looked exactly like her locket. With a growing realization, she saw that her locket wasn't a lizard at all, but a stylized dragon, obviously designed for the Viscountess Blackwell. When she looked again, she saw that if the Chinese artistry of the tattoo were taken away, the dragon on Vashon's back would be exactly like the dragon on this crest.

"In China they consider dragons to be benevolent creatures, don't they, Vashon?" she said numbly.

"Yes."

"But the English dragon is not a benevolent creature, is it? And the dragon on your back is not a Chinese dragon at all. It's the dragon on your family crest."

He slowly nodded.

"This key, how did you come by it?"

"It was in my pocket my last day in London."

"Why did you give it to me?"

His voice dropped to a quiet, harsh rasp. "Because it symbolizes everything that was good. And everything that didn't last."

She put her hand to her mouth, finally letting the shock and depression overcome her. Perhaps in the back of her mind she had held the smallest hope that she might be able to tame Vashon, to still the rage and bloodlust in him and perhaps help him find happiness. Now she could see that would be nigh to impossible. He was too strong and too angry. Love was the only thing that could overcome this kind of fury, and he would hardly accept her love, let alone return it in kind. He was right to give her the key. Things didn't last. Nothing lasted. Except unrequited love.

"Now you know why the Star is so important," he said.

She suddenly lashed out, unable to let him slip away without a fight. "No, I don't know. The only thing that's clear is that this vengeance is all wrong. It will only hurt you, Vashon. You'll never be happy seeking revenge on Peterborough. Your hatred will make you into a monster, almost the monster your brother's become."

"Perhaps I am the monster my brother is. Have you ever considered that? Half his blood runs in my veins." His face was as cold as marble.

"Then you must fight it! You don't have to be like him! It's not destined! There's a part of you that's good! I've seen it!"

"Ah, what a saintly perspective. But it's not that easy, Aurora. Maybe I don't want to fight it."

"But you've got to," she pleaded. "I see now this revenge isn't about the Blackwell title, and I see it's not about wealth, for yours must be thrice Peterborough's. Nonetheless, this retribution will never make you happy. Don't destroy everything in your path to get to him. There'll be nothing left for you if you do."

"What do you know about any of this?" he snapped, his eyes flashing. "You, with your sheltered, pitiful little life. What could you know of anything?"

He was trying to hurt her, but she shrugged off his callous words and said, "I do know what I'm speaking of, Vashon. I've seen the children at the Home, and they've had pasts much like your own. The ones that forgot and went forward are the ones that survived. The ones that didn't—that harbored their anger as you have—never did."

"I'm no foundling, Aurora."

"Not on the outside."

Their eyes met and a moment passed when she thought she might have reached him. But then, without warning, he grabbed her so forcefully he knocked the breath right out of her.

"I told you that I'm not going to change. What makes you think some by-blow of a thief is going to be the one to make me?"

His words lacerated her. She felt as if she were bleeding. She whispered painfully, "Is there no depth to which you cannot sink?"

"No, no, I can sink much farther." His arm went around her waist and he lifted her off the ground, making her meet him face-to-face. He smiled darkly. "Must you continually make me prove how cruel I can be?"

Fear crossed her face, but she hid it behind a staunch facade. "I don't force you," she told him. "It's that beast on your back, Vashon. It only mirrors the beast in your heart."

"And you jeopardize yourself every time you forget that." He smiled as if he enjoyed frightening her, then he kissed her, his lips taking hers in a mean, loveless kiss.

She moaned, hating him for his ruthlessness and hating herself for having fallen in love with him. But while he forced himself upon her, it was as if there were two men kissing her, one who could be gentle and giving, and one whose hand hurtfully gripped her chin and made her endure his wet, wretched onslaught.

When his kiss grew more bold and he thrust his tongue savagely between her teeth, she finally fought back. Her hand went up and slammed against his face, but her strength hardly touched him. He only laughed and kissed harder until she tried to hit him again. Yet this time he was ready for her. He took her hand in an iron grip and shoved it brutally behind her until she gasped from shock. With no other weapon, she found herself, little by little, forced into an unwilling surrender.

He pulled her to the bed, and she felt as if they were reenacting a dark kind of dance they had performed once before. Stiff and unyielding, she was pulled beneath him on the mattress while he continued kissing her, caressing her. His hand moved up her bosom, and she could feel him groan and harden against her thighs. She tried to get away, tried to fight again, but he finished her rebellion with one sure motion of his body as he eased himself down upon her. She tried to make him look at her; he wouldn't, instead choosing to bury his face in her throat. But her eyes, filled with betrayal, never left him.

When his fingers pulled at the gauze of her dress, searching for the flesh beneath, hurt etched itself into every smooth plane of her face. He gripped her corsage and looked to rend her bodice in two. Finally he met her gaze, and, as if taunting her, he pulled, creating a tiny rip where her dress covered the valley between her breasts.

"How do you want it, Aurora," he whispered, "rough or easy?"

Her gaze never wavered. "You know the way I want it, Vashon."

His eyes met hers and a look passed between them, her own expression fraught with supplication and pain. But now she no longer harbored any hope of reaching him. Her fate was to endure this night, then leave him, forever chained to only the memory of the man he might have been.

"Look away," he told her, his voice husky and low, her unwavering gaze finally appearing to unnerve him.

"I cannot," she whispered, hardly able to hold back the tremor in her voice.

"Why?" he demanded, his agitation growing, only promising more brutality.

"Because I—" A tear finally fell. She wiped it and saw no more reason to hide. "Because I might miss the man I love, Vashon. And you see, I see him so rarely."

As if she'd stabbed him with a knife to the gut, he pulled back, his expression filled with horror. Cold, violent rage then filled him, and she thought he might even slap her, but instead, with just as much violence, he righted himself and pointed to the door.

"Get out of here. Never show your face to me again. Do you hear?"

With a great, heart-wrenching sob she scrambled to her feet, her hand clutching her ripped bodice. "Vashon," she begged, as unwilling to be sent away as she'd been unwilling to be raped.

"Get out. You'll sail on the *Resolute* in the morning."

"Please, no," she began, but he stopped her with one deadly look. When she saw nothing before her but fury and ice, she blinked back her burning tears and stumbled to the door, her only thought that God was just as cruel as John Phipps portrayed Him to be.

25

That night rain came and Aurora watched it fall with Koonga asleep in
her arms. In the islands, the rains were gentle and brief, daily cooling
and replenishing the tropical earth. A nighttime rain was generally
viewed with trepidation, for hurricanes could rake clean islands much
bigger than Mirage. But Aurora only dared the rain to come down
harder, only begged for the wind to blow with more force. If a hurri-
cane was brewing this night, she prayed for it to come. And if instead
the sun was destined to shine in the morning, then she prayed not to see
it.

The louvers clattered with the force of the wind, but this night nothing seemed too fierce for her. There was no gust angry enough, no rain
cool enough to take away her sorrow. Desolate, she hardly felt the
spray as the rain pelted against the open windows of her room. Only
when Koonga stirred did she step away.

The Star of Aran was now a curse to be uttered only when the most
foul phrases had been already used. Thinking about the jewel, she
laughed bitterly and wiped the rain off her tearless cheeks. Twice now
she'd been abandoned for that vile emerald. Twice her hope for love had
been destroyed by the greater lure of that stone. Now suddenly she
couldn't wait to get her hands on it. She wanted to clutch the wretched
thing in her palm and see if all her pain had been worth what she'd paid
for it. And then she wanted to drop it into the ocean, an ocean as green,
fathomless, and cruel as Vashon's eyes.

But until then she had nothing to comfort her but the hard little ache
where her heart had been. And even destroying the Star wasn't going to
take that away.

She took a deep breath and hugged the slumbering monkey to her
breast. Benny would most likely come for Koonga tomorrow. She
doubted he and the monkey would come with them on the *Resolute*;

Vashon would hardly provide for her and Flossie on their returning voyage as well as he'd done on their outgoing one. Placing the creature on a pillow on the récamier, she was further saddened by the thought of how empty her days were going to be without Koonga's homely little face and amusing chatter.

A knock on the door startled her out of her melancholy state. For some reason her heart leaped at the thought that it might be Vashon, but she knew only too well he didn't knock.

"Yes?" she whispered to the closed door.

"Missa! Missa! Come quick! Is big diremma!"

She opened the door and found Tsing holding a sumptuous candelabra. In the lamplight his face appeared unusually excited.

"What is it?" she asked, becoming alarmed.

"Vashon go crazy! He go crazy! Come quick! Is big diremma!"

"But what has he done?"

"He lip up map and order more blandy! Map expensive, missa!"

"He can afford another map . . . so he's getting drunk, is he?" she asked irritably.

"Yes, missa! Come quick! Make stop!" Tsing pulled on her hand but she drew back.

"What makes you think I can do anything? Why have you come for me? Has he sent for me?"

"No, missa. But you make stop, I know it!"

"Vashon is a grown man, Tsing, and if he should desire to get drunk, there's nothing I can do."

"Missa! Missa! Rook!" He held out his long graying rattail braid. The end was sharply hacked off. "He thlew knife at me, missa! He say, 'Get blandy and get out!' and when he see no chop-chop, he thlew knife!"

"What a villain!" she exclaimed, touching the end of Tsing's braid. "Why, you should vow never to work for him again!"

"Oh, no, missa, he never done before! Is big diremma! You make stop, missa!" He pulled her out the door and down the passage.

"But I really don't know what I can do, Tsing," she implored as he beckoned her back to Vashon's apartments. "I don't have anything to do with this."

"No, missa, is not so! When Vashon thlow knife, he say ru tlying to kiwr him and he not ret you!"

She stopped. "Me trying to kill him? That's absurd! Why, he has gone mad!"

"Take, missa!" From a nearby commode he took a tray laden with decanters and thrust it into her hands. "Ru take, missa. Me want keep lest of head."

Before she knew it, Tsing had knocked on the doors. When the answering growl came from within, the doors were opened and she was pushed inside. Before she could look back the doors were soundly shut behind her.

"Leave it and get out," Vashon said in the dimness.

Aurora looked around and saw only one sparse candle lit on his desk. Next to it lay the map that he'd so ruthlessly torn up.

"I said—"

"No, don't throw another knife. It's not Tsing," she said hastily.

She saw a dark figure rise from a settee. "I thought I told you—"

"Yes," she interrupted, "but you frightened Tsing so much he refused to return and fetched me instead."

"And you should have had the prudence to be frightened also."

She looked at the shadowy figure looming in the foreground. Behind him the rain thundered down through the shuttered windows. She couldn't see his face, but she could see the sharp silhouette of the stiletto in his hand. He was terrifying, but she'd rather die than run from him again.

"I have the prudence," she said slowly, "but, unlike Tsing, I possess the faith that you won't hurt me." In the darkness she groped for a table. When she found one, she set the decanters down, only to feel the stiletto pressed against her breast.

"I see I've somehow failed to impress upon you the exact evil of my nature."

She smelled the brandy on his breath. His other arm slid across her bosom and he held her back against his chest.

She lowered her eyes. Her nerves felt as if they were on fire. She'd personally witnessed men run screaming from his presence with Vashon in such a temper, but she did her best not to show her fear.

Taking a deep breath, she felt the tip of the stiletto dig into her tender flesh. She forced herself to ignore it. Licking her lips, she said, "How odd that you should think to harm me, Vashon. Especially when Tsing tells me it's I who's out to kill you."

"You are trying to kill me," he stated as if he were completely rational.

"How am I doing that? I have no weapon."

"You have a weapon. The most dangerous weapon. This." He slid his hand to where her heart pounded wildly against her ribs.

Frightened and yet strangely exhilarated by his words, she answered, "But you must know, Vashon, with that weapon, I can win only if you let me."

He lowered the stiletto and wrapped her own palm around its handle. "Then thrust this into my back and let's be done with this agony. Or are you waiting for Josiah Peterborough to do it for you?"

She released her hand and the stiletto clattered to the floor. "You're drunk. You're talking madness. I won't listen to you."

"I'm not so drunk that I can't see what's going to happen."

"And what is going to happen?" she asked calmly.

"First," his hand lifted to her chin, "you're going to kiss me."

"Indeed? Not ever again, I vow—"

He turned her around so swiftly her neck almost snapped.

"Oh yes, you will kiss me," he whispered, "and after that sweet pleasure, we'll find my bed and there we'll stay for a very long time."

She struggled from his hold and backed toward the door. "Tsing was right. You're quite out of your mind."

"Ah, but there are worse things than madness." He reached out and gripped her waist. "Chastity, for example."

"No, Vashon! I didn't come here to be abused further!"

He pulled her into his arms. His hands cupped her delicate face and he looked at her so hungrily she gasped.

"I know why you came here, Aurora," he said. "You've come to destroy me with this love of yours. To make me fall for your artless little seductions until I no longer protect myself."

"Love or death, Vashon, it doesn't have to be one or the other," she cried out, all the emotions she held for him washing over her again like a baptism.

"You're asking me to commit suicide! To destroy myself for you!"

"No! I care for you! But I want you to have a life worth living! And if you can't love, what kind of a life will that be for you?" She suddenly sobbed.

"I've forgotten how to feel that way," he growled, hopelessness woven all through his voice. "I can never feel that way again."

"You could remember. I know it," she whispered.

"You speak with such authority," he said cynically.

"I speak with my heart, Vashon."

They faced each other, their gazes locked, both cast in a silent battle of wills. But just when she felt she would rather throw herself from the *Seabravery* than lose this battle again, he rasped, "Then show me."

She looked at him, not sure what he wanted.

"Show me," he repeated, this time more softly.

She searched his eyes and saw his terrible longing. "How? How can I show you?" she barely whispered.

"Begin with a kiss."

Trembling, she glanced down, unsure she could do it. But desperate for him and desperate for happiness, she tilted back her head and pressed a kiss on his hard, forlorn lips.

It was an awkward kiss, and when it was was over, she wondered whether he would laugh at her. He'd hardly responded, not even when she artlessly raised her hand to caress his unshaven cheek.

Still his gaze didn't leave her.

"Say it," he insisted with a whisper. "Say it and this time I won't send you away."

She was being the worst kind of fool. He was not the man for her. They could never build a life together. It was as impossible as a marriage between a lamb and a lion. This was sure to destroy her happiness rather than build it, but she could go no other way. Her feelings for him carried her along like a flood; a finger in the dike could hold them back no longer.

"I love you, Vashon," she admitted. "And the tragedy is that I cannot stop myself."

Her last words were barely discernible, yet he seemed to have heard them anyway. He grabbed her into his embrace as a dying man grasps at new life. His mouth clamped on hers, and he picked her up in one desperate motion. When he'd taken her to the bed, he fell back with her in his arms and everything she'd wanted, everything she'd dreamed of, seemed suddenly within her grasp.

He kissed her, hungry for her lips, hungry for her touch. She braced herself up on his chest and thought to pull back, if only to catch her breath, but he wouldn't permit it. His tongue burned upon hers, and his touch scalded wherever his hands chose to roam. His caress worshipped her: the curve of her back, her sweet, sumptuous derrière, her narrow waist, enticing beneath its thin drape of gauze.

She gazed at him in wonder as he undressed her, as he gently released each hook to reveal the apricot-tinted flesh beneath. Staring into those hungry green eyes, she knew what he wanted, and this time, she ached with the need to give it to him.

Slowly her hand touched his naked chest. Her fingers slid through the mat of dark hair and she reveled in the feel of him, so hard and unlike herself. Yet when he did likewise, taking both her bare breasts in his palms, the sensation jolted her back, frightening her with its boldness.

But he wouldn't allow her to retreat anymore.

"I want only abandon now, Aurora," he murmured against her hair. His hands moved up and he easily filled both of them, luxuriating in her generous flesh. Before she could protest again, his arm curved around her waist and he pulled her down onto him, crushing her soft bosom into the warm macadam of his own, and taking her lips in a long, needful kiss. His hand combed lovingly through her gilt-red tresses, then slid lower to press her hips close to his.

She whispered like a prayer, "I love you." He answered with another aching kiss and rolled atop her, pausing only to search deep into her gaze.

He must have found what he sought. With a sudden, fierce desire he possessed her, and before his lips came down to take hers one last time, he groaned with satisfaction when she whispered, "I love you, I love you," until she could speak no more.

The night rode on. The rain dwindled to a flash in the western sky, yet inside the chambers there was no other world but the whispers and sighs, kisses and caresses of their lovemaking. Twice she'd fallen asleep in his arms, and twice she'd awakened to his touch, their passion renewing itself like a kindled flame, each union outshining the glory of the last.

Finally when the lone candle sputtered in its wax, and the sun's first light burned through the mists of Mount Soufrière, peace settled upon them like a warm, soothing surf. Vashon lay against Aurora, his cheek on her belly, while she sat against the pillows, lightly tracing the tattoo on his muscular back. This morning even the dragon didn't bother her. Peterborough had stolen the Blackwell title from him. She could now understand the rage that had driven Vashon to do such a thing to his body.

"I should probably get back," she murmured, heartsick from the thought of leaving him.

"No, Sleeping Beauty, stay," he said, putting his hand possessively on her hip.

She smiled softly at his new nickname, then grew warm with the thought of what he'd done after he'd last awakened her with it. "But will the servants not be bewildered to find me gone?"

"Tsing will realize you're here."

She grew silent, disturbed by the prospect of having the servants know she was with Vashon all night, unhappy with her need to comply with propriety.

He raised himself on his arms and picked up her locket lying on the sheets. She blushed, unable to recall when the chain had broken. Dangling it before her, he said, "I wasn't able to figure out the rhyme."

"I thought as much when I saw what you did to the map." She hesitated. "But you don't need the Star, Vashon, surely you realize that. You're rich beyond most people's imagining. You can afford to leave Peterborough alone."

He nodded. "But even if I end my fight with Peterborough, he will not end his with me. Especially not now, while I have you."

"Give him the locket then."

"It's not as simple as that."

She could feel him tense. Softly, she said, "My love, he cannot find Mirage. He'll never find us. We'll stay here and start a family and never wander—"

He drew away and rolled on his back, staring morosely up at the bed's dark canopy. "If he's diligent, he can find Mirage. It's not wise to underestimate him. And there are things you still don't know, Aurora. For instance, the curse."

"What curse?" she whispered.

"I don't hold that it's true, but the Star possesses a curse. 'Whosoever shall have it, their enemies shall die.' It's written in *The Chronicles of Crom Dubh*, an ancient manuscript held at Inishmore Castle . . . where the Star originated."

"But if you don't believe this curse, then why do you even entertain it?"

"Because Peterborough believes it. He's been superstitious all along about killing his own brother. When he gets the emerald, I know he'll trade one superstition for another. He'll see me die even if he finds he has to force himself to have a hand in it."

He looked at her and brushed the strands of hair out of her eyes. "But I fear for you, *Aurore*, more than I fear for myself. So you must promise me, on everything that you hold dear, you will do what I tell you. I must keep you safe, no matter how difficult that may be."

"Just don't demand that I be sent away. That I shall never do."

"Peterborough is a danger while I have you," he repeated.

"What are you saying?" she asked. His tone disturbed her.

"I'm saying," he answered slowly, not meeting her gaze, "that you must do what I tell you. No matter what that is."

She shook her head, panic already rising in her breast. "Don't ask me to leave. Don't take me to your bed and then cast me aside."

His jaw hardened, as if he'd made a decision, a decision he knew she wouldn't like. "You have another life to return to, Aurora. It was wrong to snatch you from it. I've got to make it safe for you to return to London. I see that now."

"What you see is how much I love you!"

He faced her. "No, what I see is a woman who is deserving of more than I can give her. A woman of grace and beauty who is deluded into thinking that I am the man for her. And I see a man who has somehow been so elevated in her eyes she thinks he is deserving of her." He lowered his voice in self-loathing. "Do you know what I've done in my life? Do you know how many men I have killed?"

She thrust him away and refused to listen. "I care not how many men have fallen because of you. I'll believe to my death you had good cause—"

"Hear me out!" He ruthlessly pulled her to him. "There were times I thought I had good cause, but Josiah Peterborough is still my half brother, and half his blood runs in my veins. I can't help wondering if that doesn't color my perception of things."

"It doesn't! You're nothing like your brother!"

"But maybe I am. Maybe I'm very much like my brother. Isaac once said that the reason I've never taken that title away from Josiah was because I enjoyed torturing him more than I would enjoy a place in the peerage. And he was right, Aurora. He was right."

"I won't listen to this! No matter what you say, I will never believe you're less a man than I think you are! I love you! I couldn't love an evil man!"

He shook her, the anger and pain on his face a terrible thing to see. "I first killed a man when I was just thirteen!"

"You had cause to do it!"

"How do you know that?"

She sobbed, barely able to choke out her words. "Because that man tried to molest you, didn't he?"

Vashon stilled. His expression turned rock-hard. "Peterborough wanted me dead so that he could inherit the Blackwell title. He thought I was dead until I returned to London years ago and paid him a visit. I meant to frighten him. I told him about that man I killed so long ago when I was still a boy. I described it in great detail." His voice nearly cracked with vengeance. "Do you want to know what he said?"

Tearfully she shook her head.

"He said, 'Well done. Now I know we're brothers.' "

Vashon released her and she watched him turn away. Her heart was shattering for him. As if by instinct, she pressed against him, crushing her breasts to the dragon, wrapping his muscular torso in her arms. "That changes nothing," she whispered.

He answered in a monotone. "It was wrong of me to delude you. You're worthy of the best of men, not the worst. You should have your man Phipps, Aurora. You should have so many things."

"You told me you would not send me back," she whispered, clinging to any hope. "You said it was too dangerous to return to London."

"It is now," he answered calmly. "But I shall make it safe for you to return. You will go with Flossie to St. George's. I shall go to England to seek Peterborough."

"Don't do it, Vashon. I beg you!"

"You must have the life you were meant to live."

"I lied about my life! I lied about Phipps! I wanted to leave London. I have nothing to return to." After this pitiful confession, she bit back a sob.

"I've not done many noble things in my life, Aurora, but this time I will. You should have a little cottage. You should live an ordinary, comfortable life with an ordinary, comfortable man." He pulled her off him. "Not me. There's nothing good to come of this unholy union."

But we could have a baby! Your baby! she wanted to cry out, yet already the fight was beginning to die within her. When she met his stern emerald gaze she knew there was no changing his mind. "I'll hate you forever if you do this," she cried.

"I'd rather you hate me then. And live to tell it." He softened. "In time you'll see I was right. You'll fall to your knees in thanks that I did this."

"I will curse your name until my dying breath," she vowed, refusing to look at him, to show him how much he had hurt her.

He released a bitter laugh. "I wager you won't be alone in doing so."

Without warning, he turned and kissed her, toppling her back onto the pillows. She struggled to be released. He captured her with his gaze.

"If I'm to leave you, then I shall leave now, Vashon," she demanded furiously.

"No." A dark smile played upon his lips. "If you're to leave me, then our time now must be well spent." His hand cupped her breast. She tried to throw him off but without hesitating, his mouth found its coral-colored tip.

She closed her eyes, desperate to think of a way to thwart him, but when she felt herself spiraling down once more into sweet oblivion, she whispered the words that he'd wanted from her the very first time they'd made love. "You're a wretch and I'll hate you forever for this, do you hear? Forever . . ."

Just as she expected, he laughed; just as she feared, her fingers traitorously threaded through his long black locks and she allowed his mouth to take her own.

It was some time before they parted again. They missed the sunrise. And the sleek ominous ship that rounded Mosquito Bay on the southeast end of St. Kitts, heading swiftly for Mirage.

26

The furious knocking on the doors woke Aurora from a sound slumber. She opened her eyes and found herself lying in Vashon's embrace, his leg resting intimately between her thighs, her arm outflung across his chest in an unconscious gesture of surrender. Vashon must already have been awake, for upon hearing the banging he extricated himself from her and the bedclothes and strode to the door, unmindful of his nudity or how terrifying the dragon looked in the brilliant light of morn.

"Isaac," Aurora heard him say after he'd disappeared into the antechamber. A muffled conversation ensued and the tension grew thick. Her mortification over being discovered with Vashon was only lessened by the dread she felt at the suspicion that Isaac had come with bad news.

When she saw Vashon's face, she knew it.

He'd donned his white trousers by now, and he walked back into the bedroom, his face as grave as she'd ever seen it.

"What is it?" she cried, pulling the sheet to her breasts.

"A ship has landed near Rum Gut. Isaac said the name's the *Merry Magdalene*."

"You know this ship?"

"It belongs to a mercenary named Fontien. I didn't think he could find Mirage. But he has. He's brought my brother here, I'm sure of it. Peterborough is on the island."

She closed her eyes, overcome with terror for him, for them both.

"Get dressed," he ordered absentmindedly. He went to his desk and gathered some remaining papers and maps. "Isaac is preparing the *Seabravery*. We set sail immediately."

She watched him at his desk, suddenly consumed with the fear of losing him. All along she had discounted Peterborough, but now that he was here on Mirage his threat was so real she shook with it.

He looked up; his eyes scanned her pale face, her bed-mussed hair, her white knuckles clutching the linens to her. He softened only slightly. "Get dressed, my love. I'll admit this is a rude awakening to the most pleasurable of nights, but there's no helping it."

Numbly she rose and found her dress.

"I fear this is turning out precisely the way you predicted," she confessed, fumbling with her dress. "If we hadn't—" She took a deep breath and looked out the louvers to the Caribbean. "I've distracted you, and now you may pay with your life."

"I allowed myself the distraction." Those were the only words of comfort he offered. "Love, get ready. Finish your attire." He nodded to her dress, still partially unhooked, revealing a good portion of one creamy breast.

Distraught, she completed her toilet while he turned back to his desk. She pulled her hair into a loose knot and began to leave his apartments.

He stopped her in the antechamber. "What do you think you're doing?" he snapped.

She spun around. "I've got to get Koonga. I can't abandon her here. Benny will never forgive me."

"Where is she?"

"In my rooms."

"Leave her then. Peterborough may be in the house for all I know. Though Dragonard is big, it may be just a matter of time before he discovers where my rooms are."

"Vashon—"

"You will not retrieve her."

"Is she ready?"

Gasping at this new voice, Aurora turned again and found Isaac standing right behind her. She was sure she was going out of her mind because she'd been facing the doors all along and she'd never seen him enter.

"Where is Benny?" Vashon asked, not disturbed at all by Isaac's sudden appearance.

"He and the widow are already on St. Kitts. The *Seabravery* awaits at the docks in Basseterre."

"How shall we get to St. Kitts undetected?" she asked.

A wry smile came to Vashon's lips. "That's the least of our worries." He addressed Isaac. "Have the servants been notified to leave? Has Tsing gone also?"

"They've vacated." Isaac hesitated. "We've had a few casualties, however. Two seamen on the *Resolute* were shot in the head. I'm sure Blackwell expected us to leave on that ship."

Aurora sickened at this news. Two men were already dead. She looked at Vashon and felt she might go out of her mind with grief. The thought of his being in such danger brought her to the edge of hysterics.

Vashon nodded, then handed the captain his maps and the Venetian paper notebook. He next tucked a pistol into the waist of his trousers. "Get everyone settled on the *Seabravery*. I'll be there shortly."

"Where on earth are you going?" Isaac gasped, looking at him as if he were mad.

"Benny's monkey," he said sarcastically. "Apparently the beast has too many admirers to be left to its own devices."

"No, Vashon!" Aurora gasped.

"I agree that's a very bad idea, my friend. We've already been caught unawares." The captain turned grim.

"You can't go, Vashon! As you said yourself, Peterborough might already be in the house," she interjected, unwilling to let Vashon jeopardize himself. "Please, I beg of you, I'm the one who must retrieve Koonga."

"Take her, Isaac. I'll join you in a moment." Vashon nodded to her as if she were some kind of pet to be led away by a leash. She could have shrieked in frustration.

Isaac shook his head, obviously unhappy with the situation too, but resigned to it. He took Aurora's arm and said, "Flossie's been asking about you, girl. Come along. We've a bit of a walk ahead."

Aurora pulled away. It was unthinkable what they were asking her to do. How could she ever continue if something happened to Vashon? "No. I won't go, Vashon, until you've come back."

Vashon took her jaw like a truant child's. "Listen to me, Aurora, we've no time for debate. I made you promise to do what I told you to. Now is the time to do that."

"Oh, God, don't make me," she moaned.

"You must." Vashon dropped his hold. "I'll follow in a minute," he said to Isaac.

The captain acquiesced and began to escort Aurora out of the antechamber. She was not going to go willingly; Isaac had to drag her away.

"Vashon," she called out, fighting Isaac the entire way, "let me go with you! I beg you, I cannot lose you! Don't let me lose you!"

"You were going to hate me forever, remember?" He smiled darkly and nodded Isaac on. Aurora moaned in agony and struggled with him, but soon he brought her in front of the huge mahogany and gilt fire-screen. He pushed it aside; behind it were no hearth and fireback, but steps that led into the bowels of the earth.

"Don't do this, Vashon!" she nearly sobbed, but before she could make another protest, the captain forced her down the first steps. Her last look at Vashon saw him anxious for combat, staring at the doors leading from the antechamber, his green eyes already glittering with anger.

The years of running the streets of the Casbah gave Vashon a distinct advantage over his nemesis. He knew Dragonard and he knew how to hide. He made his way through the silent passages, his ears hearing everything—the breeze in the coconut grove outside the northwest passage, the distant slam of a shutter against the jamb, the alien sound of liquid as it fell somewhere ahead, plopping against the polished mahogany floors.

Barefoot and nimble, he crept along, the drip, drip, drip wearing heavy on his nerves. When he turned the corner, his expression hardened. He was appalled at what he saw but not surprised by it. He looked at the body tied and hung like a bat from the rafters. It was hardly disturbed at all—executed in the classic Peterborough style—one tiny slice placed carefully in the neck and the man had been doomed. As usual, Peterborough's surgical abilities were brilliant.

Vashon cut down the body and discovered it to be a young black diver from Nevis. The man had worked for him ever since he had married a servant from Mirage. Now he was dead, caught in the wrong place at the wrong time. Disgusted, Vashon laid him in the corner, then thought better of it.

"Sorry, lad," he whispered to the young man before drawing him across the passage, the large pool of blood from the dead man's neck smearing the entire passageway. He reverently stepped over the body and continued around the corner to Aurora's apartments.

Silently he opened the door. Koonga chattered in the bedroom. The sitting room preceding it was empty and undisturbed.

He walked as quiet as a cat into the bedroom. The monkey sat atop the bed's upholstered canopy shrieking at something in the corner. He looked and came face-to-face with his brother.

"So we finally meet on my terms, Vashon," Peterborough said, walking out from the bed, a pistol in each hand.

The two men stared at each other, each so much like the other, each so completely different.

"Josiah, how good it is to see you again." Vashon's voice was calm and filled with loathing.

"And you too." Josiah waved his hand at his surroundings. "I didn't know where to find you in this magnificent palace you've built here. I'm glad you found me instead." He scanned Vashon's scanty attire, remarkably crude compared with the viscount's jonquil satin waistcoat and buckskin trousers. "I see we didn't dress for the occasion."

"And what occasion is that?"

"Your funeral." Peterborough suddenly laughed.

"But I've got the girl. So how do you think I'm to die? As I see it, once I have the emerald, by all rights, the curse should dictate *your* demise."

The viscount sobered. "Where is she? The servant told us these were her apartments."

"Us?" Vashon asked.

Peterborough nodded to the door. From behind it stepped a blond young man, too precisely dressed, holding a pistol in his trembling hand.

Discounting him, Vashon turned back to Peterborough. "I assume the dead boy in the passage told you Aurora was here?"

"He didn't cooperate as quickly as I like."

"No one ever does." Vashon looked to the canopy and held out an arm to Koonga. The little monkey gratefully climbed down and held on to his neck.

Peterborough smirked. "Vicious animal. It hissed at me."

As if Koonga understood him, she hissed again.

"You leave a bad odor, Josiah," Vashon said. "Little creatures hate it."

The viscount didn't hide his annoyance. "So where is she, Vashon? I hear from Azzedine that Aurora Dayne's quite a beauty. Are you sleeping with her?"

Vashon was silent.

"She's that good? Left you speechless? Wonderful." Peterborough laughed. "I need a good woman for the voyage back. I forget how long it takes to make a crossing and how one is forced to . . . make do." His gaze slid disparagingly to the young blond man.

"What makes you think I'll give her up?" Vashon asked.

Peterborough again met his brother's gaze. "Because I shall see you dead before I leave here without her."

"Then I suppose you must kill me now."

"But if I kill you I'll never know where the girl is."

Vashon smiled. "Exactly."

"So where is she?"

"She's already gone from here. She's on her way to retrieve the emerald."

"She knows where it is?" Peterborough blanched.

"She's revealed many things," Vashon admitted.

"That emerald is mine! I shall have it at any cost!" The viscount moved forward with the pistols.

Vashon only laughed. He made a great gesture of turning around and presenting his back to him. "Shoot me, my brother! I beg you! Kill me as you should have years ago!"

Peterborough gasped and stepped back. His gaze slid between Vashon's mad laughter and the Blackwell dragon tattooed on his back. It was obvious he had never seen it before. Shock, horror, and surprise crossed his features in one fluid expression.

"Pull the trigger, Josiah. Or are you afraid?" Vashon turned and faced him once more. "Does the dragon frighten you? You thought I didn't care about the title, didn't you? How terrified you must be to find yourself so mistaken." Vashon began to stalk him. "Go ahead. Shoot me. Why are you hesitating? Because without the power of that emerald to guide you, you haven't the backbone, have you, you bloody bastard?"

"Keep your distance." Peterborough stopped him by waving one pistol. "As you yourself pointed out, if I kill you, I'll never get Aurora Dayne."

"Nor shall you, ever." Vashon flashed a smile.

"Don't be too sure, brother." Peterborough raised the pistols. "If I kill you, I needn't have the emerald at all."

Vashon paused. As if he'd choreographed the entire thing, he reached behind him, disarming and grabbing Asher in a well-schooled motion. He held the gasping man up by the collar.

"Come along, *Viscount*, shoot!" he said, holding Asher in front of him.

"Noooooo!" Asher squealed, holding his hands out for mercy.

Peterborough aimed. "I've got two pistols, Vashon. When he's gone, so will your shield be."

"Noooo!" Asher screamed like a terrified pig.

"Pray you don't miss then, Josiah." Vashon calmly held the man out further.

"I beg you! I beg you, Josiah!" Asher pleaded pitifully. When Peterborough looked as if he was ready to pull the trigger, Asher put his face in his hands and sobbed. Disgusted, Vashon heaved him up and threw him to Peterborough. Asher slammed into the viscount, and that was just enough of a diversion to allow Vashon an escape.

Practiced in running from executioners, Vashon took to the passageway like the wind. Behind him Peterborough stumbled to catch up. Vashon met the corner, then leaped across the great smear of blood left from the viscount's slaughter. As he pounded the polished floors of the passage, he heard just what he expected. Peterborough took the corner, not anticipating the blood on the floor. He skidded several feet, both pistols going off in his fall.

Koonga shrieked and clung ever tighter to Vashon's neck with the loud blasts. In seconds Vashon was gone, pulling the firescreen back into its place as if they'd never even been there.

Peterborough ran through the antechamber, covered in gunpowder and the dead boy's blood. He didn't pause until he ended in the bedroom. He spun around, looking at the five huge open windows, unable to decide which one Vashon had escaped from. But before he went farther, something familiar from the bed caught his eye. He went to the bed and saw the dragon locket glittering up from the mussed sheets. He picked it up, amazement and recognition in his beautiful green eyes. He ran his fingers over it, as if trying to recall something. When he found the secret latch, he flicked it open, obviously unsure of what he might find. When he read the inscription, he got more than he'd bargained for. He tipped his head back and laughed. The nasty sound echoed all through the empty chambers of Dragonard.

27

The mystery of Monkey Hill was solved. After they left Vashon's chambers through the underground passage, Isaac dragged Aurora through a beautiful coral cave of indescribable color, and they escaped from Mirage undetected. They went only a short distance before they reemerged through a cave on St. Kitts. Once in Basseterre, their wait aboard the *Seabravery* was agonizing, and when at last Vashon and Koonga arrived on the docks, Aurora almost wept with relief. With no time for even the briefest of reunions, they barely exchanged a glance before Vashon handed Koonga over to Benny and was called to the quarterdeck. The crew busied themselves for their departure, and Flossie took Aurora's arm and led her back to the widow's old cabin. There they shared a cup of tea and waited for full sail.

"You're terribly quiet, lovey. Is anything wrong?" Flossie asked after a long moment.

Aurora looked up from her teacup. She was so preoccupied she didn't realize what poor company she was being. "Forgive me, my thoughts were elsewhere—"

"Vashon?" the widow finished.

Letting out a deep breath, she nodded.

"I guessed as much." Flossie quietly stirred her tea.

Unable to bear much more, Aurora stood and began to pace the cabin. "I'm afraid the worst has happened. I've fallen in love with him."

"Well, take heart, lovey, that's not the *worst* that can happen."

Aurora glanced at her, then quickly looked away. She knew exactly what Flossie was hinting at.

"The worst has not happened, has it?" Flossie asked, a frown creasing her brow.

"I really don't know what you're talking about," Aurora said evasively.

"I'm talking about"—Flossie lowered her voice—"a baby. Have you missed your monthly time?"

"I—I don't know. I can't think about that now."

Flossie didn't look very relieved. "It's never too early to think of that, my dear. In fact, it's preferable to think about it before . . ."

Aurora turned away and bit her lower lip. "You think I'm terrible, don't you? I've dishonored myself and then fallen in love with the man who dishonored me."

"No, no, my dear!" Flossie hugged her. "I shall never think of you as anything but a lady, no matter what happens." She hugged her again, but Aurora quickly composed herself.

"I'll be fine, Flossie. I guess I just need to get home and forget about this terrible voyage. I had no idea any of this would happen. I suppose I was a fool to have ever left the Home."

"But you are coming to St. George's with me, aren't you? You can't be entertaining the thought of going back to that wretched orphanage? Oh, what a bloody mess this is," Flossie finally exclaimed in her usual taciturn manner. "Pardon my language, my dear. When we ever return to St. George's, I shall vow upon my grave that I've never done nor said the things I have on this voyage, but now that I've been driven to the most wretched behavior, I cannot keep quiet any longer. The man must marry you! You're too wonderful for him to leave you like this! Why, he's a villain! Not even Isaac beds a woman, then—!" Shocked by her indiscretion, Flossie stopped speaking. Her hand flew to her mouth and she blushed to the tips of her toes. After a long, painful silence, she gasped, "Oh, what you must think of me."

Aurora emphatically shook her head. "No, no. We've both been driven to do things on this voyage we might not have done otherwise." She stared at her. "Is . . . is he going to marry you?"

"Oh, heavens, I'm not sure. But he's not going to be leaving me with child!" Flossie fanned herself with her handkerchief, obviously uncomfortable with the conversation. "Oh, my dear, I hope you can forgive me. I don't admit this often, but I've been rather lonely since Mr. Lindstrom died. He was such a good, dear husband, and his memory has always been enough comfort . . . until Isaac distracted me with his . . . attentions." She almost choked on this last word.

"Don't apologize," Aurora whispered, trying to comfort her.

Flossie waved her away. "I'm not confessing for my sake, my dear. I was wrong and I know it. I'm telling you this to point out that my guilt is the only consequence I shall have to pay for my actions. You, on the other hand, have greater worries."

"There will be no baby," Aurora said. "I'm sure of it."

"As much as you'd like to think that, love, there's only one way to be sure. I'm determined that Vashon shall leave you alone on this trip. You'll stay with me from now on."

"I don't think he'll like that, Flossie."

"Pooh! Then I'll fight him tooth and nail! He's got to leave you alone! Or marry you!"

"You can't make a man like Vashon do something he doesn't want to do," Aurora said. "And you can't stop him from taking what he thinks he must have. I know that all too well."

"Well, I shall stop him. That villain."

A deep booming laugh suddenly came from the doorway. Both women whipped around to find Vashon standing with his arms crossed over his chest. Immediately Flossie stepped in front of Aurora and confronted him.

"How dare you enter my cabin unannounced!" she exclaimed. "How long have you been standing there?"

"Not long enough. Obviously," he answered with a smirk.

"Well, you've heard enough to know what I think of your behavior toward this girl. You blackguard!"

"You act as if I beat her into submission, Flossie."

"She was unschooled in the ways of the world and you took advantage of that."

He looked straight at Aurora, his gaze lingering at her bare neck. "Is that what you think?"

Furious, Aurora refused to answer him. Her emotions were all tied in knots; she was still angry from their tussle this morning, still frightened from their close brush with Peterborough, worn out from worrying about him when he went after Koonga. But she certainly wasn't about to let him bed her while he sailed to Bermuda, then leave her there without a fare-thee-well.

"She was seduced," Flossie chimed in in her stead.

"Was she, or was I?" he asked, staring ominously at Aurora.

She met his gaze, then in defiance looked away.

Impatient, he said, "Come along, wren, I have to talk to you. We've got to go to my cabin."

"She's not going anywhere with you. She's staying right here in my cabin. If you must speak to her, Vashon, you'll do so with me as chaperon."

Vashon looked at the widow as if she were out of her mind.

"I meant what I said, Vashon, I'll fight tooth and nail." Flossie put her hands on her hips.

"Madam, I hate to disappoint you, but you haven't the strength to stop me." He looked almost amused.

"I'll fight for what's right," Flossie added, moving back toward Aurora and shielding her with her large form.

"What's right," Vashon said, turning a bit more menacing, "is that Aurora and I have time together. And no one"—he moved forward—"shall deprive me of that." He looked down at the widow. "Shall I pick you up, madam, or will you step aside of your own volition?"

Flossie blanched. "Vashon," she sputtered, "you have no chivalry whatsoever."

"None," he confirmed. He raised one eyebrow as if inviting her to step aside one last time. When Flossie stood her ground, he reached for her. Flossie's eyes nearly popped from their sockets when he lifted her up by the armpits and placed her back on her feet several paces away.

When the widow was out of the way, Vashon reached to take Aurora's hand, but she pulled back.

"Flossie's not the only one who doesn't want me to go, Vashon." She gave him a daring look, and stepped away.

"Brava, Aurora!" Flossie exclaimed from the corner.

Vashon tipped his head back and studied her through half-closed lids. "You're coming with me, Aurora. You will reside in my cabin until we reach St. George's. And that is the final word. Now, you may walk out of this cabin or I can carry you. Which will it be?"

"I despise your company. I won't go willingly," she taunted.

"So be it." He reached for her and Flossie cried out in shock. Aurora kicked and scratched, but, like the pirate he was, he easily threw her over his shoulder and carried her off, not even bothering to shut the door in his wake.

When he set her down in his cabin, the silence was thunderous. She was so furious she refused to speak. Placing her arms over her chest, she stared at him as if he were anathema.

"Sit down," he told her. She didn't comply, so he pushed her back and she fell onto the dolphin-legged couch.

"Is this where you make me walk the plank, *El Draque*?"

"No, this is where I ask you where your locket is."

The lines on his face deepened and she saw he looked worried. Her hand flew to her neck. When she felt nothing, she suddenly remembered where it was. "I—I left it on the bed. That was the last time I saw it. . . ." A terrible notion occurred to her. "Peterborough, will he find it?"

Vashon didn't answer. He looked at his desk and said, "I blame myself. I should have thought to go back for it. I'm not one to overlook such things. I fear I must be getting sloppy."

She watched him go to his desk and take out his maps. A frown furrowed his brow.

"Could he decipher the rhyme?" she asked, softly going to him.

"Without your help, I doubt it." Vashon stared down at the map. The continents were massive. The Star could be on any one of them. Aurora had never seen such an impossible task.

"Let's go through what we know." Vashon nodded to the couch. She sat again and looked at him.

"We can give this up, Vashon," she said. "We can go anywhere where Peterborough can't find us and—"

"Tell me what you know about Michael Dayne again." Vashon didn't even remove his gaze from the map.

Depressed, she ran through the clues again. And again. Until the wee hours of the morning.

"I think we lived on the West End. My father was born on St. Mary's. I remember once standing outside Carlton House. I remember the ladies' satin gowns. I remember my father admiring their beautiful jewels. I remember him teaching me the rhyme. . . ."

Aurora opened her eyes and saw Vashon still studying his maps. She looked out the aft ports and saw it was almost dawn. She didn't know how long she'd slept, but certainly it was longer than Vashon had.

"You won't find it like that."

He looked up and stared at her. "Like what?" he asked.

"Without eating. Without sleeping. You won't be able to go on."

He looked back at his maps. "I will find it," he vowed.

She stretched and rose from the black-draped bed. "If anyone can, you will. But come, I see Benny left us some coffee. Take some and I'll go fetch you some dinner from the galley."

"Why are you so suddenly solicitous?"

She smirked. "Because you look terrible." She smiled at his disgruntled look and poured him a cup from the coffeepot on the drum table.

She took it to him and was just about to leave for the galley when his arm wrapped around her waist. He pulled her against him and said, "Don't go. I'm not hungry."

"You must be," she exclaimed.

"Not for food." He stood and took her hand. She dug in her heels when she saw he was leading her to the bed.

"Only you could do that with your last strength, Vashon."

"What better way to expend it?"

"No," she whispered.

He ignored her and untied his trousers.

"I said 'No.' Are you losing your hearing?"

He took her as if she'd never spoken. He kissed her and his tongue drew a ferocious response, but when they parted, she was all too anxious to hide it.

"He may kill me." He spoke as if they were a room apart, not in each other's embrace.

She composed herself and looked up at him. "You finally care whether you live or die?"

"Now that I have something to live for." He stared at her and it took her breath away. He looked at her as if she were the most precious of all jewels.

"Vashon," she whispered, "don't put yourself in jeopardy. Let's run from Peterborough, let's escape—"

His mouth cut off the rest of her plea. It was useless to try and change his mind. She knew that. But she knew too that she couldn't bear losing him.

She meant to plead with him again, yet one kiss led to another. Soon her dress fell to the floor and for a bitterly short time they did escape. To that place right between heaven and earth.

THE TRUCE

> . . . so that in love and sleep we may learn to trust one another.
> —Homer: *Odyssey*

THE
TRUCE

28

Lizzy Lizard sat and smiled
And stared across the sea
"I know the way
But cannot tell
So silly, silly me!"

They sailed north. Aurora spent the afternoons with Flossie and the nights with Vashon. He hardly slept except in the small hours of the morning when he'd spent himself on her, finally falling into a brief, fitful sleep. As the week slipped into another, she watched him drive himself harder and harder searching his maps for the Star. He couldn't last, but somehow, he endured, madly studying his maps until she could hardly bear to watch.

It was now nearing the third week. Later that evening—much later— Aurora watched Vashon rise from the bed, slip on his white trousers, and go again to his desk. She sat up, pulling the sheet to her chest, letting her hair cascade to her hip. She watched him, thinking St. George's was but a few days away, knowing it would be impossible to leave him. She lifted her hand and touched a tender place on her neck. She closed her eyes and remembered his teeth dragging against her skin in a rare moment of surrender. He didn't surrender easily, and that had made his release that much sweeter for her. She couldn't believe that in a few days they would part, maybe never to see each other again. As she watched him, staring down at the maps on his desk, she was eaten away with doubt. Especially now when he was so weary, and so angry, and pushing himself so hard.

"Shall I have Benny bring some dinner?" she asked quietly, interrupting his study.

"All right." In disgust, he pushed back and went to his bookcases. He poured himself a stiff brandy, then went to the open aft ports. A good breeze kicked up the swells, and the ship was cutting through the water at an amazing pace. That depressed her more than anything.

"It's there somewhere," he stated bleakly as if to reassure himself.

"It must be," she answered, stilling her trembling lips with her fingers. She didn't know how she would survive losing him.

"Perhaps if he gets it first, you'll finally be safe."

"Don't even think that."

He dropped his head. For the first time, she wondered if she saw him defeated.

"Vashon, let's abandon the Star."

He turned around and the wild glint in his eye frightened her. "I'll never relinquish it! What he did to me—"

"He did monstrous things," she whispered.

"You think rape is reserved only for women?"

"I know," she said, biting back a sob. "But you fought back. First with those men Josiah paid to kill you all those years ago, then in the Casbah after they sold you. You saved yourself then, so save yourself now. Peterborough won't win if you forfeit."

He turned back to the ports. The wind blew back his black locks. He looked terribly handsome in that pose: arms across his chest, feet splayed commandingly apart. But it wasn't his handsomeness that drew her to him. Nor was it his forlorn figure. Rather it was what had first made her run from him. His fierceness, perhaps even the dragon itself, lured her inescapably to his side. And she understood now that it was destined to be. Because without the dragon in him, he'd never have survived for her to love. And she did love him, with an ache so deep it brought tears to her eyes.

"Vashon," she whispered, "I'd do anything to keep you. Just tell me what I need to do, because I'm losing you, and if I do—" Her voice broke and it was all she could do not to throw herself at his feet and beg him to stop this wretched course they were on.

"Ask Benny to bring us some dinner," he said, ignoring her outburst.

Staring at his cold figure, she said bitterly, "Of course. How silly of me. I'll go right away."

He nodded. She made to leave the bed, but suddenly he stopped and turned again. "What did you say?"

"I said I'll go right away."

"No, before that."

She stiffened. How needlessly cruel he was to flail her with her indiscreet outburst. "I said, how silly of me," she repeated softly, refusing to look at him.

His eyes opened wide. " 'So silly, silly me,' " he mumbled and strode to his desk littered with maps. He shoved aside all the others except the one of the British Isles. "Where did you say your father was born?"

"Hugh Town."

"St. Mary's?"

"Yes," she answered, wrapping the sheet around her and walking over to the desk.

"St. Mary's, the Isles of Scilly, right?"

"Yes," she whispered, her eyes growing wide. The lines of the rhyme seemed to ring in her head. "So silly, *Scilly* me," she repeated in disbelief.

"Jesus. That's it. How stupid I've been."

She looked down at the map of Britain. Vashon put his finger on Land's End right at the southwest tip of England. He moved lower to Lizard Point. When he then moved his finger due west it hit St. Mary's in the Isles of Scilly. And just before Hugh Town on the eastern side of the isle was the promontory of St. Michael's Bluff.

"My God, my father's name," she gasped in shock. She looked at Vashon. "Did he leave it there, then? Oh, my soul, do you think he could still be there? Could it be possible that I might find him?"

He pulled her away from the map. "He must be dead, Aurora. Don't hope for a miracle. He would have come for you."

"But perhaps he's alive!" she cried out, irrational hope blossoming in her breast. "Perhaps he's just forgotten about me!"

He took her into his arms and quieted her. He spoke to her as if she were a child. "He's gone, Aurora. Believe me, love. He wouldn't have forgotten about you."

She started to cry. Angry and helpless, she said, "Don't go to St. George's. Go to St. Mary's instead, and take me with you! I must see for myself that he's dead!"

He looked decisive. He wasn't going to let her go.

"You cannot afford to go to Bermuda now! You don't have time to take me and Flossie there," she begged. "If you go directly to St. Mary's, you'll have the Star before Peterborough even figures it out!"

His reluctance was almost palpable.

"You must!" She grabbed him. Her eyes welled with fresh tears. "Let me see for myself that my father's dead! If you don't, nothing will stop me from following you! I'll go there if I have to swim!"

"He's dead, Aurora. Your father is dead."

"Until I see his grave, I'll believe otherwise."

He didn't say a word.

"I must find him, can't you understand that?" she said.

"I don't want to see your heart broken."

Then don't make me leave you, she wanted to cry out. Instead she looked at him, her eyes full of hurt.

"You won't find him," he said.

"But I must try."

"Then I'll take you," he said stiffly, looking as if he were completely against the idea. "We won't go to Bermuda."

She almost fell to her knees in thanks. Clutching him to her, she placed a kiss on his hard lips and almost danced around the room in her happiness. The thought of finding her father lent a joyous sparkle to her eye and an excited flush to her cheeks. With the sheet wrapped seductively around her, she seemed almost too tempting to resist. All at once, he touched her face, then kissed her so deeply and longingly, she was astonished by his passion. She grew still and lost herself in the persuasion of his lips. The sheet slipped between them until they left it behind, a silky white heap on the floor.

"Fontien says the *Seabravery*'s changing course. His ships that have spied it reported last night that they bypassed Bermuda and are now heading toward England, Land's End to be exact," Asher informed Peterborough while both men stood at the prow.

"He must have figured out where the Star is. I thought they were headed to Bermuda, but now, I don't know where they're going." Peterborough took out the dragon locket and stared at it in frustration.

"You couldn't decipher the rhyme, could you?" There was definitely a dark note of satisfaction in Asher's voice.

"I could with help from Dayne's daughter." The viscount looked ahead to the horizon where somewhere the *Seabravery* raced ahead of them. "But if I don't figure it out before Vashon's ship next makes port, I'll just have to make sure I get Aurora Dayne to help me." With that, he snatched the dangling locket back into his palm and walked away, leaving Asher frowning behind him.

In less than three weeks they pulled into the misty harbor at Hugh Town. Aurora couldn't wait to disembark. The primeval grandeur of St. Mary's beckoned her as much as the stiff, salty wind that blew in from the "roads." She looked over the Strand to the ancient coastline strewn with druid mazes and Celtic burial grounds. She paced the decks and a shiver ran down her spine. He was out there. She knew it. And she would find him.

Vashon, on the other hand, stood on the quarterdeck, staring morosely down at Aurora while she excitedly leaned on the railing at the bow of the ship.

"Could Michael Dayne really be alive?" Isaac asked as he came to stand by Vashon. He looked across the ship at Aurora, then at the desolate rocks and heath-covered downs that surrounded the tiny quay. "There can't be a hundred people on this isle, Vashon. If he's still around, he won't be too hard to find."

"He's dead."

"How do you know that?"

"Look at her." Vashon nodded to Aurora. The wind chapped her cheeks a delicious red, and her hair hung in fetching disarray down her back. With her eyes shining with hope, she looked as beautiful as Amphitrite beckoning a sailor to steer toward the rocks. Vashon scowled. "If you had a daughter like her, would you leave her at an orphanage and never return?"

Isaac frowned. "How will you ever convince her he's gone?"

"She'll have to see for herself." Vashon rubbed his jaw. "How much time have we over Peterborough?"

"You know as well as I he could be here right now. We lost a lot of time heading for St. George's."

"God, I hope not." He released a deep breath. "I need to ask something of you, Isaac."

"Anything, Vashon. You know the men of the *Leviathan* owe you. If you hadn't gone after Peterborough all these years, how many more men would be dead?"

"Then promise me, if I die, you will see Aurora returned to her former life."

Isaac looked startled. "What makes you think you might die?"

"Because . . ." He looked at Aurora on the prow and the vision seemed too much for him. He closed his eyes as if in pain. "Because now I don't want to."

"You won't—"

"No," he interrupted, his eyes snapping open. "I'm already slipping. I've let things get in the way. That's why it's taken me so long to figure the rhyme out. And that's why I made such a grievous error in leaving that damned locket at Dragonard."

"We all make mistakes, Vashon."

"And some live to tell about it." He turned to Isaac. "Promise me? She's got a fiancé back there in London. She should marry him and . . ." His voice faded as if he were having trouble finishing. After a moment, he said, ". . . and have a decent life."

"I promise, Vashon," Isaac said quietly.

"Good."

"But you're going to win. You mark my words. You're the better man. Peterborough hasn't your strength, nor your cunning. He'll fall. Men like him always do."

Vashon laughed cynically. He slapped Isaac on the back and changed the subject. "But you haven't told me, man, what are you going to do after this? Is that widow going to chase you to the ends of the earth, or are you finally going to take that woman in hand?"

"I'm afraid to say I already have."

Vashon appeared almost speechless. "You mean . . ."

Isaac came as near as a sea captain could come to blushing. "Well, you know I was never one to go wenching after I lost Rachel."

"So what happened?"

"When I finally got the old girl quiet, I realized she weren't that bad."

Vashon tipped his head back and laughed. The sound was so provocative Aurora must have heard it on the prow. She waved and Vashon captured her gaze. He acknowledged her with a smile, then turned melancholy once more.

Isaac nodded his head toward Aurora. "You could use a woman too, Vashon. It'd do you good."

"Yes." Vashon pushed back from the railing. "But then when have I ever done things that were good for me?" He grinned and said, "Are we ready?"

"As we'll ever be."

Vashon looked to the distant granite-strewn head called St. Michael's Bluff. "Then let's get the Star."

29

St. Michael's Bluff was a steep overlook that faced a bare rocky coast. The wind had been cruel, and even the heath had left its scrubbed woody stumps to face the sea and sent its spiky pink flowers leeward as if craving mercy from the elements. The only inhabitants were several dwarfed sheep that fed on the algae and fescues of the downs, and the gulls that screamed above, only increasing the tension of the men who made their way to the peak, cautious of the terrible fall that led to the beach and the great boulders scattered there.

They searched, but nothing caught their eye. There should have been a marker, a cairn, a pile of stones to direct them, but there was nothing, merely the windbeaten scurvy grass that clung tenaciously to the steep edge of the bluff, and a long fall to the beach.

But all at once excitement rose in the group. A man pointed to a large rock protruding from the bluff. A weathered tin box lay snug between it and the cliff, camouflaged by the salt-corroded surface of the granite. Two men braved the descent, and soon they were hanging on the incline, reaching desperately for the box. The cheap tin chest was eventually removed and sent, man to man, up the incline to the imposing figure who waited at the top.

The man put his hands on the coffer and they shook with emotion. At last! He broke the tiny lock and dumped the chest's contents into his palms. There was nothing but a note. On it was written:

> Only my daughter will find it.
> —Michael Seamus Dayne

Peterborough crumpled the note in his hand. The men on the incline stared at him as he stood atop the bluff. He made no attempt at all to hide his anger. He raised his fist and screamed out his fury.

* * *

"Please, take me with you, Vashon. I just want to ask about my father. If the jewel's been on the bluff all these years, what's another few hours?" Aurora clung to his arm as he was about to disembark the *Seabravery* with several of his men.

"When I know it's safe, I'll take you there. Until then, you have to wait."

Frustrated with his answer, she glanced longingly at the quay, toward the only tavern in Hugh Town, the Standing Stone.

Vashon followed her gaze, then shook his head. "You think to go in there and ask for a man probably not seen in fifteen years?"

"Vashon, I beg of you, I want so much to find him. If you only knew how much . . ." She looked desperately toward the tavern again.

He took her arms and forced her gaze to his. "I know how much, my love. I can see it on your face." He turned grim. "But I don't intend to spend any more time here than I have to. Peterborough could be on the island even as we speak. The *Merry Magdalene* could be anchored in The-Road and they could have come ashore anywhere. Until I have the Star, it's not prudent to go searching for Michael Dayne."

"I understand that. But what if you don't find the Star? I must look for him!"

He caressed her cheek. "If the Star's on that bluff, I'll find it. And then, I promise, we'll look for your father."

Her expression faltered. "But Vashon, I still fear for you. If Peterborough's on the island, you mustn't waste time here. Let me look for him while you search for the emerald."

"When I find the Star, we'll look." He placed a tender kiss on her lips, then with his chosen seamen he left for the bluff.

In silence she watched him go, her heart torn with the need to protect him and to find her father.

"The captain asks you to go belowdecks, miss."

Aurora turned to find Benny hovering solicitously around her with Koonga comfortably around his neck. She smiled tremulously. "Where is Isaac now?"

"Taking tea in the widow's cabin, miss. The widow asks that you join them."

Aurora again looked longingly toward the tavern. The sign creaked as it swung in the humid breeze.

She turned to Benny. "Vashon can't spent any more time here than necessary. I can't hold him up looking for my father. I've got to look now while he's searching for the Star."

"Miss, you can't go now! Vashon'll have my head!"

"Benny, I've got to. I've just got to!"

"No, miss," Benny began but she was already moving down the gangway.

"Benny, I'll be right back, before Vashon returns."

"No, miss!" he cried out, but by this time, she was already on the quay heading toward the Standing Stone. He had no choice but to follow.

Aurora had never been in a tavern before. She was intimidated by the dark interior, even more by the groups of men who sat at trestle tables quaffing their stout. Nonetheless, she glided across the dirt and straw-strewn floor to the man who, by his apron, had to be the taverner.

"Pardon me, good sir, but I'm looking for someone and thought I might find help here," she began.

The man eyed her with typical Cornish distrust. He wiped his bulbous nose with the back of his hand and leaned against the crude planking of the bar. He said, "Thar ain't noone here fer tha', love. We got more Irish on the lay than we know wha' ta do with. So don't need none of yourn off the ships."

Taken aback, she didn't know what to say, but behind her, Benny came to her rescue.

"You're addressing the fine lady Miss Aurora Dayne, bloke. And if she ain't addressed properlike, the owner of the *Seabravery* just may come to pay you a visit."

The tavern keeper had been about to take a sip from his mug when Benny mentioned the *Seabravery*. Upon that name he nearly spewed the contents to the floor.

"The owner of the *Seabravery*? Y' mean the—the—the *Dragon* his-self?" he stuttered in shock.

Aurora turned and gave Benny a look of amazement. She had never known Benny could be so commanding.

"The very same," Benny stated evenly.

"We-e-el, ya needn't be askin' agin. What genelmen would ya be lookin' fer, me lady?" The tavern keeper fairly oozed ingratiating sweetness. He straightened and even wiped his perennially runny nose with his apron, not his hand.

"It's my father," Aurora quickly offered. "He was born in Hugh

Town. I think he returned here. Would you know him? His name was Michael Dayne."

"Dayne? I never 'eard of tha' name."

Crestfallen, Aurora was about to thank the man when he said, " 'Course, thar were a bloke runnin' 'round here 'bout five years past."

"What was his name?" she asked excitedly.

"Don't know that."

Her disappointment grew. "Then what made you think of this man?"

"Bloke had the same red 'air you do, me lady."

Aurora stared at the man as if he had just handed her the Holy Grail.

"Miss, we've got to return to the ship," Benny whispered at her elbow. "Vashon'll speak with this man himself when he returns. But right now it's not safe for you to be here."

"No, Benny, wait!" She turned back to the tavern keeper. "What happened to this man?"

" 'E disappeared. 'Bout five years past. And we were glad to be rid of 'im, tha' we were. The bloke were as crazy as I want ta meet. 'E'd get to drinking, never talking to nobody, and lookin' more and more grievous by the year. We tol' 'im to go back to his parish, but 'e kept 'sisting tha' 'e was from here."

"Oh, God, that's he," she whispered, clutching Benny's arm for support. "But now you say he left?"

"No, don't reckon 'e left. I think 'e died, me lady. But we don't bury paupers, tha's the parish's task."

"But he was no pauper!" she exclaimed.

"Seemed like 'un to me, wanderin' 'bout, talkin' of stars. 'E were a lonely creatur', 'e were."

A lump settled in her throat, thinking about her father. What had gone wrong? Though it would always pain her to think of him as a thief, she'd found some comfort believing he was at least living well on the proceeds of that jewel, even if he'd chosen to do it without her. If she never found him, she at least wanted him to be happy, to picture him living like Bacchus, drunk on his own pleasures. But instead it seemed his last years were spent like a beggar, too crazy even for the work-house. The thought of him sitting alone in some dank corner of this tavern, drunk and miserable, gave her an inconsolable ache.

"Where did he reside?" she whispered finally, feeling the weight of depression descending upon her.

"No one really knows. 'E came down for 'is gin from the thicket near

Troy-fair. To tell true, I think 'e were livin' in one of them tombs near the maze."

"What maze?" she asked.

"The druit maze, me lady. The big 'un beside the elms, way up there." He shoved his finger behind him, in the direction of St. Michael's Bluff.

"Thank you so much," she said numbly. She turned away and began walking out. Benny thrust a coin in the man's hand and followed her back out to the docks.

"Thanks fer the blunt!" the taverner called out before they left.

"Where are you going now, miss? We've got to return to the ship!" Benny exclaimed, following her as she walked away from the harbor.

"I've got to find him. Even if he's dead. And now's the time to do it. I can't risk Vashon being caught by Peterborough if my father's gone. I just want to see if he truly is."

"But—but, miss! I can't follow you up the hill!"

Aurora turned about. Koonga was barely keeping a grip on Benny's neck while the boy tried to stay abreast. She softened and said, "I'm sorry, Benny. But I've got to go, for myself, for Vashon. Return to the ship. If you say nothing, I'll be back before anyone even realizes I'm gone."

"I can't do that, miss! I can't leave you here!"

"You have to!" she choked out, hating herself for putting him in this difficult position. She tossed him an apologetic glance, then, blocking out his cries of protest, she picked up her skirt and ran past the quay, leaving the tiny village of Hugh Town behind.

The sailor from the *Seabravery* climbed St. Michael's Bluff, wildly calling out in French. Vashon stood at the top, Dayne's crumpled note in his fist. Peterborough was nowhere to be seen. Vashon and the sailor had a quick, tense interchange in French, then Vashon turned to Isaac.

"Aurora's left the ship to search for her father." Vashon rubbed his jaw, lines of worry etched into his face. "I'm going after her. Benny left directions. Take the men back and see if anyone's seen Peterborough. From what we've found here, we know he's got to be on the island."

Isaac nodded, but instead of immediately complying, he stared at Vashon, his expression troubled.

"Don't think about Aurora, Vashon," he finally said.

The statement seemed to surprise Vashon. "What are you saying?"

"I'm saying, watch your back. Don't be distracted and we'll win this war. It will seem like you must look out for Aurora first, but if you don't, you'll be better off. Watch your back, Vashon, as you always have. It's the only way to save both yourself and Aurora." As if embarrassed by his outburst, Isaac turned a worried gaze down at the docks of Hugh Town. "That was a foolish thing she did. I hope to God she's not dead already."

Vashon's eyes filled with hatred and agony. In a voice as solemn as a prayer he said, "If she is, then he'll take me too."

He left without a farewell.

30

The Troy-fair maze consisted of little better than large rocks arranged in concentric circles on the peak of a hill. Aurora looked around, the indigo waters of Porthcressa to her right; to her left the dramatic boulders of Peninnis. Across St. Mary's Sound, the off-islands of Gugh and St. Agnes were barely visible in the mist; nowhere were there any tombs. She continued climbing, through fields of crimson clover and blooming white thrift. When she next looked up, the only structure that broke the desolate scenery was a crumbling stone enclosure that held a wretched copse of elms.

She went atop the ridge of moor and stared at the ancient crumbling walls, unsure of how to proceed. The elms were almost frightening, for where they grew above the protection of the wall, they'd become gnarled and wind pruned, like the fantasy trees in the Chinese screens she'd seen at the governor's mansion in Grand Talimen. She couldn't believe her father would live in such a strange place, but she forced aside her doubts and went toward it. Though she feared finding her father dead, she knew it was going to be far worse to find nothing at all and to watch her last chance at restoring her family crumble beneath her hands.

She took a deep breath and entered the walled garden. The purple-brown figwort was so thick it obscured everything but the contorted elms. Here and there a patch of yellow elecampane sprang up to cheer the landscape, but that was a difficult task, especially when she realized the succulent-covered bumps scattered all around were actually large Celtic tombs.

She summoned her bravery and stepped to one, tearing off its overgrown cover. The tomb was pummeled out of granite and looked to have stood since the dawn of time. She stepped quietly to another and a sudden noise frightened her, but it was only a black rabbit scurrying from its disturbed shelter. She smiled at her spooked nerves, but when she walked farther into the copse, her breath came fast and tight within her chest.

She ducked under an elm and noted how dark it had become beneath the low, gnarled trees. She moved forward, the elms growing denser with each step, and came upon a large broken-down tomb hidden among some wild privet. The tomb was the largest of them all, certainly big enough for a man to find shelter there. She bit her lower lip and brushed away the figwort from the front of the tomb. The foliage was so overgrown, she tripped. She looked down to see what had caused her to stumble and made a horrifying discovery—a pair of boots that were most definitely attached to their previous owner, a man who was now nothing more than bones and tattered clothing.

Gasping, she backed away. The dead man had to be her father, yet how would she summon the courage to uncover his body to be sure? Desperately needing Vashon, she decided to return to the ship, but a pair of hands grabbed her before she could even turn to go.

"How dare you disobey me."

She let out a cry, then almost laughed from relief, recognizing the voice. She spun and threw her arms around Vashon. He held her tightly, but only for a moment, then he pulled back.

"I'll chain you to the figurehead the next time, Aurora. I swear, I'll kill you before I'll see you do something so stupid again."

His harsh words shocked her. She looked at him, for the first time noticing his drawn features, his pale cheeks. He appeared as if he'd just been told everything he'd cherished was gone.

"But I've found him, Vashon. At least," her gaze wandered reluctantly to the spot where she'd discovered the boots, "I think I have."

His gaze followed hers. Leaving her behind, he walked to the body in the figwort and ripped away some of the overgrowth. When he bent to it, his face had the strangest expression, a blend of foreboding joy and dark triumph. He took a faded velvet purse from the skeletal fingers. He opened it and when he stood again, her eyes were drawn to his hand. Even in the dim light beneath the elms, the emerald's brilliance took her breath away. The Star of Aran was exquisite, alight with blue fire, and so large it took up most of Vashon's palm.

"It was he," she said.

" 'Only my daughter will find it'," Vashon repeated, watching her.

"What are you saying?" she whispered, finding tears in her eyes.

"He knew you'd look for him first. Dayne counted on that. You proved to be a good daughter, Aurora."

"But I didn't find him alive. . . ." The words were barely discernible. A sudden irrational grief gripped her, and she began to sob. She hadn't realized how dearly she'd wanted her father back, how desperately she'd wanted to restore what little family she possessed. Now that the hope was gone, she found it almost too much to bear.

"He wouldn't want your sorrow, my love," Vashon whispered against her hair after he took her in his arms.

"But he came to such an ignoble end, and I so wanted to find him. Now I have nothing," she said with a sob.

"No." He caressed her hair and pressed the emerald into her hand. She meant to pull back, to show him that the jewel was poor consolation for her lonely heart, but he wouldn't let her go. When her tearful gaze locked with his and he had her full attention, he whispered, "You will always have me."

She stared at him, unable to believe his words. But when his lips pressed against hers, she knew it was true. All her fears that he would abandon her fled with his needful kiss. For the first time since she'd met him, she suddenly felt the dragon might be tamed after all. Certainly if her love could ever do it, she vowed he would never want for more.

"*Aurore,*" he whispered when they parted. "we've got to get back to the ship now." He wiped the tears from her cheeks with his thumbs. "Your father left this for you, I imagine. Read it when we're back on the *Seabravery.*" He handed her a letter that was in the velvet purse.

"Wait! I must read it now," she implored and he hadn't the heart to stop her. She devoured the note with her gaze and when she was through, she suddenly felt at peace.

"What did he say to you, *mon Aurore*?" Vashon asked.

"He said he couldn't come back for me because he was too afraid of Peterborough. He felt I was safer at the Home than running scared with him. He said he loved me, Vashon." She suddenly began to cry again and he held her until her last tears were spent.

"Come. We must return," he said reluctantly when she had recovered. He held out his hand and she took it, feeling an exultant mix of joy and sorrow, especially when she looked in the direction of where her father lay near the Celtic tomb.

"How can I leave until he has a proper burial?" she asked.

"I'll send some men from the ship to shroud his body. When we sail, we'll put him out at sea."

More tears threatened to fall down her cheek. "What happened to him? Why was he so tormented? Why did he come to this wretched end?"

He held her tight. "I suspect he came to the conclusion that what he'd done hadn't been worth it. He'd escaped with the Star, yet in the end he had to sacrifice something even more valuable."

"But what was that? The locket?" she asked, confused.

"No," he answered, his gaze never wavering from her face. "You."

She wiped another tear from her cheek and again felt that odd dichotomy of sorrow and joy.

"We've got to get back. Peterborough is here. He was on the bluff before we got there."

She gasped, her blood suddenly running cold. "Why did you come after me then? I did this," she fretted. "The locket led him here, and now I've put you in jeopardy. I might lose you too. . . ."

"No." He put two fingers to her lips. "Don't say it. You won't."

She grabbed him to her. "Oh my love, please, we can't let him win now."

"But he's already won," a threatening voice rang out in their midst.

Aurora felt Vashon tense. When he forced her behind him, she stared at the figure standing in the entrance to the tombs. The man looked so much like Vashon, she might have been looking at a mirror. The only difference was that this man obviously took great pains to appear the gentleman: his green frock coat was costly and impeccably restrained; his hair was cropped fashionably close with a touch of gray at the temples that proclaimed him the elder. He was lordly and refined, what Vashon might have been. Aurora stared at Peterborough and could hardly believe that this handsome, civilized-looking man could have really brought such agony to so many lives.

"My good brother, you've found us at last." Vashon took her trembling hand and casually walked toward the entrance. Aurora followed, unsure of what Vashon was going to do.

"The *Merry Magdalene* is anchored off Porthmellon. We heard from the alehouse in Hugh Town that Aurora had come up here. Of course, I couldn't wait to meet her." Peterborough looked at her and smiled. His eyes were just like his brother's, beautiful and green. Yet Josiah's held a coldness beyond anything she'd ever seen in Vashon's. She wondered how two could look so much alike and yet be so completely different.

"How lovely it is to meet you, Miss Dayne," he continued. "You look like your father, you know, but I daresay, he didn't imagine his daugh-

ter would become such a beauty." Josiah smiled again. From his pleas-
antries, one would have supposed they were meeting for a play at Cov-
ent Garden instead of a life-or-death confrontation on a salt-scrubbed
moorland.

"I take it you discovered Dayne's note," Vashon said, stilling
Aurora's trembling hand.

"Yes, and I'm afraid Aurora here has many questions to answer for
me." Peterborough nodded behind him where a veritable battalion of
men stood, pistols in hand. A scurvy-looking man stepped forward,
obviously the pirate Fontien from the gaudy ruby stuck in his earlobe.
He meant to take Aurora, but Vashon pulled her farther behind him.

"You want the emerald, Josiah?" Vashon said. When Peterborough
laughed, Vashon opened his palm. The sight of the jewel made everyone
gasp. " 'Whosoever possesses the Star of Aran shall see his enemies die.'
Isn't that what *The Chronicles* say, my good brother?"

Peterborough blanched. It took him a moment to collect himself.
"You're outnumbered, Vashon. I believe in *The Chronicles of Crom
Dubh*, but in this instance, I cannot see how you'll win."

"Perhaps, but I shall strike a deal with you anyway. Let Aurora go
and I'll give you the emerald."

"No!" Aurora cried out.

"Vashon, you must be mad to trust me." Peterborough smiled.

"I don't trust you. But I want Aurora out of this. She should not be
involved in our conflict."

"Methinks little Miss Dayne means a great deal to you, Vashon."

"Vashon, don't do this! How can I go free, knowing—"

"Aurora, you will do as I say." Vashon pushed forward, holding the
emerald out to Peterborough. "Take it, brother. For her freedom, you
may have the Star."

"What are you about, Vashon?" Josiah narrowed his eyes.

"I want her unharmed."

"You've made my life a hell—stealing from me, setting free my property—do you know how much a healthy male slave costs, Vashon?"

"Aye, but I have money and whatever the cost, I shall pay it to see
Aurora go unharmed."

"I want you to suffer, Vashon, as I have suffered these years."

"And I have not suffered?" Vashon's control nearly lapsed. He
stepped forward, then thought better of it. He stepped back and said,
"Let her go, Josiah. This is between us, not her."

Peterborough nodded. "Hand me the emerald then, and I shall consider your request."

"When Aurora is back on the *Seabravery*."

"All right." Josiah turned to a slight figure, the only other gentleman in the group. "Asher, escort Miss Dayne to Hugh Town." He turned back to Vashon. "Is that enough for you?"

"When I see her go."

Aurora stood mutely by and allowed the young man to take her arm. She wanted to cry out in protest, but after all that had transpired on this adventure, she knew Vashon too well to argue with him now. He obviously had a plan. She just wished she knew what it was.

"I'll see you on the ship, love," he said as they walked past him. She tried to meet his eye, but he refused, as if it were too painful. She was several yards away before she suddenly had the dreadful fear his plan was to truly sacrifice himself for her. When she turned, he would still not meet her gaze, and she nearly went mad from the horror of it.

"Unhand me!" she cried out to the blond young man. She struggled, but he held fast. "Release me! Vashon, don't do this!" she implored, but to no avail. When she began to scratch, Peterborough laughed.

He stepped to them and said to the young man, "You can kill her in whatever manner you like." He then touched Aurora's smooth cheek. "You're enchanting, Miss Dayne. I regret that I'm forced to waste you on Asher here. He won't appreciate you as I could have."

"Oh, but I do appreciate her, Josiah," the man named Asher answered coolly. "In fact, I appreciated Miss Dayne so much that I sent word to the *Seabravery* that you were coming up here. I've betrayed you, Josiah. How does it feel?"

"You betray me now!" Peterborough gasped.

"You betrayed me on Mirage! You would have shot me to get to him!" Asher put a shaking hand to his pistol. He aimed it at Peterborough. "I could have grown fond of you, Josiah, but you treated me callously, and I will never forgive you for that."

"You buggering coward!" Peterborough raged. "You'll die for this!"

"So be it!" Asher retorted.

In a flash Peterborough lunged and grasped the man's weakly held weapon. Josiah pointed it, obviously not caring if he killed Asher or Aurora first. Seeing that, Vashon's self-restraint ripped apart and he attacked Peterborough in a murderous rage.

Aurora screamed and watched in terror as Vashon and Peterborough tumbled down the moor toward St. Michael's Bluff. Mindless of anything but the need to help him, she ran to them. The other pirates of the *Merry Magdalene* went to assist Peterborough, but just as Vashon looked outnumbered, the men from the *Seabravery* appeared on the mount.

The pirates clashed and soon screams of the wounded rang in the air. Aurora heard the rip of stilettos through fabric and the violent scattered explosions of gunshots. She and Asher almost clung to each other as the fight swirled around them. Never had Aurora seen the men of the *Seabravery* act as pirates, and when Isaac led them in a ferocious war cry, she couldn't fight the chill that ran down her spine. Though they had discipline, Vashon's men were every bit as ruthless as Fontien's men. The fight seemed to go on forever, but it was actually only a few minutes before the wounded, bloody pirates of the *Merry Magdalene* retreated, taking their dead comrades with them. The losers loped toward Hugh Town, the pirate Fontien forging the path, while the men of the *Seabravery* prodded them on with their sharp sabers.

That left only Peterborough.

Silhouetted against the misty sky, Vashon and Peterborough were in a grotesque dance on the promontory, fighting each other for the pistol that was in their shared grasp. Desperate to help, Aurora left Asher's side and got within a few feet of Vashon before Isaac pulled her back. In dismay she looked at him, but he only said, "It's their fight. Let them have it."

Aurora turned back to the violent scene being played out on the bluff. The emerald lay on the sand beneath them, a glittering symbol of all they were fighting for.

Though the struggle took only a moment, to Aurora it seemed like an eternity. Finally Vashon got the pistol away from Peterborough and Josiah backed away just inches from the bluff.

"I should kill you," Vashon said, still panting from his struggle.

"Go ahead, Vashon. It's what you've dreamed of," Peterborough spat. "Kill me as I would have killed you."

Aurora could hardly look at the battle of emotions in Vashon's face. He wanted to kill Peterborough, she knew that, but something held him back. That noble side of his just couldn't seem to relinquish him and allow him to shoot his own brother. Out of instinct, she stepped forward, desperate to help him, but Isaac pulled her back.

"Come on, Vashon, pull the trigger. Kill your brother as you have so many others."

Vashon gasped for air. He lifted the pistol higher; his expression frozen in a vicious mask of fury. He was barely a hair's breadth away from pulling the trigger, but then he looked at Aurora.

Their eyes met and he appeared moved by the emotions clearly written on her face. Love, horror, and shame were mixed in her expression, but the greatest of these was love. With that one glance, in the final minute of his revenge against Peterborough, Vashon suddenly seemed to change. It was as if something now meant more to him than his bloodlust for his half brother. Aurora could hardly believe it was true, but finally the dragon in him seemed to be tamed.

Breathing heavily, Vashon lowered the pistol. He stared at Peterborough, hardly able to choke out his words. "If it was ever said that I did a noble deed, then let it be proclaimed that I could not kill my own brother."

Peterborough had obviously seen the reason for Vashon's change of heart. He stared at Aurora, then lunged madly for Vashon's pistol. "If I cannot kill you, Vashon, then I shall get you where you're most vulnerable!" Josiah grabbed the pistol, and while it was still in Vashon's hand, pulled back the hammer and aimed it at Aurora.

Isaac thrust her back but there was no place to take cover in the barren landscape. The captain took out his pistol, yet before he could shoot, the men were once more in a death conflict. With a grunt of rage and terror, Vashon struggled with Josiah to take control of the gun, twisting his body in front of the barrel to shield Aurora. Before anyone could stop him, Peterborough finally had his revenge. He fired the weapon and sent the blast square into Vashon's torso.

When Vashon stumbled back, the viscount desperately scooped up the emerald. He rubbed the jewel in his palm and appeared to relish the scene before him.

Hunched over, Vashon removed his hand from his stomach. It was covered in blood. Aurora cried out and Isaac aimed his pistol at Peterborough.

A wild glint appeared in Vashon's eyes and before Isaac could kill the viscount, Vashon reached out to Peterborough.

"Take my hand, Josiah," he said. "Don't be afraid. This blood is your blood, *brother*."

Peterborough blanched.

"Take it, Josiah," Vashon gasped, the pain obviously becoming too much for him. "Take it as my atonement for the past."

"Stay away, Vashon."

"I said, take it, brother!" Vashon pushed forward.

Frightened, Peterborough backed to the edge of the bluff. Below him was the straight treacherous fall to the beach. All too aware of this, Josiah looked around for an escape. He stepped back onto the outcrop that had held Michael Dayne's box, but he misjudged his mark. He slipped and desperately reached for a horribly stunted wych elm that protruded from the cliff. Vashon was in no shape to assist him, so Isaac released Aurora and went to the edge of the cliff.

"Help me," Peterborough begged, clinging pitifully to the wych elm.

"Do you know who I am, viscount?" Isaac asked in a low monotone.

"Help me, you fool! I see you're a captain of a ship! I'll get you a thousand ships with my emerald, just help me!"

Isaac leaned down. "I'm the captain of the *Leviathan*, Lord Peterborough. I'll give you my hand so that you may climb back to the top." Isaac held out his hand, the hand that Peterborough himself had crippled. Peterborough grasped it for dear life.

The two men stayed suspended like that for a moment: Isaac not wanting to save Peterborough yet unwilling to be the one to plunge him to his death; and Peterborough pleading desperately for pity and more assistance.

In the end, the issue was decided by fate. Isaac tried to save him, but with only two fingers a solid grasp was nearly impossible.

"I can't hold on!" Josiah cried, slipping inch by inch, ever closer to the jagged granite boulders below.

When he finally fell, Isaac's only words were, "You could have."

Peterborough met his end at the rocky bottom, the emerald tumbling just beyond his limp grasp.

Horrified, they all stood at the top and stared down at Peterborough's sprawled broken figure. As if he couldn't help himself, Vashon whispered, " 'Whosoever possesses the Star of Aran shall see his enemies die.' " Vashon then crumpled to the ground.

"My love, my love," Aurora cried softly, the blood running down his shirt frightening her. Isaac's face grew grim as he saw Vashon's condition.

"My love, it will be all right," she whispered, weeping beside him, unable to keep her gaze away from his face. "It must be," she said, weeping.

"Isaac," Vashon whispered, his features taut with pain.

"I'm here, Vashon." Isaac bent down and took Aurora by the shoulders.

"You recall your promise on the *Seabravery*?"

"Vashon, don't do this." Isaac's voice shook.

"No, now's the time. You promised me. Do you recant that now?"

Isaac nearly wept with reluctance. "No, Vashon."

"Then you'll do it?"

"I'll keep by my promise."

"Good. *Aurore?*" he rasped to her.

"I'm here, my love. We'll get a surgeon—"

Vashon touched her face. His fingers became wet with her tears. "Even though the words were never spoken, you are my wife, Aurora."

"No, Vashon, no. We'll speak the words. Someday. I swear."

"This," he reached down to the emblazoned brass key still hanging around her neck, "this is all you'll have left of me. Go there."

"Vashon, don't say such things."

He turned from her and she saw a tear slip down his cheek. That more than anything affected her. He'd feared she'd make him vulnerable, and that the prophecy had come true. He finally loved her, and it had been that love that had forced him to spare her life at the expense of his own. She began to sob madly until Isaac pulled her off him. Cook, who served as the *Seabravery*'s surgeon, arrived on the bluff and began quickly ministering to Vashon's wounds. Other seamen arrived to help also, and soon she was lost in the pandemonium.

"Come along, Aurora," Isaac said numbly. "I've got to return you to London."

"No, I cannot go," she cried, watching Cook bandage Vashon while another seaman took off his shirt and placed it under his head.

"I've got to take you. He made me promise. We've got to go now."

"I won't."

Isaac roughly grabbed her arm. "Don't you see he's dying? Don't you see he doesn't want you around for you to see him like this?"

"But I must be around. I love him," she sobbed.

Her tears softened him, but he stood by his promise. "It's what he wishes, Aurora. Do as he wishes." He pulled her away.

"Please, let me be there when he goes. Let me hold him. I have nothing but him." She wept bitterly and fought him. He nearly lifted her off her feet to drag her unwilling body along the heath-covered down. There were men everywhere on the bluff now. He snapped an order to a few oncoming men to return to the ship to help prepare her for sail.

"I beg of you, Isaac, I would rather you kill me than force me from him now!" she lashed out, viciously pulling his arm.

"I gave him my word, Aurora."

"I have nothing to return to. I have nothing to live for," she cried. "Don't do this to me!"

"He wanted you to go on. You will go on."

"Don't make me." She wept in a small wretched voice. "Don't make me live without him."

"My child." Isaac finally broke down and wiped the tears streaming down his own cheeks. He held her to his burly chest. She wept against him and he rasped the cruelest words he'd ever had to speak.

"You must."

THE DRAGON TAMED

The beggar begs by God's command,
And gifts awake when givers sleep,
Swords cannot cut the giving hand
Nor stab the love that orphans keep.

—Ralph Waldo Emerson:
Fragments on Nature and Life

31

Aurora stood at the door to Peterborough's former residence, Blackwell House, the London mansion of the titled Blackwells. She was pale, her eyes swollen as if she still spent long hours weeping. To Isaac, she looked as tragic and inconsolable as that afternoon when they had sailed from Hugh Town, leaving Vashon behind on that bluff covered in blood and swarming with the *Seabravery*'s men.

But this day, when Isaac watched her stare up at the enormous wainscoted front doors of the mansion, he was struck by the subtle difference in her face. Gone was the stiff armor of propriety she'd used so frequently on their voyage; gone too was that air of offended innocence that Vashon had found so titillating and yet so annoying.

He had always thought of Aurora as beautiful, but today her beauty haunted him. Her face held a softness that he'd never seen before and a strength that looked as if not even a tidal wave could break it. Isaac considered himself an old hardened Jew, callused by brutality and prejudice, too jaded to appreciate the sublime things like beauty and grace. But even he found himself inspired by the fact that both this woman's softness and her strength came from loving a man as hard and brutal and wild as Vashon.

"Use the key," he whispered, urging her forward.

Aurora stared at him, then impulsively took his hand. In their shared grief, Isaac had become the father she never had. He smiled at her and squeezed her hand. Finally she found the courage to look down at the brass key in her hand. Holding her breath, she fitted the key in the enormous brass lock.

Isaac opened the doors and led her into a huge marbled hall with a staircase that looked grand enough to be in a Roman temple. But everything was dark, for all the shutters on the house were closed, verifying the previous occupant's expected long absence.

In silence she sauntered through a great saloon done entirely in red and gold, the furniture looking ghostlike with its dust shrouds of linen. They went from room to room, each more elegant and more abandoned.

The house depressed her. There were no servants to fling open a window and let in some fresh air, nor to light the lusters when evening came to call. The house was the finest she'd ever been in, but as she wandered its passages and formal rooms, she couldn't picture herself living there. There were no dragons on the carpets, no gilt dolphin feet on the settees. The beds weren't draped in muslin; instead they were dressed in fine silk brocades.

Vashon was nowhere to be found. She couldn't picture him anywhere, not on the tapestried fauteuils in the saloon, not having his breakfast in the Wedgwood morning room, nor reading a book in the Egyptian-inspired library. He was not there. She could find evidence only of Peterborough.

She'd seen enough. She'd asked Isaac to escort her out when they came to a small mahogany door that led up to the fifth-floor attic rooms. To satisfy her curiosity, she lifted her skirt and mounted the stairs, only to find herself in an old, unkempt nursery. Dust grayed everything from the rotting lace curtains at the dormer windows to the painted floor cloth that had once been bright blue. There was a schoolroom beyond, and she was just about to walk to it when her skirt caught on something. She stopped and looked down.

It was a small wooden rocking horse, a dear little toy, obviously well used and well loved. She brushed away some of the dust with her hand and revealed chipped blue paint, faded to the color of a robin's egg. The horse had a real mane and tail. Enchanted, she tried to set the thing in motion, but one of its runners was split off and it wouldn't move.

She tried not to think of him as a little boy, riding his rocking horse in the nursery, impressing his nanny with his talent. She tried desperately not to think of him, but when her hand lovingly ran over the cracked leather saddle and she saw the name "Vashon" painted in gold lettering on its cantle, she couldn't stop the lone tear from escaping and christening the little horse. In her pain she wanted to hug that little rocking horse to her breast and sit in a corner, never to rise again. And for one wild moment she thought of doing just that before Isaac touched her arm and bade her rise.

"There's more to see beyond this room," he said.

She shook her head. "I don't want to see any more. I can't find him, Isaac. He's not here," she said with a truth that stabbed her like a knife.

Vashon wasn't there. She could only picture him on Mirage, running along the surf, or eating genips beneath the silk-cotton tree. And smiling at her with that dazzling, dangerous smile. That man with his long black hair and sinful earring didn't belong in this staid, aristocratic mansion, and even the little boy who owned the rocking horse was gone, for that tame and innocent child had long been excised from Vashon in the streets of Algiers.

Taking one last look at the little broken rocking horse, she asked, "Would you mind taking me to the Phipps-Bluefield Home, Isaac?"

"Why there, Aurora?"

"I'm going back," she said with a finality that surprised even her. "It's what he wanted, wasn't it, for me to return to my former life?"

"Vashon wanted that in essence, but not literally. I think he wanted you to live here, Aurora."

"I couldn't."

"If it's the funds you're worried about—"

"No. I have a place back at the Home. They can use me, and I need to be busy."

Isaac stayed respectfully silent.

She took a deep breath, needing to collect herself. It was very hard for her to speak. "How strangely life works. When I first left the Home, Isaac, I thought the emptiness within me was because I had never found out who that little girl was that Michael Dayne left at the orphanage so long ago. But now that I've found her, still there's that emptiness. And the only time it ever left . . ." Tears stung her eyes. She ignored them, then shook her head, unwilling to go on.

"Come with Flossie and me to St. George's. Don't stay here in London where you have no friends, child."

She looked up at him, and suddenly realized how dear he and Flossie had become to her after this terrible adventure. But she had to refuse his offer. They were to be married and already had a tumultuous relationship. They didn't need her in the middle of it.

"No, thank you, captain. The Home waits for me. Don't take me away from my purpose."

"You didn't kill him. You know that, don't you, Aurora?"

She turned away. Her face was so consciously without expression it appeared ready to crack. "I believed in my heart that living without caring and emotion was not living at all. I forced him to feel what he did not want to feel." Her voice lowered to a hush. "He told me not to love him."

"You didn't kill him."

She glanced at Isaac, then away. Her voice wavered. "I beg you, take me away from this place. I can't stand to stay here another minute." To prove her point, she fled down the stairs all the way to the marble hall. She dropped the brass key on a gilt console and was out the door before Isaac could stop her.

"He's been in such a fine temper since you've been back. I daren't ask him for another shilling. But, oh, Aurora, would you ask him? We must have some more milk. I don't know how the children will fare when it gets colder if we don't have it." Faith held her hands out in supplication, and Aurora put down her pen.

A month had passed since she'd left Hugh Town. John had taken her back into the Home and now, when she thought by all rights things should be better, they were worse. It was as if John knew everything that had happened to her on her voyage. That was impossible, she knew, but something had given her away; perhaps it was the way she didn't shrink from confrontation now, or the cool, level, knowledgeable way she met his eye when he spoke to her. She wasn't the same, and he hated it. And now he made everything more onerous. When before he was testy, now he was outright belligerent.

"I'll talk to him." She nodded. "Did you get the notices from Queenhithe?"

"No ship today. The only ships that have docked are the *Tenacious* and the *Sleeping Beauty*."

Aurora jumped upon hearing the latter name. A flood of bittersweet memories came back to her, but she pushed them away, forcing herself to concentrate on the matters at hand. She didn't think of Vashon during the day. That was reserved for night, when it was dark and she was alone. Then she pictured him as she'd seen him that very first time on the *Seabravery*, caped in black, his eyes cold and frightening and mysterious. She'd known so little about him then, only that he was dangerous. Yet she'd grown to love him. Her eyes clouded when she thought of that last look he had given her, right before he'd lowered that pistol away from Peterborough. She cherished that look, for it was the essence of all his love for her, but, too, there were nights when she found that memory so painful she wondered if her love wouldn't destroy her as well.

Faith stared at her and grew glum seeing her so far away. "The ship that you wait for, it will come one day, I know it," she whispered.

Aurora came out of her reverie and tried to smile at the girl. She knew she was foolish to even look for the return of the *Seabravery*, but for some reason she'd been overcome with a torturous hope that it might return. She refused to even express her next hope for it was too crazy and too wrenching. Still, every day she looked at the notices from Queenhithe.

"I'll go speak with John this very minute."

Faith sighed in despair. "He grew worse while you were away. Today he's rambling about the Dark Continent, sure he can take Wilberforce's message to the heathens. I'm sorry I'm too lily-livered to speak with him myself. I just can't face him again this morning."

"If only we could buy this place from him. Pray, let him do his calling then. What a blessing that would be—to everyone but the heathens, that is." Aurora rolled her eyes.

Faith giggled. "How glad I am that you've come back, Aurora. It was terrible without you, quite terrible."

Aurora smiled softly.

"Oh, I forgot!" Faith opened wide her eyes. "While you were taking the children to the rag fair for their coats, a gentleman came to see you, Aurora. He was—"

Aurora almost grabbed her. "Did he have long black hair? Or a hoop through his ear? Was he frightening?"

Faith looked overwhelmed with all her strange questions. Shocked, she stuttered, "No, Aurora."

She slumped to her chair, believing surely she was going mad with her desire to see Vashon again.

"He said he'd return at three to discuss something with you. From his appearance I think he might have been titled. He was finely dressed and restrained in his manners." She lowered her voice. "I suspect his case is like that of the other gentlemen who visit here. His mistress has inconvenienced him with a child."

"I see," Aurora answered numbly, chastising herself for her foolish notions. "Then tell the gentleman when he returns that I'll speak with him in the parlor."

"I will." Faith studied her. "Are you all right, Aurora? Ever since you've returned you seem so distant and sad."

Aurora stood and squeezed both of Faith's hands. She was going to have to confess her state at some point, so she resolved herself to begin now. "On the contrary, I feel a great joy. Knowing my circumstances as you do, you may not see this the way I see it. I'm going to have a baby, Faith. And though the future is uncertain, I beg you to be happy for me."

Faith gasped.

Aurora trembled a smile. "Do I shame you?"

"You never could!" Faith protested.

"I suppose this means I may have to leave. When John finds out, he will be most displeased."

"You know I hardly make more than my bed and board, Aurora, but what I have is yours, for you and the babe."

"No, no. I have friends who I believe will help me. But they're not in London. I hate to leave the Home again. If John will let me stay, I would like to stay."

"Oh, I shudder to think how Mr. Phipps will take this revelation."

Taking a deep breath, Aurora opened the door. "Well, he shall know it this afternoon. Wish me good luck."

Faith watched her go in stunned silence.

She was tired, broken with a weariness that went beyond the physical into the spiritual.

Aurora climbed the stairs to her garret room, wondering what was going to happen to her, to the Home, to Faith. She hadn't been able to tell John about the baby. After she'd asked for the money, he rambled to her about the true message in St. Paul's teachings. "Let the women learn in silence with all subjection!" he'd ranted, and she knew it was not the time to mention her condition.

But for the first time John mentioned to her his trip to Africa and his plans for selling the Home. She'd been shocked, for though John had his failings, he was far better a master than many would be. To let the Home fall into uncaring hands was a fate too terrible to contemplate, yet she had a worse one waiting for her. She was sure John was going to ask her to marry him again. He planned to take her with him to Africa, he'd all but said that, and knowing that, she would be forced to flee to St. George's earlier than she'd imagined.

She eased herself down on her little bed and drew the patched comforter over her. She was too exhausted to solve all her problems, but this one was serious. If she fled to St. George's, what would happen to Faith and the children under a new owner? Would the man be kind? And if he was not, who would be there to challenge him?

She rolled over and closed her eyes. She would have to do something. That was her last thought before she fell into a deep dreamless slumber.

"Wake up, Aurora! The gentleman's here to see you!"

Aurora opened her eyes and sat up. Faith stood in the doorway at the top of the stairs, a frenzied expression on her face. Aurora thought she'd only just closed her eyes, but she'd obviously been asleep for hours.

"Tell him I'll be right down," she said, scrambling out of bed and pulling her hair back into its neat bun. She made a quick overall appraisal of her appearance in her cracked looking glass, then flew down the stairs.

It was so terribly difficult to deal with the peerage. She hated it, having to pretend they were not the monsters they were, gladly accepting their unwanted progeny as if they were some kind of refuse. But she always kept her temper, for those who paid for the Home at least kept the children off the parish. Everyone knew that children on the parish never lived past their first birthday, for they were usually starved, and given cheap paregoric whenever they wailed for sustenance.

With that thought heavy on her mind, she put a smile on her face and went to the closed doors of the parlor. She would take the man's babe and she would even thank him for it. He would never know how much she loathed him.

"Good day to you, sir," she said as she rushed into the parlor. The man was standing with his back to her, staring solemnly out the soot-covered window. He certainly was a finely dressed gentleman. His blue coat of superfine fit like a glove. He was tall with broad shoulders, but slim, slimmer than Vashon had been. And his hair was most certainly not in a queue, for though it was jet black as his had been it was cut into a fashionable Byronic crop.

"Have you a child, sir, for whom you need a place?" she asked, but still the man did not turn around.

He was beginning to intrigue her. His grave stance, his reluctance to turn around, gave her pause.

"Good sir? How may I help you?" she whispered, suddenly overcome with a wild, sweet yearning.

The man lifted his hand and she saw something in it—a brass key exactly like the key she'd left in the hall at Peterborough's mansion.

She clutched the door. It couldn't be him. In her state, she must be seeing things.

He turned around. There was no disputing it. It was him.

Trembling in disbelief, she wanted to convince herself that it was a mirage, but no matter how she tried, she saw only the man she loved. Some might have thought it was his brother, for he now looked just like Peterborough, tamed and civilized. But as Aurora stood by the door, she knew the man before her was not Josiah. This man's eyes reflected a joy and a warmth that only Vashon's would have.

It was Vashon.

Their gazes finally met. His expression spoke eloquently to her, telling her of a longing and a love that he had never been able to put into words.

Her first steps were the hardest. She had to force herself to believe in this vision before her, this ghost wrought from her own terrible need. But the closer she walked, the more she knew it was true, and by the time she flung herself into his embrace, she knew he was real. In ecstatic disbelief, she felt his arms go around her, and she felt him warm and alive and hugging her so tightly it was as if nothing in the world could every pry him from her.

"My God, I thought you were lost to me forever. I killed you," she suddenly wept, unable to take her eyes off him. "So are you an angel then, come to take me to heaven?"

"You didn't kill me," he said.

"I saw Peterborough fire the shot. I saw the blood."

"Am I not worse for it?"

She stared at him, joy, hope and fear mingled into one tragic emotion. She couldn't take her gaze from his face as if by moving her gaze away he might disappear forever. And if that were to happen now, she knew she couldn't endure losing him twice, and her only hope then would be to join him.

"Look at me, love. I am all too mortal."

She lowered her eyes and studied him. He did look worse. He was much too thin for his frame. His face looked almost gaunt and his bronzed skin was gone, but to anyone who didn't know him, he might be merely sporting a lordly pallor.

"If I touch you, will you vanish?"

"Touch me and see for yourself."

She ran her hand down his chest. It was hard and warm and thrummed with the beating of his heart. She laughed and cried in the same breath. "How could fate be so merciful?"

"I had to survive, don't you see?" He took her face in his palms.

She shook her head and her tears fell over his hands.

"I finally had something to survive for."

She closed her eyes, and with unspeakable relief she let him hold her. She placed her cheek against his chest and felt the strong, reassuring beat of his heart. She would never want for another thing as long as she had him.

When her tears were finally spent, he pulled her away and studied her with the same intensity she'd studied him. It was as if he couldn't bear to miss a detail. But out of the blue, something in her appearance struck his fancy and he tipped back his head and laughed. It was a beautiful sound.

"And what are you laughing at, good sir?" she asked smartly, all the while wondering if she could ever bear closing her eyes in sleep again if that meant she had to part with him.

"When Isaac returned to Hugh Town and told me how you insisted on returning here, I must admit I expected to find you in a rather sorry state. But to look at you now, I can't believe you ever missed me. Why you're actually getting plump."

She met his gaze. Her eyes held the slightest hesitation, but that alone spoke volumes.

He inhaled sharply, understanding flooding his features.

She hardly needed to say her next words. "I fear it's not the state of my mind that has me growing plump."

He stepped back and leaned on John Phipps's desk. Crossing his arms over his chest, he perused her. "And what shall we name this babe? Is it a boy or girl?"

"I cannot tell you that now, sir." She smiled softly. "But regardless, I do have the name picked out. I hope it will be agreeable to you."

"And what name is that?" he asked, puzzled.

She reverently lowered her voice. "I should like very much that this child's name be Blackwell. For its father is the viscount, you know."

He reached for her. When she was in his arms once more, he said, "I like that name. It's been used too infrequently in my family." He sobered and looked down at her, his face the most handsome in the world. "I told you how I felt on that bluff, *Aurore*. The words were never spoken, but they shall be now, both loud and clear. We shall marry in the cathedral of your choosing and we shall have everyone there to hear those words, Flossie, Isaac, even the Regent if you wish."

"The Regent! He wants you twisted!"

He glanced at her, obviously surprised at the slang she'd picked up on the *Seabravery*. "On the contrary, I've secured a complete pardon. He owed me that, at least, for all I've done for him. And he's pro-claimed me the Viscount Blackwell, renouncing Josiah's evil deeds. I promise you, from now on, we'll live the quiet life here in London. I will be the most stuffy peer in town."

"Good heavens! I can't even imagine that!"

"Well, you must imagine it. Everything will be changed now. The pirate Vashon is gone."

"But you cannot take away the dragon," she said, running her hands down his back. "You'll never be rid of it, Vashon, and in the future, when I look at you across a crowded ballroom, I'll know it's there, for my eyes only."

"The dragon will be the only thing to stay."

"But we must have Mirage. We cannot give up Mirage."

"Mirage will stay also. If you wish it."

"And Isaac shall marry us quietly aboard the *Seabravery* while we return home. I could not have you unhappy in London, my lord. You belong, *we belong*, at Dragonard."

"Is there anything else you desire, my greedy viscountess?" He laughed.

"Yes. One last thing. I beg you, buy me the Home as a wedding gift. And allow me to rename it simply 'The Bluefield Home for Little Wan-derers.'"

"It shall be done. But what has happened to your illustrious Phipps?"

"Is that a note of jealousy in your voice?" She smiled. "I suspect John will now be the one to have an adventure ahead of him. Especially when he learns of my upcoming nuptials."

He smirked, then kissed her with a passion that took her breath away. It was a long time before they parted, but when they did, he shook his head. "I'm afraid one thing has changed. The *Seabravery*'s gone. She's the *Sleeping Beauty* now."

So that was why he had escaped the notices at Queenhithe. She laughed and fell into his arms. She never wanted him to let her go.

He stroked her hair, and they stood in each other's arms for another long moment. Finally he said, "I love you, *mon Aurore*. When you came upon my ship that very first day, I thought I was the one who had captured you. But now I see it very differently."

She stopped at his words, unable to believe he had really said them. "What did you say?" she whispered.

"I said I love you. You think you forced me to feel it, but you didn't.

In the end I found I couldn't help myself." He stroked her cheek with the back of his hand. "When death came to take me on that bluff, the only thing stopping him was my love for you. And in that tug of war, I finally knew what truly made me strong."

"And what was that, my love?"

He held her tight. "You."